For my grandparents, and my grandchildren

Matthew 13:35

Author's note:

This book is a test for all who read it.

Please send all thoughts, questions, concerns, insights, grievances, wonderings, criticisms, congratulations, adulations, subpoenas, death threats, interrogations, solicitations, well wishes, and spam to:

prodigalsonauthor@gmail.com

This is a work of fiction.
Any similarities to people, things, or ideas,
alive, dead, or inanimate,
are intentional, even when they are not.
They are intended in good faith for those who act in good faith,
and are protected under parody law, fair use, and the first amendment
for those who get a little cranky sometimes.

The breathing exercises contained herein should not be practiced in situations where transient loss-of-consciousness would be an issue, like while driving or in water. Play, but don't be stupid.

"The history of the world is none other than the progress of the consciousness of freedom."
- Georg Wilhelm Friedrich Hegel

"Technological enlargement is a process toward excess. As a part of his spiritual health, man should make as his first object the recognition of pattern as a means to avoid excess and achieve equilibrium."
- Marshall McLuhan, The Global Village

"GOD IS DEAD. God remains dead. And we have killed him. How shall we comfort ourselves, the murderers of all murderers? What was holiest and mightiest of all that the world has yet owned has bled to death under our knives: who will wipe this blood off us? What water is there for us to clean ourselves? What festivals of atonement, what sacred games shall we have to invent? Is not the greatness of this deed too great for us? Must we ourselves not become gods simply to appear worthy of it?"
- Friedrich Nietzsche, The Gay Science, 1882

PART ONE.
DEPARTURE.

ONE

EXTERNAL ALGORITHM 5129-OLI
Instructions for Living a Life:
1) Observe
2) Be Astonished
3) Tell About It

    A bloodcurdling scream echoed through Theo's dispassionate ears as he slid his broadsword out of the peasant leader's chest. He watched in a frenzied buzz of glorious satisfaction as the leader of the now-failed uprising tumbled off the cliff, a corpse lost to the rocks and foaming surf below.

    He turned, slowly, to face the peasant leader's wife. Cowering near the foot of a nearby tree, she tried and failed to shield her infant child from him. The salty sea air intermingled with the smell of exposed flesh, mixing in Theo's nostrils as he stalked towards the peasant girl. She frantically pushed herself further against the tree, woven blouse falling off her shoulder, gray-blue eyes fearfully tracking his every move. Savoring every second, Theo raised his sword and slowly traced the tip down her cheek, which grew visibly flush despite the mud-stained face that was the hallmark of the laboring classes. Quivering in fear, she opened her mouth to protest.

    "Honey, come set the table!"

    "Why can't the butler do it?" Theo yelled back without taking off his headset.

    "Just shut off your game and come help me."

An annoyed Theo saved his game, then took off his headset. He'd almost beaten *Princely Defense*, and he hated being interrupted.

"NOW, THEODORE. You know I don't like that game, don't make me take it away!"

Theo winced. His mother was the only one who ever used his full name. Even his father called him Theo, but he'd been away overseeing the construction of the first Martian Aerodome, and Theo hadn't heard his father's voice in over a year.

"COMING!" Theo started to roll his eyes, felt guilty, then craned his neck and looked around, trying and failing to convince himself that he hadn't had the contemptuous impulse in the first place. He walked down the narrow hallway, ignoring the NFTs and family gifs he hadn't actively seen in who knows how long, and entered the dining room. One of the four place settings was already done.

"I did one so you could copy it. I know you probably don't remember what it should look like since the butler usually does it—he's at the Nerd Herd specialist for repairs. The good silver is over there." She gestured to the 3D-printed walnut-textured plastic cabinet.

"And I hope I don't have to tell you not to talk back like that when our guests are here."

Theo nodded, avoiding her expectant gaze and the firmly pursed lips he knew sat just below them. She nodded, satisfied, and returned to the kitchen. Theo set the table, completely ignoring the place setting his mother had prepared. He remembered perfectly well the etiquette lessons that were drilled into his head at age 9 during the infamous "Manners Week" at school. His class was one of the first to utilize a revolutionary new technology called NeuroComs, which, as the Teaching Facilitators explained, allowed them to "imprint" information into his memory directly, among other things. It was regarded as a wild success, but after that week, it seemed to Theo that everyone got significantly more dull.

"And remember to look up anything you don't understand." She shouted from the kitchen. "We all have this technology, so you'll be expected to use it to keep up."

The doorbell rang.

"They're here! Quick, run and get dressed—that blue jumpsuit I laid out for you."

Theo sullenly plodded to his room to change, steeling himself for the evening to come. Since his father was away on business, his mother had taken it upon herself to maintain the family's social maneuvering on the Moon. Both she and Theo's father came from middle class families, and were only able to join the Moon-bound group for the Exodus of 2029 because they "knew the right people". In the nine years since, Theo's father had risen to the top of his field, and now oversaw the construction of new colonies, specifically the domes used to insulate their extra-terrestrial communities from the elements (or lack thereof).

Tonight's guest, as his mother had briefed him, was Robert Ditto, a newly declared candidate and frontrunner for Head Programmer in the upcoming bi-world election, and his wife Eleanor. Bob was the CEO of Malum Inc., the corporation that developed the NeuroComs. As a result of his position, he became their lead public advocate, eventually spearheading their integration into schools and society in general, exponentially increasing the bandwidth with which people could interact with ever-more-ubiquitous computing technologies.

Theo had been repeatedly briefed by his mother that it would be advantageous for the two families to be in contact, given that the infrastructure of the Aerodome communities Theo's father built were highly reliant on the algorithms embedded in the Head Programmer's digital counterpart, the Societal Operating System.

As he changed from his haptic suit into the latest in gender-irrelevant fashion, he could hear the Dittos in the entry hall, praising the interior design of the cookie cutter 3D-printed-out-of-moon-dust house, reaffirming each other's compliments with complimentary affirmation. Theo took a breath, tried his best to smile with his eyes, and walked out into the hall.

"Mr. and Mrs. Ditto, pleasure to meet you." Theo said cordially, holding out his hand to shake as he had been imprinted to do.

"Ah, Theo! I've heard so much about you. Actually it's Dr. Ditto, but you can call me Bob."

Bob grabbed Theo's hand and executed the ideal handshake perfectly—thumb down, firm grip, 3 pumps while maintaining eye contact, then a slight linger to convey warmth, ending with a simultaneous break of both eye and hand contact.

Mrs. Ditto reached out her hand as well. "And you can call me Ellie. My, how you've grown!"

Theo shook. Almost as firm, but more moderated, and somehow much statelier. Theo controlled his face as he attempted to fight back the annoying thought that she had never seen him before.

"You have a lovely home! It's much quieter in the Outer Ring, isn't it Bob?" offered Ellie.

"That it is! Peaceful. Don't know why they put the Head Programmer's house in the center of the Residential Dome, when it's so much better out here!" laughed Bob.

You mean the Head Programmer's mansion? It's three times as big as any other house here. Theo thought, maintaining his smile. *You can see it no matter where you are in the Dome.*

Violet chuckled and grinned. "We do love it here—it's perfect for us." She shifted gears.

"The dining room is through here. Theodore, would you go bring in the salads from the kitchen? My sincerest apologies, our butler is in the shop for repairs. His gyro has been off-kilter, and we couldn't have him rolling around, leaning everywhere."

Happy to leave the room, if only for just a second, Theo went into the kitchen and picked up two pre-fixed salad plates.

"Violet, I'd be happy to give it a look if it were here. Takes me back to my old days taking apart laptops in my father's garage." He laughed, a deeply resonant, unforced laugh. Ellie and Violet joined in. Theo set the salads down in front of Bob and Ellie and went back to get the other two for himself and his mother.

"This looks delicious Vi. May I call you Vi? Lovely. Pardon my asking, but if your butler's in the shop, who made this wonderful salad?" Ellie inquired with a practiced twinkle in her eye.

"Well, I'm a bit embarrassed to admit it" said Theo's mother nervously, as Theo placed the other two salads and took his seat at the table, "but I did".

"How wonderful! A real meal made by human hands. I can't remember the last time, can you Bob?" Ellie reveled.

Bob shook his head in wonder. "Must have been back on Earth, a few months at least! If you don't count my morning coffee." Everyone laughed again. Theo did his best to join in.

☕

As they ate, Theo grew more and more comfortable. *The Dittos are nice people,* he thought. *Nicer than I'd expected.* However, something about them appealed to him on a level he couldn't quite elucidate, and that made him uneasy. He shook his head. *Keep quiet,* he thought, *they'll be gone in an hour or two. Then I can get back to my game.*

He remained silent as his mother engaged them in pleasantries, and they responded to every one as though it were the most important question in the world, and *rightly* so. But just as he found himself increasingly ingratiated to the strangers in his house, something else kindled inside him that grew less and less stable as the opportunities for escalation were avoided and re-avoided. He couldn't stand it any longer. Theo cut in-

"My mother tells me you're leading in the polls to be Head Programmer. How is that going?"

The three adults froze. Theo's mother glared at him, then started sweetly, "Theodore, that's impolite. I apologize Bob--"

Bob stepped in- "Don't mention it. I think we've had enough small talk to graduate to... bigger questions." He grinned. Theo's eyes lit up. Bob continued.

"It's going well! Ellie and I have been very fortunate to be in the position we're in. Polls are showing we've gained an unprecedented amount of popular Earthling support with the announcement of our 'Future, Faster' Disruption Initiative—our NeuroCom-For-All program especially—so we couldn't be happier." He glanced at Ellie, smiling.

"Campaigning is tiring, but I think ultimately the OS will see that I'm the best man for the job."

"You mean the people?" asked Violet, thinking she misheard. "The people vote to decide who will be Head Programmer."

"Common misconception!" Bob bounced back with a seasoned politician's ease. "The people vote, of course, but the OS is the ultimate decider. The algorithm it uses gives very strong weight to the decision of the people, in direct correlation to the magnitude of the symbolic social role the position of Head Programmer plays. However, it takes into account a number of other inputs, most of which the average voter would be unaware of."

"Like what?" Asked Theo, genuinely fascinated.

"Well, the Head Programmer is, in all functionality, the human counterpart to the OS. And its machine learning algorithms have grown complex enough that it's impossible to fully understand it. Luckily I have a whole team of experts to give our best guess."

"Best guess?" Theo asked, doubling down. "So, you're just guessing what the OS wants in a human counterpart?" Violet nudged Theo's leg under the table. He ignored it.

Bob laughed. "An informed and educated guess, but a guess nonetheless. Programming has gotten significantly more complex since the quantum supremacy revolution of the 20s- but that's all technical mumbo-jumbo, I won't get into that. The point is, the OS doesn't operate in finite absolutes the way that computers have for the past century; it also deals in probabilities. The quantum side of the OS generates possibilities grounded in probability, and the classical, binary side executes based on those options. You can think of it like a left brain, right brain dynamic- it is built on a neural net, after all. But because it uses probability, and we can't possibly consider all the options the quantum processor sets forward, using solely pure reason and logic is extremely inefficient, and therefore inappropriate to our purposes."

Theo replied, processing. "So, what does that mean, exactly? I mean, how do you improve your chances of getting elected—or picked— by the algorithm?"

Violet glared at Theo. Bob looked at Ellie, seemingly asking without words how to reply. She looked at Violet (who had softened her face just in time), turned to Theo, then returned to her husband. She smiled, and nodded.

Bob seemed almost relieved, even excited. "Well—our team doesn't only consist of programmers. We have health experts, psychologists, ex-secret agents, even a Buddhist monk."

Violet was aghast, but hid it well from everyone except Theo. She laughed lightheartedly at all the silliness. "A Monk? But didn't the OS determine that religions are just earth-bound fancy? Narratives built around our inability to explain what we don't understand?"

Bob smiled- "Buddhism isn't a religion, it's a philosophy—a shamelessly escapist one at that—but Aum just teaches me meditation. It's one of the many ways I'm being trained to maximize my stable potential. My team has determined that mental stability and physical health are two of the qualities most highly valued by the OS in a counterpart. Since it's been allowed access to the biometrics of all candidates, I've been meditating regularly, taking 5-HTP supplements to maintain my mood, keeping a strict daily routine of work and exercise, having biweekly microbiome implants--"

Theo was engrossed. He couldn't remember the last time he'd had the opportunity to talk this freely to an adult, and he was utterly compelled to press further. He cut in, unable to restrain himself. "Microbiome implants? Like fecal transplants? I've heard those can be—"

"THEODORE."

Theo froze. He realized a bit too late that talk about fecal matter wasn't necessarily dinner conversation. He backtracked as quickly as he could.

"Sorry- uh—sorry…"

After too many seconds of tense silence, Bob let out a pained chuckle, and Violet tried to pick up the broken remains of the conversation. "You said you have ex-secret agents? How can they help? Protection?"

Bob eased back in as best he could after that hard stoppage of conversation. "Protection, yes, but also microexpression training, body language, that sort of thing."

Violet decided they were finished with this minefield of a conversation. "That's all *very* interesting. I'm sure the OS knows what's best. Theodore, would you mind clearing the table and bringing in the main course?"

Theo, head down, quickly did as he was told. He brought in four steaks, cooked in an air fryer to a perfect medium rare.

Violet stood as Theo set the food down in front of their guests. With as much natural gravitas as she could muster, she began her rehearsed spiel. "Bob, Ellie- *This* is no ordinary meat. As you know, Theodore Sr. is on Mars overseeing the construction of the new Aerodome. Any food you eat has to be brought with you, as you can imagine, and since they are there for such a long time, he and the boys in the lab built a machine that made what is sitting in front of you."

Ellie started. "Made... the meat?"

Violet smiled, butterflies of pride swarming her abdomen as she elaborated. "In the kitchen is a first edition, domestic sized meat printer. Completely synthetic, but one hundred percent real meat, right in your own home. No cruelty, all real." She ended with the tagline she had thought up and practiced in front of the mirror, and took her seat.

Ellie hesitated, but Bob cut in. "I love it! What a time we live in, don't you think honey? I can't wait to try it."

Violet hid a sigh of relief, and smiled. "Dig in everyone!"

They did. After the initial praises were sung of how "it tastes like the real thing" and "it's cooked perfectly, you've really outdone yourself", the conversation settled into one more relaxed. Wine was brought out, and the three adults loosened up considerably.

"I tell you Vi, it's probably a good thing your butler is on the mend- otherwise I'd have to be more careful what I say. He's hooked up to the OS, you know."

Theodore's mother let a knowing smile creep across her face, quickly hidden by her glass of wine as she took a sip. "The thought had occurred to me."

"Pros and cons to everything" added Ellie, nodding thoughtfully. Violet and Bob agreed. "Indeed", "Truer words, never spoken".

Quite suddenly Ellie turned to Theo.

"So Theodore- Theo. Any ladies in your life?"

Bob tacked on, a mischievous twinkle in his eye. "Or men?".

The three adults chuckled and exchanged slight glances, in the way that one does when adults want to get entertainment out of an outnumbered child's lack of life experience, then all attention was focused on Theo.

Theo froze, taken aback a bit by the sudden shift in attention towards him. After the fecal incident, he was ready to eat his food, clear the table, and get back to his game as soon as he could. All he could manage to squeak out was "I... I don't really get out much."

Ellie smiled warmly- "No one at school catching your eye?"

Theo grew steadier. "Well, since the whole NeuroCom switch, I don't really talk to anyone at school anymore. We all just download our knowledge deposits and leave."

Bob laughed. "I guess we didn't consider that when we were making it! That's the trouble when you invent something with so many applications. Hah, strange times have stranger consequences!" He shook his head. "But I'm sure you'll find someone Theo- what did they say when we were growing up? There's an--"

The other adults joined in. "An App for that!!"

They all laughed, reveling in the nostalgia.

Suddenly, what felt like a bolt of lightning shot through Violet's temple. For a split second, she was paralyzed, unable to make a sound or perceive anything other than blinding pain. She saw red, every inch of her being throbbed violently, screaming to separate from the source of the agony. She thought the backs of her eyes would explode out the back of her skull, then as quickly as it came on, it was over. She looked around. No one had noticed anything was amiss. To bring it up would spoil the evening, so, still trembling slightly, she took a sip of wine, trying to hide what had just happened.

But Theo had noticed. The only one not laughing, he saw his mother freeze, seemingly go into a pained trance, and recover quicker than either of them had realized something happened. Before he could ask what was wrong, Ellie cut in.

"So, Theo, any idea which college you want to drop out of?"

Theo was still too jarred to say anything, so he just shook his head.

"Well, you don't want to graduate—wouldn't that be awful? To spend all that time just *learning*, with no disruptive ideas to show for it? What a shame. But I digress- so do you have any idea what you want to be when you grow up?

Bob took another sizable sip of his wine. "Ellie, stop pestering the kid. He's what, 13? He doesn't know yet."

Ellie looked annoyedly at Bob. Theo did his best to dispel the tension that suddenly had appeared surrounding him.

"I'm not sure- I went to the doctor a few months ago. That could be cool... to get assigned there. We don't get to take our OS Career Placement Assessments until we turn 18. Which is pretty soon, I guess, since I'm 16—and my next birthday's in a couple days.

Bob backpedaled, probably less swiftly than he normally would. "Ah, 16, of course, sorry- I see it now. Happy birthday. You're a strong young man. Don't know how relevant doctors will be, what with nanobot medicine and bedside manner algorithms accelerating as they are. Soon they'll go the same way as the lawyer- remember lawyers? From before the Phlogiston Network integrated its smart contracts into the OS? Good times. You could get away with *a lot*. But that's the beauty of the young generation, isn't it?" He opened up to the rest of the table for approval, filled to the brim with a confidence that seemed not to need said approval. "Blind idealism. You don't know the rules yet, so you aren't afraid to break them."

Theo shifted awkwardly in his seat as Bob monologued. Out of the corner of his eye he watched his mother, lightly smiling and chuckling along to Bob's nostalgic waxing. *Is she ok?* She seemed alright, but it still didn't sit right with him. *Something's off—is it me? How can I fix it?* Helpless, he scrounged around for an idea substantial enough to matter, but subtle enough that she'd be the only one to see what he was doing. *Oh, right!*

Look up Phlogiston, he thought. His NeuroCom responded with the requested information as though he were remembering something long forgotten. *Oh yeah. The luminiferous ether, thought to be the undetectable medium through which all matter passes until it was abandoned in the early 20th century. A blockchain-based network of the same name constructed a trust-free economic internet which...* He opened his mouth to contribute what he'd learned, but before he could, Ellie, to move the conversation along more than anything else, gave Bob the affirmation he was looking for.

"Truly. Oh, would you look at the time. If Bob is going to keep to his circadian schedule, we really must be going. Thank you for the wonderful dinner Vi- may I help clear the table?"

Theo's mother, only recently having caught up to the conversation, and a little nauseous, was suddenly grateful for the night's abrupt end. "Please, don't give it another thought. Theodore will take care of it, won't you Theodore?"

"Of course, mom." Said Theo, still hiding his concern.

"I'll walk you to the door."

Within two minutes, Ellie Ditto had gotten Bob out of his seat, made their way to the door, and were in an autonomous taxi-rover back to their home in the centermost Residential Ring, adjacent to the Head Programmer's Mansion. Theo cleared the table without a word. His mother came back into the kitchen, and immediately went to the sink to get a cup of water. She drank, slowly.

"Hey mom, you ok?" Theo asked, tiptoeing.

"Yes sweetie" she replied, waving him off. "Just a bit too much wine. Go ahead back to your room and play your game. I'll finish up here."

Theo almost protested, then remembering where he was in his game, and how much he hated doing the dishes, chirped "Ok, thanks mom! Goodnight!" and left the kitchen.

Violet took another sip of water, took a deep breath to quell her shaking hands, and started on the dishes, wishing the butler wasn't broken.

TWO

EXTERNAL ALGORITHM 2239-HDT
"The language of friendship is not words, but meanings."

"I wonder what we learned today." Theo mused, scratching behind his ear.

"Beats me," shrugged his best friend. "They only give names to the Learning Weeks that everyone's parents have specifically advocated for."

"God forbid we have a Synthesis Discussion once in a while. We haven't had one of those in years."

"My dad's brought that up, but apparently not enough other parents have. I asked the Facilitator about it. Apparently, they're not worth the time investment."

"That's dumb. If they told us what we learned, we'd at least be able to talk about it outside learning hours."

Theo and Govinda took their time leaving the Educational Facility, not because they liked being there, but because they were always dizzy for the few minutes that followed a knowledge deposit. It was located in the Retail Ring, the outermost ring of the Central Dome of the Aerodome Complex, right next to the tunnel that connected it and the Residential Dome. Theo had never had the occasion to explore the inner rings of the Central Dome, but Govinda had been dragged there by his father a few times right after the Exodus and assured him it wasn't that interesting. Apparently, inside the Retail Ring lay the Corporate Ring, and at the center of the Corporate Ring lay the Governmental Node that housed the Moon's OS. In Govinda's words, however, anything within the Retail

Ring was "Just a bunch of computers and blinking lights." Theo shrugged, and took him at his word.

"Dude, I had the best dream last night." Govinda blurted out.

"Yeah?" Theo encouraged.

"Remember the classrooms we had on Earth? With all the people and the little tables and stuff?"

"The tables attached to the chairs? You'd always try to melt your crayons onto them on sunny days, until all the teachers collectively sat you away from the windows."

"I forgot about that! Good times. Anyway, remember those active shooter drills they made us do?"

"Where we all had to crawl under the chair-tables?"

"Yeah. I had a dream that someone was actually shooting up the school, and they broke down the door to our classroom. Everyone was cowering under their tables and screaming and stuff, but I immediately, like, sprang into action. I hucked a table at the guy to distract him, then I tackled him to the ground and beat the crap out of him. I was a total hero, and everyone was worshiping me and screaming my name, and by the time the cops came Ms. Anima and I were full-on making out."

"Ms. Anima? Our second-grade teacher?"

"Yeah—but I was like, me now, not me in second grade."

"Ahhh okay. Still a 'lil bit weird, but that's cool though. I wish I could remember my dreams like that."

In an hour they'd made their way through the Residential Rings, stopping at Govinda's house in the Middle Ring so he could change clothes, then at Theo's in the Outer Ring so he could do the same. They hopped the fence behind Theo's house and started walking. In minutes, they were at their favorite spot, taking turns throwing rocks at the side of the Aerodome.

What on the surface seemed a terribly irresponsible thing for the two boys to do, given that the smallest crack in the dome's surface would result in the prompt evacuation of all breathable air and the horrifically painful death of all those who called the Aerodome Complex home, was in fact akin to stabbing a suit of armor with a paper straw. These paper straws, however, made the most satisfying *klunk* when they made contact with the hexagonally patterned decimeter-thick inner layer of a state-of-the-art polymer, before dropping into the drainage fissure that let out in the Sea of Tranquility, where all the domes of the Aerodome Complex were located.

Theo played the events of the previous night over and over in his mind. The look of complete shock and vulnerability that painted his mother's face was a hauntingly terrifying expression, the existence of which he'd never even considered, much less seen before. It had lasted less than a second, but the memory of it filled him with an unsteadiness that increasingly shook him to his core the more he replayed it.

He couldn't get past the speed at which she returned to normal- it was a capacity he'd never had the occasion to observe. With that level of control over herself and her reactions, what else could she have hidden from him over the years? It was at times like these, when life's frustrations left little room for control, that Theo would run off to the edge of the dome and hurl rocks at plastic. Govinda came along, of course, because that's what friends do. They had gone to school together, vacationed together, worked through life's hardships and celebrated its victories together. And, when circumstances required it, they destroyed things together.

"They were all laughing, then my mom just froze. Then a second later, she came back, and acted like nothing had happened."

Klunk.

"What do you mean, came back?"

Klunk.

"Well, it was like she was in a trance or something. I don't know. Bob and Ellie left almost immediately after, but for the rest of the night my mom still seemed distracted. I asked if she was ok and she said she was fine, so, I don't know."

Klunk.

"Weird."

"Yeah, really weird."

Klunk.

"Did Bob drink a ton?"

Klunk.
"A lot."
Govinda laughed, "Yeah, he does that. I don't know how the OS isn't picking up on that in his biometrics." He lobbed a softball-sized hunk of moon rock.
KLUNK.
"Hell yeah." Govinda did a little dance.
"What were you aiming at?"
"Earth. What else am I gonna aim at?"
"I dunno. There's stars and stuff."
"Where? Your dad's tinted plastic blocks all the nice stuff that can't hurt us, on top of solar radiation."
"At least my dad's invention isn't itchy."
Govinda's father, Sid, was one of the other lead programmers credited with the development of the NeuroComs. One of the major dramatic controversies used in the initial promotion of the device was a parallel drawn between Bob Ditto and Steve Jobs, and Sid and Steve Wozniak. The two were friends, but in the spirit of "All press is good press", they concocted this feud to draw the public eye—although, having lived through it behind the scenes, both Theo and Govinda agreed it was an apt characterization.
"Have you seen Cute Nose recently?" Govinda asked.
"No, not for a few weeks." Theo replied.
"I saw her two days ago for a few seconds. She cut her hair."
"Yeah? How short?"
"Like to her shoulders. She looked good."
"Nice. I wish I'd seen her."
"Yeah dude. Made my whole day."
Klunk.
"I bet she smells good."
Klunk.
Klunk.
 "What are your thoughts on love?" Theo asked.
"What about it?"

"Like why do we have it? Why is it there?"

Klunk.

"It's a function of familiarity over time, catalyzed by commitment, so that we can reliably reproduce. Plus some pheromones and—"

"No, not like literally, more like... I don't know. Do you think you'll ever find it?"

"Of course, our parents did."

Klunk.

"They say they did, but where are we supposed to find it? We don't interact with anyone at school anymore. We're there, we go under for a half hour while new neural pathways are burned into our brains, then we leave. There's no familiarity, time or anything there."

"I don't know dude, maybe later in life, like at our jobs or something. Why are you so stuck on this?"

Klunk.

Theo considered. "They brought it up at dinner, then when I said I don't interact with anyone at school anymore, Bob just laughed and said they hadn't thought about it when they were designing the NeuroComs. Then they just brushed it off saying I could always use an app."

Govinda harrumphed. "Old people. Apps are pretty much vintage now."

Klunkshhhhhhhh.

"Did you just throw gravel?"

"Hehe yeah."

"Hah, nice."

Klunkshhhhhh.

"What really gets me though isn't the fact that they didn't see it coming, it's that they were so blasé about it. I don't want to meet someone with an app, or some algorithm that matches me to a stranger based on personality or common interests- I want... I don't know, something more. Some spark of something spontaneous, a... what's the word from Film Week.... A meet-cute. I want a story to tell at dinner parties of a line I used, or something stupid I did that caught her attention and endeared me to her."

"I don't know man, I think you're overthinking this. Whoever you end up with, you probably won't meet them for years, and you won't be the same *you* you are now. Just focus on growing into that you right now, and when she comes, you'll be ready."

"But I don't know what I need to do to grow into that person. We don't get our Career Assessments for another year, and I can't predict where it'll put me. How am I supposed to get ahead of that?"

"We just gotta wait and trust the process. That's the way it's set up. I'm sure Cute Nose is doing the same thing."

"Yeah, well, that's easy to say, and *way* harder to do. You're saying I should not only distract myself from all my biological urges, but also forge an identity by predicting what society will value in a future that's getting more uncertain by the day, making constructive choices, and not messing my life up irrevocably. Even though by the time I get good at whatever career the OS ends up assigning me to, some robot will be on the market that does it better and quicker than I'll ever be able to."

"You could always be the one to make the robots?"

"Until there's a robot for that. I wish we never left Earth."

Klunk.

Klunk.

"Could be worse", offered Govinda.

"You could say that about anything", Theo shot back.

"Well yeah, obviously, but you don't have to be a dick about it, I've got all the same problems too." replied Govinda.

Klunk.

Govinda continued. "All I'm saying is, it's worth remembering how good we have it. We got to be part of the Exodus, and now we live at the forefront of human civilization. People stuck on Earth aren't as lucky- my dad says hardly anyone can afford a NeuroCom there, but we get them for free through school. I know Bob wants to give them to everyone, but dad says that'll take years, if not decades. Their kids will still have to go to school for 9 hours and learn the old-fashioned way—typing with their fingers."

"Yeah, well, they won't have these itchy *(Klunk.)* skull implants either."

"We have literally all of human knowledge at our fingertips—"

"So do they."

"Not all the time. My dad says more than half of the Earth's surface still doesn't have Wifi."

"OK, I'll give them that. That's a travesty."

Klunk.

Klunkshhhhhh.

Klunk.

Theo mused. "Do you ever think about how everyone experiences hardship differently?"

"No, but continue."

"Thanks for that. Well like, you ever think about how everyone compares what they're going through to the worst thing they've ever gone through? Like, we're coming up on the 100th anniversary of the start of World War Two. The Jews and Gypsies—"

"and Gays"

"and Gays, and people who helped them, and probably other people I don't remember, all went through really terrible stuff in concentration camps and stuff. So, everything after that must have seemed like a vacation in comparison."

"Makes sense so far."

"So if, say, one day, a Holocaust survivor went to get a sandwich, but they were out of ham—"

"Jews can't eat ham."

"Fine, turkey, whatever, the meat doesn't matter."

"Matters to them."

Theo stared at Govinda.

"Sorry, continue. Still with ya."

"Ok, so like they'd be bummed, but then they'd get roast beef, which isn't their favorite, but because they'd probably end up consciously or subconsciously comparing it to the time they were only allowed a half cup of gruel a day for 6 years, they'd enjoy their sandwich. But if a prince, who'd never known a day's work in his life, always got what he wanted, and never knew anything other than perfection suddenly found out there was a turkey shortage and his daily turkey sandwich had to be replaced with roast beef, it'd be the worst thing he'd ever experienced."

"I think I see where you're going with this, and you're treading on some dangerous ground here bud."

"I'm not saying it's right, or a good thing, but on the day of the sandwich switch the prince would feel a lot more like the Jew in the camp than the one in the deli, just slightly bummed about a sandwich."

"I think you aren't giving the prince enough credit. Would he really be that self-involved?"

"You're missing the point- never mind. Forget I said anything."

Klunk.

Klunk.

Klunkssssssssh.

Klunk.

"What made you think of that?" asked Govinda.

"The Earthlings not having Wifi."

"Ah, yeah, I see it now."

Klunk.

Klunk.

"It just sucks that in order for everything to seem so great, you have to go through something really shitty beforehand so you have something to compare it to."

"Yeah, I suppose."

"Maybe life on Earth really would be better."

DING DING.

A ringtone sounded out of nowhere, as millions of self-transforming nanobots arranged themselves out of thin air into a small speaker. Theo and Govinda looked at each other in shock and surprise— they'd heard of foglet technology, but it wasn't available to the public yet, even in the highest social circles of Aerodome complexes.

THEODORE FREEMAN JUNIOR. ACKNOWLEDGE.
"Uh… yeah? That's me."
VOICE PATTERN RECOGNIZED. PLAYING MESSAGE.
THEODORE. THIS IS A MESSAGE FROM THE AERODOME CIVILIAN POLICE. THERE HAS BEEN AN INCIDENT INVOLVING YOUR MOTHER. SHE IS ALIVE. PLEASE RETURN HOME AT ONCE.

THREE

EXTERNAL ALGORITHM 0042-ALC
In sterquiliniis invenitur.
Translation: In filth it will be found.
—or—
That which you need most will be found where you least want to look.

Theo sprinted home, Govinda close behind. He burst through the front door.

"MOM?" Theo shrieked.

"In here!" A male voice called out from his mother's room.

The two boys dashed down through the living room and turned the corner to see Theo's mother unconscious in bed, hair matted with blood, covered in dark purple and green bruises. She was hooked up to an IV drip, and sitting next to her was the primary care physician of the Outer Ring, typing into a tablet. Standing next to him was Sid, Govinda's father.

Trying to catch his breath, but not wanting to waste time, Theo gasped "What... what happened?"

The two adults looked at each other for a second, then turned back to Theo. The class of people that found themselves on the moon at this point in time weren't particularly well versed in this type of difficult conversation. Govinda's father began.

"Theo, I don't really know the right way to tell you this, so I'm just going to come out and say it. A half an hour ago, your mother was seen by the neighbors clutching her head and screaming. A few minutes later, she jumped off your roof... headfirst. On Earth, the fall would have… um—but with the moon's reduced gravity she was just knocked unconscious."

Theo's whole world screeched to a halt. He was flung into space with nothing and no one, surrounded at once by silence and the deafening roar of every thought he didn't want to let in. He was in a place beyond time, a place of fear, confusion, anger, resentment, sadness, hopelessness. He found himself on the side of a planet-sized mountain of ice, frigid, exposed, unable to get any traction. After what seemed like ages, he came up for air and found his way back to the world.

"No… No, she couldn't. Was she… she could've been cleaning the roof? And she just slipped, or…" As he said it, he knew it wasn't true, but it didn't feel right to accept that his mother would do such a thing.

"I know Theo, I know. No one saw this coming. What's important is she's going to be ok. Doctor Moreau here is running a few tests to try to figure out what may have caused this sudden change in behavior."

Doctor Moreau looked up from his tablet. "Theo, there's nothing conclusive yet, but we'll let you know as soon as we know anything. I'm taking your mother's diagnostics and running a full scan, but it will take a few days to fully analyze. In the meantime, I recommend a week's stay in the Restorative VR Spa. It's very cost-effective. She'll be essentially unconscious, and unable to attempt to harm herself further."

"That, um, ok." Processed Theo. "I don't know how… or… has anyone told my dad yet?"

"We've sent a message to him", Govinda's father offered. "We have yet to hear a reply, but as soon as we hear anything, you'll be the first to know."

"OK." Theo reassured himself. It seemed like the situation was under control. His father would hear the message, and come back as quickly as he could. He might even commandeer a ship and fly it all the way back on his own. "I've never heard of this VR spa. What's going to happen to her there?"

Dr. Moreau calmly explained. "Whatever happened to your mother, she was undergoing severe emotional trauma when she… well, you know. At this new, state-of-the-art VR spa, she will experience all the relaxing effects of treatment at an analog spa- massage, hot stones, sauna, et cetera- without her needing to move a muscle or even be conscious. She will essentially be asleep for a week, allowing her body to heal itself in whatever way it needs to, with a little help from a new, state-of-the-art soothing program developed by the physiomental health engineers at NeuroCom. It's very cost-effective."

"Some of my best programmers oversaw the development of this program." Sid added. "Your mother will be safe there."

Theo didn't know what to say or do. Everything about this situation was foreign to him. Parents were there to protect him until he grew up, whenever that was. His father was off providing, and his mother was here caring for him. Now, with his mother unconscious and his father out of reach, he felt alone. Utterly alone.

Sid saw the look on Theo's face, and placed a hand on his shoulder. "I know this is a lot for you to process right now. No one should have to go through something like this."

Theo nodded absentmindedly, and Dr. Moreau picked up where Govinda's dad left off. "Theo, in the case of an emergency, your parents have designated Sid here to be your legal guardian- that's why he was called here in the first place. Because you're still a minor, for the time your mother is in the spa, you will be living with him. Does that sound all right to you?"

The way Theo saw it, he didn't have much of a choice, so again, he just nodded.

"Good." Sid said with a semi-forced smile. He glanced at Govinda, then returned to Theo with renewed energy. "As a matter of fact, I have to take a business trip to Earth for the next few days- why don't you come along?"

Theo could see they were just trying to cheer him up, but it was all too much—he just wanted to curl up in a ball, in a dark room, until this was all over. In fact, that image alone gave him comfort, so he settled into it.

Govinda flicked him on the shoulder and Theo came back. "Go dude, it's a good distraction."

"Can Govinda come?" Theo asked, trying to at least be involved in the planning of what was happening to him.

The adults exchanged glances again, which Govinda saw, quickly cutting in—

"I've got school dude. For now, you just go have fun, and I'll keep an eye out for Cute Nose. We'll fill each other in when you get back."

Theo looked around. His mother lying on the bed, the subtle beeping of the medical equipment (annoying in its quietness), the three people around him who he felt both grateful for and indignant toward for either helping or coddling him, he couldn't tell which. All he knew was that he wanted to be anywhere but here.

"When do we leave?"

FOUR

EXTERNAL ALGORITHM 5230-CAM
"It is by going down into the abyss that we recover the treasures of life. Where you stumble, there lies your treasure."

STRONGBACK RETRACT. ENGINE CHILL NOMINAL.
A mechanical human voice echoed in Theo's ears.

At 7:56 am UTC (Coordinated Universal Time), Theo found himself being strapped into a back-row seat in the cockpit of the OriginX Rocket Charon. He had only been given a few hours to pack a small suitcase of clothes for the journey before getting picked up by Govinda's father and shuttled to the launch pad just outside the Aerodome. He was still in a bit of a daze from the events of the day before. His lack of sleep made it feel like the day hadn't yet ended at all, so there was, as of yet, no separation between the horror of the previous day's events and the adventure that awaited him. At Govinda's goading, he had agreed to spend the next week visiting Earth on a business trip with his father. For Theo, Earth was just a distant memory, a pretty ornament hanging in the sky. The Great Exodus occurred when he was 8, so he barely remembered any of it. In fact, now that he thought about it, he wasn't even sure what caused the Exodus in the first place. *Oh well,* he thought, *there had to have been a good reason, otherwise it wouldn't have happened.*

I wonder what Earth will be like when we get there, he thought, trying to distract himself from the surrounding commotion. He knew about Earth history—he'd learned it in school. They lived in large governed societies, not privatized communities, like him. For the last few thousand years there had been wars of nation-states and ideas, unimaginable bloodshed, struggles between groups and individuals. The only constant, he had been taught, was the savagery that came with a lack of control over one's animal instincts. The people of the Moon, and the upper classes in general, got that way and stayed there because they were able to value logic and reason over anger and lust. Everyone had access to these answers, but those who took the initiative to find and follow the idea of delayed gratification were rewarded, and justly so. *Maybe that's why the Exodus happened,* Theo thought, giving it his own personal stamp of approval. *The people who actually put in the effort got tired of dealing with the lazier, impulsive ones, so they made their own community away from everyone else. That makes about as much sense as anything else.*

"Ready Theo?" Sid sat down in the seat to the right of Theo, strapping himself in. Theo nodded.

"I know you're not, but there's no need to be nervous. Captain Green will take care of everything." He raised his voice so as to be heard over the sounds of the pre-takeoff mechanics. "WON'T YOU BILL?"

"WHAT? YEAH! THIS THE KID? EVERYTHING'S GONNA BE SMOOTH AS WARM BUTTER ON TOAST."

If Theo wasn't nervous before, he definitely was now, after everyone had felt the need to reassure him. Anything that was really safe didn't require reassurance. And now he was hungry, too.

Sid kept talking. "The trip to Earth will take about 55 hours- we'll have about 2 days in space, and land off the coast of Los Angeles at about 7 AM local time. For now, just sit back, and enjoy the ride."

Theo nodded, and turned to look forward again. Nerves buzzed all over his body, growing in intensity and irritatingness by the second. He felt his pulse quickening, and could hear his heart thud louder and louder between his ears, and the butterflies trapped in his gut started flying around. He took a deep breath, something his father had always reminded him to do if he was ever stressed. It seemed to slow the acceleration of his anxiety.

T-MINUS ONE MINUTE TO LAUNCH. COMMENCE STARTUP. PREPARE FOR FINAL COUNTDOWN.

There were six seats in the cockpit, in three rows of two. Theo and Sid were in the back row, Captain Bill and what looked to be the copilot were in the front row, and two people who Sid had introduced as coworkers were in the middle row. He knew precious little about them, but all five of his companions were talking and laughing lightheartedly like they weren't about to be launched into space in a tin can at multiple times the speed of sound. Either they were all stupid, or they knew something Theo didn't. *They've all probably made this trip dozens of times,* Theo told himself. *If they aren't nervous, there's no reason for me to be.* Despite his ironclad reasoning, Theo was still unable to relax. He had no idea why.

T-MINUS 15 SECONDS.

Captain Bill turned around. "Ready team?"

"Woohoo!" "Hell yeah!" "Who are you calling team?"

Bill laughed- "Remember Dave, no holding your arms above your head. I don't wanna have to pop your shoulder back in again."

Dave, who was in the second row, put his arms up defiantly to make a point, then put them down again when it got the laugh he was aiming for.

10 SECONDS.

Theo took another deep breath and pushed himself as far back into his seat as he could- he didn't want any sort of whiplash. He wasn't sure if that was something that happened, but taking every precaution he could think of made him feel a little better.

5. (Here we go.)

4.

3. (Is my seatbelt pinching?)

2. (Was it like this before or did I just notice now?)

1. (I have to pee.)

LIFTOFF. SEMPER FI, AND RISE.

With a muffled roar, Theo and the rest of his companions were thrust into the backs of their seats. With all the hooting and hollering that had filled the last few minutes, Theo was unnerved by the relative silence that overtook the cabin. With great difficulty he turned his head to look at Sid. Only the tip of his nose was visible through the plexiglass of his helmet, which fogged and faded in an almost meditative rhythm. Facing front again, the rest of the crew sat stoically, vibrating to and fro like stiff ragdolls as the capsule shot them further and further away from the only home Theo had known for the past nine years.

He wished he could look back at it. He imagined the grey, lightly terraformed rock he had come to love shrinking below him, with Cute Nose looking up and waving frantically, screaming for him to come back. When he'd returned from his mission, they'd finally be together, hug each other tight, and do whatever else people did when they were being together. *I bet she has a nice voice. Maybe even a little lisp—that'd be cute.* He chuckled wistfully, trying to dwell on the feeling, but the cruel rumbling of the rocket yanked him out of his fantasy in seconds.

I hope my mom is OK.
I hope Govinda checks on her while I'm gone.
I bet he will.

The two had been friends since they'd met at camp the summer before the Exodus, and other than his mother, Govinda was the only real constant he'd had in his life. Immediately Theo added his father to that list, but the more he considered his place in that group, the guiltier he felt. He shook his head and went back to thinking about Govinda.

He remembered the first time he'd seen his best friend- Theo was six, Govinda a young seven, and neither wanted to be at sleepaway camp. Theo had spent the first day in tears, hiding from the counselor who was hunting him, forcing him to have *fun*. He had just wanted to be back home with his mother and father, watching TV and doing the same comforting, boring things they always did. He and his mother would each sit on a couch, and Theo's dad would settle into his La-Z-Boy as they ate dinner and watched whatever movie they'd picked for that night.

But none of that familiarity was at camp. Camp was filled with loud and raucous strangers, all seeming to know something he didn't. Already, he'd seen two kids start bleeding, he'd gotten four mosquito bites, and he'd watched a group of girls all scream after an older boy mooned them. He was back hiding under his bunk, almost out of tears to cry, when he heard the sound of feet coming down the hall. He froze.

From beneath his bed, he saw two legs come into the room, not big enough to belong to a counselor. He squeezed his stuffed wombat closer to his chest and tried to keep still until this kid left. The strange legs walked over to the bed, and climbed the ladder to the top bunk. Theo closed his eyes and screamed internally, wishing with every ounce of his wishing power that this kid would just leave so he could be alone and miserable again. The springs of the top bunk squeaked as Theo's worst enemy laid down and seemed to be settling in. Theo was livid, but stayed silent. There were still 11 days left of this horror, and he didn't want to be known as the crying kid for the rest of it. He wiped his eyes with his wombat, and got ready to dig in for the long haul. He couldn't crawl out now- then the kid would ask why he was under the bed, and why his eyes were red, and was that snot on his wombat, and what even is a wombat, and then he'd be known as the bed-hiding red-eyed crying wombat sniffer for the rest of his life. He sniffled a little.

The top bunk squeaked.

"Hello? Someone in here?"

Theo froze. He knew he shouldn't have sniffled. He heard the squeal of the top bunk's springs straining under the small child's weight, and then the light tapping of said child coming down the ladder. He jumped down the last few rungs with a *thunk*.

Theo watched as the kid slowly walked around the room.

"I know you're here. I heard you." said the hunter, stalking its prey. Theo shrunk back away from the light. There was no possible way this could get any worse.

The kid turned to face the bunk. Theo watched his world ending—the knobbly knees, uneven white socks, and dirty sneakers stalked closer and closer to his hiding spot until they stopped, a mere foot from Theo's still dripping nose.

A small hand reached down from above—in it, a half-opened chocolate bar.

"You want some?"

Theo didn't want to give up his position, but he couldn't get his mother's words out of his head. Six hours earlier, Theo had clung tight to his mother's leg, a few feet from the door of the bus, begging her not to make him go to camp. She gently pulled him off, knelt down, looked him in the eye, and said—

"Theodore, no one said making friends was easy. But every strong relationship starts with trusting someone, and giving someone the opportunity to trust you. You can do this."

"I don't need friends. I have my wombat," he'd said, frowning.

Back under the bed, six hours later, the sentiment was still the same.

But he really wanted chocolate.

He reached up and broke off a piece.

Knobbly Knees spoke again. "I'm Govinda! Assuming this is your bunk, looks like we're gonna be bunkmates."

Theo nibbled on his chocolate. It was good. No nuts.

"I thought we weren't supposed to bring snacks." Theo said feebly, still hiding.

"Yeah, well, I'm not gonna go two weeks without chocolate. They barely have any candy here. And the candy they do have, you have to buy. I don't have any money, I'm seven! So I brought some. You can have some too, since I told you about it, but don't tell anyone else. I don't have enough for everyone."

"Ok." Theo said, unsure of everything except that having more chocolate in the future would be a good thing.

"What's your name?" asked Govinda's knees.

"Theo" said Theo.

"Hey Theo. You wanna come out? I think someone threw up under there last year. They probably cleaned it up, but still, I wouldn't wanna be down there."

Theo scrambled out from under the bed, with all the speed and agility of a nighttime rat who suddenly found itself in a beam of light. He recovered himself just enough to give his face and nose another rough wipe with his stuffed wombat as he stood up. For the first time, he looked at his chocolate dealer. An unwashed bowl cut sat on top of a ruddy face covered in chocolate, dirt, or both. The face grinned to reveal a missing tooth, and more chocolate that didn't make it all the way down.

"You weren't here last year. Is it your first time?"

Theo nodded sullenly. He looked back at his hiding place.

"Don't worry, no one threw up under there. As far as I know. I just wanted to get you out from under there. It's my second year. I hated it the first time I was here, but it got fun pretty quick. You wanna play some frisbee golf?"

Theo shifted. He didn't particularly want to do anything. But this kid seemed nice, and gave him chocolate.

"Ok."

Govinda bounded up his ladder. "Cool! You don't smell like camp yet. Put on some bug spray. Then the mosquitos won't bother you." He tossed a bottle down to Theo, who had to throw his wombat on his bed so he could catch it.

"What's that? Some kind of beaver? Where's its tail?"

"It's a wombat."

"It doesn't look like a bat. But that's cool. Come on, we gotta go before all the frisbees get taken. I like frisbee golf cause the course takes you away from all the loud people."

Theo sprayed himself all over with the bug spray and threw it on Govinda's bed. It smelled weird. Without a word, the two walked down the hall of the cabin dorm and opened the door into the blinding light and deafening roar of the first day of camp.

And everything went quiet. Theo blinked as the interior of the cockpit lit up. Still strapped into his seat, he started to feel himself lightly bouncing between the back of his seat and his seatbelt.

The two adults in the middle row unstrapped themselves and went out the rear door. The copilot took out a checklist and Captain Bill Green began flipping switches and talking through the radio to ground control. Sid leaned over and tapped Theo's arm with the back of his hand.

"Hey-- the hard part's over. Now its smooth sailing until we land. You get through that OK?"

Theo turned a little towards Sid, held back by the bulk of his space suit and the straps, gave a thumbs up, and went back to the position of least effort, facing forward with arms on armrests.

"Good. I knew you would. I'm gonna go take care of some work stuff—while we're cruising you're free to go wherever you want. Just don't flip any switches or anything. If you have any questions, feel free to ask. Okay Theo?"

Theo gave another thumbs up. Sid nodded and turned to go out the rear door. But before he reached it, he heard a loud snore.

Theo, so exhausted by the events of the past day, had fallen asleep in his chair.

FIVE

EXTERNAL ALGORITHM 7362-WAT
"The attitude of faith is to let go, and become open to the truth, whatever that might turn out to be."

    For the few seconds before Theo opened his eyes, he was blissfully ignorant of everything that was happening to him. Very quickly, he realized he was weightless, which meant he wasn't waking up in his bed at home. He opened his eyes and found himself in a small closet, strapped to the wall in a sleeping bag. His arms, limp just a few seconds before, had been floating like those of a dead man in a koi pond, sticking out of the armholes in the bag. He was on a space shuttle, and none of what had happened to him in the past 36 hours was a dream. Weightless, he tried to sink deeper into his bag. It didn't work. He ground his teeth together in frustration, and tried to cry, but he had no tears left from the day before. He had to pee.

    He unzipped himself from his bag, took a deep breath, and opened the door of his sleeping closet. He found himself in a round hallway with walls covered in light blue handles and patches of rough Velcro. He looked about- there were doors on either side of him, one three meters to the left, and another about four meters to the right. He pushed off to the left, and immediately slammed into the ceiling. *This is harder than it looks in movies,* he thought.

    After a minute or two of trial and error he reached the door, and with the press of a thankfully labelled button, it slid open to reveal more hallways above, below, and in front of him. Instantly he heard voices from ahead, so he launched himself in that direction. As he floated along the hallway, he started to be able to make out who was talking- He recognized two voices- Sid, who at the moment was laughing at something said by Dave, the one who wouldn't keep his arms down.

"I see your point, it's just a stupid point!" said Sid, calming himself down enough to speak.

"I don't think you do! We can't fix a problem if we don't know what the problem is!" bellowed Dave, incredulously.

"Maybe you should have brought that up before the company spent a couple million flying us to Earth HQ?" said a new, female sounding voice he hadn't heard yet. "And isn't your job to find and fix bugs?"

"If this were just a bug, I could write a script to find it and fix it in an hour. Which is what I DID, and it didn't find anything! The problem isn't with my code."

Sid cut in. "Well, whatever this issue is, we need to fix it before it gets any worse. There were 16 incidents yesterday on the moon alone, and the doc is swamped. I have a few—oh, hey Theo! How'd you sleep?"

Theo had reached the three adults, who seemed to be sitting around a square table despite the lack of gravity. There was Sid, who he knew, sitting opposite a young looking, mid-20s male with a very punchable face. On the opposite side of the table from Theo sat an athletic-looking woman either in her late 20s or early 30s, with hair pulled back into a tight ponytail.

"Ok." replied Theo. "Where's the bathroom?"

Sid pointed- "Right back the way you came, in the same hallway as the sleeping bags. Printout of a poop emoji on the door- use the yellow tube for #1 and the hole and handles for #2. There are instructions on the inside of the door that we put there as a joke, but they should work well enough as real ones. Need me to show you?"

"No, I've got it. Thanks." Theo nodded and went back the way he came.

"Oh, and there's TP and disinfectant wipes on the wall for when you're done." Sid shouted after him.

"Thanks!" Theo shouted over his shoulder as he went through the doorway again. He reached the bathroom, opened the door, and saw the yellow tube Velcroed to the wall, which he took down. He shut the door, and immediately saw the instructional card Sid was talking about. The top half, labelled with a bolded, underlined, and italicized *#1*, said "OPEN IT UP, STICK IT IN, AND DON'T ENJOY THE SUCTION TOO MUCH." He blushed and chuckled. When he finished, he disinfected everything and put the card back on the door. He went back to the table room.

"Everything go alright in there?" Dave asked, a little louder than he needed to.

"Yup. Great instructions too." Theo said, unsure of what to do next.

Sid saved him- "Theo, let me introduce you to these guys- this is Dave, idiot savant, emphasis on the idiot- my protégé and greatest annoyance."

Dave puffed out his chest, smiled, and bowed in a gesture of mock humility. "What he means is—"

Sid cut him off. "And this is Dr. Rita Patrick, our chief medical specialist."

The woman offered a hand, which Theo shook after a second of maneuvering himself to the table. He overshot, but quickly grabbed his end of the table to steady himself. As he shook and pulled himself back, she spoke.

"You can call me Rita. There's a switch on your bench that should allow you to sit, by the way. It activates a magnet that attracts the metal wiring in the sitting area of your suit."

Theo came to a sitting position a few inches above the bench, found a switch, and flipped it. With a startling jolt his suit pulled him down to the bench. He let out a small yelp as embarrassment flooded his cheeks.

Dave laughed, and Rita stifled a chuckle. "Takes you by surprise the first time. Happens to the best of us. Hungry?"

Theo was grateful for the compassion, but a little resentful that he felt he needed it. He buried these thoughts and nodded. Rita reached behind her and pulled out three silvery packages, two with small white cap-looking attachments.

"These are yours. PB&J, creamed spinach, and a mango smoothie".

"Thanks" Theo said, taking them. He ripped open the package labelled 'PB&J' to reveal a tortilla folded over into a quesadilla-style envelope. Noting the confused look on his face, Sid explained.

"Tortillas last way longer than bread. It's a short enough flight to have bread, but we're on a budget. Dave, you wanna hydrate his spinach?"

Dave, who took a second to realize it wasn't really a question, grabbed Theo's spinach packet and spun around on his bench. He stuck the white cap into an opening on the wall, made a few selections on the adjacent screen, and pressed a big red button. With a low but satisfying *gzzzztztz*, the bag inflated slightly. When it was done, Dave gave it back to Theo, then did the same with his smoothie.

Wanting to eat rather than talk, Theo asked "So what's this business trip for?", before biting into his grown-up Uncrustable.

Dave laughed. "That's my question too- Sid, you wanna tell him?"

Sid kicked Dave under the table. Dave whined.

"Owwwwww!"

Sid ignored him. "Well, that is a bit of a mystery. We have a new update coming out for the NeuroComs soon, but we've gotten reports of a few inconsistencies across our platform. As of now, our main headquarters is still Earth HQ, so that's where we'll have the best chance of fixing the problem quickly enough that we won't have to push back the release date."

Theo nodded, camel chewing to get the peanut butter out of all his nooks and crannies. He swallowed and asked, overenunciating. "What thorts of inconthithtencies?"

Sid hesitated, and looked at Rita, then Dave, then his plate. Theo realized he had accidentally struck a chord that may have been better left unstruck.

"Nevermind, I was just curious. You don't have to—"

"No, no, it's alright" acquiesced Sid. "I'm just not sure how best to explain it. We've gotten some reports from employees on Earth of glitches in our terminals—the programs our coders use to write our code. Um---"

Dave cut in, apparently helping out Sid. "You know what bugs are? Little bits of a code that aren't quite right, and cause problems that compound on each other the more a program iterates through that buggy line? Well, we've had more of those than usual lately, but the problem is, none of our coders will cop to admitting they messed up. So, either they're lying and getting worse at their jobs at a staggering rate, or..."

"Or... we don't know. But we hire only the best coders to work for us— either they average six failed startups apiece, or we poached them from the top of the Big Four tech conglomerates. Dave may think they're lying, but I know these guys- they're the best of the best. There's no way they got that careless, that quickly. At this point all we have to go on is what they've told us, which is just them covering their asses—Oop, sorry about that. Don't tell your mom."

Theo froze. He'd never heard an adult curse in front of him before. His mother said cursing was a sign of an inactive imagination. But his mom respected Sid, and he was widely thought to be one of the greatest innovators of their time. That didn't make sense. He took a chance. "Your -ass- is safe with me."

The three adults burst out laughing. Dave stuck his hand out for a high five, which Theo slapped emphatically. They calmed down and Sid continued, with a lighter, somewhat relieved energy.

"Oh good, I'm glad you've kept a little bit of your dad's rebellious streak. Your mother is a fantastically intelligent and kind woman, but your father was always the one who got her to loosen up."

"Say what you want with us kid. Welcome to the world- here you can be different people with different people." Dave tacked on.

Theo's eyes and mouth were agape and smiling in astonishment at the sudden change in energy of the group, and how openly and candidly they talked to him about his parents. He fixed his face, but noted that the feeling of community he'd picked up on between the three adults, once separate from the dynamic between him and Sid, now felt as though it was beginning to encompass him as well. He felt a surge of well-being and confidence wash over the kneejerk reaction to receiving pity he'd been soaked in for the past two days. For a brief second, he felt great, and something inside him reached out to capitalize on that feeling.

"So if it's not the coders, what the fuck could it be?"

Sid and Rita winced. Dave snickered. *Too much.*

Sid grabbed a bag of trail mix. "Well, it could be a glitch in our operating system. But out of nowhere, when things have been running smoothly for so long, that doesn't make sense. Once we get down there, we'll be able to see the problems in action, and figure out where to go from there."

Theo finished his sandwich and moved on to the smoothie. "Is it possible you got hacked?"

Sid laughed. "That's fun to think about, but we go to great lengths to make sure that's not possible. No one can adjust our code without being in our facility, since we run a completely closed system—we don't even have Wi-fi. We have multi-factor biological and informational authentication systems keeping non-employees out of the facility, as well as IQ and personality tests to determine who we hire, so unless we got on the bad side of a ghost who can go through walls, then turn solid and code, I think we can safely say that's not what happened."

He downed the rest of the trail mix and flicked the switch on his seat, floating up a few inches.

"Dave, we should probably get back to work. Theo, there's a laptop Velcroed to the wall outside the bathroom with some movies on it if you get bored of floating around. Rita?"

She stared at Sid, daring him to give her an order.

"You do you."

Sid and Dave got up and floated over to a large Ziploc garbage bag, where they threw away their empty meal packets. Dave stuck a fist out, Theo pounded it, and the two floated back in the direction of the sleeping closets. Theo looked at his creamed spinach, ambivalent.

"You don't have to eat that if you don't want to. I hate spinach." Said Rita, pulling a spoonful of something brown out of her package.

Theo resealed his spinach. "What's that?"

Rita smiled and spoke with a half full mouth. "Chocolate cake. I'd offer you some, but I want it."

Theo chuckled halfheartedly. Rita noticed and started rooting around behind her. "I think you have one here somewhere. Yeah, here it is—scheduled for tonight. You want it now?"

Theo made a face, not saying yes, not saying no. Rita frisbeed it over to him.

"That's what I thought."

Theo opened his cake, took off the plastic spoon that was taped to the bag, and pulled out a bite. It was so moist and dense, not what he'd expected from bagged space cake. He chuckled mournfully.

"What?" Rita asked.

Theo shrugged, and shoveled another bite of moist space cake into his mouth. "It's my birthday today. It's just… not how I expected to spend it."

Rita processed for a second, then asked "How old are you?"

"17." He replied, pouring all of his morose focus into his cake.

Rita thought for a second, then flipped her bench switch and started floating away from her bench. "Come with me. We've got time, so I might as well show you now."

Theo swallowed uncomfortably, flipped his switch, and followed Rita down the hallway toward the sleeping closets. Right before they went through the door, they went down a level. As Theo floated down and forward, Rita opened a door in front of them to reveal a room with six black sets of robot legs strapped to a wall, opposite six sets of robot torsos of varying sizes. Theo dropped his cake. It just floated there.

"When we get to Earth, there will be six times the gravity you're used to. These suits should help you support your own weight while you adjust."

Theo floated around the room, looking at each pair of appendages. Now that he saw them closer, he realized that they weren't full legs and arms, but rather were built to strap on to existing ones.

"Which ones are mine?" asked Theo.

Rita pointed to the further of the two smaller pairs. "Try that one on. See how it fits."

Theo took his legs off the wall and strapped himself in. They fit perfectly. He did the same with the arms. He looked down at himself. He looked awesome. He pulled himself against the far wall and launched himself off, palms face down like Iron Man.

Rita laughed. "That exoskeleton was made for Govinda. Luckily you two are the same size."

Theo reached the other end of the room. He'd completely forgotten about his best friend ever since they'd lifted off. And now that he thought about it, it was eminently clear that Govinda was supposed to be here, not him. This suit fit both of them, right now. It was probably made specially for him, for this trip. A dense pulse of guilt increasingly throbbed in Theo for wearing it, for sleeping where Govinda was supposed to sleep, for eating what Govinda was supposed to eat. He looked at the bag of cake that was still floating a few feet from where he'd left it. That was Govinda's cake. He pushed himself back to the other end of the room and started unstrapping himself.

"Done already?" He jumped- he'd forgotten Rita was there.

"Yeah" said Theo, coolly. "I wanna get back to this cake."

Rita gave an accepting chuckle, and the two left the room.

○

After getting back to the kitchen, the two finished their cake, and Rita left to go do an inventory of their medical supplies. Theo, now alone and unsure what to do, floated around to explore the ship. He went up the hallway from the kitchen, and found the empty cockpit. He doubled back, and went up where he'd gone down earlier with Rita. There was nothing interesting up there, just more handles, Velcro, and printouts of bad Millennial and Gen Z memes. At the far end of that section of the spacecraft Sid and Dave were both on laptops, arguing about something. He didn't want to disturb them, so he went back down to the sleeping closet hallway. He found the laptop Sid had told him about, returned to his closet, and opened it.

Cozied up in his wall bag, he scrolled through and barely recognized any of the titles. *1776... 1984... 2001: A Space Odyssey... Brave New World... nah.* Theo sighed.

DittoCon 2038?

Now that I've met the guy, this could be interesting. He pressed play.

Bob Ditto stood alone on a vast black stage. With the press of a small button hidden in his hand, a two-story screen lit up behind him, revealing the Malum Inc. logo- a chrome caduceus with an apple core replacing the orb that traditionally sits atop the central staff. The darkened audience erupted into applause. As they roared with approval, he pointed to someone in the front row, exchanging grins, before looking out over the crowd. He pressed his hands together in a prayer position and lent a slight bow of humility, before raising a hand to quell the crowd. They quieted to a murmur, and he spoke.

"I guess you've heard the rumors then."

A ripple of laughter echoed through the audience as he threw them a knowing wink. Something was yelled out from the audience that Theo couldn't quite make out.

"What rumor?" Bob repeated, slathered in false incredulity. "What rumor. This guy!"

An aftershock of laughter filled the auditorium.

Of course they'd heard it, it was purposely leaked months ago to test the waters, affirmed Theo.

"I'm gonna be honest with you…" started Bob, as everyone in the room chuckled. "I'm nervous."

The audience went silent. He continued.

"Let me tell you why. I'm nervous because with each passing day, thousands of people are losing their jobs to automation. I'm nervous because the gap between the rich and the poor has never been wider. I'm nervous because you cannot program human decency into the Societal Operating System, and let me be honest one more time—it is advancing in its capabilities, faster than ever."

An anxious murmur rose from the audience. Bob called out over the crowd.

"Now let me tell you why I'm not nervous."

The mob of lanyard-wearers fell silent again.

"I'm not nervous, because we have never been better equipped to deal with these problems. Our current Head Programmer has guided the OS in developing and integrating a job placement routine that has reassigned over a billion displaced workers. The rich are richer, yes, but so are the lowest income levels of society—in the past ten years, we've eradicated extreme poverty throughout the world, and through Science, we've made sure that no one in the world has to go to bed hungry. Ever."

The audience erupted into cheers.

"Yes! Cheer! That's to be celebrated! Never before have we faced so much change, and made so much progress, in so little a time. But, we still have a major problem ahead of us."

The atmosphere shrank to a whisper as he continued.

"Like I said before, the Societal Operating System is increasing in its capabilities, in ways faster and more complex than we're able to understand. As a species we have created something so useful, so *powerful*, that the possibility has arisen that sometime soon we may end up in the passenger seat to our own offspring, just along for the ride. Our current Head Programmer has taken a few modest steps to make sure that doesn't happen, but I think it's clear to anyone who's paying attention—HE IS NOT. DOING. ENOUGH!"

The crowd started to quake in anticipation.

"SO! It is with profound excitement, that I hereby declare my official candidacy to represent you as Head Programmer of the Societal Operating System!"

Ecstatic screams and bellows of approval flooded the auditorium, so much so that Theo had to remove his headset for a second until it died down.

The man can work a crowd, I'll give him that. He lowered the volume and tuned back in.

"As you all know, I have done my best to address this issue through the free market. It has been a long, hard slog through the trenches, but through Malum's flagship product, the NeuroCom, I have begun to bridge the gap between man and machine."

Theo rolled his eyes. *Sure, you did. It's not like Sid had anything to do with it.*

Bob clicked the button in his hand, and the screen behind him flashed to a picture of a mud hut sitting on the front lawn of a mansion.

"What does this picture look like to you?"

He paused for dramatic effect, before pointing to another audience member and grinning like he was trying to get the spotlight to reflect off his teeth into the audience's eyes.

"No, it's not a house in need of a sauna upgrade, I know how you love your sauna Joe!" he said with a wink. "When I look at this picture, I see the world. Some are lucky enough to live in lavish houses, while others' whole houses would fit in the garage of the lucky few. And this gap is widening ever faster.

It's true, that this is partially due to the improvements offered by having a NeuroCom. That one little chip can put you lightyears ahead of the competition. Imagine being able to look something up on a search engine the same way you try to remember something you saw a few seconds ago. Having all of human knowledge at your fingertips is nothing compared to having all of human knowledge next to your neurons."

The crowd chuckled. He continued.

"But currently, only those who are already fortunate can afford this upgrade. So, we face a double problem, that compounds on itself daily. On one hand, the gap between the fortunate and the downtrodden is growing exponentially as a result of this miracle technology. Those with the upgrade are vastly more effective and productive. But on the other hand, we can't level the playing field by removing them—the Societal Operating System grows smarter and more complex by the second, and every second we waste is a second in which we fall further behind, and chance losing our freedom at the hands of our own creation. What are we to do?"

Theo's eyelids hung heavy. He already knew what was coming, but the audience was just starting to get it.

"It seems obvious to me—we have no choice but to accelerate our efforts forward. With that in mind, I would like to announce the foundational Disruption Initiative on which I am running. As Head Programmer, I pledge to bring us into the Future, FASTER, by giving everyone access to NeuroComs, absolutely FREE."

The audience went berserk. In between the bellows and hollers of approval that followed the initial gasps, an uproarious applause shook the auditorium to its foundation. The once dark crowd was suddenly filled with the glow of phone screens on faces. In seconds, the whole world had heard the news, and simultaneously, a few weeks later, Theo had drifted off to sleep.

Still, the video continued.

"Now that that's out of the way, let me tell you about the newest revolutionary NeuroCom update." Bob said as he clicked his little button. "We've heard you, and we've taken the initiative of rebuilding our software from the ground up…"

◯

When Theo opened his eyes, the hallway outside his closet was dark. The movie laptop, still Velcroed to the wall in front of him, had died. He'd been out for a while. Half asleep, he unzipped himself and took the laptop off the wall. He floated down the hall, glancing into his shipmates' closets- they were all zipped up and fast asleep. He drifted over to the bathroom and plugged the laptop in to the opposite wall to charge. Out of the corner of his eye, through the window in the hatch to his left, he saw a faint glow.

That wasn't there a second ago, thought Theo. He floated over to the hatch and opened it. He cringed as it slid open, louder than he'd remembered, and floated through to the next hallway.

The ship was deathly silent. He looked below him to the hall where Rita had shown him the exoskeletons- pitch black. He looked above to the hallway where he'd seen Sid and Dave working- just as lifeless. He kept propelling himself forward until he reached the kitchen. There were a few small red buttons lit up on the hydrator, but those were always like that. Then, movement, out of the corner of his eye, through the small hatch window in the cockpit. He turned and pushed himself toward the door.

Probably just Captain Green running through a checklist before we land tomorrow.

But he'd seen Captain Green asleep in his closet, along with everyone else on the ship.

Theo floated over to the hatch window, and peered in. He stifled a gasp.

Floating in the center of the cockpit was a woman he'd never seen before. In fact, she was unlike anything he'd ever seen before. She wasn't a woman. She couldn't be. She was *glowing*. He could see *through* her. She wasn't wearing any clothes, and she seemed to be made up of what he could only describe as lightly wafting energy, flavored with semi-transparent shades of purple, blue, silver, and white. There was a flowing silver cord coming from her navel that seemed to go straight through the front of the cockpit.

Theo watched in horrified confusion and curiosity as this strange being floated around the cockpit, searching for something. After a second, without any sort of external force, she floated over to a panel on the side the cockpit. Theo watched, enthralled, as she took two fingers and stuck them a few inches *into* the panel. She was motionless for what felt like an eternity as Theo looked on, all sense of agency having dissipated and been replaced by sheer wonder. Then, without warning, she removed her fingers and turned to look directly into Theo's eyes. He froze. In the space of less than a second, her eyes betrayed a look of terrified recognition, and the once-loose silver cord suddenly pulled taut and whisked her through the front of the rocket, out into oblivion.

Theo floated, stunned. *Was she messing with the rocket? What was she doing? How was she there? What WAS she?* He gathered his wits about him and opened the cockpit hatch. He pushed himself over to the panel that she had touched- nothing seemed out of the ordinary. He maneuvered over to where the silver cord had pulled her through the control panel and scanned for any sort of damage or residue, something. Nothing. He looked out the window at the never-ending blackness of space, a million thoughts racing through his head all at once. *What was she? Am I dreaming? Whatever that was, it was impossible. I should tell Captain Green. But he'd never believe me. I should at least tell Sid. But what if it's nothing? He'll think I'm crazy for the rest of the trip. If I tell Dave, he'd just laugh. I won't tell Dave. But what about Rita? No, same thing as Sid. I haven't even met the copilot yet; I can't tell him. Talk about a bad first impression. Should I tell Sid though? What if it is something? But it can't be, it's impossible. But maybe...*

Theo, lost in thought, paralyzed by fear, confusion, and the possibility of harsh derision from the only stability at his disposal, floated back to his closet. Safely confined in his chrysalis, he stayed awake for hours, playing the memory of what he had seen over and over in his head, until he finally sank deep, into a quiet, dreamless slumber.

SIX

EXTERNAL ALGORITHM 2638-MUR
Whatever can go wrong, will go wrong.

Theo woke to a knock. He peered out the small plastic window to see Sid gesturing for him to open the door. He did, a bit resentful of being woken up despite how well rested he was.

"We just passed the ISS and the inner Van Allen belt, so we're about T-minus 4 hours from splashdown. I let you sleep as long as I could."

Theo nodded as his nervous butterflies started waking up.

"Go ahead and grab a bite to eat, and get your exoskeleton on. Rita said she showed you where? Good. You'll need to be ready and strapped in in the cockpit in 30 minutes."

Theo nodded again, and Sid floated away, leaving Theo alone.

Theo made his way to the kitchen. He rummaged through the food box Rita had used the day before, finding the only three food packets left- another PB&J quesadilla, applesauce, and dehydrated kale. He left the kale in the box, hydrated his applesauce, and headed down a level. He'd finished his applesauce and was starting on his quesadilla when he got to the exoskeleton storage room. The hatch slid open, and he nearly choked on his space sandwich when he saw the only person on the ship he hadn't met yet- a gruff, stocky man of few words with hair so curly it looked like a slinky factory had exploded on his head.

"You know you really shouldn't be eating anywhere other than the kitchen. Crumbs or any sort of liquid could cause problems if they found their way into the mechanics."

Theo froze, mid bite. After a second, he swallowed the food that was already in his mouth. Through a peanut butter glazed mouth, Theo managed to eek out "Tschorry".

The man finished strapping on his leg braces and smiled. "I'm just messin' with ya, I don't care. It is true though. Hank Thompson, copilot."

He reached out his hand to shake. Theo reached out his hand, noticed a bit of peanut butter on it. He licked it off, and began to offer it again. He thought better of it, wiped his hand on his pant leg, then offered it a third time. Amid all the action, Hank had clenched his hand into a fist, and Theo gave him an embarrassed fist bump.

Hank gestured to the only torso-leg pairing left on the wall. "Looks like that one's yours. Better suit up, we gotta be strapped in in.... 17 minutes."

Theo grunted, and shoved the rest of his space sandwich into his mouth, careful not to let any crumbs float away. He maneuvered over to his suit and started putting it on.

"When's the last time you were on Earth?" Hank asked.

"Brefrore thre Exrodous", Theo managed to say through the peanut butter.

"That long ago... wow. You may have a little trouble on the first day or two. Gravity's pretty strong there. The suits should help you stand and walk, but your heart will be working triple time pumping blood up to your brain. Try to take it easy. Don't force anything."

Theo swallowed a bit. "Thanks".

Hank nodded. "Don't mention it. Take it from me- the first time I went back, I'd been on the moon for a little over a year. The first day I couldn't stand up without passing out."

Theo wheeled around, aghast. Rita had given him the impression the suit would take care of any problems he'd run into. No one told him the change in gravity would be *that* drastic. Hank wasn't looking at him, strapping himself into his torso, a relaxed expression of focus defining his face. He kept talking.

"But you're young. You should be able to adjust much quicker than I did."

Theo turned his focus back to getting his suit on. "Rita didn't say anything about passing out."

"Maybe she didn't wanna scare you. Personally, I think a little fear is a good thing. Makes things more exciting. And it helps ya keep things in perspective- reminds ya that there are things we don't understand and can't control."

"I saw something last night". Theo blurted out, unable to stop himself.

Hank paused for a second, then resumed what he was doing, still not looking at Theo. "What'd ya see?"

With an air of 'no turning back now', Theo took a deep breath, and replayed the events of the night before to Hank. He told him about the glow, the woman, the string, and her reaching into the side panel. During this Hank finished putting on his suit, but kept listening, looking slightly down and away from Theo.

"Then she turned, looked at me, and got pulled out of the front of the ship. I don't know if she was a ghost, or I was dreaming, or what, but I didn't know who to tell. But I felt like I had to tell somebody, then you said the thing about things we don't understand and..." Theo trailed off.

Hank's expression turned coarse. If he looked at all friendly before, he looked deeply concerned now. He took a deep breath, then another. He started to speak, and shook his head, still refusing to look at Theo. Theo's hand twitched, his space sandwich wanting to give him another bite, his conscience forcing him to wait until he'd gotten Hank's response. After an eternity, Hank cleared his throat.

"I'm glad you told me that. No idea what that was, but it's good to know. Stranger things have happened. I'll see if anything was off on Bill's checklist."

With that, Hank floated over to the hatch, and with a brusque "See ya up there" he disappeared around the corner.

Theo looked around. He wasn't sure if Hank liked him, hated him, or didn't care. Whatever it was, he was glad he hadn't been dismissed outright. Hank had listened to what he had to say. He thought about what Hank had said before about fear- he had been terrified to tell anyone about what he had seen the night before. Hank addressed that fear, placed it in a category as something to be respected and engaged with, rather than avoided and buried, and when Theo tried to work within that framework, he didn't ridicule him, or dismiss his concerns like adults usually did. He treated them with the same seriousness and consideration that Sid or Rita would receive. He hoped Hank liked him. He liked Hank.

Theo finished strapping his skeleton on and made his way up to the cockpit. Fully suited up, he pushed himself through the hatch, and strapped himself into his seat, not quite as nervous as he thought he would be.

Sid tapped him on the arm to get his attention. "You finally met Hank, I hear."

Theo's face flushed, but he kept facing forward so Sid couldn't see. "Yep. He's a really cool guy. Will he be with us the whole trip?"

Sid chuckled. "Not while we're on the ground, but he and Bill are in charge of flying us back at the end of the week."

"Good." Theo sighed. "I wanna talk to both of them more."

"There'll be plenty of time for that when we're moonbound." Sid reassured him.

Theo gave a thumbs up, and settled in.

"Theo here yet?" Bill shouted back, to which Sid responded "Yup."

"Alright, sealing the hatch door. Everyone say goodbye to the booster. Detaching."

An Alcoholics-Anonymous style "*Bye Booster*" filled the cabin, as everyone on board felt their propulsion system separate itself from the capsule. Theo couldn't see it, but imagined it drifting further and further away from them, until it was just a speck on the horizon, and it finally disappeared.

"It'll land on its own so we can refill it and use it again for our trip back." Sid explained.

Theo nodded. He knew nothing about rockets, other than what he had personally experienced. You don't get imprinted with rocketry knowledge until secondary physics, which was supposed to be next semester.

That could be interesting, Theo thought. *Maybe I'll end up being placed in a rocketry career.*

"Oh, and we just got a message this morning from the bi-world legislature" Sid added. "They've picked up a few inconsistencies of their own with the evolution of the OS, and they've asked us to take a look at it while we're here."

Theo gave him a thumbs up, and settled in. Despite everything, he was looking forward to the next week. He didn't really have a picture in his head of what it was going to look like, but he liked the idea of being on the inside of things, seeing the inner workings of the structures holding up society that other people weren't typically allowed to see. The thought popped into his head of whether or not, given the choice, he would go back and stop the events of the last week given all the things he was now going to be allowed to do as a result. He cut off the coal supply to that train of thought. He didn't like where it was going.

For a little over three hours, Theo looked out the window in wonder as the horizon of the Earth came into view, larger than he could have ever imagined. He knew the planet he was born on was bigger than the moon, but it had never really hit him until now how *much* bigger, or for that matter how much more colorful. What in his mind was just a little blue and green marble in the sky was now a huge curved expanse, where deep blue oceans met land covered in all shades of green, tan, brown, grey, white, and black. Snow-capped mountains peeked out below and between wispy clouds, sloping down into brownish then greenish earth. A finely textured ocean stretched out to his left, covered here and there by clouds, until his gaze drifted up to the horizon, where a subconsciously shifting deep blue met a band of blurry white, with the thinnest line of effervescent royal blue separating the clouds from the blackness that stretched further than the mind could think.

"Oh--Theo, Hank told me to tell you everything on the checklist was nominal- I mean normal. We'll keep a lookout for anything strange, but we don't anticipate anything." Captain Bill shouted back.

"Thanks!" Theo sent back up, both beaming with pride and relaxed reassurance.

"What's that about?" Sid asked.

"I saw something weird last night. A shiny ghost lady was in here. She reached into that panel, then got pulled out of the cockpit super fast. It's stupid, and probably nothing, but I didn't wanna not tell anyone. I don't think I was dreaming though."

Sid was quiet for a second. "Pulled?"

"Yeah, there was a silver stringy thing coming out of her stomach. Like an umbilical cord. It pulled her out."

Sid, suddenly lost in thought, cocked his head to the side and murmured "That's... so curious".

Dave, sitting in front of him, cut in. "Hey Sid, think it's the Bohus?"

Sid snapped out of it and laughed, swiftly kicking Dave's chair. "Shut up Dave. They can hear you."

"Who're the Bohus?" Theo asked after the scuffle had subsided.

Sid chuckled. "Tovu Va Bohu- they're a fringe group of eco-terrorists that turned up a little after the Exodus. They live on the internet and make empty threats. They claim to have supernatural powers that they can use to return the earth to a state of ecological balance and utopia. And they don't like Malum very much, to say the least."

"We've gotten a few threats over the past few years, but nothing's come of 'em. Maybe something would, if they'd ever leave the cave they live in." Dave added, before looking up and around, shielding his face with his arms. "Sorry, I forgot you can hear me-- I didn't mean it, I swear!"

Sid laughed. "Look out Dave, you're in for it now. They're going to give you bad dreams and doxx you on 8chan."

Theo laughed nervously. "You guys get threats? Why would anyone do that?"

Sid calmed down a bit. "Just basic rebel hippie stuff. They say we're widening the gap between the rich and the poor, and we're a power-hungry company that only cares about profits."

"Well, some of that stuff *is* happening—but Bob's trying to address it in his campaign, right?" Theo asked cautiously.

"It's more than that though," added Dave. "Apparently we're tainting the *perfect humanity* that nature created."

Sid chimed in. "It's true—we are a for-profit company, and having a NeuroCom implant means you're able to learn and access information faster, which has led to an advantage over non-implanted competition, but that's not all we do. Fixing paralyzed limbs, restoring sight to the blind, emotional regulation… but our main focus is bridging the gap between humans and computers, so when we eventually create an artificial intelligence that's sentient—or at least more intelligent than we are—we can *work* with it rather than be forced to *compete* with it. Part of humanity's 'perfection', if you want to think of it that way, is our ability to adapt."

Dave cut in again. "But those Bohu freaks want everyone to stay completely human, and if you don't, you're deemed a traitor to your species. Anyone with an implant is automatically impure, and in their eyes, no longer human. I think they're just mad at being left behind."

Sid reached out a hand, pacifying Dave a bit. "I don't necessarily know if that's fair to say. There are two sides to every story. No side is more or less valid than the other."

Now they're defending them?

"Unless they're schizo cave dwelling eco-terrorists...?" Dave asked slowly.

"Uhhhhhhh…. I mean…" Sid stuttered with a grin you could hear, as the whole cabin descended into laughter.

Without warning, the whole capsule shook slightly and shut down. Everything electronic turned off, and the entire cabin turned silent as the grave. After about five seconds, everything started to come back on. Dave was the first to speak.

"What the fuck was that?"

Captain Bill looked around as lights came back on one after another. His center console screen flicked on, and he started tapping it.

"I…" he said, checking three things at once, "have no idea. System rebooting. Hank, check drogue and secondary chutes."

"Both still online. Navigation?"

"Seems nominal so far. Could it be a high energy solar ray?" Bill asked.

"Anyone see any stars, lines, any sort of distortion in their vision?" Rita asked the whole cabin.

Everyone replied with various negations. Bill and Hank kept flipping switches and typing things into their console.

"Bill." Hank said gravely.

Everyone was silent. His tone was anything but encouraging. He continued.

"We seem to have lost communication with ground control. Trying to reestablish."

Everyone was silent. No one wanted to say what they were thinking. No one wanted to say anything until they knew for certain what was going on. The capsule started shaking.

"Entering the atmosphere. Communication still severed." Hank said, attempting poorly to suppress his nerves.

Theo, body shaking and heart pounding, looked out the window. White streaks flashed past the window, growing wider and longer as they gained speed and the atmosphere thickened around them. *I feel hot. Is anyone else hot?*

"We've drifted slightly off course. Attempting to correct." Bill said, voice shaking. He typed into his console. "Un—" he swallowed. "Unable to correct without jeopardizing reentry parachute position. Recommend we continue as normal, while attempting to establish communication."

"Affirmative." Hank said. "How far off course are we?"

"Calculating." Bill typed into his console. "Projected landing, 55 miles south of target."

"55 miles is slightly??" Theo yelled over the rumble of the freefalling capsule. No one responded. His unsteadiness growing, he glanced out the window again. Just below them were giant, looming clouds, so huge they dwarfed mountains. What would have filled him with childlike wonder a few minutes ago now gave him an increasing sense of how terrifyingly small and fragile he was with each passing second. Everything outside was suddenly blanketed in motionless white as they shot through a cloud, only to return a few seconds later to the same terrifying freefall as before, with nothing but open air between them and the ocean below. The capsule shuddered.

"Bill, the drogue chutes have been deployed." Hank said, uneasy.

"Did you deploy them?"

"No."

"Neither did I. I think someone else is in control of this capsule."

The cabin was frozen in time despite the frightening speed with which they were closing in on the surface of the planet. They were cut off from Ground Control, hurtling toward an unknown destination for unknown reasons, controlled by someone or something of which they were completely unaware. After a few seconds that seemed much longer, Sid spoke.

"If they wanted us to crash, they wouldn't have opened our parachutes. I think the best course of action is to keep our wits about us until they let us land and we have more information."

No one spoke, but no one had a better suggestion. The capsule shook again, and lurched upward.

"Secondary parachutes deployed." Hank said, out of nothing but duty.

"Apart from trajectory, communication, and control, everything is nominal." Bill joked, shakily.

No one laughed. No one felt like it.

"500 meters to splashdown." Hank said after an uncomfortable silence, eyeing his console.

Theo looked out the window to see three inflatable speedboats racing towards them. He turned back to face the front of the capsule.

"300 meters."

Theo had the strangest feeling that everyone was thinking the same thing, but no one wanted to say it. He took a deep breath, trying to quell the panic that was starting to set in, like his father had taught him. For the first time in his life, it didn't work.

"100 meters. Prepare for splashdown."

Theo shut his eyes, preparing for the worst. He was ready to be slammed against his seat, seatbelt pinching everything, drawing blood. He steeled himself for the whiplash... but it never came. They hit the water like a marble dropped on a pillow. The slight bounce would have been fun, if he weren't so focused on the uncertainty that was currently defining whatever the next few minutes would hold.

He heard shouting outside the capsule as they bobbed up and down. He was immediately struck by how heavy his body felt. Glued to his seat, he tried to lift an arm, but could only sustain it for a few seconds.

Suddenly, the capsule door was violently wrenched open. Blinded by the sunlight pouring through it, he felt someone remove his seatbelt and pull him out of his seat.

All the blood rushed away from his head and toward his feet as his captors pulled him by his armpits across the threshold of the Charon capsule into the crisp sea air. Louder than hell itself, two gunshots echoed inside the capsule. The last thing that came into view before he was swallowed by blackness was the most musclebound woman he had ever seen, standing over him, a gun on either hip, her right eye covered with a blood red eyepatch.

PART 2.
INITIATION.

SEVEN

EXTERNAL ALGORITHM 724-RUM
"Be grateful for whoever comes, because each has been sent as a guide from beyond."

A strange smell jolted Theo awake. The smell of burnt gunpowder, 3D printed polymer and recycled air was just a memory, now supplanted by something new, something... weird. *No, not new...* he thought. *Long forgotten?* Musty and dry, but textured, and somehow more... vivacious. Crisp. Toasty even. There was something else there too—he couldn't quite put his finger on it, but it smelled good. It seemed to clear his sinuses the way a hot mug of mint tea did, but it was more woody, stronger, heavier. He flashed back to his days at camp, going on hikes, jumping into the pond below the waterfall, riding a zipline tied between two—trees! The spiky kind! *Were they pine or fir? I could never tell the difference.*

Thrilled by a smell he had been separated from for nearly a decade, it took him a second to remember the circumstances that brought him to where he was. Come to think of it, he still had no idea where he was. He opened his eyes to see the dusty inside of a forest green canvas tent. He was lying on a cot—taut, scratchy, and forest green, the same color and material as the tent. He looked around, noticing how much heavier his head was than usual. To his left was another cot, empty. The floor and frame of the tent were wood, old but sturdy, with a square wooden pole in the center of the floor stretching up to the ridge of the tent roof. He tried to sit up, his vision swirled, and he instantly saw stars. His heart started pounding, he felt faint, and he collapsed back onto the cot, breathing hard. His head hurt. Straining against gravity, he reached his hand to the area on his scalp right behind his ear, and was startled to find gauze and surgical tape.

Did I get hit? I don't remember that, he thought. His heart sunk.
They took out my NeuroCom.
Theo heard footsteps crunching dirt outside his tent.
And my exoskeleton's gone.

The footsteps got louder; the crunching dirt replaced by a hollow thudding of heels on wood. He pretended to go back to sleep. The footsteps entered the tent, and a female voice spoke, a few feet from Theo.

"See, I told you he's still out."

Another responded. "Well, he'd better wake up soon, or there's no way we'll get the doctor to help us."

The doctor? Theo thought. *Do they mean Rita?*

"I'm gonna check his pulse. Make sure he's still alive."

Theo tried to stay calm as the stranger grabbed his wrist. His anxiety only grew as he felt his pulse running wild under the fingers of his captor.

"Shit. It's going crazy. Something's wrong. Is he having a nightmare?"

"Who cares? Let this Bougie die—less of them can only be a good thing."

"We can't do that, Butler told us to keep him safe."

"Why is that again?"

"Some things are on a need-to-know basis. Some of us don't need to know."

"Yeah, yeah, efficiency not secrecy, keep parroting that bullshit... Should I go get a tranquilizer, or what?"

Theo's eyes flew open. "I'm awake! No tranquilizer, I'm awake!"

The two women screamed. Theo sized up his captors. Both looked around 5' 4", one with a tight ponytail, the other with a loose top-bun. Both were fit, wearing yoga pants and sports bras, and looked a bit unkempt. *I'd probably be nervous if I weren't already freaking out,* he thought.

Their screams turned into laughter.

"Oh, thank god." Said Top Bun, who'd taken his pulse. "That's a relief." She turned to Ponytail.

"Go get Butler. She'll want to know he's up."

"Why do I have to go?", asked Ponytail.

"Well, one of us has to. I can go if you don't want to."

"No, no, I'll go. I just don't like the way you told me what to do. You're not my superior, comrade."

"I never said I was."

"Well, the way you said it made it seem like you were."

"I'm sorry! That wasn't my intention…"

"Well… okay, fine. Just watch your microaggressions. Your internalized hierarchies are showing."

"I will, I'm sorry."

Ponytail left. Top Bun sighed to relax herself, then turned to get a look at Theo.

"You're kinda cute, for a Bougie."

A confused Theo looked around, unsure what to do, or if he should even do anything. He had no idea where he was, what was going on, or how long he had been asleep. He couldn't even sit up, and now he was trapped in a tent by a strange (albeit alluring) woman, with no clue as to whether or not any of his companions, besides Rita, were still alive. The beginnings of tears started welling up his front side. His frustration morphed into the beginnings of anger, and the tears retreated.

"Where… where am I?"

The stranger hesitated for a second, then spoke.

"I'm not really supposed to talk to you until Butler gets here."

"Who's Butler?", Theo pressed further.

Top Bun said nothing.

Theo wanted to jump out of bed and shake his captor until he got some answers, but according to gravity, that wasn't an option. Maybe when this Butler person got here, he could get some answers, or at least some food. His stomach growled.

"I'm about to meet her, right?" He kept going, whether she'd respond or not. "I might as well know who I'm talking to."

She started to say something, then pressed her lips together and shook her head. The two remained in silence, interrupted only by the sound of Theo's annoyed stomach, until the sound of boots crunching on dirt, then wood, drew close to them. The tent flap flew open, and in walked a short woman with short hair and the most intense, piercing eyes Theo had ever seen. She was dressed in a white linen shirt and pants, wearing an earth-toned scarf with a repeating pattern of seven different flower-looking symbols. She looked to be about 60, and carried herself with a matching level of gravitas, but one could tell that just beneath the surface dwelt the spritely energy of someone half her age. At once disarming and engrossing, she squatted down next to Theo.

"So... you're the boy, hm?"

Theo waited for more to come, but none did. She pursed her lips expectantly. Theo opened his mouth, no idea what was about to come out.

"...No?"

The air around them froze as all attention turned toward Butler. No one moved a muscle. Her face, stoic as stone, scanned the boy in the bed before shattering into a smile as she laughed, releasing all the tension in the tent.

"Very good. You show promise already. I had my doubts when the general said you'd fainted within seconds of leaving the capsule, but there is a strength in you yet. My name is Butler."

She reached out her hand to shake. Theo, purely out of reflex, raised his to shake as well, albeit with great difficulty. As their hands met, guilt washed over him. He pulled his hand away as soon as he could, stirred up all the courage he could muster, and let loose.

"Where's Sid? And Rita? Where's everyone else? What happened to the rocket? How... How...." Theo's speech failed him as his vision blurred and his heart began to pound. He breathed faster and harder, harder and faster, no longer able to control the intensity of the very functions that kept him alive, and were now turning against him. Stars crowded his vision, which narrowed into blackness by the second.

Butler sprang up. "Panic attack. Greta, elevate his legs. Carson, go get him some water. Boy, listen. Breathe with me. All the way in. All the way out. All the way in. All the way out."

Theo did his best to follow along with Butler's breathing, just slightly slower than his own, as she stared calmly, directly into his eyes. Top Bun/Greta, grabbed a pillow off the other cot and stuck it under his feet, and almost immediately the stars went away. By the time Ponytail/Carson got back with a bottle of water, Theo was breathing normally. Butler took the bottle and handed it to him.

"You okay? That was scary." Butler said soothingly.

Hands shaking, Theo sipped from the water bottle. "Where are my friends?" He asked gravely.

Butler's face shifted from an expression of comfort to one of stern consideration.

"All in good time. Let's get you some food." She turned and gave a quick nod to Carson and Greta, who nodded back and left the tent. After they left, she went outside, returning a second later with a stool, which she placed against the center pole of the tent. As she sat down, she leaned against the pole in a fashion best described as 'relaxed and disinterested'. A furious storm whipped up inside of Theo, one he knew would only start to quell once he got some answers. He opened his mouth to speak, and—

"I suppose you have a few questions you'd like answers to," cut off Butler.

Knock my legs out from under me, why don't you? thought a stunned Theo. *Not like you haven't already. Think you're a mind reader, do you?* He recovered himself quickly, and with a shaky voice, responded.

"Yeah. And—" She cut him off.

"I can't tell you everything you want to know right now, but what I can tell you, I will. First of all, your friend Rita, the doctor, is safe. She is here with us. You'll be able to see her soon."

Theo's annoyance was displaced internally by a huge sigh of relief. *So, Rita is safe. That just leaves the other four.*

"Your tech-savvy friends, I believe their names are Sid and David? They are safe as well. They've been transported safely to another one of our other camps. Unfortunately for your two pilot friends, my general deemed them a liability to our cause, and took it upon herself to deal with them. I want you to know that that order was never given, and she has been punished accordingly."

Hank and Bill are dead? Theo's brain, furiously attempting to piece all this chaos together, hit a wall. Greta and Carson entered, carrying a colorfully scrumptious looking tray of chickpeas, strawberries, walnuts, kale, and pinto beans.

"Ah, very good. Here you are. Sit up so you can eat." Butler instructed.

Theo, still in a daze, did as he was told. His vision darkened, stars appeared, and he immediately fell back on his cot.

"Oh dear, I was worried this would happen. Your heart is weak from underuse. We'll have to work on that first."

First? thought Theo. *What other plans do they have cooked up for me?*

Butler stood up to leave. She stopped at the tent flap, and turned to face Theo.

"I have important matters to attend to, but I want you to know you were not a part of our plan. We had no idea you would be on that rocket, and we are sorry you've become mixed up in all of this- in our eyes, you are a blameless victim. In addition, I hope you do not think of us as inhumane monsters, who killed your friends, and are now holding you captive, though at the moment you have every right to do so. As soon as you are able, you will be free to wander and explore the camp as you please, with a few common exceptions. As for your recently deceased friends, well… what do you animal eaters say—you have to crack a few eggs to make an omelet. I am not an unreasonable person, and should you prove yourself trustworthy, I may even let you in on our… omelet. We shall see. For now, rest easy and rest well, Theodore."

She left.

EIGHT

EXTERNAL ALGORITHM 2529-MAT
"For to everyone who has, more will be given, and he will have an abundance; but from the one who does not have, even what he does have will be taken away."

For the first few days, there wasn't much Theo could do besides eat and lay in bed, doing breathing exercises that were supposed to help strengthen his heart. They began with controlled hyperventilation, "Like you're running", as Greta put it. After about 30 breaths he began to feel tingly. After 60, he was amazed to feel his whole body seem to start vibrating. At 75, he was instructed to allow a slow and full unforced exhale, like he was letting the air out of a balloon from the smallest possible hole, then lie in complete stillness as he resisted the urge to breathe for one, two, sometimes three full minutes. Then he would breathe in again, and (this took some practice) push the ab muscles around his gut and his diaphragm out and down towards his feet while holding his breath. He would do this when he woke up and went to bed, over and over for about 30-45 minutes, or until the vibrating turned to full body shakes. After a few days, he was astonished to find he could sit up, and stay up. His vision still blurred a bit when he was vertical, and he still felt lightheaded, but he seemed to be growing more comfortable with it, and these symptoms lessened as the days continued to pass.

He was surprised by the treatment he was getting from his captors. Knowing he needed protein and calcium to help build up muscle and bone density, they tripled his chickpea ration, and someone had found a bottle of mixed berry flavored Tums in the medical hut for him to supplement with. They brought him as much water as he wanted, whenever he wanted it. He was surprised at how delicious the water was- after the first day or two he found that it reinvigorated him in a way he'd never felt before. He relished the cool, pure mineral taste, as it wetted his lips, flooded his mouth, and continued downward on its selfless journey to keep his body working smoothly and efficiently. *It must come from a spring or something,* he thought. *I'm used to recycled moon water, this is fresh, directly from the earth.* Even colors were more vivid than he was used to, and he found that when he was hydrated, he was more focused on the present moment than the past or the future. Drinking it gave him a vague, reminiscent sense of connection to the world he was born on, and had been away from. He didn't know what he was expecting, but given what he had learned about the savage and tribal cultures of Earth in school, this level of kind treatment definitely wasn't it.

After the first week, around the time Theo was able to sit up on his own, Rita began to visit him. She'd had her own problems adjusting to Earth, but she was more used to making the adjustment than Theo was, despite the lack of exoskeleton support. She was a welcome sight, and though he'd only known her a few more days than everyone else, the fact that she was a friend rather than a captor made all the difference, and as a result, they grew close quickly.

Theo and Rita proved to be supportive and helpful companions to each other in the early weeks of their stay in camp. He listened intently as Rita complained about how creepy Dave was—always staring when he thought she wasn't looking, then looking away when Sid would give him a nudge, urging him back to work. It was a nice break from reality, talking about the old normal as if it was still happening, and Theo was happy to oblige. In return, Rita gave Theo regular updates on the phases of the moon—it wasn't much, but it was all Theo had to reassure himself of his mother's well-being. If the moon was changing, then surely his mother was changing for the better too.

As a doctor, Rita was able to help Theo exercise, in ways adjusted to his condition. The two found that the periods of exercise in which they were together provided an excellent strategic opportunity for sharing information they were able to glean from conversations they'd had—or overheard—when they weren't being interrupted by Carson or Greta, who seemed to be the two assigned to keep tabs on the prisoners.

They were indeed in the den of the eco-terrorist group known as Tovu Va Bohu. The camp they were staying at was an ancillary base—one of many, as far as they could tell—in an abandoned Boy Scout camp on Catalina Island, 26 miles off the coast of Los Angeles. Sid and Dave had been taken to a camp somewhere on the mainland, the reason for which they hadn't yet ascertained. The two decided, however, that given everything they didn't yet know, and the supreme disadvantage under which they were operating, the most important thing to do at the moment was to continue gathering information, and get Theo to an acceptable level of physical autonomy.

The Bohus, as they called themselves, had removed and destroyed their NeuroComs and exoskeletons, so they couldn't be used or tracked by anyone trying to locate them or their base. There was very little modern technology in camp- their philosophy called for the eschewing of all large-scale technological advances, and all small-scale ones that weren't strictly necessary for the accomplishment of their goal. The goal in question, despite Theo and Rita's best efforts, remained elusive.

Rita, who'd been able to walk on her own after the first week, took it upon herself to explore the camp and report back to Theo everything she'd learned. The camp itself was not very big- there was a dirt road running down the center of camp, stretching a little over 500 meters from the shore of Cherry Cove to where it met a fire road that carved along the hillside in both directions up and away from camp. She had been instructed by Carson and Greta that it would be wise not to explore further in that direction, as the further you get away from camp, the more likely you will be to run into the local—poisonous—wildlife.

The tents were the furthest part of camp inland, save for a building that seemed to be used for storage. Rita had tried to sneak a peek inside as a Bohu member left the building, but she had yet to succeed. In the opposite direction there were a number of small buildings scattered along both sides of the road, which bisected the cliffs and ran straight to the salt flats and the small red and white lighthouse at the edge of the cove, only making a small detour to go around the largest building in camp, which Rita had found out was the dining hall. On the side of the hill, overlooking the lighthouse, salt flats and the shallows of the cove, was an amphitheater of wood and dirt. Rita relayed that occasionally, a few Bohus would light a campfire there at night, and talk informally about their cause, waxing poetic about the state of society. She told Theo that she hadn't yet built up enough of a rapport with the Bohus involved to join their hangouts, but she was working on it.

There was a building on the side of the hill, just inland of the amphitheater, that had a short road leading up to it. This building intrigued the two of them more than any other- not only were they not allowed to enter, but neither were the vast majority of the Bohus. Butler and the eye patched woman, who went by the name Odin, were the only two who were seen regularly entering and exiting the building multiple times per day. It seemed that no one without access knew what was inside, and no one with access was willing to say.

The days passed slowly, but shortened as Theo found his routine. Carson would bring him breakfast and dinner, leaving immediately after she dropped off his food, and returning about a half hour later for the dishes. Chatterbox Greta, on the other hand, brought Theo his lunch every day, during which he could hardly get a word in edgewise. As he ate, he would occasionally tell her about life on the moon, while she would usually spend the time telling him about old girlfriends (all crazy, except one), her family (they hadn't spoken in a few years), and anything fun or interesting that had happened in camp.

Every day, just before Theo received his lunch, he would hear noises coming from the dining hall- loud, guttural noises from dozens of throats, sometimes screaming, sometimes crying, sometimes bellowing, always laughing. Greta told him that was their "primal screaming" practice- a slight, older woman named Marianne had joined the Bohu ranks a little over a year ago, and with her she brought a number of new age wellness practices she'd picked up, all of which were quickly embraced by the majority of the Bohus.

"That's why I'm always so relaxed when I bring you your lunch", Greta would say with a huge relaxing sigh. "It loosens you up like nothing else. When you're up and about you HAVE to try it." Theo, enjoying her lackadaisical demeanor in spite of himself, agreed.

Theo took every opportunity he had to learn the ins and outs of camp life, using all the care, caution, and manners he'd learned as a child to stay on the proprietous, unsuspicious side of curiosity. Greta proved to be a great source of information, which could be relayed back to Rita. Apparently, the structure of the Tovu Va Bohu organization was less stratified than they'd expected. Everyone was considered equal, and were to be treated the same, Greta had explained. When asked about the building on the hill, however, her attitude turned matter-of-fact, and ever-so-slightly indignant.

"Some things are on a need-to-know basis, for the good of our cause. Some of us don't need to know" was her reply, every time. "Butler says we all have our functions in support of our mission, and if something isn't relevant to your function, there's no reason to bother about it. It's about efficiency, not secrecy." Then she'd change the subject.

Once however, after a particularly intense sounding primal screaming session, he found he was able to breach the subject of Butler and Odin.

"It seems like if anyone's in charge, they are." Theo noted, cautiously.

"I mean, not really. Butler's been in the organization since the beginning- she knew Michel, the founder. And Odin joined not long after, so the two of them really know what we're about. A lot of us have just joined in the last year or two since the Apophis disaster, so we're still learning the ropes, and they're helping us, but really we're all equals, we're all comrades in the fight for Nature."

"What's the Apophis disaster?" Theo asked, between bites.

Greta's jaw dropped. She stared at him, eyebrows peaked toward the center in disbelief.

"You know, the Apophis disaster. Two years ago…?"

Theo shrugged and shook his head.

"Big meteor? Russia? Seriously??"

"Never heard of it. Was it bad?" he asked.

Greta's face turned grave. Theo stopped, mid-chew. Greta lowered her voice, and looked him dead in the eyes.

"Yeah, it was really bad. Millions of people died."

Theo's heart sank.

"What happened?" he asked, attempting to balance the earnestness and horror in his tone.

Greta took a deep breath, and let out a tense, frustrated sigh.

"I can't believe you don't know about this. Just goes to show how much the Bougies care about us here on Earth."

There was an uncomfortable silence, while Theo searched for something to say, but nothing came. Greta took another breath, and reset, invigorated.

"But you had nothing to do with it. Of course. Sorry. You were too young. Just born on the wrong side in the wrong time."

There was another silence, which Theo broke.

"Soooooo....... What happened?"

"Oh, right, sorry." Greta said, shaking her head to reset herself further.

"So, I don't know everything exactly, but here's what I know. Apophis was this huge asteroid. Like a quarter mile across. Huge. There was a bit of a scare that it would hit Earth in 2029, and cause a lot of major destruction, but it didn't, and NASA figured that out ahead of time, which was good. But they also said it would come back again in the next few decades, 2036, 2068, kinda spaced out, but within our lifetimes. It freaked a lot of people out, especially you rich people, who ended up abandoning us and moving up to the moon just in case."

Theo sat, stunned. *What?* He snapped back outward, as Greta continued.

"So, NASA did a ton of math and figured out we weren't in any danger in 2036 or 2068, so all the REASONABLE people figured, c'est la vie, let's just go on with our lives. But Russia disagreed. They said that their scientists knew FOR SURE, it was gonna hit in 2068. All the

American scientists tried to convince them otherwise, Germany, even China tried to convince them. The International Council for the Exploration of Space tried to monitor Russian space activity, but they dropped out of the Council so no one could even have a chance of seeing what they were doing. There were a few whistleblowers, but they all '*disappeared*', and in late March of 2036, we found out what they'd been preparing."

Greta paused dramatically. After a second, he realized what she was waiting for, so he asked.

"Then what happened?"

Greta leaned in close.

"They nuked it. Shot up huge nucular bombs to blow that thing out of existence so it couldn't come back and hit us. But like, there were so many other things they could have done—even if it was gonna hit us! But it wasn't, and they still…"

Greta held back tears, remembering something. Sensing there was more, Theo took her hand and squeezed it. She squeezed back and smiled.

"Thanks. Sorry. So, they blew it up, but it just blew up into chunks. Most of them flew away, but some ended up being blown towards Earth. Most of them were so small it didn't matter, they disintegrated on entry and didn't hit anything, but six big chunks flew across the sky like crazy balls of dragon fire. Two flew into the Pacific Ocean, and caused a tsunami that wiped out Maui. One hit Libya directly in a natural gas reserve, which lit up a pipeline that ran like a fuse and destroyed like half of their capital city. Same thing happened in Ethiopia, and both of them were supposed to join the G20 that year. One landed in the Gulf of Mexico, flooding everything around it, and one landed somewhere in Canada, where there weren't a lot of people, thank GOD. The power grid went down, the stock market tanked, people were rioting and looting- I don't blame them honestly. The Bougies made the OS care more about personal property than human life, so it's only fair. So many people lost their homes and their savings, and family members—burn it all down, I say. And then everyone wanted to start a war with Russia, but for some reason no one did. Probably a good thing. I hate war. Anyway, I was in Austin when it happened. But just a month before I was in New Orleans for Mardi Gras, and if I had been there just a month later, who knows if I would've made it out in time…"

After Greta finished talking, she just sat in silence, staring blankly at the floor, living in the memory of the story she'd just told. Theo, having just finished his food, just sat there, unsure of what to say. Finally, he spoke.

"I… I'm sorry. I had no idea."

Greta looked up and gave a sorry shrug.

"It's not *your* fault. But we didn't hear a *single word* from your people up there. I mean, they said the basic stuff they had to say, like 'it's a tragedy' and 'we're doing everything we can', but they made it super clear that we're on our own down here. The OS sent out rations and cleanup crews and stuff, but like always, there weren't enough, and there were other problems, bigger problems. Kids lost their parents. Parents lost their kids. You can't fix that."

Greta wiped a tear from her eye and stood up.

"I should go. I've got Bohu stuff. I'm glad I met you Theo. I was beginning to think you guys were all bad."

And with that, she took his tray and left the tent, leaving Theo alone.

Theo leaned back against his pillow, parsing through what he'd just heard. How come he hadn't heard of such a huge disaster? Surely there must have been some effect on him, on their society up there. *Hang on,* he thought. *Dad left for Mars in 2036, just over two years ago. Could there be any connection there? If the Exodus was to avoid this—Apophis—the first time, could they be trying to distance themselves further from Earth? I don't see how that would help- unless the goal was to ensure the survival of some humanity, rather than protecting all of it. That doesn't seem fair. These people, the people I've met so far, were kind. They've cared for me, fed me generously, especially Greta. She's been through so much; I'm surprised she's as well adjusted as she is. A bit emotional, a few boundary issues maybe, but she's a genuinely good person. They deserved as much of a chance as we did.*

But they killed Hank and Bill.

He shook off the thought. *Greta didn't. She couldn't. It was that crazy general, Odin. Greta would never, I don't think. Carson, I'm not sure. I haven't talked to her enough. Seems like she was perfectly happy to let me die when I got here. But Greta, probably not. And from what I've heard, neither would most of the people in this camp- Marianne just wanted to do her hippie screaming and stuff away from society, with people who would enjoy it. That's not a big deal. It doesn't hurt anyone; Greta says it relaxes her and makes her feel better about everything. I don't see any reason why they shouldn't be allowed to do that stuff if it doesn't hurt anyone.*

But they killed Hank and Bill.

He shook it away again. *Butler said she punished Odin, she said they weren't supposed to be killed. Maybe they were supposed to be here with me and Rita, or with Sid and Dave, wherever they are. But Rita's seen Odin walking around. I wonder what the punishment was. Maybe I'll ask Butler the next time I see her.*

A few hours later, when Rita visited him to help him exercise, he didn't mention the story. *Did Rita know about this? Probably. Sid definitely did. Did he tell Govinda? You'd think he'd have told me if he did. Why haven't they told me about this?*

As he fell asleep that night, and every night for the next week, his mind was plagued by the same cyclical thoughts—*Why wouldn't anyone up there tell me? But the Bohus did. But they killed Hank and Bill. But they never mentioned it either. Why wouldn't anyone up there tell me?*

NINE

EXTERNAL ALGORITHM 1859-TWA
A person with a new idea is a crank until the idea succeeds.

"Butler's called everyone to the amphitheater—including you." Carson took Theo's empty dinner tray off his lap, and turned to leave.

"Me? Why?" he asked.

Carson shrugged.

"Beats me. I'd start heading over now if I were you."

It had been over three weeks since the crash, and Theo was just starting to get used to his crutches. He couldn't yet stand on his own, but he could be fully upright without getting lightheaded now, so he was excited with his progress, slow as it was. He swung his feet over the side of his cot, and reached under his bed to grab his crutches. Straining against gravity, he hoisted himself up, and exited the tent.

He entered the open air, then crutched a few feet until he was confronted by his current nemesis—the three wooden stairs that bridged the tent platform and the dirt road that ran down the center of the camp. Heart pumping, mind focused, he heaved one crutch down a step. Success. The other crutch matched it seconds later. *This isn't so hard,* he thought. Brimming with a confidence that had eluded him for the past three weeks, he swung a crutch down to the next step. Before he realized it, the bottom point of crutch landed directly on the crack between two boards, sliding out from under him at lightning speed. In a split second, he tumbled down the stairs, landing bruised and red-faced in a cloud of dust and embarrassment. A few passing Bohus witnessed his botched descent, and ran over to help him up. He waved them off, but thanked them. Confused, and a little indignant, they headed off in the direction of the amphitheater at their original, much quicker pace.

Theo made his way to the amphitheater, following the flow of the crowd through the darkening camp. As of yet, he hadn't ventured more than a few feet from his tent, but so far Rita's description of the camp had been pretty accurate, he thought. He was surprised by the amount of people in the camp. Rita's best estimates had it at around 50, but so far he had seen well over 100 walking in the same direction as him. Some gave him odd looks—a few curious, a few almost hateful—but for the most part they paid him no mind.

An intense orange glow rose up from behind the dining hall. *There must be a campfire,* he thought. As he rounded the dining hall, Theo stopped, stunned by the sight that came into view.

It was a bonfire unlike any he'd ever seen—flames fifteen feet high, crackling and roaring in all its mesmerizing, destructive glory. He could now make out the sound of bongo drums, multiple players beating out a complex polyrhythm, now keeping the beat, now throwing in an accent, now supporting the others, now going wild, and all the while silhouettes danced to the beat in eccentric movement against the bonfire, strange, lovely, relaxed, tense, now limbs outstretched, now held in tight. There was no order to them, moves were rarely repeated, but when they were, they seemed to have little relation to their previous usage. Curious, wild, and beautiful, some slumbering, unfamiliar impulse impelled Theo closer.

As Theo approached the revels, he discovered that something within him wanted to join in, but he had no idea what he would do, how he would move, how people would respond. His gut butterflies woke up, and he decided that for the moment, he was grateful to be on crutches. Dancing would be a task for future Theo.

When he reached the amphitheater, a few Bohus he hadn't met yet helped him up the stairs. As he reached stage level, a silhouette stopped dancing, turned from the fire and rushed towards him. He was so surprised he nearly lost his balance, but when she reached him, Greta helped him steady himself.

"I'm so glad you were able to come! Butler hasn't given a speech in months, something really big must be happening!"

"Huh" was all Theo could say. It was all so overwhelming- the crowd, the music, the dancing, and most of all the bonfire that drew him in with its unpredictability and beckoning warm glow.

"Here, come sit in the front row, you shouldn't climb more steps than you have to."

Greta, more pushing than directing, maneuvered Theo to the corner seat at the far end of the front row.

"Save me the seat next to you, I'm gonna dance!" Greta shouted over the din with a mischievous grin, and bounded back towards the fire with an ecstasy totally novel to Theo. He looked around. Everyone was talking to each other, not paying much attention to him, but everyone in their own way just seemed so... *happy*. It was so unlike anything he was used to. In the Aerodome, people would walk around, blank faced, not happy, not sad, just... determined. Like there was always somewhere to be, and something to do. The problem was, he now realized, that once you got to that place or did that thing, the next logical step was always to find the next place to go, or the next thing to do, putting off that gratification further, with the idea, be it hope or historical knowledge, that if you kept on, eventually you would reach the point where you could start cashing in, and it would be that much sweeter.

But what he was seeing now flew in the face of that idea. Greta dancing in front of the fire looked happier, more ecstatic, more fulfilled than he had ever thought anyone could be. She moved wildly, freely, grounded and connected, and never focused on the moment beyond the one she was in.

Same with all the other dancers. They all had that same quality of spontaneity, dancing with that sense of release, laughing and exchanging energy with the other dancers—except one. One woman, who looked younger than the rest, had her eyes closed. She was not moving wildly. Her movements were controlled, precise. But she somehow seemed more relaxed than the rest of them. She moved like water, each posture flowed into the next, speeding up right before each downbeat, slowing down right after, allowing herself to fly and float and fly in a mode of receptive peace with the beat. Theo, realizing he'd been holding his breath, exhaled. Next to her, all the other dancers seemed like they were flailing rather than dancing.

The drums stopped all at once. Theo snapped out of his flame dance trance and looked around. Greta scampered over to Theo and sat down. The other dancer was nowhere to be seen.

"Is Rita here?" he asked.

"No, she's taking care of Inanna!" whispered Greta, only half-paying attention.

"Who's Inanna?" Theo asked.

"She tried to spend the night in the forest to practice being one with Nature, but she got bitten by a rattlesnake just outside of camp. I guess she didn't set her intention strongly enough." Greta replied, still distracted. "Ooh! Shush, it's starting!"

Out from behind the fire strode Butler. Her short hair shone bright as the bonfire reflected off it, her face all but obscured by shadow. A wild round of applause, hoots and hollers rose up- she held out her hands, giving the universal signal to stop, but nevertheless, they persisted. After a second, she called out, and the applause died down.

"All right, all right, let's settle down comrades. You know I'm not a fan of applause and all it implies, but I honor and respect that you wish to give it." She scanned the crowd, and continued.

"I see our numbers have grown considerably in the last few months. You- what is your name?" She beckoned to a girl in the third row, who couldn't have been older than 19.

"Dany."

"And what brought you here Dany?"

She shifted uncomfortably in her seat. The girl next to her took her right hand and squeezed it, saying "It's all right", a sentiment echoed shortly thereafter by everyone around them- "We're here for you", "No wrong answers". She gulped in some air and began.

"I'm from Mobile—Alabama. I lost my family in the floods. I, uh, bounced around a bit until I met Leary—" she gestured behind her to a young man in a flannel shirt. He put his comforting hand on her shoulder, which she covered with hers.

"He told me he was on his way to find you guys, and so we decided to come here together."

Butler smiled and looked up at Leary. "You're treating her well?"

"Yes ma'am!" He nodded. "My momma raised me right."

"Damn right she did. And Dany'll let us know if she didn't" She added fiercely, before allowing a sly grin and a twinkle in her eye to set the whole crowd laughing and Leary blushing.

"To Dany, Leary, and all the rest of you—welcome home."

The crowd whooped and applauded, Dany and Leary were swarmed in a group hug. Butler allowed the rise in energy to reach its peak, then as soon as it began to dissipate, she caught everyone's attention again.

"It's wonderful to see the comradery and support in this group. It's beyond anything Michel and I would have ever expected- but we *are* here for a higher purpose, are we not?"

At this point Butler paused, and walked slowly across the front of the bonfire, every step thoughtful, measured, and in control. Crickets chirped, the bonfire crackled, and every eye in the crowd followed her in rapt silence as she slowly crunched dirt towards Theo. She drew closer, until she couldn't have been more than 10 feet away, then turned to face the audience again. But for a second before, just a second, she glanced at him, reading his expression as her piercing eyes lit up in the firelight. Theo had been just as taken with her as the crowd had, and in this glance, he suddenly became aware of himself again. Guilt washed over him, and he found he was ashamed that he'd been so engaged with the group that had captured him and killed his friends. He took a breath and resolved to keep his guard up. Butler returned to the crowd.

"Many of you are here because you are tired of being treated as tools in a plan that we had no hand in creating. Those who built the current system had one goal in mind- progress. They subject the people within it to conditions that cause unhappiness, then give them drugs to take it away. They claim to be free and happy, but their ideas of what freedom and happiness are comes from the system that is limiting their freedom, limiting their happiness. The only way to know what true freedom and true happiness are is to live outside the system, as all you wonderful, beautiful people do."

There was a murmur of agreement from the crowd. Butler stopped in her tracks, and raised her chin to survey the audience.

"HOWEVER- there is one among you who was so deep within the system, so painfully aware of its shortcomings, and so painfully unable to escape it... until recently. The love and support needed to achieve the levels of freedom and happiness with which you are all familiar, he has likely never felt. But despite all that, we do not pity him. We do not pity him because he does not need it. I can tell you, in the time I have known this young man, I have seen more strength, more resilience, more potential- than I have seen in a single person, in many years."

Theo's heart sunk. He looked around. There weren't many men in camp- a few scattered throughout the crowd, but none of them seemed to know who she was talking about.

"Theodore? Will you come up here please?"

Thrust into a self-aware state of shock and frustration, Theo disassociated, looking upon himself as an outside observer, just a member of the crowd unable to stop himself from following instructions. Greta pulled him up, handed him his crutches, and nudged him toward Butler. She waved, and someone brought out two stools, and set them in front of the bonfire. A murmur of concern welled up in the crowd. As he limped towards the fire, he heard a hiss, followed by someone in the back yelling "BOUGIE!", which was swiftly followed by a few laughs and corresponding admonishment. As he sat, Butler addressed the crowd.

"Now, now, we'll have none of that. He is no less a victim of circumstance than any of you."

Theo, reclaiming his mind and shivering in fearful anticipation, leaned towards the fire, hoping it would calm him. Its warmth wrapped him in a blanket of comfort, as small tendrils of white-hot flame leapt out to lick his bare skin, one after the other, just missing him, thrilling him in its destructive power and his control over it.

"Most of you should be aware by now that Theodore was on the rocket that we brought down three weeks ago. We did not know he would be there, but by some fortunate twist of fate, he was." Butler spoke to the crowd calmly, matter-of-factly.

"However, no sooner were we aware of his presence, than we were also aware of the powerful gift he holds within him."

Theo turned away from the fire. *Gift? What gift?*

"Many of you have, by now, been made aware of the operation that brought us this boy, but in order for you all to understand what I have come to understand, you must know not only how we brought down the rocket, but also the greater plan within which it fits."

The crowd brimmed with an air of nervous excitement.

"Shall I tell you?" Butler said, reveling in the suspense.

A resounding "YES!" descended upon the stage. Each member of the crowd knew their parts, and they knew them well- but, in a moment, they would be face to face with the image of everything they'd been working toward.

"Alright!" Butler shouted over the ever-raucous crowd, who went silent in an instant.

"As we are all aware, the Industrial Revolution and its consequences have been a disaster for the human race. Never before has it been more evident, and the tension between the technological world and the natural world grows with every passing day.

Both our world and theirs claim to strive for greater freedom for everyone, but according to the Bougie worldview, a "free" man is essentially no more than a tool within a greater social machine. He is only allowed a certain set of freedoms; freedoms that are primarily designed to serve not the needs of the individual, but instead the social machine they claim to want to free themselves from."

The crowd murmured in resentful indignation and support of what was being said, though Theo didn't quite catch all of it. Butler continued.

"We, on the other hand, believe in humanity. We look on each and every one of you as a beautiful, whole creature, at once divine and human, perfect just the way you are. Is it so much to ask that the system view us as people, rather than tools for some industrial purpose?"

Again, the crowd roared, this time "NO!", quickly followed by self-contained shushing. Theo could feel the entire crowd on the edge of their seats, leaning forward, waiting to hear what she'd say next.

"So. It is with this in mind that we take our next step in giving a voice to the voiceless. But in fighting a system so vast and corrupt, compromises must be made. If this revolution of Nature over blind progress could be accomplished by diplomatic means, it would have been so by now. Believe me, it has been tried. So…"

Butler paused, allowing herself a slight grin.

"…We took their rocket."

The crowd burst into applause. Butler once again, allowed it to rise and fall, and continued with her momentum.

"How did we do it? Well, we used a few of their weapons against them, as well as a few of our own. You are all familiar with our spiritual prodigy Simone? Stand up Simone, let everyone see you!"

A few rows from the back, a young woman stood up. Theo squinted his eyes, trying to get a glimpse, and as another Bohu brought a torch near to provide some light, Theo was stunned. He knew—he didn't know how he knew, but he knew— this was the woman he had seen that night on the rocket. There was no doubt in his mind. Her shape, her demeanor, the soft but strong glint behind her eyes—this was she. As she waved to the applauding crowd, he saw in her the same control and relaxed precision of the dancer from a few minutes before.

"We couldn't have done it without Simone. Building off her profound abilities, we were able to extend her range of Astral Projection to the point at which she was able to travel into the rocket, as it was approaching Earth, and short out its backup security relay. One more round of applause for Simone."

She sat, gracefully, as the crowd rippled in support. Butler continued without skipping a beat.

"Once the rocket entered the atmosphere, our base on Mt. Wilson fired an electromagnetic pulse that shut down all its electrical and primary security systems long enough for us to take control. A light push in the right direction, and gravity did the rest."

Butler took a small bow, was greeted with applause, and returned the applause given by the audience. *So that's what happened,* thought Theo. *I did see something—but why did they bring us down? What was the point?* He scanned the audience. *They sure like clapping a lot.*

"Why did we bring down the rocket? What was the point? For that, I must remind you of the immense problem we are facing as a society. You all remember our good friend Robert Ditto?"

The crowd erupted in hisses. *Bob? What does he have to do with this?* Theo's brain went into high alert. *Do they know I know him? I hope not. If they find out, there's no telling what they would do to me.*

"Bob Ditto, the head of NeuroCom, current frontrunner for *Head Programmer*? I'm sure you all see the hellish symbolism there. With the announcement of his 'Future, Faster' Initiative, it has become eminently clear that time is running out much more quickly than previously thought. Thus, it is similarly clear that we must *necessarily* co-accelerate our efforts against him and everything he represents."

The crowd responded with a resounding mix of boos and applause. Butler doubled down, egging them on towards frenzy.

"Yes, yes, Bob Ditto, that Snake, that Usurper of Nature! The agent of the system itself, builder of the enemy and traitor to humanity, wishes to '*upgrade*' all of us, against our will, with his poisonous NeuroCom-For-All decree! He wishes to infect us all with his rusty device, which he knows very well is flawed, even dangerous, but refuses to cease or even slow in his quest to aid the OS in taking over everything we hold dear, everything that makes us, US. Why even our dear, brainwashed Theodore here is aware of the dangers it holds. His own mother, unconscious and under intense medical care, all because of a beta test gone wrong!"

The crowd, booing and jeering along with Butler's rant, now gasped and turned silent. All eyes turned toward Theo to gauge his reaction. Theo froze. *What beta test?* He looked out at the audience, frightened, vulnerable, then stared directly at the ground. An eternity passed, and Theo stayed silent. He didn't care about these people and their judgements. He was furious at them, and everything they had put him through. He was supposed to have been following Sid on his business trip, he should have been home weeks ago. He should be having dinner with his recovered mother, playing his video games, as the newly fixed butler took care of all the household chores. The crowd began to whisper in confusion as they anticipated a reaction that would never come. Butler watched this unfold, and continued.

"The beta test in question, recently announced by Ditto himself at his shamelessly self-indulgent *DittoCon*, consists of bug-filled, deterministic, fascist hogwash. Pre-programmed behavioral modifications. They say that over a period of weeks to months you'll be able to build new neural pathways that allow you to be more empathetic, more analytical, more creative, whatever your free little heart desires."

The crowd clamored uncomfortably.

"But we see the truth—this is nothing more than the latest attempt by a corrupt and outdated system to control the disgruntled masses. When they say empathetic, we hear submissive. When they say analytical, we hear automated. When they say creative, we hear satiated! There is no terror these people cannot frame as beneficial."

The crowd, now on the verge of frenzy, was about to lose it. Theo held his breath, praying for the chaos to quell.

"HOWEVER!" she shouted above the raucous din. In a matter of seconds, the crowd fell silent again.

"We have something they do not."

Theo, now finding himself thinking along the same lines as the crowd, had to stop himself from asking the question out loud. *What?*

"We have the brains behind the system itself."

Sid.

"Bob's cofounder, Sid, and his highly skilled, prodigal apprentice David, are at our Mount Wilson base as we speak. They were the targets on the rocket we brought down, and after hearing what we had to say, they have graciously agreed to join our cause."

The crowd blew up, but Theo didn't hear it. *Sid and Dave joined them? That's not possible... is it?*

Theo flashed back to the rocket.

You can be different people with different people.

Dave's words echoed in his mind, followed by Sid's.

There are two sides to every story. No side is more or less valid than the other.

He stared at the firelit dirt between his feet, bewildered.

"Just as a captive dog takes on the personality of its owner, a machine takes on the values and assumptions of its creator—that innovation, improvement, and technological progress above all else, is the goal. It is with their help that we will gain control of the OS, and for the first time in history it will serve our purposes over theirs—the promotion of the welfare of the communal masses rather than the ego-driven elite. For too long we have lived and died in the shadow of the Bourgeois controlled OS. For too long we have been dragged along, fed scraps, been told that we should be grateful for what we have, when what we have is *not enough*. But there is one more thing we have in abundance that they do not, comrades—that beautiful, world-building, unifying quality of LOVE. Once we have torn down the system, it is up to us to extend that love to all, friend and enemy alike, and build it back *better,* for *everyone*. We will be oppressed no longer- and they will no longer be our oppressors. And finally, with the elimination of category, when we are all *truly* equal, we will all be free to be free!"

The crowd rose to their feet with a deafening roar. Theo covered his ears and stared at the ground. It was all he could do. He had no idea who to trust, what to do, how to be. All he knew was that he wanted to be away from this place, away from the noise, away from the strangers who hated him, or at best, tolerated him.

"BUT."

A hush fell over the crowd. Butler brought them down as quickly as she had riled them up.

"We are not there yet. Lucky for us, we have Theodore here."

Theo looked up. *What now? This couldn't possibly get any worse.*

"Theodore here is a perfect example of the type of person we will encounter once we have triumphed. He is a victim of the system, born at the top, by the same chance that we found ourselves on the bottom. His entire worldview, up until three weeks ago, was conditioned by the false society he grew up in. As a result of that, you must all keep in mind that any lack of knowledge or custom on his part was arrived at through NO FAULT OF HIS OWN, taught to him by the corrupt system that he profited off of, yes, but had no recourse to yield away from. He came to us with a weak heart, and a weak body. He could not sit up, much less stand—his society had not prepared him for an Earthly return, they saw no need of it, the reason for which all of you are aware, but it seems Theodore was not. Our dear friend Greta, say hi Greta—"

Greta stood up, bubbly as ever, and waved to the crowd.

"Greta, one of Theodore's caretakers, has relayed to me that he was not aware of the Apophis disaster of two years ago, nor the scare that caused the Abdication of the Elite seven years before. They didn't tell him. Not in school, not in passing—no mention of it in the slightest. Lying by omission is still lying, isn't it Theodore?"

Butler turned to Theo, who had been staring at his feet, a pained look on his face. He did nothing.

"Theodore, look at me."

He didn't move. She could say what she wanted, but he wouldn't move. Butler squatted down so she was on an eye level with him.

"I would like all of us here to promise, that for the duration of your stay, no—for the duration of your life—we swear, never to lie to you. You will receive nothing but the utmost truth from all of us. Isn't that right everyone?"

The crowd murmured. They were being put on the spot the same way Theo was, but in a few seconds, one person after another began shouting down to him.

"I promise."
"I promise too!"
"Yeah, me too!"
"I swear!"

On and on and on people from the stands threw their support to Theo, growing in number and volume, until a chorus of "I promise you Theodore!"'s and "You can trust me Theodore!"'s rang out across the cove. Theo just sat, stunned by the sudden turn of events. A nervous sense of strength, though still tinged with worry, washed over him. But now, rather than worry regarding his well-being, his gut butterflies fluttered in anticipation of what this new shift in his daily interactions would be like now that he was known by every single person in the camp.

Butler, who stood up and was applauding the crowd, brought up one hand, and the cheering wound down. She turned towards Theo, and squatted down again.

"Now Theodore- we do not want to make you one of us. You are free to commit to our cause if you wish, but not yet. At this very moment, the only commitment we want you to make is to yourself. We want you to commit to thinking for yourself, not the way you were taught. We want you to commit to being all that you can be, and to maximize the gift that you've been given. Are you willing to commit to that?"

Theo shifted. All attention was on him again. After a brief pause, he swallowed the lump in his throat and responded.

"You keep talking about my gift... What gift?"

Butler was stunned. She looked down for a second, then immediately burst out laughing. Through her laughter, she stood up, and replied.

"Oh, my dear boy, of course. I'm so sorry, I didn't get around to saying it. You remember our mutual friend Simone?"

She gestured to the top of the crowd. Theo nodded, not sure where this was going.

"You saw her in her astral form, while you were on the material plane. The ability to do that is so incredibly rare, even among us, who have lived among nature and engaged with the spirit world for decades, if not generations. For someone raised so separated, that you were able to do so is a sign that you have an unparalleled strength of spirit—a strength that we would consider a privilege to be allowed to cultivate."

The crowd began to whisper again.

"Did I just hear her right? He saw Simone?"

"I don't believe it, there's no way he could do that. I've been training for years and I can't do that."

"My great-grandma was a psychic in Iceland. She could see into the astral plane, and her best friend was a gnome."

Butler turned back to Theo, her face soft, but expectant. She posed the question again.

"So Theodore—will you commit to being all that you can be? With our help? And once this is all over, we will do everything we can to return you to your home, and your mother."

Theo looked at her. He scanned her face for any sign of deception, but he found none. He turned to look at the crowd. They were all looking hopefully back at him, waiting to hear his answer. Greta was practically bouncing up and down in her seat with excitement. He swallowed.

"Mmm… I guess so. Yeah."

The crowd exploded with a joyous cheer, louder than ever before. Theo was nearly knocked backwards into the fire as the roar of approval hit him with a wall of sound. His face turned to one of shock, and quite without intending it, he broke out into a smile. He laughed, and the crowd rushed down to hug him, and to wish him well.

"Welcome home Theodore! Until you go back to yours, of course."

"Sorry about before, so glad you're with us Theodore!"

"If you need anything, I'm here for ya!"

The kind words of love and support continued for a few minutes, until it became clear that Butler had nothing more to say. The Bohus began to disperse, but Theo stayed and watched Butler shake hands and give encouraging words to those that chose to approach her. Greta gave Theo a big hug, and left to go to her nighttime meditation. Once everyone besides the loiterers had left the amphitheater, Theo picked up his crutches and caught up to Butler. Before he could say anything, Butler spoke.

"Ah Theodore- before you say anything, I wanted to apologize for the way I may have put you on the spot there. You're a very smart young man—I'm sure you've noticed by now how much these people appreciate a flair for the dramatic."

Theo was taken aback- he hadn't expected to hear such an outright recognition, unprompted.

"No, I... of course. I see that."

They were both silent as they made their way down the stairs together. Theo ruminated on how easily Butler had just gotten him to dismiss what had seemed to him, in the moment, to be the biggest affront since they took down the rocket. She had addressed the issue quickly and without hesitation, catching him off guard, and immediately followed it up with a compliment that, had he denied the apology, would have constituted a similar denial of his own abilities. *She's good,* thought Theo. *She could beat the Sun Tzu DLC expansion of Princely Defense in a nanosecond. I have to be very careful around her, but she can't know I see through her tactics. She seems to think I pride myself on my skills. I can play into that.*

"Hey, did you mean what you said about... you know... my gift or whatever?" Theo asked, with all the coy nonchalance he could muster. Butler answered, stoic as ever, no longer playing to a crowd.

"Of course. I would never joke about that sort of thing. It's a blessing you know. And besides, we all promised to never lie to you, and we meant it."

Theo studied her face. *She does seem like she means it.*

"Ok... cool. Um, can I ask you something?"

"Of course."

"How... how did you know about my mom's condition?" he squeaked out, just loud enough for Butler to hear.

Butler's right cheek lifted in a barely detectable smile. "Our dear Simone is a powerful spirit. She can go far beyond the Aerodome Complex, if she so chooses. And soon you'll be able to as well. You may even get as far as your father's workspace on Mars."

Theo gaped at Butler in unfeigned disbelief as her sly grin became noticeable. *She knows a lot more than she lets on. I need to be careful.*

After a few dozen yards, they reached the turnoff for the limited access building, and Butler split off from Theo.

"See you soon, Theodore. I'm glad to see you're getting your strength back. Soon you'll have more than you know what to do with."

As she turned back up the sloping driveway, Theo called out to her.

"Butler?"

She turned and looked at him, some semblance of a pleasant expression on her face. He took a deep breath.

"Since you promised not to lie to me… How did you punish Odin for killing Hank and Bill?"

"Ah, yes…" she nodded, without a second's hesitation. "You've seen her eyepatch?"

Theo nodded.

"She used to wear it as an intimidation tactic. Now she needs it."

With that, Butler turned, and disappeared into the building, leaving Theo stunned and anxious at the base of the driveway.

TEN

EXTERNAL ALGORITHM 4334-JUN
"Until you make the unconscious conscious, it will direct your life and you will call it fate."

That night, Theo had a dream, more vivid than any he had ever had before.

He's in a dark, shadowy pit, a hundred feet deep.

Above, there are silhouettes of people, shoveling straw into the pit.

He looks around—he's surrounded by camels.

His feet and hands feel wet—why are his hands on the ground?

He looks down, and sees the reflection of a camel's face staring back at him in the rising water.

Straw lands on his reflection. He looks up to see that many of the other camels are eating the straw, growing fat as the water begins to rise around them.

He is annoyed—he doesn't want to eat the straw, so he doesn't.

He tries to climb out of the pit, but he can't.

The falling straw piles onto his back, growing heavier and heavier.

He strains under the weight; he tries to shake it off, but it will not leave him.

He sees how fat and happy the other camels are, but still, he refuses to eat.

The water reaches his shoulder level.

A few of the fatter camels can no longer support themselves, they collapse beneath the water and drown.

The wet straw weighs him down, he cannot swim, and just as it rises higher than his neck can stretch, he hears a loud CRACK as his back finally breaks.

He contorts uncontrollably as a life-endingly excruciating pain courses through his flailing body, until his hand hits a wall and he steadies himself... with giant paws.

He swims to the surface.

He can feel the water swishing against his mane- he is now a lion named Leo.

He digs his claws into a wall and looks around.

Dead camels float all around him, but three other lions have found their way to the wall of the pit.

As the water continues to rise, the people above begin throwing rocks at the lions.

The defiant lions climb the side of the pit towards the top, aided by the rising water, dodging and smacking away the rocks that get too close.

One lion gets distracted, is hit by a rock between the eyes, and sinks into the murky depths.

Another tries to climb above the waterline, loses its grip, and is lost to the water.

The third takes the briefest of rests, and is swiftly swallowed by the rising tide.

Leo climbs his way to the top of the pit, avoiding rocks, climbing at the pace of the water.

As he climbs over the top, he finds that he is no longer a lion, but a baby without a name, and that the person he had been planning to destroy is a mechanical automaton, which has shorted out in the overflowing water.

He sees a cord coming out of the back of the automaton; it leads off into the setting sun of the vast desert surrounding him.

As he crawls toward the horizon, he sees many other babies escaping their own pits, following cords of their own, in wonder and considered determination.

ELEVEN

EXTERNAL ALGORITHM 1764-YEA
"In dreams begins responsibility."

Theo awoke to the sound of knuckles rapping on the wood just outside his tent. He had no memory of his dream.

"Theodore, you up?"

A voice he hadn't heard before called from outside. It was low, with a gruff bite to it, but still light and feminine.

"Yeah- who is that?"

"I've been instructed to bring you to the Mine."

Theo propped himself up on his elbows, semi-annoyed.

"What about breakfast?"

"No breakfast. Hurry up."

Theo muttered to himself as he pulled on his pants and shirt. He grabbed his crutches from under his bed and heaved himself outside the tent.

He flung the tent flap open, and all intentions of using a snide remark regarding his denied breakfast evaporated. In front of him stood Odin, chiseled out of granite. She was dressed like an Amazon, with black leather sandals strapped to her feet and running up her ankles like a Greek Olympian, leading to a dark tunic that seemed to want to burst at the seams. Now that he saw her up close, he noticed that she had small scars covering her face, and an ear that more closely resembled a stalk of cauliflower than an ear—and then there was the blood red eyepatch. No sooner did he look at it, than he looked away. That was not a conversation he was ready to have anytime soon.

Odin turned and walked briskly towards the cove, giving off the impression that the time spent doing this mildly annoying chore could be much better spent elsewhere. Theo followed, struggling to keep up on his crutches.

"Where are we going?" he shouted, in a vain attempt to slow them down.

"I told you—the Mine." Shouted Odin over her shoulder, speeding up if anything.

"What's—the Mine?" Theo said, struggling to breathe, talk, walk, and crutch all at the same time.

"It's a mine" replied Odin. Under her breath, but just loud enough so Theo could hear, she added "Stop talking, it slows you down."

For the next few minutes, they wound their way silently through the camp. When they reached the dining hall, they took a left onto a short trail leading along the hillside. Finally, they reached a cave that Theo had never paid a second glance, though he could now see that caged work lights were strung along the inside of it, leading down into the depths of the hill.

"I've got shit to take care of, just follow the lights." Odin said with more than a hint of irritation.

"What? Why am I—" Theo tried to ask, but Odin paid him no mind, turned, and jogged briskly across the salt flats directly toward the limited access building, out of earshot in a matter of seconds.

Theo turned back to the cave. His stomach growled. *I want breakfast,* he thought. His stomach growled again, as if to say "Me too, dumbass." He took a sigh of resignation and limped into the mine.

Almost immediately he felt the temperature drop. The air smelled of wet metal and mud, and there was an annoying buzzing coming from the lights. *I wish they'd turn those off, it's giving me a headache*, he thought. *I'd rather take my chances in the dark than have to listen to that fucking buzz for one more second.*

He made his way deeper and down, deeper and down, into the depths of the mountain. After a hundred or so feet, the work lights strung along the ceiling became his only source of light. *I'd still rather be in the dark than have to listen to that damn buzzing*, he chuckled. He kept crutching. *Is this a mountain or a hill? Where's the line between a mountain and a hill? I'm gonna call this a mountain. It's funner, and more dramatic.*

After limping what was, in his estimation, a few hundred feet, he came to a fork in the cave, one leading up, another continuing down. The lights continued on the downward slope, so he rolled his eyes and continued down the slope. As the space between his back and the fork lengthened, he began to hear another buzzing coming from in front of him, subtler than the lights. It grew louder and louder until he realized it wasn't buzzing, it was a rumbling and sputtering, almost like an engine. He saw the lights turn a corner into a brightness that illuminated the space preceding it, and as he reached the corner and turned, he was surprised to find that he was in a well-lit room, with a generator sputtering just to the right of the entrance.

The room was roughly 20 feet by 20 feet, ceilings about 8 feet high, with walls of grey rock and a floor of mahogany soil. Two sleeping cots lay side by side in the center of the room on top of a large, finely detailed violet Persian-style rug. In the near-right corner, closest to the generator, was a pile of pillows and blankets, all earth toned and much nicer than any he had seen before in camp. In the back-right corner was a folding table piled high with books and candles, and in the back-left there was another, covered with what looked like medical equipment—IVs, drip bags on poles, syringes, apnea machines and the like. As he scanned the room from left to right, he took in posters and paintings of humans in various forms that had been nailed into the walls—the skeletal system, muscular system, and a poster with the same seven flower looking symbols he'd seen on Butler's scarf, running up the center of what Theo now realized was an astral body, just like he had seen on the rocket. Next to that was a similar poster with not seven, but ten symbols (Hebrew, he guessed) enclosed in circles, arranged symmetrically in three columns of three, four, and three, mapped onto a human body. Theo recognized other paintings, from his lessons on the long-obsolete religions— among them two black and white dragons chasing each other's tails at the base of the Bodhi tree, forming a yin and yang, the Mother Earth caring for her children, the Norse world tree Yggdrasil stretching through the nine realms with the great snake coiled at the bottom, tearing at its roots with its terrible fangs.

"You're less impressive than I thought you would be."

Theo whirled to his left and saw Simone, sitting in a rocking chair, a pen behind her ear, one leg over the other. In one hand she held a mug of tea from which she was currently sipping, and in the other was a book with a title Theo could just barely make out—*The Alchemist*.

Theo sputtered. *That's no way to say hello.*

"Yeah, well nice... pen." he shot back, immediately regretting everything.

"Hmph" she said disapprovingly.

She closed her book and placed it on the small side table next to her. Taking her time, she uncrossed and re-crossed her legs in the opposite direction. After the whole affair, she leaned back in her chair, smoothed out the tie-dyed sundress she had on, and looked up at Theo, who had been watching in awkward agony.

"I'm changing all the He's to She's." she offered, coolly, waiting to gauge his response like a jaguar peering out of the undergrowth.

Confusion replaced Theo's nervousness, but only for a second, until the nerves surged back and the two feelings intermingled in an extrasensory stew that seemed bent on making him look stupid.

"Why?"

Simone cocked her head down an inch and raised an eyebrow as if to say "Are you serious?", and upon realizing he was, she rolled her eyes and looked around the room, as though looking at Theo was a burden she was not willing to bear for the time being. Theo shifted on his crutches.

"Because women want to read books where they're the hero sometimes too, and in case you haven't noticed—which is definitely the impression I have so far by the way, you aren't doing yourself many favors—there aren't that many of them lying around. So, I have to make do with what I'm given, like *usual,* like we've had to for *all of time. Is that okay with you, **sir**?"*

This sudden attack struck Theo like a gut punch. He tried and failed to imagine what could have brought on this sudden ambush. Thoroughly annoyed and feeling a new-tasting anger bubbling up from somewhere unfamiliar inside him, he bit back.

"Did I do something wrong? You don't know me. And I don't know you, for that matter. And the way things are going, I don't really feel like I want to get to know you— so far you seem like a thoroughly unpleasant person."

"Hah." Simone laughed, leaning back in her chair. "Yeah, that's right, you don't know me. But I do know you, Moon Boy. Mommy loved you, maybe a bit too much, Daddy paid for whatever you two wanted, including the robot butler—it's fixed by the way, your mom hasn't picked it up yet. Still at the *spa*. But none of that really matters. Some of the shit Butler said last night was true—about you being a victim of circumstance and whatnot—but we both know that everyone has the freedom to choose what side they're on. Right and wrong, the oppressors and the oppressed. You're just one of the rare cases where you were born on the side of the oppressors, so if you stay neutral, you're siding with them by inaction. And we both know you haven't done anything resembling making an actual choice in your life, have you? Yeah, you decide what cereal to eat, and what VR game to play next, but can you name a single thing you've done that was difficult, and not in line with your Bougie industrial 'progress at all costs' mindset? That you did for any reason other than that someone told you to, or that it was just the 'next thing'?"

Simone's eyes drilled into Theo's during this relentless barrage, slashing every pulsing artery of common decency to which Theo was accustomed. A wave of realization welled up inside him, a mix of fury, resentment, paralysis, and frustration that sent the beginnings of tears shooting up his front side and out under his eyes. Unable to speak, unable to do anything, he turned and let the storm fall for the few seconds before his vision blurred into blackness, and he fainted.

◯

When he came to, he groaned. He was still in that horrible room. That horrible girl was sitting next to him in a chair, reading her dumb book with her stupid pen behind her horrible ear. He was lying on the left cot in the center of the room. He sat up, and was disheartened to see that his crutches were out of reach, leaning against the wall in front of him.

"Good morning star shine." Simone said with sarcastic placidity, putting down her book. Theo said nothing.

"Hello?"

Theo harrumphed and rolled over on his side, facing away from her.

"Look—sorry. That might've been a little harsh. But from your reaction it seemed like something you needed to hear."

Theo gritted his teeth, furious.

"Well, here's something you need to hear—you're an asshole."

Simone chuckled.

"Thank you, I've worked very hard to become one." Theo rolled back over to look at her, exasperated.

"So why did Odin bring me here? What is this fuckin' place?"

Simone's face turned stern. "I'm supposed to help you get in touch with your 'gift', remember? Butler's orders. And try to be respectful of the Sanctum."

Theo bit his tongue, trying not to say something about the muddy smell and the annoying sound of the generator, lest he have to suffer her wrath again.

"So…" he began, trying his best to turn over a new leaf. "What do *you* think about my… gift… or whatever?"

Simone shrugged. "I don't know—but you did see me on that rocket, which I'll admit was weird. We can definitely find out. If you don't have one, I'll know pretty quick."

Theo kneaded his lips together, musing. He hated this girl, a feeling all the more exacerbated by its contrast against his initial feelings of intrigue and interest for her on the rocket and at the bonfire. Then again, he had no idea how long he was going to be kept on this island. If he could learn to do what she could do, with the astral spirity stuff, maybe he could see how Sid and Dave were faring, or even check on his mom, or possibly his dad. And he could stop at any time. What else did he have to do?

"All right, it's worth a shot, I guess. What do I do first?"

Simone hopped up, and grabbed a few of the pillows from the pillow corner. She brought them back to Theo, so he could prop himself up on the cot.

"So, what do you know about energy?"

"Uh, what do you want to know? It can't be created or destroyed, it can be both a wave and a particle, it's essentially unstable matter..."

"Ahhh, science. Right. Ok, well what do you know about esoteric energy?"

Theo looked at her with the same "are you serious" look she had given him not a few minutes before.

"Got it." She said. "Ok, well think of it this way. You know what oxygen is, right?"

"Yeah, I know what oxygen is." Theo shot back, quickly and snarkily. *Does she think I'm a child? I've learned via NeuroCom for years, and she hasn't—I know way more than she does.*

"Right, so all life needs oxygen. The Chinese mystics called it *chi*, the Hebrew mystics called it *ruach*, the Hindus called it *prana,* the Greeks called it *pneuma,* but anyway— but I like to call it energy, since among other things, that's what it provides to the body, through a process called—"

"Glycolysis, as a part of oxidative phosphorylation, yeah, I know. In the mitochondria. They're—"

"*The powerhouse of the cell.*" The two said in unison. Theo was unable to suppress a look of surprise, which was returned with a look of 'yeah, now are you gonna shut up and let me teach you?'.

"You know that breathing exercise you've been doing?"

Theo nodded, unsure of where she was going with this.

"I taught that to Greta to teach to you. That's increasing your ability to store oxygen throughout your body. You've been doing it every day?"

Theo nodded.

"Good. Then you should have gotten rid of a lot of your inflammation and blockages by now. Alright. First, hold out your hand, palm up."

Theo did. "Like this?"

"Yeah. Good. Now feel the inside of your hand with your mind."

Theo let his hand drop. "With my mind?"

"Yeah, with your mind, the same way you check if you have to pee or not. Just feel the blood and electrical impulses coursing through your hand."

Theo took a gruff sigh, cleared his throat, and held up his hand. He closed his eyes.

He saw the backs of his eyelids. His eyes wouldn't stop twitching, so he squeezed his eyes shut even tighter.

"Stop trying. Just breathe and observe." Simone said quietly, calmly. "Stay calm."

Theo took a deep breath, then jumped a little as he felt Simone's finger lightly tap his palm. He flexed his hand slightly, and just like that he became aware that his hand had been buzzing, vibrating, just toeing the threshold of the noticeable. He could feel the tiny little twitches of every muscle in his hand, and the light exchange of pressure as blood swooshed by them, syncopated against his heartbeat. He opened his eyes, surprised.

"I feel it!"

Simone chuckled. "Yeah, good. Now think of something that makes you anxious."

"I'd really rather not."

"Do it. It's important—you don't even have to tell me what it is, just think about it and keep thinking about it."

Theo scanned her face—she wasn't going to budge. He closed his eyes.

His mind quickly flooded with possibilities. *When am I going to get off this island? When am I going to get to go home? I haven't seen Rita in a few days, where is she?* His gut butterflies suddenly raged wild, undercutting his ability to breathe.

Is my mother ok?

Simone, seeing on Theo's face that he'd stumbled onto something vital, leaned in.

"Focus on that feeling. Not the thought now, but the physical manifestation of that feeling of anxiety. Where is it localized?"

"I don't know, everywhere?" Theo said, increasingly short of breath. *I don't want to think about this anymore. Shit, now that I have, the more I try not to, the more I will. Fuck, I haven't heard from her in weeks, and she hasn't heard from me—she must be worried sick.*

"It's not in your foot, is it? Where is it strongest?" Simone pressed over his increasing mental noise.

Did Simone say she was still in the spa?

"Fuck, I don't know—my chest? No- my stomach area."

It's been more than week; she must have really liked it there. Dr. Moreau did say it was cost-effective.

"Right—now focus on the center of that feeling, and tie that feeling, through your spine, to the part of your brain right above where your throat and nasal passage meet. Breathe deeply and slowly, and tell the communication between the two to slow down."

Theo, on the verge of panic, didn't have the mental energy to do anything but obey. He slammed his eyes shut, felt the *thump thump thump*ing of the back of his head and the tightness in the back of his neck, reverberating against the frenzied, deafening roar of his gut butterflies screaming at him that everything was wrong, building and exploding off of each other in an exponentially increasing feedback loop from hell. With every last bit of willpower he had left, he focused on his spine between the small of his back and his nasal passage, where he could picture the electric commerce whirring in both directions at light speed. He took a deep breath in, as slow as he could, and exhaled just as slowly. The growth of the feeling seemed to slow, but was by no means decreasing.

"Now keep doing that, and relax all your muscles—starting with your shoulders, neck, and abs."

Theo opened his eyes to protest, and upon realizing it wasn't his biggest concern at the moment, shut them again. He breathed slowly, in and out, in and out, willing the back and forth to slow, releasing his muscles as much as he could muster. To his surprise, after no more than a dozen breaths, he was able to open his eyes with a sense of relative calm and balance. He looked at his hand for a second, then turned to Simone.

"What was that?"

"That's a demonstration of your willpower—the active power you hold over yourself. You used your mind to dampen the stress response in something called your hypothalamic-pituitary-adrenal axis. The more you practice controlling it, the more it'll grow."

"Huh…" Theo was speechless. The two sat for a second, Theo processing, Simone watching him.

"I feel like a psychic," said Theo, with an air of meta-self-satisfaction.

Simone laughed. "You're not wrong!" "Technically." She added.

Theo stretched out on the cot again, still dubious, but ceding caution away step by step.

"So, what does this have to do with the astral stuff Butler was talking about?"

"That's one way you can drive a wedge between your evolution-built, material self and your higher, eternal self—or the part of you that thinks, and the other part of you that observes you thinking. When you exert restrictive control over your biological processes, you practice putting yourself more in a pattern of identifying with the observing part, the part that isn't subject to entropy and is common among all conscious beings."

They were silent again.

"Huh" said Theo.

"Yup" said Simone.

"This isn't how I was expecting this to go." Theo mentioned after a second.

"What were you expecting?" asked Simone.

"I dunno—For one thing I remember learning in school that hippies love crystals. I don't see any crystals in here."

Simone laughed. "Those are… complicated. But for your purposes, Strauss and I have agreed to take a more scientific approach."

Theo rolled his head to the side, looking up at her.

"Strauss? I haven't met her yet."

"You'll meet *him* soon. I think you'll like him. He's a super old Austrian guy who lived in Argentina for most of his life. Shitty family, but such a great heart." Simone, lost in thought for a second, regained herself.

"I think that's enough for today. Keep practicing the breathing and the control thing I showed you. Once you've got that down I'll show you what's next."

Theo sat up and swung his legs off the bed. Now with a dozen questions, he settled on one.

"When will I be able to astral project?" Theo queried, before coolly adding "or... whatever?"

Simone rolled her eyes, and considered for a second.

"If you're as special as Butler claims you are, sooner rather than later."

With that, Simone picked up her book and pen, and returned to her rocking chair in the corner. Theo cleared his throat.

"Oh, right. Sorry." Simone hopped up, and walked Theo's crutches over to him from their leaning place by the entrance.

"Oh, one more thing," she added, as Theo got to his feet. "I want you to start writing down your dreams as soon as you wake up. Ask Greta or Carson. They can get you some office supplies."

Theo nodded, and Simone returned to her book nook, fixated with unflinching resolve on the task at hand.

As he crutched out of the mine a few minutes later, Theo looked up to see the daytime moon looking back down on him.

I'm coming Mom, he thought. *As soon as I can, I'm coming home.*

◌

When Theo awoke the next day, he couldn't remember any of his dreams. Having already started the day off poorly, he chalked the whole thing up as a wash, and spent most of it moping.

The next morning, he immediately rolled over to grab the pen and notebook, opened it up, and paused. All he could remember was seeing himself going over Niagara Falls in a washing machine. *It's better than yesterday,* he shrugged, before writing "going over Niagara Falls in a washing machine", and returning his journal to its newfound place under his cot. He did his daily breathing exercises, and just as he was finishing, Carson brought in a breakfast of oatmeal, fresh berries, assorted nuts, and of course, water.

"How's your morning going, Carson?" Theo chirped. His breathwork had put him in a great mood, and interrupting her clockwork sour attitude made the light-hearted impulse all the more entertaining. She stopped, surprised.

"Same as any other morning" she sneered, before hurrying out of the tent. Theo chuckled to himself, and ate his breakfast.

When he finished, he decided to go for a walk around camp. He left the tray for Carson to pick up, grabbed his crutches, and ventured out. He made his way down the wooden steps of his tent (victoriously), and crutched along the path towards the beach. He passed a few tent complexes, where people were hanging out, having just woken up. A few waved at him, and he waved back. *It's really easy to be nice from a distance,* he thought.

He passed two gated gardens that Greta had told him used to be shooting ranges for the Boy Scouts. He saw rows of berries and mushrooms and stalks of corn- but none of the other protein sources he'd grown accustomed to eating. *There must be some other garden somewhere else where they grow all that,* he decided. He kept crutching toward the beach, taking in the sweet salty smell of the sea air, listening to the light breeze tousle the treetops on either side of the camp, feeling the recently awoken sun start cloaking him in its warm, comforting rays. A familiar voice sounded in Theo's left ear.

"Theo!"

He turned, and was elated to see Rita jogging towards him, having recently exited a building just this side of the dining hall.

"I haven't seen you in days!" Theo said, surprised and relieved to see his friend.

"I know, I'm sorry!" she replied, reaching him. "Now that you're able to get around on your own, they've moved me to their medical building. Apparently, these people have a ton of medicine, but no doctor, so I've been overloaded with untreated patients."

Theo's eyebrows raised in excitement.

"Oh yeah, you're helping them too! I heard about Inanna and the snakebite."

"Oh, yeah, poor girl." she replied, slightly out of breath. "Wait— what do you mean, 'too'?"

Theo eagerly burst back at her.

"That's right, you weren't at the bonfire! I have so much to tell you. Sid and Dave—"

She cut him off.

"Let's talk about this later, ok? I'm in the middle of a procedure right now—Inanna's actually. She's really having a rough go of it. I'm just running to the supply building to grab some equipment. Meet me at your tent in about an hour? I have a lot to tell you too."

Theo nodded.

"Great," she said. "I'm glad to see you're on your feet."

With that, she jogged inland.

Theo, still processing a bit, began to crutch back toward the beach. *She has a lot to tell me? I wonder what it is...*

His train of thought switched to a completely different track as he rounded the dining hall and the ocean came into view. Endorphins flooded his body as he saw the sea, the recently risen sun reflecting down upon it, brightly painting its ever-shifting ripples with every color of the rainbow. A few dozen Bohus were on the beach doing yoga, led by a short, rail-thin older woman that he guessed was Marianne. As he got closer, he saw Greta in the crowd, as well as Simone, Dany, and Leary. They all moved and breathed as one—except Leary, who kept looking around to see if he was doing it right. Theo wanted to go up behind him and tell him that it didn't matter, and yes, he was, probably; but upon realizing that would disturb the class, and might attract the attention of Simone or Greta, both of whom could be an obstacle in his sneaking off to talk to Rita later, he stopped just shy of the salt flats, among a line of palm trees. He watched for a minute, took a deep breath, and made his way back to the tent.

A little over an hour later, after Theo had practiced his "butterfly wrangling" as he'd decided to call it, Rita entered his tent.

"Sorry I couldn't talk before, couldn't arouse suspicion." Rita said.

"No worries, I understand." Theo said, slightly surprised at his unintentional use of hippie vernacular. He switched to business mode. "What have you found out?"

Rita sat on the cot opposite him.

"Ok. So, you know that building right before the fire road, in the back of the camp? Since I agreed to help their patients, they've granted me access to that building during the day—it's where they keep all their supplies. Sacks of grain, wheat, medical equipment—but more than that. They've got 6 ATVs parked in there, with enough gasoline to fuel them for a year or two. They've got walkie talkies, canoes, kayaks, all the stuff you'd expect at a camp for kids, but they also have cases upon cases of ammunition—I haven't seen any guns, but they must have them stashed away somewhere."

"Maybe in the limited access building by the amphitheater?" Theo conjectured. "No one seems to know what's in there, but it makes sense that Butler and Odin would want to limit access to that sort of thing."

"Good point. I bet they're there. I'll try to find out more when I can." Rita agreed. "Oh—what was it you were going to tell me?"

Theo took a deep preparatory breath, and relayed to her everything he could remember about the night of the bonfire—the plan, how they brought down the rocket, where they took Sid and Dave, and that they'd apparently agreed to help Tovu Va Bohu take over control of the OS. Rita sat there without making a sound, listening, considering. When he was done, she spoke.

"I've known Sid for a long time... I can't see him doing that. Dave, maybe—he's always been a stupid kid out for himself, despite his knack for coding. But not Sid. We'll have to keep our ear to the ground and find out anything we can about what's going on at their camp, without arousing suspicion." She kneaded her fingers into her temples, and continued.

"The only problem I'm seeing is that there's no way to bring that up organically. Maybe you could ask Greta? No, she's loose lipped, but she's not stupid. That'd definitely get back to Butler and Odin, and that's the last thing we want."

Theo shook his head. "I'm not sure if that's even something she'd know. It seems like they have a strict policy of only sharing necessary information. I'm not sure who would know anything about the other camp, apart from Butler and Odin."

A light bulb lit up in Theo's head—then he switched it off. Rita noticed.

"What? What was that?" She asked, excitedly.

"Well, I don't know… it could be something?" Theo lifted his head and spoke quickly in a raised tone, as one does when bringing up an idea one knows will be contentious, so as to propose the idea without putting one's full support behind it.

"Butler claimed in front of the whole camp that I have some sort of gift… like a spiritual gift? They want to help me develop it. I don't know if it's a real thing, but Simone—she's the one who's supposed to be teaching me—she's able to do some weird and crazy stuff. Maybe if I let them teach me, I'll eventually learn to do that too? Then I can use it for us—like to see inside the limited access building, or look at the camp where they're keeping Sid and Dave?"

Theo finished, voice twittering and teetering with nerves. Rita sat, staring at the floor, elbows to knees, one hand over her mouth, thinking. Finally, she removed her hand, and spoke.

"I'm hesitant to say yes… only because I have no basis of understanding for what they'll be doing to you or teaching you."

She paused, then continued on, still staring at the floor.

"You said this girl—Simone—travelled into our rocket, and shorted out our security relay. Taking our being here as evidence of that being true, and Butler's point of telling the entire camp that you may be able to do the same, I suppose it may be possible. However—"

Rita took a deep breath, then sighed.

"Butler seems to be incredibly smart. Far more intelligent and cunning than she lets on. I'm not entirely convinced that this isn't all a part of some unknown plan to convert you to their side. Not that that's something they could do, but you get what I mean. All that being said—I don't really see any other options. I'm not going to tell you not to pursue this, but if you think it's a risk you're willing to take, I won't stand in your way. I just ask that you keep me updated on any new developments. I don't want you—I don't know, there's just so many unknowns. It's up to you."

Rita, having said everything she needed to say, raised her head to look at Theo. He looked away, as his butterfly friends began to wake up in his gut. Almost reflexively, he stopped them in their tracks with the technique he'd been practicing for the better part of an hour. Reflecting on how immediately useful what he'd learned so far was proving to be, he met her gaze. He spoke calmly, resolutely.

"I think... I think I should do this. We don't know if anyone's coming for us, or even if anyone knows where we are. If someone were going to come for us, you'd think they'd have gotten here by now—I'd rather I take the chance myself than keep waiting here for someone else to take it for me."

The two sat in solemn silence. Neither spoke, neither wanted to. All that could be said had been said, and all that still needed to be said could not be confined to the paltry language the two captives had inherited. Both felt, however, what the other was thinking.

Just after the long silence peaked and began to last too long, Rita took a quick, invigorating breath, and slapped her hands on her knees.

"Well, I guess that's enough of that. How's your progress coming? You can get around on your own now, you want to learn a few other exercises?"

Theo, happy to have moved on, nodded excitedly. Rita spent the next few minutes showing him how to do some bicep curls with his crutches, as well as knee pushups, and a few stretches to keep himself limber. Once it seemed like he had the technique down, the two agreed to meet in secret every few days to exchange information, and said their goodbyes.

TWELVE

EXTERNAL ALGORITHM 0515-PRV
Drink water from your own cistern, and flowing water from your own spring.

Theo's next few days in camp went slowly. Each was broken up by the arrival of his meals, but apart from that welcome interruption, Theo was left on his own. Had he found himself in similar circumstances no more than a few months ago, with little stimulation and even less supervision, he would have gone mad in a matter of minutes, but his newfound sense of purpose and direction kept him busy. Get strong, get home. With Greta's help, he was able to install a hook in the top beam of his tent, on which he could hang his crutch and practice assisted squats to strengthen his legs. Any time not spent eating or sleeping, he was exercising some part of his body or mind. Unable to do more than two or three at a time, he did 50 pushups spread throughout the first day, a number he steadily improved on as the days passed. He'd work his nerves up on purpose, to higher and more unbearable states of unease, just to see how quickly he could bring himself down again. Every victory spurred him on, every failure doubly so.

It was during this period that Theo learned the bittersweet lesson that children on Earth, who are always told to lower their expectations, learn much sooner than children on the Moon, who are constantly reminded of their infinite potential—that the sweetest satisfaction in life comes from accomplishing that which was previously thought impossible.

His dreams grew longer and more vivid as late spring turned to early summer. His nights were peppered with increasingly coherent images of an older, stronger Theo flying over the camp, finding Simone's sanctum beneath his house on the moon, a third person perspective of child Theo and his parents watch current Theo on TV. All these found their homes in his journal.

After two weeks of intense practice and exercise, Theo could stand on his own. He could not yet walk, but his quick progress motivated him all the more to continue. One morning, he woke to find a small piece of paper taped to the center pole of his tent. Scrawled on it was a single word:

Lighthouse

Theo scribbled what he remembered from last night's dreams into his journal, took a few minutes to breathe, then grabbed his crutches and made his way through the camp to the beach. He arrived just as the yoga class (which he'd found out was a daily occurrence, rain or shine) was finishing. He waited on the edge of the salt flats between the palm trees until he began to see towels roll up and people meandering back toward camp. He crutched against the current of Bohus streaming back towards the dining hall, returning waves with nods and smiles as he received them, keeping his eye on the red and white-striped wooden lighthouse. As he reached the back of the throng, Greta appeared out of nowhere and let out a little scream of excitement.

"Theo! No way! You just missed sunrise yoga—come say hi to Marianne!"

Greta led him through the Bohu stragglers to the lighthouse, where he was relieved to see Simone and another young woman in her early twenties talking to Marianne. Greta gave Marianne a quick tap on the shoulder. Marianne turned to face him, and her eyes lit up. She reached out an excited hand to shake. He took it and executed the ritual he'd long since committed to muscle memory. She winced, but recovered quickly as they let each let go.

"Mmmmm, firm grip. I see they taught you a few *habits* up there."

Theo chuckled nervously, not sure whether that was a good thing or a bad thing. Marianne sensed his apprehension and laughed, a light, musical sound, untethered to any supposition or predilection apart from itself.

"Oh relax--don't worry darling, as soon as you're off those crutches we'll see what we can do to help you learn how to *enjoy* yourself. Lovely to meet you dear. Now, I want BREAKFAST."

Without another word, the flighty little sprite of a human was off and away. Theo couldn't help but grin as he watched her scamper between those of her students that seemed less determined to get to food, FAST. Theo chuckled.

"She's fun. I like her."

"I do too." Greta sighed. "She operates at such a high vibration—being around her just makes me feel *better*, you know?" She turned to Theo. "OH! I almost forgot—I was gonna ask you at lunch, but a few people are gathering around the campfire tonight to talk! Nothing serious, just talking. Might be a good opportunity for you to meet people, hear what we're about, listen, maybe learn some stuff? I learn something every time I go."

Theo's heart jumped into his throat. *Rita's never gonna believe this. Play it cool, Theo, play it cool.*

"Yeah, uh, sure. I'd love to come."

Greta squealed in excitement.

"YAY! I'm so excited. Sparks up at sundown. See you then! FOOD TIME."

Greta gave Theo a tight hug, then raced into camp through the remaining crowd, darting between people like she was in a Marianne-imitating contest. He turned back to the lighthouse to find Simone staring past him, giggling at Greta playing dodge-the-camper, while the other girl looked directly at him with a mix of disapproval and smug satisfaction. Simone saw this and rolled her eyes.

"Theo, this is my sister, Karen." Said Simone.

"Your pleasure, I'm sure." Added Karen.

Theo nodded. "Yeah, uh, nice to meet you."

"Hmph." Replied Karen, unimpressed.

Simone smacked her on the arm. "I told her what I was teaching you today and she said she wanted to watch the first part. You don't mind, do you?"

Karen smacked her back.

"I have every right to be here. Look, I even brought him a towel."

Karen picked up a hot pink towel from the ground, which was now covered in sand. She tossed it to Theo, who, still dependent on his crutches, had no choice but to let it hit him square in the chest and drop back onto the beach. Simone picked it up, and brushed it off.

"You done?"

Karen eyed Theo suspiciously.

"We'll see."

Theo shifted on his crutches.

"Sorry, what are we doing today?"

"Right—follow me."

The three of them walked across the beach and onto a pier that stretched a few dozen meters out, Simone leading the way, Karen in the back. Theo struggled to maintain his balance as he crutched forward on the swaying platform, until they stopped about halfway out. Simone turned to him.

"You've been practicing?"

"Every day." Theo nodded. "I'm getting pretty good at it."

"Good." Simone placed her hands on her hips, and faced out toward the water. She looked around, with an air of nervousness that Theo hadn't seen in her before.

"So, ok. So sometimes your limbic system, your fight or flight, gets triggered by outside sources. Most of the time, actually. Thinking about something that makes you anxious is one thing, but there are times when no matter what you do, the threat is still there, and you have to keep your cool."

Karen snickered. Theo looked at her, confused, then looked back at Simone, unable to hide his unease.

"What are you building to? What are we doing today?"

His butterflies started rustling.

"I can see you're getting nervous, and you're not controlling it." Simone said. "I don't think you're ready for this."

"Bullshit!" said Karen. "That's the whole point! Stop tiptoeing, push him in!"

Theo swiveled, and quicker than he could say "What?", Karen stepped toward him in a huff, and shoved him, crutches and all, off the dock and into the ice-cold Pacific surf.

As Theo plunged shoulder first into the frigid depths, his vision was replaced by a flash blinding white light, then complete darkness. Then the cold hit. He was unable to pay any attention to his slowly returning vision as his butterflies instantly morphed into a snake that whipped mercilessly at his guts with its tail, constricted his spine, and sank its fangs deep into the back of his brain. His body flung its disparate parts about in any attempt to escape the unbearable cold, no rhyme or reason to their direction, only fear. As he bobbed back up to the surface, he could hear sounds coming from his left—laughing, yelling, both? He didn't know or care. He opened his eyes wide and screamed and gasped for air, only to find that his breath was so fast and shallow that at any given moment he was practically holding it. He could hear Simone yelling in his direction, but he couldn't make out what she was saying before he sank below the surface again. His feet touched mud, and a glimpse of hope flashed amid his overwhelming terror as he erected through the surface, the agitated waters lapping against his raised chin. He steadied himself with his arms, gulped in a mass of air, and Simone's voice echoed in his ears.

"DO IT!"

Theo slammed his eyes shut, but the cold seemed so much worse with his eyes closed that he was forced to wedge them open again. He heaved all the air out of his lungs, then gulped in more, fuller and deeper than he had ever taken before. He slowed his breath, forcing all his attention toward the psychic snake that had taken over his body. With each successive breath, he forced the snake to loosen its grip, ever so slightly. It dug its fangs deeper into his brain, trying to keep hold, but Theo refused to back down. In a flash he saw himself in his cabin, breathing, doing squats and push-ups, growing stronger every day than the day before, and redoubled his efforts to vanquish the villain in his mind. Eyes crushed shut, everything, even time itself was gone, nothing existed but him, this snake, and the cold, and he was stronger than both. He felt it writhing up his back, screaming in pain as he willed it away. It was not welcome, and with each breath, he banished its control from him, never to return. An eternity passed. He felt its fangs dissolve out of his head and its body collapse off his spine, before it drifted away in the surf, dead. He opened his eyes, and looked at Simone, his mind screaming with excitement.

"I did it!" he shouted, still a bit in shock. Then, quite inexplicably and uncontrollably, he started laughing.

"You did!" she said back, no more than 10 feet away. Karen, still cackling, said something to Simone that Theo couldn't hear, then walked off the pier towards the camp.

"What was that?" Theo said, now able to moderate his volume.

"Oh nothing. You did well! Sorry about her—let's get you out of there. Where are your crutches?"

Theo's crutches had washed up on the beach right next to the dock. Theo pushed away the freezing water with his arms as he waded towards the beach, aided by the miniature waves. Simone ran ahead, and waded in as far as her waist, handing Theo his crutches so he could make his way out. She spread out the towel in a particularly sunny patch, and Theo laid down to warm up. Simone sat down next to him.

"So, how did that feel?" she asked.

Theo, still euphoric from the whole experience, laughed loudly for a reason and at a volume he didn't quite understand.

"I mean, terrifying. Then scary. Then terrifying again, then… well… really cool. Like weirdly—empowering. I don't know, that may sound stupid, but—"

"No, it's not stupid at all. That's exactly how it's supposed to feel."

Theo stared at the innocent-looking water as it lapped lightly against the sand. He chuckled, entertained by the lie he'd uncovered.

"What?" Simone asked.

"Oh, nothing" he said with a loud smile. "I won't have to do that again, will I?"

"I mean, I won't let Karen push you in again, if that's what you mean." Simone retorted.

"Yeah—don't take this the wrong way, but so far I really don't like your sister."

Simone turned to look out at the horizon.

"You know…" she began, thoughtfully. "…Not many people do."

The two laughed, and Theo laid back down, splaying out his limbs to receive the sun. Simone leaned back on her elbows.

"I'll be honest," she began, "Before she pushed you in, I wasn't sure you'd be able to do it, but you got in control much quicker than I thought you would, even when I was being optimistic."

"…Thanks?"

Simone flicked sand in his direction.

"You know what I mean."

"Yeah, yeah, I do. Now let me get warm."

"Right, sorry."

After a minute or two of silent sunbathing, Theo felt warm enough to focus on other things. He rolled his head over to look at Simone, who had begun meditating beside him.

"So, if that was lesson two, what's lesson three?" he asked.

Simone opened her eyes.

"You think you're ready?"

"Tell me what it is, then I'll decide."

"Hmm, no. I'm your teacher, I'll decide."

Simone posed and postured, imitating thinking in the way you do when your mind is made up and you just want to infuriate the other person. Theo rolled his eyes.

"Alright, sit up."

"Sit up? Why? Do I have to?"

"You wanna do this or not?"

"Yeah, yeah, alright."

Theo sat up, cross-legged, matching Simone's posture.

"OK, now close your eyes." Theo did.

"What do you see?" Simone asked.

"Uhhh... nothing?" Theo replied, dryly.

"Bullshit. Your eyes still work, they're just closed. What do you see?"

Theo sighed, and played along.

"Blackness. Well, it's not really black. More really dark red, with like some orange on it."

"Hmmm, interesting. Ok."

Theo opened his eyes.

"Interesting? What's interesting?"

"Nothing. Just keep going, and keep describing what you see."

Theo reset himself, and continued looking at the backs of his eyelids.

"Ok, so still the dark red. But... but it's almost like the red is static that's on top of the black. Oh shit—"

Simone expected him to open his eyes again, but he didn't.

"The orange is like... flashing. It can't decide if its orange or yellow."

"What shape is it?"

"It doesn't really have one? Wait, no. It's like a t. Like a lowercase t, or a cross. But like a fat t, like a plus sign. And it's bubbly. It fills up practically the whole space. Everywhere but the corners"

"Bubbly?"

"Yeah, like it's not a block letter, it's more... I don't know, the only word that fits it is bubbly."

He opened his eyes.

"How was that?"

Simone nodded, thinking.

"Good, good. Keep doing that—make it a part of your daily practice. Just watch the lights behind your eyes. If anything interesting happens, write it down."

Theo nodded, and opened his mouth to respond. Before he could, Simone cut him off.

"Oh yeah, have you been recording your dreams?"

"Yeah, Greta got me some writing stuff, like you told me. I don't remember much though."

"Good. That's fine, the more you do it the more you'll remember. Write this stuff down in there too, so it's all in one place."

Theo nodded. Simone stood up and brushed the sand off her clothes.

"That's all for today. Next time bring your dream journal, so we can talk about them."

Theo leaned back on his elbows, and craned his neck to look at her behind him.

"That's it?" he asked, more incredulous than he intended.

"What, you wanna go in the water again?" she challenged.

"No ma'am." He balked.

"That's what I thought. I've got work to do—you can get up on your own?"

"I'm not completely helpless," Theo retorted as he grabbed a crutch and showed it off.

Simone smiled and gave a quick nod.

"See ya, Theo."

She turned to walk back towards the camp.

"Hey Simone--?" Theo called after her. She turned and looked expectantly.

"What do you mean by interesting?"

Simone puzzled for a second, then looked back at him.

"What?"

"You said if anything interesting happens write it down. Like what… interesting…?"

"Oh—just anything new or unexpected," she answered, matter-of-factly. "Anything else?"

Theo shook his head no.

"Great. See you tonight then."

"Tonight?"

She grinned, and without a word, turned and walked back toward the dining hall, leaving Theo laying on the beach, in the sun, on top of a hot pink towel he didn't own.

○

As the blinding corona of the setting sun dipped below the horizon, flint struck steel, and Theo made his way up the steps to the amphitheater.

"Theo! I'm so glad you made it!" Greta squealed, as he reached the stage level. "I saved you this stool, next to me."

Theo nodded, and crutched to his seat on the far side of the fire, offering nods of acknowledgement to Dany and Leary as he passed them.

A man with a voice like warm caramel syrup leaned back from his position of tending the fire, and reached out a strong hand to shake. Theo obliged.

"Hello Theodore. My name is Paulo."

"Nice to meet you Paulo- I actually go by Theo, if that's all right."

"So it is. Theo- meaning *Of God*, I believe. Excellent. You are welcome here. You know dear Greta, and this is Dany, and Leary."

"Oh yeah, I remember you two from the bonfire. I'm so sorry about what happened to your family."

"Thank you. That's kind of you to say." Said Dany.

"How've you been likin' your stay in camp so far?" Leary asked, putting his arm around Dany.

"I've been having a decent time actually, apart from the whole crutches thing." Theo replied. "It's nicer than I'd expected. And almost everyone is nicer than I'd expected too. I heard a few stories about you guys before I got here—right before, actually. I heard you guys lived in caves, but the tents are, well… better."

"Not much better." Simone interjected as she helped a gaunt young woman up the steps to the stage. Leary leapt up to help, but Simone waved him away.

"Inanna! So lovely to see you! How are you feeling?" asked Paulo, helping Inanna to her seat. Leary scowled.

That's Inanna? Theo thought. *She looks terrible.*

"Grateful, thank you." Inanna replied.

"As always. You are truly an inspiration. Hello, darling Simone. Thank you for helping her—we've missed her so."

"Of course!" Simone replied, kissing him on both cheeks before sitting down on a stool next to him. An uncomfortable dejection kindled in the deep recesses of Theo's gut, mirroring the movements of the coals crackling before him. Theo groaned, caught himself, and turned it into clearing his throat. *That was weird...*

"Inanna. Tell us your story." asked Paulo, snapping Theo outward again.

"Of course. Inanna is eternally grateful for Dr. Rita. She really took care of Inanna. Inanna is amazed at how blessed she is. The snakebite wasn't too deep, so Inanna didn't need antivenom, but Dr. Rita was able to treat Inanna using tetanus antibodies extracted from Dr. Rita's own blood. Inanna doesn't understand it, but she is here now, and that's what matters."

Theo surreptitiously leaned toward Greta.

"Why is she talking like that?" whispered Theo.

"Theo?" asked Paulo. "Do you have something to say? There are no secrets in the Circle of Conscientização."

Theo blushed.

"The...? Um. Yeah, no, I was just wondering... why is she—"

"You can talk to her." Paulo guided. "Direct communication is a key part of our Circle."

Is interrupting a part of your circle?

"Oh, sorry. OK... um... why are you talking like that, Inanna?"

Inanna gave a slow, graceful nod.

"Inanna does not speak of herself as though she were herself, because Inanna is not herself. Inanna is everything. It helps Inanna remember, in the present, that she is not Inanna."

Is anyone else buying this? Theo looked around the circle, and was met with looks of deliberate peace and sincerity. It made him uneasy.

"Ok—great. Cool. Thank you." Theo said quickly, ready to move on.

Inanna gave Theo a slight bow in return. Paulo continued.

"Please, Inanna, continue with your story. Tell us of the lesson you learned."

Inanna bowed to Paulo.

"Of course. Inanna had begun to feel too dependent in the industrial life and all its luxuries. Inanna felt a separation from Nature, and to strengthen her connection, she decided she would spend a night away from the trappings of society. She removed all her clothes and bathed in sage smoke. She cleansed her aura thrice and thrice again, charged her amethysts and black obsidian, and set her intention to safety and openness and love for all things. Once the preparations were made, she wandered into the wild. She found a lovely place to rest in the hills, beneath a wise old tree, and lay down to sleep. She awoke to a sliding on her leg, and upon seeing a snake crossing her leg, jumped, and could not stop herself. The snake was frightened, and rightly so, and in its fear, it sank its fangs into Inanna's heel. Inanna tried to apologize for disturbing the snake, but it disappeared, and Inanna had to make her way back to the camp. The clear lesson is that I—she, did not set her intention for peace strongly enough."

"Knew it." Whispered Greta to herself.

Inanna continued. "If she had properly prepared, then perhaps Inanna and the snake could have been friends."

Theo chuckled, stifling it a little too late. All eyes turned to him.

"Theo? Do you have something to add?" asked Paulo, cautiously.

"No, sorry." Theo replied. "Please, continue."

Paulo cleared his throat.

"Theo, it is clear you are new here, and we welcome you. But the Circle of Conscientização is a place of safety and honesty. If you have something to say, you must say it."

Theo scanned the circle for permission, and was met with nods and the same creepy looks of peace.

"Ok... I mean... wait, sorry. What's the point of this Circle? I don't want to speak out of turn."

Paulo nodded thoughtfully.

"Of course. A very valid question. We seek to grow our conscientização, our critical awareness of the world around us, thereby freeing ourselves and others from oppression."

"Ok. Got it. Then I don't think it's out of line for me to point out that no matter what, I don't think Inanna and the snake were every going to be friends. Like... it's a *snake*. It has no interest in being friends—it has no interests apart from not dying and finding a snake wife and finding out what mouse it's going to eat next. It's not a matter of intention, because the snake doesn't care about your intention. It's a matter of using logic to decide not to go into the woods without proper protection against snakes."

The crackling campfire seemed to roar amid the vacuum of silence that fell over the circle. Dany and Leary looked at each other, then at the ground. Greta was frozen, staring at the fire. Simone might as well have been a million miles away, gazing deep into the white-hot coals. Inanna gave a pained whimper.

"Theo," began Paulo. "These are not the sort of fear-based conversations that are welcome in the Circle of Conscientização. We will forgive you, because you are new, but this is the exact sort of oppression we are trying to free ourselves from—this... *attitude* of dismissal and minimization of other's experiences is just a small part of the atmosphere of oppression that we are fighting against."

"I'm not trying to minimize anything" Theo stammered. "Really. I'm really sorry you got bitten by a snake, Inanna. That sucks. I thought I was just doing the whole 'critical awareness' thing you were talking about."

Theo looked around the circle for approval, and received none. Everyone looked at the ground, except Simone and Paulo. Paulo looked at Theo, and Simone was still staring into the fire.

"Ah, I see." Nodded Paulo thoughtfully. "It is because of your upbringing that you do not understand. When we speak of critical awareness, we speak of it specifically in reference to the narratives of manufactured consent of the oppressor class- the class you come from. It is everyone's first task to listen to the oppressed, and take them at their word. Their power lies in their truth. Inanna here lost her parents in the floods, and her brother to a dangerous OS work assignment. When she speaks, our first task is to let her know that her experience is valid, and she is being heard. That is all."

Theo was starting to get a little annoyed. He hated being lectured at, especially when it didn't make sense to him.

"Ok, just so I know what we're doing—we aren't focused on solutions yet, just emotional catharsis right now, right?"

"I do not know this word, 'catharsis', but I can tell you, you are wrong, because we *are* focused on solutions." Paulo replied with an infuriating calmness. "There are two sides, oppressor and oppressed, and my job as the orchestrator of these discussions is to guide us all away from the oppressive, paternalistic way of thinking that you have just exhibited—through no fault of your own—where one person knows better than another. We are all trying to figure these things out together."

Theo felt his blood boil. *How dare he talk down to me?* Theo glanced at Simone, who hadn't taken her eyes off the dancing flames. *Why doesn't she say anything?*

"But doesn't that just make *you* the person who knows better than everyone else?" Theo retorted. "Who keeps you accountable?"

Simone looked up at Theo, surprised. For the first time, Paulo stammered.

"I keep myself accountable... and so does everyone else." He paused, taking a deep breath to calm himself down. "I am sorry to do this Theodore, but if you are not willing to engage in the set rules of the Circle of Conscientização, then I must ask you to leave. Go."

Theo looked around in disbelief at the other members of the circle, searching for a single hint of backup, but none came. Four pairs of eyes were pointed directly at the ground, and Simone had returned to her flame-induced trance. Shaking his head, Theo picked up his crutches, and hoisted himself up. He crutched his way to the stairs, before turning to face the group one last time.

"I'm sorry if I offended you Inanna. I'm glad you're feeling better."

Inanna sniffled, and gave him a nod.

"Inanna forgives you and thanks you, not because she wants to, but because she has to."

As Theo descended the stairs, away from the warmth of the fire, he heard Greta apologizing to Paulo on his behalf.

THIRTEEN

EXTERNAL ALGORITHM 9883-STI
"Today's policies and political activity treat people like pawns. More than ever before, attempts will be made to use people like cogs in a wheel. People will be handled like puppets on a string, and everyone will think that this reflects the greatest progress imaginable."

    Over the next few days, Theo grew less and less dependent on his crutches. Every morning he would walk from his tent in the back of the camp down to the beach, to watch the sun and its preceding colors find the horizon. He looked forward to the mornings when there were clouds—he decided they provided an unpredictably exciting canvas for the rising sun to play off of, texturing its rays in all sorts of surprising and pleasing prismatic configurations.

    He told Rita about what had happened at the campfire, but given how it had played out, they both agreed there probably wasn't a lot of valuable information being exchanged there. Rita admonished him for being so critical of Inanna, and he agreed that if he were to have the opportunity again, he'd have to take one for the team and play along with whatever game they were playing. It seemed that the best strategy was for both of them to keep their heads down, and ingratiate themselves to the Bohus, who proved to be a rather accepting bunch, as long as certain guidelines were kept to.

    After watching the sun rise, Theo would make his way back to his tent, where he would practice "eyelid gazing" as he'd named it, until Carson arrived with his breakfast. In the first few days, he observed that the colors he was seeing seemed to have a sort of layering aspect to them.

In the back was just blackness, with red static on top of it. On top of that, he discovered, was the color of whatever light source was on the opposite side of his eyelids, which filled up nearly his entire field of vision apart from the corners, making the fat, bubbly cross. At first, he experimented with covering his closed eyes, and looking around to see how it changed things, but the most peculiar thing he found came about a week in while butterfly wrangling, when he impulsively decided to switch his attention to his vision. He had been breathing deeply for almost 30 minutes, give or take, when he noticed that a new phenomenon was emerging.

Just outside the center of his vision, faintly protoplasmic greens and purples and bright white-yellows were coalescing and disappearing, like shadows of ripples on the bottom of a pool on a sunny day. They would swirl and comb around his visual field, washing over and feeding into each other in waves from the outside in, growing brighter and more intense as they enclosed each other, nearing a blinding pinpoint brilliance before suddenly shrinking out of existence. To his dismay, whenever he shifted his gaze to look at them, they disappeared, instantly. He wrote this down, and begrudgingly contented himself with his peripheral vision.

A week to the day after Karen pushed him off the dock, he woke up to another note:

Mine

About an hour later, having watched the sun rise, completed his breathing, and realizing no breakfast was coming, Theo turned the corner and entered Simone's sanctum.

"No crutches today?" he heard from his left. There sat Simone, book in one hand, tea in the other, pen behind her ear.

"Nope. Red pen today?"

"Yup." She turned her book towards Theo, showing him the title—*The Myth of Mental Illness*. "Makes it easier to get through the parts on female hysteria. You bring your journal?"

Theo nodded, showing her the notebook in his right hand.

"Hey, so, about what happened at the campfire—"

Simone cut him off.

"Don't worry about it—you didn't know the deal there," she replied dismissively. "Not your fault. And it's not like what you were saying didn't make sense. C'mere, sit. Tell me what you came up with."

Theo stuttered, and decided the best thing to do was just to drop it. He walked over to the left cot, and sat. He opened up his journal and flipped through it.

"Not a ton," he began. "I'm not really sure what I'm supposed to be looking for, or if I'm doing it right—"

"There's no such thing as doing it right." Simone cut him off. "Just read to me what you've written. From the beginning."

Theo started to offer more caveats in protest, then realized he didn't have anything to say. He flipped to the front page and started reading with all the enthusiasm of a used napkin.

"Ummm, well, the first night I went over Niagara Falls in a washing machine... that was about it... then the next night—"

"You were in the washing machine?" she interrogated.

"Yeah," he said, defensively. "The door was open—I could see myself in it. I watched myself go over the edge and fall all the way down. I don't remember if I hit the bottom or not."

"Third person, good, good." She said, musing. "Continue."

Theo's attention darted confusedly between her and the book as he set himself and began reading again.

"Then the next night, I was back home on the moon, and I found a trapdoor that was only visible to me, and I went down it, and then I was in here, and then... um..."

Theo stopped. He'd reached the part where Simone had showed up.

"Then that was it—I mean—I woke up."

He was silent. Simone eyed him suspiciously. Theo shuddered, recognizing it as the same look Karen had given him a week before.

"That's it?" she asked, probing.

"Yup." He said, unable to meet her gaze.

Simone paused for a second, then raised her chin as she spoke defiantly.

"I don't believe you."

Theo stuttered as Simone heaved herself out of her chair, and started walking toward him with the evident purpose of taking his journal and reading it herself. Theo hid it behind him and spoke quickly, trying to diffuse and appease all at once.

"No—fine, you were there, and then you did some stuff, but I didn't do anything, nothing happened, nothing weird… happened. I didn't do anything."

Simone stopped. In the span of a second her face completely morphed through an expression of sudden self-consciousness, then flattery, then anxiousness, then to one of anger. She planted her feet, crossed her arms, and glared at Theo, daggers in her eyes.

"What did I do?"

Theo cowered. "Nothing!"

She took a step forward.

"Theodore—what did I do in your dream?"

Theo slammed his notebook shut and scrambled off the cot

"I don't wanna do this anymore," he said hurriedly, as he made a beeline for the passageway out of the mine. Simone's arms collapsed to her sides and she grasped for whatever words would come.

"Wait!"

Theo stopped, just shy of the doorway. Simone continued, stuttering, with no idea what would come out next.

"Look, I… I'm sorry. That might have been a bit too forceful—it's… it's my fault. Please come back?"

Theo turned slowly to face her general direction. He didn't want to look at her, but out of the corner of his eye he saw her feet. They were shoeless and covered in dirt, but there was an unmistakable daintiness to them that didn't seem at all to match his experience of her thus far. He could see her small toes clutching onto the dirt floor, tense with anticipation, awaiting his reply. He clenched his dream journal tighter in his hand, and spoke slowly, shakily.

"If I'm gonna learn this stuff, it has to be on my terms. I only share what I want to share."

Simone nodded. "Ok, sure. Fine."

"And I don't know why, but the stuff in this journal feels really personal. I don't know what it means, or why you're making me do it, but I feel way too vulnerable telling you everything in my head and not knowing anything about you. You gotta share stuff with me too, ok?"

At this, Simone hesitated. After a second of silence, Theo looked up at her, pressing expectantly for a response with his eyes. She looked away and down, searching for any way out. She sucked at her gums and relented.

"Fine. Same goes for me too though. I don't have to share anything I don't want to."

"Good." Theo nodded. "Fine." He walked back to the cot, slowly, but with purpose. He sat down, then put his closed notebook on his lap.

"Your turn."

Simone looked at him, confused.

"Huh?"

"Your turn. Dream for a dream. Your turn." Theo looked at her expectantly.

Simone crossed her arms.

"I don't have to tell you anything I don't want to." She said, matter-of-factly.

"I never said you did," stated Theo. "But fair is fair. Dream for a dream."

The two glared at each other, each challenging the other to back down. Finally, Simone relented.

"Fine."

She grabbed her chair, and pulled it closer to the cot. She sat down, and immediately crossed her arms and legs. In between huffs and sighs, she shifted, unable to find a comfortable position. Finally, she shook her head, wrung her hands, and blew out her mouth in a rather dramatic display of self-control.

"So. A dream?" she asked, combatively.

"Yup. Any dream." Theo said, nonresponsive.

Simone thought for a second, then leaned to the side of her chair.

"Ok, how about this one? I'm a tarantula. Big ol' hairy spider. A giant scary buff man steals my baby girl and runs off with it, so I chase him. He gets to the ocean, goes in about waist deep, and repeatedly tries to drown it. I try to go in to save it, but every time I touch the water, the part of my leg that gets wet dissolves. Analyze that, Freud."

Simone, apparently finished, cocked her head to the side, and looked at him keenly, sucking on her top side teeth. Theo frowned, then shook his head.

"I dunno. You're the expert. What do you think it means?"

Simone gawped at him.

"That's not what we said. Dream for a dream. Your words." She shot back.

"Fine." Theo said bluntly, and a little annoyed. "Analyze mine, then we'll do yours."

Simone scoffed. She uncrossed and recrossed her legs, thinking.

"Not much to analyze with what you've given me. Washing machine, Niagara Falls, just sounds like you're struggling with a bed wetting problem."

"I do not—" Theo stopped himself. Simone grinned.

"Oh, you're... got it." He forced himself to move on. "Ok, fine, how about this one. It felt kinda meaty right when I woke up from it."

He flipped through his journal, and found the page.

"So—I think this was two nights ago. I was flying around over the camp, but I wasn't me. I was like an older, stronger version of me. I took a huge running start, and I could run, like *really* run, then I jumped and I flew around. And I just felt super confident and strong while I did it. And part of the time I was him, and other parts of the time I was on the ground, watching him while I'm a child, holding my mom's hand. And I didn't write this down at the time but now I'm remembering that I wanted to go be that guy that I was watching, but my mom wouldn't let go of my hand, so I couldn't, even though I kept pulling harder and harder. I don't remember if I got away from her or not."

Theo finished, and looked at Simone. She was staring at the floor, hand over her mouth. After a few seconds, she moved her hand to the base of her throat, and began fiddling with pearls that weren't there as she spoke.

"So...hmmm. That sounds good to me. Like, you said I'm the expert—I'm not. I know more than you, let's get that straight, but I'm no expert, so this could be completely off base. It sounds like you've made an idealized version of yourself, which is good. It gives you something to strive for. But it also sounds like you aren't him yet. Duh."

She glanced up at Theo, who was scowling.

"Sorry. Force of habit. Good thing is, you want to be him, and you're trying to be, but some part of you is trying to stop that from happening."

Simone said something under her breath that Theo couldn't quite make out.

"What was that?" he asked, confused.

Before she could answer, they both froze at the sound of voices approaching from the mine shaft, underscored by swift footsteps. Simone turned to Theo.

"We'll have to pause for a bit. This is good though."

Theo nodded and gulped, as Butler and Odin strode in from around the corner, quickly followed by a very old, very bald man dressed solely in overalls, with a big bushy white moustache and eyebrows to match.

All three stopped when they saw Theo. Butler whispered something to the other two, who whispered back. She smiled.

"Ah, Theodore. Good to see you're here. Simone has been teaching you well, I trust?"

Theo nodded.

"Yeah, she's a fantastic teacher."

"He's a great student." Simone added. "A bit feisty, but that's good. It takes a bit of that to really get the hang of things."

Theo looked at her, surprised. *Feisty? Not the first word I'd use to describe myself.*

Butler laughed. There was something not quite genuine about it that Theo couldn't put his finger on, but noted, then shrugged off.

"We're in the middle of a lesson. Did you need something?" Simone asked, more politely than Theo had ever heard her speak.

Butler nodded, then took out a small piece of paper.

"Yes, as a matter of fact. A mission. Unfortunately, Theodore will have to leave for the time being."

Odin stepped forward and looked around the room.

"Where are your crutches?" she growled.

"I... uh... I don't need them anymore?" Theo asked, unaware that it wasn't a question.

Odin gritted her teeth, fuming. She made a start toward Theo, but heeled like a trained rottweiler as Butler spoke, softly, acceptingly.

"That's wonderful to hear. I'm so glad you're making progress."

Odin glanced at Butler, annoyed and uncertain.

"Unfortunately, today's lesson will have to be cut short. A pressing matter has just come up, and it's time sensitive." She gestured for Theo to leave. Theo stood, rubbing his arm sheepishly.

"Um... well it's just that—"

"Come on, speak up. We don't have all day!" bit Odin.

Theo jumped a bit, then sped up.

"It's just that if I'm gonna learn to do all the stuff Simone's doing, maybe I should watch her do it?"

Silence fell on the room. The first to break it was Odin, who did the human equivalent of snarling, swiftly cut off by Butler.

"Perhaps another time."

Theo's heart dropped.

"I agree with Theo," came a voice to his right. Simone had left her chair, and was now standing right next to him. She continued.

"Theo's been making fantastic progress, much quicker than I'd anticipated. I think it would really help him if he had a picture of what he was working toward."

Butler studied Simone, whose eyes were wide as she plead on behalf of Theo. She thought for a second, whispered to the other two adults, then turned back towards the two teens.

"Very well. But he is not to be involved. He is to stand... over there." She pointed over to the corner where Simone's chair usually sat.

Theo nodded, looking back and forth between Simone and Butler.

"Sure! Great! Yeah, absolutely. Won't move a muscle."

He walked over to the corner, notebook in hand. The three adults watched him do it, then Butler and Odin turned their attentions to Simone. They walked over to her, handed her the piece of paper, and Butler began talking in hushed tones as Odin moved the right-side cot out of the way. The old man waddled over towards Theo, eyes sparkling with curiosity.

"Hallo! So, you are the Theodore that I've been hearing about? So pleasant to be finally meeting you!"

He grabbed Theo's hand, and shook it vigorously.

"Uh, yeah! Theo—um... sorry... you are—"

The old man let go of Theo's hand and slapped himself in the forehead.

"Ah! Yes. Theo. Of Course. I am Strauss. Pleasure. Anysing you need, I vill get for you."

He took Theo's hand again, kneeled painfully, and kissed the back of it. Theo laughed nervously, then helped the old man back up.

"So, what's going on?" Theo asked tentatively.

"Ah. Yes. So." Strauss turned to stand (or rather crouch) beside Theo, and whispered conspiratorially to him.

"Ve have just had a major breaksroo vis the primary mission." Strauss doubled down on the secretive nature of their discussion, in the way gossipers do when their most common claim is to hate gossip.

"Ve have located the headquarters of the Primary Societal Operating System."

"The OS?"

Theo was stunned. The location of the OS's central mainframe was well known to be a secret, known only to the handful of programmers responsible for its maintenance. Even Theo had to admit, he was curious.

"Where is it?"

Strauss looked up at Theo, giddy, unable to contain himself.

"*Yellowstone National Park.* Isn't it ingenious? The ultimate in mutually assured destructions. Any physical attack capable of its destroyal vould almost definitely result in the annihilation of all of the life on the planet! Hee hee!"

Strauss danced a jig as Theo processed the implications of what he'd just heard.

"So... What's Simone doing? She's not destroying it, is she?"

Strauss stopped his little dance and laughed.

"Hee hee, no, of course not! That would be foolish und stupid. Don't be stupid, stupid!"

Strauss rapped his knuckles on Theo's skull a few times before he moved out of the way. Strauss grinned up at Theo with an almost hungry look in his eye, before turning to look at Simone, who was laying down on the remaining cot as Butler and Odin gave her instructions.

"No, she is just going to fly over there, give it a look around, see vat there is to see. Qvick trip. No stress. Bing bang boom."

Butler and Odin turned to him and nodded.

"Off to verk! Stay over there, handsome boy!"

He half-waddled, half-scampered over to the medical table. Theo watched in awe and confusion as he strapped what looked like a sleep apnea mask onto Simone, who had begun meditating supine on the cot. Strauss pressed a button, and Theo saw her relax. Her breathing slowed as the air began to flow. He set the button on a small table he'd brought over and wheeled over an IV stand with four separate bags, each filled with clear liquid, hanging off it. With a speed and precision Theo wouldn't have expected from the weird old man, in less than 30 seconds he'd inserted an IV into the recumbent Simone's right arm, and hooked up all four bags via a slow drip. The three adults stepped back, and none of them moved, watching her intently.

"What's going on?" Theo asked, as tentatively and quietly as he could muster.

"SHHHHH" shot back Odin.

You could hear a pin drop as everyone waited on bated breath. For what, Theo had no idea. But they weren't moving, so neither would he.

Simone's breath was slow, weirdly slow, but Theo resisted the urge to bring it up. *Maybe that's just how people breathe when they're unconscious... or whatever Simone is right now. She's astral projecting, I know that, but she hasn't told me what happens to your body while that happens. I guess I'll see.*

For minutes, everyone in the room stood in silence, gaze fixed on the motionless girl in the center of the room.

She twitched.

Odin looked at Butler, who looked at Strauss, who never stopped staring at Simone. Theo watched them all.

She twitched again.

"Has this happened before?" Butler whispered to Strauss.

"No, but nussing to vorry about." He mumbled through his moustache, just loud enough for everyone to hear.

For a full minute, there was no movement at all in the room. Then suddenly, Simone began convulsing. Her body started to shake uncontrollably, IV drip tubes flailing to and fro, whipping the frightened adults next to her. She screamed an inhuman, bloodcurdling scream.

"Shit. SHIT. HOLD HER DOWN" ordered Strauss with a voice full of fear and fire. Butler thrust her forearm down on Simone's upper chest as she held down Simone's quaking left arm, while Odin grabbed hold of her wildly kicking legs without a second's hesitation. Strauss grabbed her right arm and pulled out the IV as quickly and smoothly as he could.

"Seal the DMT, don't waste it!" Butler shouted, but Strauss had already sealed the bags and dropped them on the table before returning to Simone's side with a small cylinder in his fist. He removed the cap, and plunged the Epi-Pen into her leg. She froze, then after a few seconds, she began to shake, less violently, and her eyes flew open. Tears flooded her cheeks as she regained consciousness, and curled up in the fetal position, hyperventilating.

"MILK." Commanded Strauss. Odin and Butler looked at him, confused.

"MILK. NOW!" He glared at Odin, who realized what he was saying, then sprinted out of the room. Strauss turned his attention back to Simone.

"You're ok. You're ok my darling. Can you speak?"

Simone tried, found she couldn't, and descended back into hyperventilation. Strauss leaned over her, rubbing her back.

"You're ok. You're ok. It's ok. It's all over. You are here, in your body, it is good..."

Theo watched all this transpire, frozen in the corner. Strauss continued to calm her down, while Butler stood awkwardly a few feet away, looking concerned and lost in furious thought. About five minutes later, Odin returned, carrying a jug of milk.

"They only had whole milk, I hope that's ok. They asked if I wanted almond—"

"It is fine, give it here." Strauss ordered. He snatched the carton out of her hand, raced over to the medical table, grabbed Simone's tea mug, emptied its contents against the wall, and filled it with milk. He gave it to Simone, who removed her apnea mask, took the mug, and drank. It seemed to calm her down. After a minute or two Strauss spoke to Simone as tenderly as he could.

"Somesing went wrong?"

She nodded furiously, fighting back tears.

Strauss nodded understandingly. He turned to Butler and Odin.

"She vill need time to recover before the debrief. I vill let you know ven she is ready."

Odin began to protest. Butler did as well, but as soon as she halted the impulse, Odin followed suit.

"Shouldn't take too long. Bye-bye."

The two most powerful people in camp exited the room, annoyed.

Theo watched them go, then edged his way toward the cot. Strauss noticed. He whispered to Simone, who hesitated, then nodded.

"You can come. Just not too close." Strauss said.

Theo walked cautiously and came to a stop a few feet from the cot, where Simone was finishing her milk.

"More?" Strauss asked softly, perched on the edge of the cot like a mother with a sick child. Simone nodded, and a smile crept across her face. Strauss looked up at Theo, and swung his head in the direction of the milk jug. He took the hint and brought it over. He unscrewed the cap, and poured it into Simone's mug. When finished, he replaced the cap, and continued to hold on to the jug. For a few minutes, Simone continued to breathe and sip in silence while the other two stood, holding space for her.

"You feeling better?" Strauss asked after a few minutes had passed, and Simone had seemed to grow more stable. Simone nodded.

"Good enough to tell me vat happened?" Strauss asked gingerly.

Simone took a sip of her milk, then nodded.

"I found it."

"You found it?" Strauss asked, incredulous.

She nodded again.

"I found it. Right where we thought it would be. Took longer than I thought to get there, but once I did, it was hard to miss it. Rusty Winnebago with a trapdoor. Weird, really."

Theo's brow furled. *Winnebago?* She continued.

"And it's an Airstream, not a Winnebago. Anyway, I went down, it's down like, 100 feet I'd say. Maybe 120. Really deep. Then there was a door—biometrics, ID, the whole nine. I had just gotten through the door when I suddenly felt… I don't know, it's hard to describe."

She looked down, more pained than discouraged.

"Please try." Strauss pleaded.

"It was… like an electric shock. But not—like, whatever the opposite of an electric shock is. I was frozen, like all the energy had been sapped from me. I thought for sure I wasn't going to be able to get back."

"Back?" Theo asked, before he knew what he was doing. The two looked up at him with a mix of surprise and forgiveness. Strauss replied.

"Back—into her material body. It is always a possibility that ven you project across long distances you may lose contact. That is why ve train vis the silver string."

Simone nodded, and continued. "If I hadn't had the string, I don't think I would've gotten back. But I did." She looked at the used Epi-Pen next to her leg. She picked it up.

"This do it?" she asked Strauss. He nodded.

"That vas the little tugger!"

Simone chuckled, and turned her attention back to her milk. Strauss looked down on her like a doting father, then turned to Theo.

"She vill need to rest. Probably best if you make yourself busy elsevhere."

Theo stifled his shock at the directness of his dismissal, which was immediately replaced by the of-courseness with which every altruist is familiar. He put down the milk, and went over to the corner, where he had long since dropped his notebook. He returned to the bed to bid them both goodbye, only to find that Simone had sunk into a light, dreamless sleep. Strauss grinned as he watched Theo watch her.

"Do not vorry. You have much to learn, handsome smart boy. She enjoys teaching you."

Strauss gave him a wink, and Theo, more bashful than uncomfortable, nodded and left.

When he reached the mouth of the mine, he was surprised to see Butler standing there, flipping through a thick stack of paper. She looked up.

"Ah, Theodore. I hope you found the experience... educational."

Theo nodded. *Why is my throat so dry?*

"Good. I'm sure you're aware that everything that occurred in that room is to be held in the strictest confidence." Her tone shifted to a lighter one. "And I'm very glad to see you're able get around on your own. No more need for breakfast in bed, hmm?" Butler looked at him, with an subtly forceful glint that inferred more than Theo was able to take in.

"I, uh... I guess not."

Butler nodded.

"Very good. Off you go—I think Marianne's primal yelling class is about to begin in the dining hall, if that interests you. Perhaps you could think of it as... extra credit."

Butler chuckled at her barely-a-joke. Theo smiled and chuckled along as best he could, then bade her farewell as he walked toward the dining hall, head still swirling.

FOURTEEN

EXTERNAL ALGORITHM 1885-NIE

Out of every one of their complaints sounds revenge; in their praise there is always a sting, and to be a judge seems bliss to them.

But thus I counsel you, my friends: Mistrust all in whom the impulse to punish is powerful! They are people of a low sort and stock; the hangman and the bloodhound look out of their faces. Mistrust all who talk much of their justice! Verily, their souls lack more than honey. And when they call themselves the good and the just, do not forget that they would be pharisees, if only they had —power.

Theo spent the next few days trying to piece together what had occurred in the sanctum. He paid very little mind to the lesson he had supposedly been learning before they were interrupted—he kept returning to the objective, systematic manner with which Butler and Odin had treated Simone. As far as he could tell, they didn't seem to have any real appreciation for Simone's talents. They were focused solely on how she could be used to further their goals, even to the point that after everything had gone wrong, and she was hyperventilating, unable to speak, Strauss still had to tell them to give her space, and remind them to treat her as a subjective entity. It seemed completely antithetical to the way that Butler had presented herself at the bonfire a couple weeks before. The two seemed irreconcilable.

Deep in the pit of his stomach, he was furious. Not just at them, though they deserved it, but also at himself. Why hadn't he done anything? Simone was lying on the cot, screaming, crying, curled up in a ball, and he had just *stood there*. Strauss had handled the whole thing—all he'd done was pour some milk after the fact.

He consoled himself with the thought that had he stepped forward and said something, there's no telling what Butler, or worse, Odin, would have done. Still, it didn't sit right.

He'd told Rita what had happened, who again cautioned him in every possible way. She agreed that Bodin (they'd initially combined the names in a denigrating "celebrity couple-esque" game, but found it a very useful shorthand for referring to the two as one entity) hadn't reacted in a way that instilled any sense of well-intention or security. The newfound knowledge of the location of the OS, however, was the greatest source of anxiety for the two. Neither had any idea how they'd found it, or the specifics of the eventual plan that concerned it. All they knew for sure, was that there was a plan, and it was moving forward more quickly than either of them wished it to.

Theo was finding himself more and more integrated into camp life as the days blended on. He still kept the strict routine that he'd developed over the past few weeks of breathing, meditation, and exercise—it was comforting to have that pattern to steady himself amidst all the other uncertainty in his day-to-day life. Since the day after the incident in the sanctum, Theo no longer had his meals brought to him, which meant that whenever he wanted to eat, he would have to go to the dining hall, where the entire camp congregated around mealtime.

The first time he'd walked into the dining hall, he was immediately flagged down by Greta, who had just finished filling her plate. She pointed to a table at the opposite end of the room from the kitchen, by the window, and gestured for him to join once he'd gotten his food. Uncertain, he queued through without incident (the server recognized him and gave him his adjusted portion) and he made his way to the table where Greta sat, observing a conversation between a springy-haired woman in her early 30s and Leary, whom he'd recognized from the bonfire.

"You can't know what it's like! And assuming you do is an impediment to everything we're working toward."

"So, my opinion doesn't matter? I have no value to contribute to the conversation?"

"You've contributed enough." Scoffed the springy-haired woman. Dany, who was sitting next to Leary, raised her hand slightly.

"Robin, I don't understand that though... what did Leary do in all this?"

As Theo took a seat next to Greta, the springy-haired woman, whose name was evidently Robin, turned to Dany and spoke in a much softer, kinder tone.

"It's not that he did anything in particular, it's that the group that he belongs to built everything wrong with the world, without letting anyone else weigh in. Now we're giving everyone else a shot, and making up for lost time. It's only fair."

Leary pushed his lips together, unable to come up with a response. Dany grabbed his arm and rubbed his back.

"Maybe she's right, Lear" she proposed in her soft, fairylike lilt.

"But I'm helping... I'm on her side—I'm on your side!"

"Then be on our side, *silently*." Robin retorted.

"I thought silence was violence." he muttered into his plate. Dany rubbed his back in support as he grabbed a fork and speared a chickpea. Robin turned her attention to the new table member.

"Speak of the devil. Theodore, right?"

Theo froze, mid chew, and nodded.

"I heard you got pretty violent at the campfire."

"That wasn't his fault" Greta interjected. "He didn't know the protocol there. I should have told him beforehand."

"Hmmm. Doesn't know how to defend himself either apparently. Or he's too fragile. So, what do *you* think of the cause, Richie Rich?"

Theo swallowed and looked around. He glanced at Greta, who nodded encouragingly, then Leary, who was still staring at his food, defeated.

"I don't really know yet. I know you guys are all about nature and stuff, which I like, but I don't really know what else you do, or like, what you're trying to do."

Robin harrumphed disapprovingly.

"Typical Bougie ambivalence. Don't know what you think but keep acting on it anyway."

Theo pushed his food around his plate with his fork, muttering.

"What's that, moneybags?" pressed Robin.

"I was just saying, if you tell me what I don't know, then I can tell you what I think about it." Theo responded as calmly as he could, trying to contain his annoyance.

Robin took a sharp inhale, then spoke calmly, with more than a hint of condescension.

"Justice for those facing injustice. Equality for those who don't have it. Freedom from oppression. Having a society based on compassion, that rewards love for your fellow man. Do you object to any of that, your majesty?"

"Those all sound like pretty decent goals to me. I don't know why anyone would have objections to any of them. Is that what Butler's plan is working towards?"

Robin nodded confidently.

"Then how does she plan to get there?" Theo asked, genuinely interested.

"By tearing down the old system, and replacing it with a new one, *obviously*." Robin replied. "This one was built on oppression and cruelty, and it's outlived its welcome anyway. It's unfair, and it's up to us to make things right. And, if you're not with us, then you're against us."

In no movie, ever, is it the good guy that says that. But there is bad stuff going on, clearly. And if there's bad stuff going on, then it's the good people who usually try to stop it.

"So then, how does she plan on doing that? By getting control of the OS? What's she gonna do with it once she has it?"

Greta cut in.

"I think that's enough of that. Give him a break Robin, he's barely been here a month. He'll see that what we're doing here is the right thing, eventually. And you heard what Butler said, he's a victim of circumstance. He didn't choose to live up there any more than we chose to live down here."

Robin rolled her eyes and looked away.

"Fine."

Everyone but Robin took a bite in awkward silence before she finally broke the tension.

"How about we talk about something else? There's a rumor going around that Simone is sick. You know anything about that Theodore?"

Theo choked on his food, annoyed he hadn't been able to get in a peaceful bite since he sat down. *What could she be talking about? The mishap with the mission? No one's supposed to know about that.*

"No—last time I saw her was yesterday. She taught me a few things, then I left." He said, unwittingly. Then he quickly added, "Why? What have you heard?"

Robin leaned in to the table, much in the same way Strauss had the day before.

"WELL. Karen said she didn't see her at all yesterday, and she wasn't at sunrise yoga this morning. She never misses sunrise yoga. The last time she missed yoga, she was super sick, but even then, she told Karen about it. Something MUST be up."

Of course she's friends with Karen, Theo thought to himself.

"You really haven't heard anything?" Robin pierced Theo. "What's she teaching you anyway?"

Theo shrugged.

"A lot of weird stuff, I don't really know what it's all doing. Some breathing, some stuff she calls 'visualization'… and I record my dreams and stuff. Not sure why, but she seems to know what it's all about." He returned to his food.

"Hmmm. Weird." She said, reflectively. "Weird girl. You guys know how she got here right? I know I'm the only one who was here when she arrived, but you've all heard the story, right?"

Everyone at the table shook their heads. Theo's ears perked up, though he tried to hide it. Robin's eyes gleamed with superior anticipation.

"OK. So. They were in Cancun for vacation with their mom when Apophis hit, and the Gulf flooded. Simone drags Karen into the rental car while she's drugged out on Ambien, *abandons their mom,* and next thing Karen knows, they're driving North through Mexico City, trying to make it to the border so they can find their dad. Karen's all like 'we have to go back, we can't just leave mom', but Simone won't even consider it. They finally reach the border, and they can't get through, so they stay just south of it in Sonora where they meet Strauss, the Nazi fuck."

Robin spat on the floor.

"Then he brainwashes her with all his science-y spirity bullshit, and he suggests that they all come here. Simone won't take no for an answer, no matter what Karen says, so she went and Karen *had* to follow her—to make sure she stays safe. Totally out of control."

Robin leaned back on her bench, allowing everyone else to bask in the inside wisdom she'd just bestowed upon them. No one said anything—least of all Theo. *That's insane,* he reflected. *She abandoned her mother? There's gotta be more to it than that… Then again… how much do I really know about her? She never talks about herself. Maybe it could be true.*

Dany piped up in her mousey voice, tentatively, but gaining confidence as she went along.

"I just wanna say, I think all of us have been through a rather difficult time in the past few years, and I don't think any of us should judge anyone for what they've had to do. I know Leary and I have been through some rough stuff that we wish we hadn't had to deal with, but we certainly wouldn't want to be judged for them. It just seems… wrong."

All attention turned to Robin, waiting to see her reaction. She thought for a second, then turned her attention to Dany, the care and understanding in her tone this time absent.

"I don't know what you did, but the reality is, you don't have to *do* anything. No one *had* to oppress anyone else, but they did. Everyone needs to be held accountable for their actions, otherwise any chance at *real* progress is thrown out the window. So share what you had to do or don't, but just know that whatever it was that you did, you *did.* There's always another option."

No one dared to speak as Dany shrank back into her seat. Leary put his arm around her to comfort her. He turned to Robin, fire in his eyes.

"Like you're so innocent? You have no idea what we've been through—what about you? Everyone's here for a reason, what are you running from?"

"Watch it, big scary man" Robin replied, coolly. "I never said I was innocent. I own the things I've done. I came from an upper-class family—not moon-level like Richie Rich over there, but we were taken care of and very comfortable. My family got to where they were by profiting off the backs of the poor and overworked. It took years for me to come to terms with that, but now I'm owning it, and taking *responsibility* for my complicity. So why am I here? I'm here for the cause—to tear down the broken system, so we can build a better one, the *right* one. The *fair* one."

Leary bit his tongue, then relented.

"Sounds to me like you're just compensating for feeling guilty."

"Yeah, I am. And I should be." Robin riposted. "And you should be too. And you, and you, and everyone who has in any way profited off of the system of hierarchical oppression we were born into. It's basic compassion."

Greta cut in, audibly stressed.

"I think that's enough for one breakfast!" She pivoted. "Theo, great to see you're off your crutches! You gonna come to Marianne's screaming seminar today?"

Theo nodded, swallowing the food that was in his mouth.

"Yeah, I think so. I only really know what you've told me about it, but I'm interested to see what it's like."

"Non-committal bougie" muttered Robin, just barely audibly. Everyone ignored her.

"Great. I really think you'll enjoy it." Greta said, eyes gleaming.

Theo did enjoy it. He found it a little weird—it started with a few physical exercises to "loosen up his instrument", which he thought made him look really stupid. His self-consciousness receded quickly though, as he allowed himself to be lost in the crowd of other stupid-looking people. Once they were "loose", Marianne, standing on a table on the ocean side of the dining hall, led them in a call and response sort of exercise, making guttural noises, high pitched screams, laughs, nasal sirens—each one weirder than the last, but Greta's unrestricted enthusiasm as she stood next to Theo seemed to allow him an unspoken permission to commit to the furthest edges of his comfort zone. Finally, the class ended with the "free-scream", a period lasting about ten minutes where everyone just "did what felt right". At first Theo returned to his self-conscious appraisal of his environment, carefully observing so as to tailor his behavior accordingly, but upon looking around, he found he had no basis of commonality to build upon. People were screaming, crying, laughing, rolling around of the floor, jumping up and down—everyone seemed to be doing their own thing, irrespective of what the person next to them was doing. He spent the majority of the time humming and vocalizing rather quietly and embarrassedly, but as he felt the end of the session arriving, he began to worry that he'd missed out, and let out a constricted "Woohoo!" that sent sparks of contention through his whole body. He fought the restrictive side of it, and let out a louder one, then even louder. He laughed, and let out a completely unabashed "WOOHOO!!!!", just as Marianne clapped and the room quieted down. A few ripples of laughter spread around the suddenly silent room, quickly followed by a growing applause that Marianne encouraged from atop her table.

"Lovely! I love seeing new faces, making new progress, finding new strength. Everyone welcome Theo! Lovely, lovely work today, everyone!"

She clapped, and the resounding applause resurged.

"That's all for today, you're free to end your practice however you wish."

She hopped down from the table, and darted over to Theo quicker than seemed humanly possible.

"Beautiful work today darling. Really beautiful. I saw you really release some tension there. You'll continue to come, I hope? Lots of experience to gain, lots of joy to be had?"

Marianne grinned hopefully up at Theo.

"I... uh... yeah! I'm all for joy!"

Marianne giggled.

"Yay! Oh yay, I'm so excited. We're going to have so much fun. Fun? Fun. Yes? YES!"

This last word she bellowed as loud as she could, arms extended upward, projecting victory and excitement, at which Theo, nearly knocked off his heels in surprise, couldn't help but laugh. She grinned at him again.

"Remember dear, anything is possible when you allow yourself the freedom to find it! See you soon!"

With a wink, she scampered away, disappearing into the crowd in mere seconds.

Theo, reveling in the strange new experience he'd just had, left the dining hall, people still bellowing and screaming behind him. He walked back towards his tent, mind and body loose, endorphins pumping, repeating what Marianne had said over and over in his head.

Anything is possible if you allow yourself the freedom to find it.

He felt a sense of renewal, a sense of excitement, a sense of wanting to allow himself the freedom to be free. He explored his mind, brainstorming ways he could do just that as he passed the garden on his right, until the entrance to his tent came into view, a few dozen yards in front of him. He set his mind, all his focus, on that point, and steeled himself. His fists clenched, his teeth gritted, all his muscles twitched in anticipation. He dug his right foot into the dirt behind him, and pushed off, thrusting himself forward into a full sprint, reveling in a feeling of power and autonomy he hadn't felt in well over a month. Almost immediately, his legs buckled, and he tumbled into the dirt.

As quickly as he could, he brushed himself off and looked around. A few people had seen his fall, and they were rushing over to see if he was all right. He waved them off, and limped back to his tent.

I guess not anything is possible, he thought. *At least not yet.*

But this is progress.

FIFTEEN

EXTERNAL ALGORITHM 1324-PRO
[Spare the rod, spoil the child...]

Every morning for the next three weeks, the first move Theo made when he woke up was to check his tent pole for a note from Simone. Every morning, he collapsed back into bed, disappointed.

He hadn't seen or heard from her since the mission-gone-wrong. There were whispers around camp—that she'd been spotted near the mine under cover of night, or in the hills surrounding the cove—but no one could corroborate them. When questioned about it, Strauss would refuse to give any direct answers, though it had been noticed that he had been taking slightly more food than usual at each meal, and "saving some for later".

Butler and Odin were strangely silent on the subject as well, though most people in camp were too nervous to bring it up the few times they were out and about in the open. Rumor had it, they were increasingly spending more and more time in the limited access building. There was even speculation that they were sleeping in there a few nights a week—but that was little more than hearsay. All Theo knew was that he was worried.

He and Rita had begun decreasing the frequency of their meetings, due to a frustrating lack of new information, and a wish to not arouse any undue suspicion during this lull of novelty. They had each independently noticed that a frightening proportion of Bohu members made a habit of finding excitement and intrigue where in actuality there was none, sometimes completely blowing past the generally accepted level of anecdotal embellishment to the point of completely fabricating truths about people and events, just to see what would happen and what would stick. These pot-stirrers were treated with enthusiasm and curiosity whenever they entered a group of talkers, but as soon as they left, the general attitude toward them quickly turned sour. Taking into account that fragile atmosphere, the two decided that they should only be seen together when absolutely necessary.

Now that Theo could get around on his own, he had been added to the chore rotation in camp. He was to spend a few hours a day in the garden, watering the crops, flipping topsoil, pruning, and picking what was ripe. He was annoyed at first, but after finding out that his options were either that or post-meal dishwashing, he was more than happy with his assignment. He'd have to spend the first few days being taught how to correctly care for the plants, but he didn't mind that so much.

The first morning he was to report to work, he did his morning breathing and exercise routine, occasionally distracted by wonderings regarding Simone's well-being. It was difficult not to think of her during his practice, as she had been the reason for his doing them in the first place. But each time, eventually he had to force the decision to shake off the thought, and concentrate solely on himself.

He had his breakfast, walked back and forth across camp a few times, testing the edges of his briskness, and finally turned off the main path into the garden. He walked down the rows of plants, eyeing the berries, carrots, and tomatoes as he passed them. Past the tomatoes were stalks of corn a few feet high, and as he approached, a familiar face stood up from behind the backmost row.

"Carson!" he chirped, slightly more upbeat than he meant it to be.

She turned to him, and the determined grin of satisfaction that one gets when one is working hard on something they enjoy dropped off her face.

"What are you doing here?" she asked.

Theo frowned, confused.

"I'm supposed to start working here this morning."

"You're who I'm training?" Carson asked, annoyed.

Theo shrugged sheepishly.

"Are there any other new people in camp?"

Carson looked around for someone to complain to, but no one was there. She heaved a sigh, and waved him over.

"Fine, over here." She said, burdensome.

Theo walked over, a bit on edge, unsure of what he'd done to pivot her mood downward so quickly.

"We're pruning the tomato plants today."

"Great, do I get clippers or something?" Theo asked hurriedly.

"Slow down, George Washington. Ain't no cherry trees getting chopped right now. You'll get 'em when you're ready."

She knelt down next to a tomato plant.

"See this?" She pointed to the base of the plant. Theo squatted down next to her and nodded.

"That's the leader. It's the central branch of the plant, the strongest part. It has the most direct connection all the way down to the roots. Rule number one: Never cut the leader."

She pointed to a small offshoot further up the plant.

"See this flower cluster?"

Theo peered through the leaves, and spotted a cluster of four or five small yellow flowers.

"Those can only grow on the leader. If you see a big branch, and it doesn't have flowers on it, it's a sucker."

"What's a sucker?" Theo asked.

"It's called a sucker because it sucks energy away from the rest of the plant, without providing any fruit. Suckers get pruned."

Theo searched a plant next to the one they were looking at. He pointed at a small branch.

"Like that one?"

Carson shook her head.

"Good guess, but see how the leaves are really wide? That's a sun leaf."

She pointed to another one.

"See how this one's leaves are thinner, and kinda shriveled near the leader? That's a sucker."

She snipped it off.

"There are two kinds of tomato plants- determinate and indeterminate. We grow indeterminate plants- given the right circumstances, there's really no limit to how tall they can grow. As long as you prune off the suckers, it'll keep growing taller and taller, but if you let them accumulate, there won't be enough nutrition to reach the top of the leader and it'll stop growing."

Theo took all this in, and traced the plant's growth from where it met the dirt, up the leader's verdant stalk, covered in light white fuzz, until it split off into two. After a quick scan of the plant as a whole, he turned to Carson.

"It looks like this plant has two leaders."

Carson looked up in light surprise.

"Yeah, they all do. Good eye—how'd you figure that out?"

Theo surveyed the multiple rows of tomatoes, realizing that they all shared some facsimile of a Y structure.

"The base splits into two strong looking branches, but they both have flowers on them."

Carson nodded, a hint of a smile creeping across her face.

"Good—yeah, we grow them like that on purpose. Each plant, when it's young, only has one leader, but as it gets bigger, the suckers—if they're allowed to grow out—can end up becoming leaders themselves and flowering."

"So why don't you let them all grow, if they can all bear fruit?"

"Because the plant is stronger if there aren't many leaders. It's more efficient with its energy, and can grow much bigger because of that. Once it's at the biggest manageable size for its environment, and if it can get enough nutrition, we can be more relaxed about the suckers, but until then, we've gotta stay vigilant, and only keep the leaders and sun leaves."

"So then why two? If the less leaders the stronger, why not one?"

"Because ultimately the point of the plant is to bear fruit. Three would overextend the plant's ability to provide enough nutrition to itself, but two allows for almost double the amount of flowering clusters that a single leader plant would, as long as the root structure is big enough. And, if something were to happen to one leader—a grasshopper, deer, squirrel or something gnaws it off, or it gets diseased—we still have one strong leader to keep the plant growing."

"Huh." Theo scanned the plants, then turned his attention to Carson. She was focused intently on one of the plants, going branch by branch up the stalk, every now and then snipping one off, as she was instructing Theo.

"Most people would say that a single leader plant is the strongest kind, and that your typical root structure can't support a double leader growing pattern. But that's only for the typical root structure—I've found a way around that."

Theo watched as she worked her way up each stalk. Each movement, each look of consideration was slow, methodical, not wasting time, not rushing. Each snip was delicate, precise, and definite—imbued with of the kind of relaxed intensity that spawns from the twin virtues of experience and understanding. She continued.

"When we have the beginnings of new plants, we have to be kinda harsh, dig them up, and prune off everything below the top four-ish inches, and replant most of it underground, so we get around twice the initial root structure as we would if we just let them grow normally. Gives them a health jumpstart right at the beginning of the growing season, and a much better chance at success. Before I got here, we were ending up with less than half of the tomatoes we get now."

Theo nodded, still transfixed by the effortless concentration he was witnessing as she finished one plant and moved on to the next. She pulled another pair of clippers off her belt and handed them up to Theo.

"Just go down the line, and cut off any suckers at the base that are touching the ground. They never get sun, and are just begging for mildew or fungus to grow on them."

Theo nodded, took the clippers, and knelt down to begin his task. Seemed simple enough. Any tiny branches touching the ground, snip 'em.

"You know a lot about tomatoes." He offered.

Carson nodded, never looking away from her work.

"My dad and I would work in his garden every Sunday—he'd always say 'The Lord says we're not supposed to work on Sundays, but the plants don't know what day of the week it is. They just want to grow.' He taught me everything I know."

Theo glanced over toward her. *This is the most I've gotten out of her the entire time I've been here.* He turned back to his plant, trying not to make a big deal out of it.

"You, uh, did you grow stuff besides tomatoes with him?" Theo asked, fumbling.

Carson nodded, and swallowed. She responded, voice a bit shaky.

"All kinds of things—potatoes, corn, carrots, berries. He loved his flowers though. He had this rose bush that was his favorite. It was the only one I wasn't allowed to touch—every rose on it, once it had fully bloomed, he gave to my mom. She had a fresh rose in the center of the dinner table 6 months out of the year. One time—" She chuckled. "One time when I was six, I decided one was fully bloomed and tried to pick it for my mom, but one of the thorns stuck me in my finger. I started bleeding, crying, and I got so mad I started to kick the bush because it had hurt me. My dad heard me screaming, ran outside and pulled me away. He didn't get mad though—he bandaged up my finger, and explained that the rose bush was alive too, and it was only doing what it was supposed to do when it felt threatened. I argued, and told him it was our plant, and it shouldn't hurt the people that own it. He just shook his head and explained to me 'No, bud, the flower and us, we're partners. We help it grow strong, and it rewards us afterwards with how beautiful it becomes. Just like you, bud. I'm feeding you, clothing you, and sending you to school so you can grow big and strong, and my reward is seeing how beautiful and strong I helped you become.' He always knew what to say."

She shook her head, then doubled back down on her work. After a second, she froze.

"Sorry, I didn't mean to—" she started.

"No, I loved it—I mean, thanks… for sharing that." Theo floundered. The two worked in silence for a minute.

"I wish I had a memory like that with my dad." Theo mentioned, as casually as he could. "He was always so focused on his work, then when he got home, he was usually too tired for anything other than eating or watching TV."

Carson took a slight inhale, then released it.

"Well, he worked hard enough that you we able to abdicate with the rest of 'em, so it's not a big loss, apparently."

Theo bit his tongue. He still hadn't gotten used to the vague air of resentment that clouded most of his interactions in camp. He tried to maneuver around it.

"Yeah, I had it pretty good, but still. It's a tradeoff I'd want the choice to consider, you know?"

"Hmph. Maybe. A lot of people would want the choice, but you don't know the value of something until you don't have it."

"That's true." Theo replied. "I haven't talked to my dad in over two years, now I even miss the boring stuff."

"My dad's been gone for six, and it's the boring stuff I miss most of all." Carson shot back, strangely casual. Immediately, she realized what she'd said, then focused all her attention on her plants. Theo, seeing this reaction, realized the gravity of what she'd just said. He went back to his plant, and stayed silent. After a few seconds, Carson's arms dropped, and she spoke.

"Sorry, I didn't mean to—"

"No, no, please. Sorry if I pushed you to—"

"No, you didn't—"

"You don't have to talk about anything you don't want to—"

"No, I know, sorry, you're just…" Carson trailed off.

Theo shook his head, not knowing what to do or say.

"Just…?"

Carson avoided looking at him, and glared at her tomato plant.

"You're… UGH. You're annoyingly easy to talk to."

Theo couldn't help but laugh.

"Sorry?"

Carson stopped her work to gather her thoughts.

"No! It's just… Most of the people here kinda suck, and I was kinda… sorta… hoping you would too."

Theo, unable to hide his surprise, said nothing, for fear of ruining whatever it was that just happened. Carson anxiously elaborated.

"You're a good listener, and most of the people here, they just wait until it's their turn to talk. I don't know if it's some Bougie thing, or what, but I wanted to hate you, and you're making it really hard."

Theo tried, poorly, to stifle a chuckle. Carson blushed, and returned to her work, distracted.

"Well, whatever it is, it's not a Bougie thing, or whatever you said." Theo responded after a second. "People up there like to hear themselves talk just as much as people down here, as far as I can tell."

He returned to his plants, but after a few seconds, he noticed Carson snickering. He turned to her and laughed nervously. Her giggles grew, until she stamped them down, and got a hold of herself.

"What was that?" Theo asked, self-conscious.

Carson shook her head. "Nothing." She smirked. "So people just suck everywhere, huh?"

Theo let out a chuckle of relief and nodded. "Yup, seems that way."

The two kept working in silence, broken only by Theo asking an occasional question about pruning. After the day's work had been done, he gave her the clippers back, and the two parted ways—Theo toward the dining hall for Marianne's class, Carson inland toward the tents.

○

Now that Theo could contribute, he found his schedule practically filled up. He'd wake up, do his morning routine—occasionally joining the yoga class at dawn—have breakfast, work in the garden, scream with Marianne, then have lunch. Every day he hoped that the space between his lunch and dinner would find itself suddenly filled by a note taped to his tent pole, but instead he usually ended up napping and exercising. A brief post-lunch siesta gave him the time he needed to digest, and when he woke up, he found himself full of enough energy to work out hard for a couple of hours.

Purely to give himself something to do, he'd set a goal—to be able to jog from one end of the camp to the other. Whenever it popped into his head, a bittersweet chuckle would find its way up his gullet. A light jog was something he'd taken for granted his whole life, even found boring—but now, that baby step back to completely unrestrained autonomy was a treasure toward which he directed all his vital energy. In his dreams he would bound through forests, up hills and down, legs pumping, never tiring, jumping over logs, ducking under branches—then he'd wake up, sigh, do a few warmup jumps, and start his powerwalking laps.

His efforts didn't go unnoticed. Every now and then, people would cheer him on from their tents, or come up and try to walk with him. He tuned them out. Walking was awkward, sometimes painful, but all the more reason to keep going. *One day*, he thought, *one day I'll be able to run faster and longer than anyone here.*

After three weeks of jumping, squatting, and powerwalking, he finally had enough leg strength to complete the weighty bounce required to jog sustainably. He could powerwalk with the best of them, but now he could bounce from one bent leg to the other, each supporting his weight, shifting balance front to back, side to side.

On his second day of jogging the length of the camp (a painfully slow jog by anyone else's standards, but a victory for Theo), he nearly fell when he saw Butler waving at him. He trotted over, painfully.

"You're really moving along there, aren't you?" she projected as he drew closer.

He nodded, panting.

"I'm very impressed with your progress. You're really coming into your own."

Theo wiped off some sweat, and nodded.

"Yeah, I guess so."

"Carson says you've been picking up gardening rather quickly too, hmm? Making yourself indispensable?"

"I don't know about that. Doing my best, I guess."

"Indeed. Well, contributions shouldn't go unrewarded, in my opinion. I assume you're growing a bit tired of the back and forth across camp? It has come to my attention that leg strength can plateau without… shocks to the system."

Theo's butterflies woke up.

"Maybe... what do you have in mind?"

Butler's face broke into a smile. She laughed. It seemed genuine, but felt very unnatural.

Maybe that's just the way she is, Theo thought.

She handed him a piece of paper. He unfolded it. It was a triangle with a tail. He looked up at her, confused.

"Odin has pointed out that nothing develops functional leg strength like running up hills. I've taken the liberty of drawing up a map of a loop you may use if you would like, once you are able. Turn right on the fire road at the inland end of camp, and follow the coast."

She leaned over the map, and pointed at the lines Theo now realized were trails.

"Turn left at Watertank Road, then left again onto the Goat Whiskers trail. You may run the loop in the other direction if you would like, but take great care never to go off this loop. Use of this road is a privilege, not a right, hmm? I will know if you leave it. I have eyes everywhere. Understand?"

Theo stared at the map. He shook himself back out of his head and nodded furiously.

"Yes. I understand. Uh, thank you."

Butler smiled.

"Of course, Theodore. I've made the necessary staff aware of your privileges. Glad to see you are meshing well with the rest of the campers. You will let me know if you hear of any issues?"

Theo looked up from the map again, confused.

"Like what?"

"Oh, just anything that seems worth mentioning." Butler replied, nonchalantly. "Don't worry about it, just if something comes up. Enjoy your jog."

Butler turned in the direction of her building. Theo thanked her, and started walking towards his tent, when a thought occurred to him, and he called after her.

"Hey Butler?"

She stopped, and turned expectantly. Theo jogged over, painfully.

"Have, uh…" he began in a low tone, "have you heard from Simone at all?"

Butler searched her mind for a second, then began.

"This is all confidential, of course."

"Of course." Theo assured her.

Butler continued. "She has been… recovering from the most recent mission. It seems to have done a number on her. Don't worry though, she'll be back to working capacity in no time, and you'll be able to continue your lessons with her post haste. Is there anything else?"

Theo shook his head.

"Very good. Best of luck in your progress, Theodore."

She paused for a second, then began again.

"Oh, Theodore—if you're free, I would very much like to lunch with you at some point in the near future. I would be very interested to hear what you think of our camp—at a time that wouldn't interfere with your duties, of course."

Theo was struck dumb. *What could she want to know? Something about the OS? I don't know anything about that. Or about the camp? What would I know that she doesn't? I can't very well say no…*

"Of course—I'd love to." He squeaked.

Butler beamed.

"Excellent. I look forward to it. Be well, Theodore."

She gave him a quick nod, and walked briskly away.

SIXTEEN

EXTERNAL ALGORITHM 1914-MIU
"In every walk with nature, one receives far more than he seeks."

After a couple weeks of working together, Theo had made a practice of allowing Carson the space to open up, acting as a sounding board for those rare situations where Carson felt like sharing what was on her mind. He quickly learned that he had to be careful to offer his thoughts only when they were asked for, or else she would shut down, hardly speaking to him for the rest of the day. Despite these small setbacks, Theo was surprised and pleased at how quickly they'd become friends, given their rocky start and Carson's taciturn attitude.

The tomatoes seemed to be growing swimmingly, thanks to Theo's efforts and Carson's watchful eye. Theo's chest warmed with pride whenever Carson noted that they were on track for a record harvest.

He enjoyed his gardening work more and more as his knowledge blossomed, fertilized by Carson's stern but careful direction. He found the seemingly antithetical combination of ruthlessness and delicate care for the cultivation of their crop particularly engaging. The essentially sadistic snipping of promising buds that were too far divorced from their leaders, contrasted against the nurturing support and careful positioning of the remaining branches in areas of adequate sunlight, was a dichotomy that he found especially difficult to reconcile. Carson explained that both, however, were necessary for the plant to grow as strong as possible. Theo begrudgingly said he understood, and acted like he did, but still found the information difficult to integrate.

Once he had gotten a handle on all the basic duties of their job, the conversation between the two dried up, except for those rare occurrences when Carson spoke first. Try as he might, besides complaining about the other campers (which both admitted early on that they didn't enjoy doing or listening to), Theo had little success in starting a dialogue. They came from completely different worlds, and thus had very little common ground. Usually, his attempts at conversation went something along the lines of

"Do you like video games?"
"Not really."
"Oh. Ok… They're pretty fun."
"I bet."
After which, they'd return to their work. Or something like—
"You know some people think the world is flat."
"Yeah, well, you're the one who's seen it from the moon—is it?"
"No."
"That's what I thought."

Neither wanted to dig into the invisible divide that separated their two worlds. They both valued a particular level of discretion when it came to topics of particular sensitivity. Both were aware that breaching an unresolvable subject would render the work environment saturated with high, spoken tension rather than low, unspoken tension. Since they knew they had to work together every day, just the possibility of the former was enough for both of them to default to the latter.

One morning, however, a rather productive conversation between the two occurred. It began like this:

"You know how walnuts are shaped like brains?" asked Carson, quite unprompted.

"Yeah, I noticed that. It's kinda cool." replied Theo.

"It's more than cool. Not only do they look like brains, they're full of omega-3s and other brain-healthy nutrients."

"That's interesting- like a mirroring thing."

"Yeah, and it's not just walnuts. Tomatoes have four chambers, like our hearts, and they're good for heart health, sliced carrots look like eyes and they're great for eyesight—it's everywhere. I think it's called the Doctrine of Signatures, or something like that."

"That's really interesting actually. Crazy how things like that just happen by chance."

"Not by chance, really."

"Right, sorry—evolution."

"I'm not even sure evolution could do something like that."

"What do you mean?" Theo asked.

"Well, the more you think about it, it's so weirdly poetic, it's kinda funny. Almost like the existence of that pattern is just some kind of big joke."

"Well, if there's a joke, that implies that someone set it up. Do you believe in all that old stuff?"

Carson shrugged.

"I don't know... my dad did. He was the smartest guy I ever met. I always just kinda adopted whatever he thought was true."

"Well like what, specifically though? Christian, Muslim, Jewish, Pagan...?"

"No, no none of that—well, technically Muslim, I guess. But I don't know, I never really gave it much thought. I went to pray at the mosque every Friday with my dad, but I didn't really enjoy it. Now that he's gone, it just makes me feel closer to his memory..."

Carson trailed off, lost in thought. Theo gulped. He could go one of two ways, but somehow leaving her in silence felt wrong—he chose the less confrontational route.

"How, um... how did your dad..."

Carson started, then hesitated. Theo jumped back in.

"Sorry, you don't have to if—"

"No, no. He, uh..." her voice caught in her throat. "It was kind of a buildup of things... Just after the first Apophis scare he lost his job... In the scramble following the Abdication, a lot of companies rushed into automating their workforce. He was one of the first to be let go. We didn't have a lot of money—we weren't poor, but we weren't struggling—but when my dad tried to find a new job, he found out that pretty much everything he was qualified for had been automated. He didn't have any formal training—he could make friends with anyone, but he was never great with numbers. Tried coding, couldn't get it. Soon the only entry-level jobs left were in hospitality, so when I was 14 I suggested he become a bartender, only to find out he was 15 years sober—he used to be an alcoholic and went cold turkey the second my mom got pregnant with me. Said he didn't know what it meant to be a man until that moment, and couldn't risk falling back into his old habits. My mom and I were his whole world, and his purpose in life was to take care of us. I tried to tell him we could take care of ourselves, he didn't have to do it all himself, but eventually it became too much for him—the OS couldn't match him with an existing occupation, so he had nowhere to turn, he felt like he couldn't provide for us, and…"

    Carson stopped, and wiped her eyes with the back of her gloved hand. Theo, unsure what to do, walked over and put a supportive hand on her shoulder. She didn't move, but Theo felt weird removing it, so he didn't.

    "He sounds like a great man." Theo said.

    She nodded and smiled at the ground.

    "He was. I remember whenever I was mad at him, he'd make me stop and take a deep breath, then explain what the problem was. It made me furious."

    Theo chuckled, and took his hand off her shoulder.

    "My dad did the same thing. Breath and all."

    Carson looked up at him, smiling gratefully, the trail of a tear still glistening on her cheek.

    "You're gonna be a good dad, Theo."

    "Really?"

    She nodded. "Yeah. I can tell."

    Theo, unable to restrain his smile, turned back to his tomato plant. "Thanks."

    As the two continued their work in silence, the atmosphere turned eerie. Both were reflecting on the more magnitudinous points in their conversation, and both became aware that they were thinking about the same things. Theo, unable to stand the mounting tension anymore, spoke.

"My mom tried to."

"What?" Carson stopped her work and looked toward Theo. He didn't look away from his work.

"What your dad… my mom tried to. A couple days before I came here."

Carson took a deep inhale.

"Wow… I… I'm so sorry."

"Yeah. Thanks."

"So that's what Butler was talking about at that bonfire?"

Theo nodded. Carson thought for a second.

"That's terrible. No one should have to go through that."

"You can say that again." Theo chuckled, bitterly.

"Nah, I think once is enough." Carson giggled.

Theo burst out laughing.

Jolted by Theo's sudden reaction, Carson joined in, the two chortled and giggled and tittered and cackled until they had to brace themselves against the ground they were laughing so hard.

"Why are we laughing??" Theo asked incredulously between guffaws.

"I don't know! It's terrible!" Carson responded, gasping for air.

The two calmed down, after receiving strange looks from those passing by the garden. They returned to their work, exchanging knowing grins in solidarity against the Bohus that started whispering when they passed them. As they neared the end of the day's checklist, Carson posed a question to Theo, one he'd always thought about, but for which he had yet to find an answer.

"Theo?"

"Yeah?"

"Why do bad things happen to good people?"

Theo thought for a second, then gave up.

"Because of whatever comes after, I guess? I don't know."

"Yeah, I don't think anyone does." Carson replied with a shrug, as she pruned the last sucker off the last plant of the day.

◌

After nearly a month of intense daily practice, Theo had reached the point where he could jog nonstop across the camp and back, a full kilometer. The first day he accomplished the feat, the kitchen staff rewarded him at dinner with a whopping mound of whipped cream on top of his berry ration. Robin questioned whether or not he should have gotten it in the first place, but the rest of the people at his table congratulated him, so he let them steal a fingerful.

A few days prior, when his goal was in sight, he decided that his personal reward would be to allow himself to explore the loop for which Butler had given him a map. When the day finally arrived, he rushed through his morning routine and gardening duties, skipped Marianne's screaming class for the first time (to study the map), and distractedly fended off Greta's admonishments during lunch regarding his absence. He laid down for his post-lunch nap, but he was too excited to sleep. After trying and failing to sleep for about 20 minutes, he contented himself with a few rounds of breathing, then set off toward the back of camp.

As Theo passed the storage building and reached the fire road at the back of the camp, he looked around. Not a single person had asked where he was going, what he was doing, or even gave him a second look. He suddenly found himself filled with a giddy sense of glee that lasted the whole first leg of the loop. He grinned in wonder as he walked up the fire road toward the ocean, getting a better overhead view of the camp with every step. He passed the bathrooms, then the tent complexes, where he could see little people talking to each other, laughing, arguing, all totally unaware of the observer up above. He passed the gardens, where it struck him again how small they were—it didn't seem like they could feed a camp of over 100 people on any sort of regular basis. He passed the medical building and imagined Rita inside, treating injuries or doing inventory. *She does inventory a lot,* Theo chuckled to himself. *Oh*—He caught himself. *I need to tell her about this map. This definitely counts as news.*

He passed over the dining hall, then the limited access building, the salt flats, the amphitheater, and finally reached a turnout that brought him out overlooking the ocean. He stopped for a minute, and breathed in the salty sea air, taking in the spacious blue majesty of what lay before him. Just beyond it, peeking through the horizon, he saw inklings of land. With that one image, the miles of ocean and the land beyond, it struck him— he was a prisoner. As nice as these people were, he was not here by choice. *Well, it was a choice,* he thought. *Just not my choice.* He resolved to continue on, and took in the sign stuck into the side of the hill.

He glanced down at his map. *She said I could go either direction I wanted. May as well go in reverse the first time.*

He started hiking up the hill. Immediately he was struck by the steepness. The red dirt crunched beneath his feet and dug between his toes. His legs strained against the incline. Cacti and half dead bushes mocked him from either side as he pushed himself higher and higher along the shallow V carved through the trail by years of runoff. Soaked in sweat, he reached the top of the first crest and took a deep inhale of victory, which got sucked out of him like a vacuum when he saw what the trail had in store.

Up and up he climbed, heaving and panting, vast sea to his right, prison to his left, forcing himself to go on. His legs cried out in pain as he meandered deeper through the waist-high brush, following only the path beaten into the ground by those nameless wanderers that had come before him. He reached another crest, and took his time on the brief decline before reaching the uphill anaconda that had come into view. As he ascended, he wheezed and strained, relishing the painful thrill of pushing himself to his limit and further, his chaparral surroundings growing taller in harmonic accord with his spirit. The knee-high cactus and waist-high brush were now accompanied by trees that towered over him, threatening to push him off the trail with their overhanging invasiveness.

He proceeded in this way, up and down and sometimes flat, fast and slow but never stopping, further up and further inland, until the camp behind him was barely discernable next to the magnificent, subtly swirling sea that embraced it in its hilly cradle. He ducked under a gnarled white tree that had had a very long, hard life, when he heard it.

It was light—a lilting, high pitched sustained sound. In his curiosity, he forgot the pain in his legs and chest, and rounded the final corner of the trail to see… another sign. He pushed himself up the last few feet, hands against knees, and gasped for air as he read it.

The arrow pointed to the trail he had just ascended. He turned to face the ocean, and looked at his map. Where he'd come from was to his right, the road Butler had told him to keep to was to his left. He looked around, saw no one, and heard it again.

It was *singing*.

And it was coming from the road directly behind him.

He looked around again. No one was there. Apart from the voice, he was completely alone.

He turned around, and walked up the forbidden road.

SEVENTEEN

EXTERNAL ALGORITHM 9987-JUN
"I use the term *enantiodromia* to describe <u>the emergence of the unconscious opposite</u>, with particular relation to its chronological sequence. This characteristic phenomenon occurs almost universally wherever an extreme one-sided tendency dominates the conscious life; for this involves the gradual development of an equally strong, unconscious counterposition, <u>which first becomes manifest in an inhibition of conscious activities, and subsequently leads to an interruption of conscious direction.</u>"

As Theo drew nearer, the song grew clearer, and he began to make out the words.

> *I had a dream, of a mountain peak high*
> *I was rolling a boulder up towards the sky*
> *Nearing the summit, my feet always fail*
> *And back down I tumble like Jill with her pail*

Theo walked as quickly as he could on quiet feet, drawn by the angelic voice.

> *All the while, above, an invisible friend*
> *Soaring on high, biding time on the wind*
> *Watches my journey, and using its song*

Waxes melancholic and follows along
Ah

The light, lilting ah drifted through the air like a wistful leaf surrendered to the wind, flying and falling, at once hopeful and mournful.

At the base of the mountain I start up again
Knowing full well what awaits at the end
And again near the top of this imperfect life
I roll down again to continue in strife

But above it all my friend still remains
Singing its song despite sorrow and pain
How can it live without taking or giving
Just riding the tune of the life it is living
Ah

The road turned slightly up and to the left, and as Theo reached the zenith, his breath left him as he saw a familiar sundress through the trees on the side of the road. He stopped just shy of them as Simone's voice rang out over the valley below.

Away, Away! For I will fly to thee
Teach me the ways of your life in the trees
Gliding above and engaging at will
But still taking the time when it's time to be still

All the while it sings
Ah   .

Her voice rang out again, until she paused, seemingly lost in thought. Theo didn't dare breathe. Then, quietly, she sang, almost to herself.

You lie there in slumber, I sit here awake
I can't help but wonder, was this a mistake?
Can I close off my feelings, and still be connected?
And if that's the mistake, can they be resurrected?

And what of my mountain? Is it worth the climb?
Could I get to that songbird if I had the time?
Was it a vision, or a waking dream?
Fled is that music: —do I wake or sleep?

She finished. She knelt down; Theo's view now completely obstructed by his hiding tree. He shifted slightly, to get a better look at what she was doing, when suddenly—

CRACK

A twig beneath Theo's foot split in two, way louder than seemed possible. Simone's head whipped to glare directly toward Theo, eyes both angry and terrified.

"WHO'S THERE?" she ordered. Theo stood stalk still, frozen in place.

"I know you're there, I heard you." She said, twisting onto her knees, then standing. With a shaky voice she added, "I know Krav Maga!"

"No—no, don't! I'm coming out!" Theo raised his hands and walked slowly out from behind his hiding spot to see Simone in a ready karate stance, in the center of a bed of multicolored flowers and herbs—tulips and daisies, roses and rosemary, and nearly a dozen other kinds Theo didn't know the names of. When he came into view, she let her arms drop, which Theo took as permission to do the same.

"Oh, it's just you." She said, with a slight hint of annoyed relief. Immediately, her defenses shot back up again.

"Were you spying on me?"

"No! I mean I guess, but no! I didn't know it was you, I just heard the singing." He said, warily. Simone folded her arms.

"Hmph. Creep. What are you even doing here? You're not allowed to leave the camp."

"Butler gave me permission." He shot back. "And I could ask you the same thing. Where have you *been*? No one in camp has heard from you in weeks. Karen's been worried sick, and I..."

He went silent before he finished the thought. Simone rocked back on her heels, and bit her lip. Through slitted eyes, she peered at Theo, sticking out her lower jaw and sucking her upper teeth, the way she does when she's thinking something over. Then, quite suddenly, something in her relented. She turned away from him and knelt down next to a bed of lavender.

"I had to get away. Something... just didn't feel right after what happened. Don't—no, stay there."

Theo, who'd been edging closer, stopped in his tracks. He raised his hands again in acquiescence. She said nothing, and returned to inspecting her flowers. Theo, not knowing what to do, slowly sat down, legs crossed, watching her work. She looked up, brow furrowed, then went back to what she was doing.

For a few minutes, neither spoke, her tending her plants, Theo watching. Even with his weeks of gardening experience, he couldn't really tell what she was doing. Whatever it was, she seemed to be doing it very intently.

"What was that song?" Theo asked tentatively, once he'd given up on figuring out what she was doing.

"My mom used to sing it to me when I was little." She said, without stopping what she was doing. *Her mother- the one she abandoned?* he thought.

"It's beautiful. What's it from?" he asked innocently.

"Some musical. She loved musicals." She replied, distractedly.

"Well, I bet she'd love to hear you sing it. You have a beautiful voice."

She looked up at him with suspicion, then rolled her eyes and returned to her work. Despite the gesture, Theo noticed a small smile peeking out of the corner of her mouth.

With all the tact of a dump truck, a barely encouraged Theo pressed his luck.

"Where is your mom? You've never talked about her."

Simone stopped what she was doing and stared at the ground, hair obscuring her face. Theo fluttered nervously.

Dammit. After a few painful seconds, she spoke.

"What did Karen tell you?"

Theo gulped. Feigning ignorance clearly wasn't going to be a useful strategy.

"Karen? Nothing. Robin said something…" he started, and was cut off—

"*Robin?* Fuckin' Robin! I hate her. Always has her nose in other people's business, doesn't have a clue that she annoys everyone around her, sensationalizes everything… I wish I could take her dumb face and slam it over and over again into a brick fucking—" Simone stopped, suddenly overcome by self-awareness. Shaking, she started to backtrack.

"I… uh… that's not—" Theo cut her off, with no idea what to say.

"Hey—no. If it's any consolation, I think that's something a lot of people would love to see."

Simone, eyes watery, looked near to where Theo was sitting, and after taking in what he said, she was unable to stifle a chuckle that nudged the tear nestled below her eye to run down her cheek. She pulled a stalk of lavender toward her and smelled it. It seemed to calm her down. With renewed caution, Theo started again.

"She, uh" he gulped. "She told me what Karen told her, but it didn't really seem to me like something you would do. Like, at all. You're strong—and sometimes scary honestly—but I can tell it never comes from a malicious place. You have a good heart. You're not the type to abandon anyone."

As Theo spoke, the earnestness of his belief and the terror of being wrong raced against each other, each clawing the lead from the other quicker and more violently, until his whole being was enveloped by throbbing uncertainty. He finished, and turned his attention outward toward her, praying with his eyes to receive the news that what he'd said was true.

She started weeping, softly. Theo looked on in horrified silence as he waited for her to speak. After a few seconds, she wiped her tears and responded.

"Clearly you don't know me as well as you think you do."

Theo struggled to take this in. She sniffed, pulling herself together, and continued.

"I did what I had to do."

Simone, now stone faced, yanked a sprig of lavender off the bush, and crushed one of its needles between her fingers. Theo watched.

"So... you did?" He asked, voice unsteady.

She nodded briefly, crushing another needle.

"I didn't have a choice."

"Why?" Theo asked, pleading.

She took a deep sigh.

"If we stayed with her, we would have died. For background, she was a drunk—not so bad when we were younger, though she didn't really know what she was doing then either. Once we hit puberty, she tried to be the "fun mom", and ended up the opposite. She was napping after blacking out, so was my sister. We were staying at a hotel on the beach in Tulum—my dad had to fly back home early for work, so it was just the three of us. I was the only one awake, felt the impact, and turned on the news to see if it was an earthquake. Turns out New Orleans had already been destroyed, and the wave was due to hit us in less than 15 minutes. I tried to wake both of them up, but we couldn't get my mom to budge. Karen was crying, told me to keep trying, but I could tell we were out of time. I grabbed the keys from her purse and we left her there. 5 minutes after we left, the hotel was underwater. So you're wrong. My heart's as black as they come."

As she finished, she yanked another sprig off the bush and ripped it in half. Theo stared at the ground.

"No."

She looked up.

"What?"

"No. You did what you had to do to save your sister's life. Her being ungrateful for it doesn't make what you did wrong."

She froze. As she thawed, her head tilted slightly to the side, and she let the lavender fall from her hand. Unsure what to do, Theo repeated himself.

"You have a good heart."

Theo, still staring at the ground, glanced up at her for a second. She hadn't moved. He stared at his feet. They were really dirty. There was a sizeable grain of dirt under his big toenail. He started picking at it, when suddenly he felt a thin pair of arms around him, squeezing. Simone had made her way the few feet over to him, sat down, and hugged him. He went rigid. When she was done, she let go and pulled her knees in toward her, hugging them, mouth resting on her thighs. Neither said anything. Simone sniffled. Theo just sat there.

For a few minutes, they just sat. It was awkward, but neither wanted it to end. Eventually a thought occurred to Theo.

"So is the rest of it true then?"

Simone turned to look at him.

"Huh?"

"The rest of the story. Fighting your way through Mexico, getting turned away at the border, meeting Strauss, all that?"

She nodded.

"Yeah, pretty much. I don't know what she told you, but all that sounds right."

Theo leaned back, hands to dirt.

"Wow. That's insane."

"It's my life." She replied, matter-of-factly. Theo shook his head in disbelief.

"Your life is insane."

She gave an affirming shrug, then leaned back, hands to dirt. The two listened to the birds for a time, until Theo broke the silence.

"There's one thing I don't get though."

Simone turned to him, eyebrows raised.

"What?"

"You were trying to cross the border to get to your dad, right?"

She nodded.

"Then you met Strauss, who—the word Robin used was brainwash, but I doubt that's accurate—taught you all the spiritual stuff you know, and brought you here."

She laughed.

"Brainwash? That's rich. She's more brainwashed than anyone. But yeah, sorry, you were saying?"

Theo continued. "Are you still trying to get to your dad? Or are you happy here?"

Simone's gaze dropped. She sucked on her teeth.

"That's what I've been trying to figure out the past few weeks. Everyone's been so nice here. I love Strauss, Marianne, and everyone, but this isn't where I saw myself when I got here. I originally came here because it's technically across the border. It solved our problem. But then Strauss told Butler the stuff he'd taught me, and she started giving me special privileges in order to help them, and I guess I lost track of time. Then a few weeks ago, I guess I woke up."

Theo nodded.

"I've been thinking about what happened every day since." He admitted. "Watching it was horrible. I can't imagine what it must have felt like."

She nodded.

"It was terrifying. Then coming back, it was like something inside me that had split off was trying to claw its way back. I don't know what, but I think it had had enough of me doing what I was doing, being…" she trailed off, then shook her head. "I don't know."

"Used." He said. "They were using you as a tool for their plan, whatever it is, I still don't know. But you didn't see their faces when you had just come back. Butler couldn't look at you. She was just thinking. Odin just stood there, staring at her for orders. Made me furious. I wish I'd done something."

"I'm glad you didn't." she said. "Odin would've snapped you like a twig."

Theo laughed. "True, but still."

Simone sat up, and curled into a ball again. Theo mirrored her, slightly more relaxed.

"I don't even know what it's all for. Maybe I'd agree with them if I knew what they were doing, but they only tell me what I need to know for what they need me to do."

"So you don't know what their plan is either?" Theo asked.

She shook her head.

"No. I don't think anyone but Butler does. Strauss might, but he's so old and his brain is so addled from drugs I don't know if I trust his judgement anymore. I mean I trust him, but I… I don't wanna let them use me."

"I won't let them." Theo said, reassuringly.

"My hero." She smirked and rolled her eyes.

He changed the subject, embarrassed.

"Why do you think Butler had you teach me?"

"Two projectors are better than one, I'm sure." She said, thoughtfully. "You said she gave you permission to come up here?"

He nodded.

"Sounds like she's trying to court you the same way she did to me. Make you feel special, give you a few privileges, then she asks for a small favor. You're grateful, so you say 'sure', then the favors get bigger and bigger, and suddenly you can't say no. If it weren't for Strauss, I don't know if I would've been able to step away for the last few weeks like I have."

"But isn't he the reason you're here in the first place?"

"Yeah," she conceded, "but I hardly think he could've seen this coming."

"I guess." He replied.

The two twiddled the dirt and grass surrounding them, as they reflected on their predicament. After a minute, Simone perked up.

"I think it's clear what we have to do."

Theo turned toward her, no idea what she was talking about.

"And that is…?"

"We need to get off this island."

Theo's heart leapt into his chest. He bit his lip, silent, not sure if it was a test.

"Think about it." She elaborated. "We're in the same position. Neither of us is here on purpose, especially you. Neither of us wants to stay here. So, let's leave. I'm sure Strauss will help us. I don't know if he'd want to come—he can if he wants—but we can figure that out later. I doubt your doctor friend wants to stay either. We can steal a boat, and once we're on the mainland, we can figure out what to do next. But first we have to get away from Butler. And Odin. That's the most important thing."

Theo paced along with her, thought for thought. It all made sense. But still, he saw problems.

"But it's more complicated than that. There's still Sid and Dave to account for. They're at the other camp. If we escape, we have to go get them before anything else."

Simone's face dropped. Theo noticed.

"What?"

She shook her head.

"Sorry, Theo." She said, full of remorse.

"Sorry...? Sorry for what? Are they ok?"

"What? Oh, yeah, no, they're fine—well, alive at least. It's just, your friend Dave... He's the one that gave them the location of the OS."

Theo's heart dropped.

"Fuck, the way you said that, I thought you were gonna tell me they're dead."

"Oh no—sorry! No, they're both still alive—as far as I know."

"Thank goodness—So then, Dave's on their side now?"

She nodded.

"Either he is, or they've broken him enough that we can't trust him."

Theo took this in.

"What about Sid?" he asked, voice full of worry.

"As far as I know, he hasn't told them anything. But from what Butler's said it sounds like he's helping them in some way. I'm not sure how, or if he even is. I'm sorry, I wish I could tell you more."

Theo nodded mournfully. Rita's instincts had been right about Dave. But the issue remained— they needed to escape.

"Well, we can't make it seem like anything's up." He stated. "I think we need to figure out who we can trust. Rita for sure, you think Strauss?"

She nodded. "Positive."

Theo returned the nod. "Carson maybe, I'd have to talk to her more, but that's slow going. I don't even know if she'd want to leave. Greta I really like, but I don't think she has any intentions of leaving." His tone turned somber. "What about Karen?"

Simone inhaled, and held her breath. With a difficult sigh, she replied.

"I honestly don't know. She's my sister, and I love her, but I just don't know."

"Ok." Theo mused. "Then for now, we shouldn't tell her. Just act like everything is normal."

Simone nodded with a tense brow.

"Where do they keep those inflatable motor boats they took us in?" he asked.

"In the supply building, near the back of the camp. It'll be pretty nearly impossible to get that to the beach unnoticed."

"Not even at night?"

She shook her head.

"The building gets locked at night. Butler has the only key."

Theo shook his head, stumped.

"Well, that's a problem. When do they get brought out?"

"Almost never" she lamented.

"Then the best we can do is to keep our eyes out for an opportunity."

She nodded. Theo looked at the horizon. The sun was starting to set—he had been away from camp for a long time.

"I need to get back to camp. This is the first time I've been allowed to leave—I can't push it."

Simone nodded mournfully as Theo got up. He started to turn back to camp, then stopped. Simone got to her feet. Theo turned around, and to Simone's surprise, he hugged her. She wrapped her arms around him and squeezed, neither wanting to let go, but both knowing that for both of their sakes, they had to. They separated, and he took her by the arms.

"I'm trusting you, ok?" he begged softly, staring into her eyes with the unforced sincerity of a soul in crisis. She nodded slightly.

"I'm trusting you too."

Theo nodded, took a deep breath, and turned to head back to camp. Just as he had rounded his hiding tree, Simone called after him.

"Oh, Theo—?"

He jogged back and peeked out from behind the tree.

"Sorry, it just occurred to me. Butler knows I'm up here. If she asks, I'll have to tell her you found me. If we're gonna act like nothing's up, at least. But I'm telling you, so, I hope that's ok."

Theo looked away for a second, thinking. He looked back at her.

"OK. No, that's good actually. I can work with that. Thanks." He paused. "Tell her we talked about gardening. That's plausible enough. Anything else?"

She shook her head quickly.

"Nope."

"Alright then." He nodded. "See you at our next lesson."

He turned and went back down the way he came, unable to believe his luck.

EIGHTEEN

EXTERNAL ALGORITHM 1945-SOL

"Gradually, it was disclosed to me that the line separating good and evil passes not through states, nor between classes, nor between political parties either—but right through every human heart—and through all human hearts. This line shifts. Inside us, it oscillates within the years. And even within hearts overwhelmed by evil, one small bridgehead of good is retained. And even in the best of all hearts, there remains... an unuprooted small corner of evil.

Since then I have come to understand the truth of all the religions of the world: They struggle with the *evil inside a human being* (inside every human being). It is impossible to expel evil from the world in its entirety, but it is possible to constrict it within each person."

When Theo returned to camp, nothing was amiss. He ate his dinner in silence, paying little mind to Robin's cathartic crusading, and went to bed early, mind racing as he stared into the darkness above.

Simone is on our side. I have to tell Rita. She's gonna talk to Strauss, I'll have to see what she finds out about him. He's a weird guy, but seems to prioritize Simone's well-being over anyone else's, which is a good sign. He should be good.

I mentioned Carson to Simone, but I don't know how she feels about everything here. We haven't talked about the cause at all—but she doesn't like most of the people here, so something else must be keeping her. That'll take some work.

A bug landed on his face. He blew on it. It didn't move. Annoyed, he removed his arm from its comfortable position and waved it off.

Karen's the wild card. Simone already had to leave her mother behind, I don't know if she could do that to her sister too. But she knows her way better than I do. I'm glad we decided not to say anything to her just yet. Nothing's set in stone yet anyway.

I'm getting ahead of myself. We don't even have a way to get off of the island yet. We know where the boats are, but we don't know when they're used or how we could get access to one. Ear to the ground, that's the name of the game. Ear to the ground.

Multiple voices and the sound of feet on dirt entered his awareness. Vigilant, Theo monitored them as best he could before they passed his tent and disappeared out of earshot. He settled back into his cot.

Butler's going to find out I left the trail. Even if she doesn't, I need to prepare like she will. I heard the singing... is that an excuse? I can't tell her I didn't leave the trail. So, I have to admit to doing it. Maybe fessing up could even buy me some trust, get me into her good graces. The more she trusts me, the more I'll be able to move freely around the camp, and the more likely I'll be able to spot holes in security. But I can't get too close, too quick. I need to ease into it, that'll be less likely to arouse suspicion. The more I can tell the truth with her, the less she'll suspect I'm lying.

He smiled at the darkness.

What's that thing from the tutorial of Princely Defense? Keep your friends close and your enemies closer.

Nervous, but satisfied, he settled in to sleep.

◯

For two days, nothing seemed out of the ordinary. He'd heard nothing from Butler, and his days continued on as normal. He wasn't sure whether or not he should run up the fire road again. If he didn't, that would arouse suspicion, because who wouldn't want that extra taste of freedom? If he did, Butler could also grow suspicious, because of how long he would be away from camp for any given period of time. He eventually settled on a compromise—he would go back and forth along the fire road in between the camp and the start of the trail, claiming that the full loop was "too much for him", and he would "work up to it". That way he could rely on his now-secondary goal of increasing his physical fitness even further.

On the third day of his new alliance, he tried easing into a conversation about the Bohu cause with Carson. Obstinately and frustratingly neutral, she said she didn't care all that much about Butler and what she was trying to accomplish, but didn't give a clear position one way or the other. He tried to pivot to her future plans, but this attempt was similarly derailed.

"So if you don't care all that much about what the Bohu's are doing, where do you see yourself in five years?"

"I don't really think about it all that much" was her reply. "I just wanna make sure we have a good harvest."

Frustrated, Theo decided to drop the issue for now, resigning himself to his chore. The next day, however, as they were planting wooden stakes to brace against the corn, a brisk knock on the rifle range frame echoed through the garden. Peering over the corn, Butler's keen eyes met his. Doing his best to keep his butterflies calm, he walked over.

"Hey Butler." He said, with as neutral a tone as possible. *Dammit, no opinion is more suspicious than having one. Focus up Theo, it's game time.*

"Hello, Theodore." She replied. "Looks like the crops are coming along nicely. How is he doing Carson?"

"A bit talkative, but other than that, he's been really helpful" came Carson's voice out from behind the corn.

Butler laughed. Sort of.

"Wonderful to hear." She turned her attention back to Theo. "Well, if you're in a talkative mood, I think today would be a splendid day to have lunch, hmm?"

She knows. It's time. Keep it together Theo.

"Oh, uh, lunch? Yeah, sure. Today works."

Maybe a little too nervous?

"Excellent. Shall we?" Butler asked, composed.

"Oh... now?"

She nodded. "If I'm not mistaken, you should be done in a few minutes anyway. Carson managed on her own before you, I'd imagine she can finish up without you for one day."

"Oh, uh…" Theo looked back at Carson, who had gotten to her feet. She shrugged.

"I'm good."

"Excellent. This way." Butler turned and waited for Theo as he set down all his tools and went around the rifle range structure to meet her. Once he did, they set off in the direction of the dining hall. She kept them at a pace that was either leisurely, or calculated—Theo couldn't tell.

"I do tire of chickpeas," Butler mused.

"What?"

"Chickpeas. Why, do you call them Garbanzo beans? I've never liked that term. GarBANZO—far too chaotic. But chickpea… there's a measured elegance to it. Chick-pea."

"Oh… uh, sure."

"But to the point, I do wish we had more variety in our meals."

"Hmm…" Theo considered nervously. "I guess I'd agree. But beggars can't be choosers I suppose."

"Quite right." She agreed. "However, if a better option existed, do you think a beggar resigned to that attitude would know about it? Having never asked?"

"Is there a better option?" Theo parried. "If anyone would be aware of one in this camp, my guess is it would probably be you."

Slowly, Butler smiled and let out a chuckle.

"Of course. Unfortunately for both of us, that's what's on the menu today. And tomorrow. And tomorrow and tomorrow."

Theo allowed himself to chuckle at the seemingly innocuous exchange. As they approached the dining hall, Butler veered off to the left.

"We're not going into the dining hall?"

"Oh, no, I don't eat in there," replied Butler. "You must understand, if we ate there, we'd be constantly interrupted, gossiped about, leered at—it's in everyone's best interest that we maintain our distance."

"So where are we going?"

They turned the corner around the dining hall, and Theo knew even before she told him. Directly ahead of them, drawing closer with each step, was the limited access building.

"I've never been in there before." He said, nervously.

"I'm aware." Butler grinned.

"Am I allowed?" he asked, unsure. Butler slowed, and glanced at Theo.

"Should you be?"

Theo's mind raced.

"Uh... yes?"

Butler nodded, and continued walking.

"Good. I hoped so."

They crossed in front of the dining hall, and walked along the cliffside in tense silence. Theo's heart pounded in his ears.

"What's in there?" he asked. *Why is my throat so dry?*

"You'll see in a minute. Wouldn't want to ruin the surprise." Butler said, shooting a knowing glance toward Theo.

"Ok." He said, at a loss. The two closed in on the building to a light soundtrack of bare feet crunching on dirt. They reached the door. Butler pulled a single key out of her deep linen pocket, inserted it into the lock, and turned. The door swung open.

Theo was superbly underwhelmed. There was a rectangular wooden table in the center of the room encircled by eight chairs, and a corduroy sofa up against the wall opposite the entrance. In the center of the back wall to the left was a cheap bookcase with less than a dozen books scattered throughout its shelves. A coffee maker sat on a small table in the corner, next to a mug that said WORLD'S GREATEST DAD. A few potted plants and small trees were placed along the walls and in the corners, enlivening the space a bit. Next to the sofa were a few drab grey filing cabinets that counterbalanced the vivifying effects of the plants, while the soft buzzing of fluorescent lights filled the room.

"Not impressed?" asked Butler, after reading the look on Theo's face. He couldn't help but laugh.

"I... I honestly don't know what I expected. But not this."

Butler allowed a balanced 'I suppose' grin to peek out.

"A bit plain, I know." She said, gesturing him toward the table. "But I prefer it that way. No frills. Less distractions. Much better for getting work done."

A knock on the door. Theo paused, but she waved at him to go ahead and sit in the end seat. She opened the door, to reveal Odin holding two trays of food. Butler let her in, and with a surprising absence of ill-feeling toward Theo, she placed the trays on the table and promptly left. Butler locked the door, and sat down in the adjacent seat to Theo.

"Honey?"

"What?"

"Would you care for some honey?" asked Butler. "It's especially good with the walnuts."

"Oh... yeah" he nodded, as Butler fished a bear of honey out of her deep linen pocket and handed it to him. He squeezed some, but not too much, onto the side of his plate for dipping, then gave it back to her. She did the same.

"I so wish we had enough for all the campers to have some. It really makes a difference, I think. You'll have to tell me if you agree. I think we should set up a few beehives as our next community project. What do you think?"

Theo nodded as he chewed. Butler continued.

"Of course, we'll need to train someone to take care of them. Perhaps I'll send out for a Beekeeping book for our next shipment."

"Shipment?" Theo asked, curious.

Butler took a bite, chewed a few times, then swallowed.

"Yes—we occasionally get shipments from the mainland. I'm sure you've noticed that our gardens are conspicuously small for the amount of food we consume as a group?"

Theo's eyebrows raised as he nodded. He shoveled a forkful of chickpeas into his mouth, so she'd have to continue talking.

"Of course you did. The shipments provide us with all the things we can't produce here in sufficient quantities. Beans, rice, walnuts, chickpeas—it takes more than you'd think to feed over a hundred people.

Maybe once you get a bit stronger, you'll be able to come along and help with the pick-up. Would you like that?"

He nodded, swallowing.

"Where do the shipments come in? The beach?" he asked.

"Another part of the island. We get there by the fire roads—but all in good time. Once you're ready. Speaking of which, have you tried out the hiking route I showed you?"

And so it begins, he thought.

He nodded.

"Yeah, I went up for the first time a few days ago. It was really tiring though, I think I'm going to just do laps between the camp and the Goat Whiskers trailhead while I build up to that."

"That sounds like a very prudent approach." Butler replied. "But that first time, you were able to accomplish the whole loop?"

She knows. She has to be building to it. She knows. I have to beat her to it.

"Yeah, I did. It took a long time though. Steep trails are way more tiring than I expected. But to tell you the truth, I did stop partway through… and I may have left the loop you showed me. Sorry—not may have. I did. I heard singing, which turned out to be Simone, and I walked a little bit up the trail to see where it was coming from. Only like 100 feet, not far. Then I came right back."

Butler listened to this intently, chewing slowly, digesting every word. When Theo finished, he scanned her face for any sign of a response. To his astonishment, she was surprised.

"Really… Well, I appreciate you telling me. Simone hadn't mentioned it. Of course, I haven't seen her in that time, but that is curious. She's been spending a lot of time up in that garden of hers. But don't worry about your little exploration, it's perfectly understandable. I've already forgotten it." Butler reassured Theo.

Shit, did I just put Simone in hot water? I need to fix this, now.

"We talked about that, actually. I mean mostly we talked about gardening, but she also said that she was still shaken from what happened in the sanctum. To be completely honest, she seemed relieved that I'd found her—gave her a chance to get out of her head for a bit. I think... I think if she and I continued our lessons, and if she knew she wouldn't have to do any of her—missions—for a while, she'd get back to operating capacity more quickly. At least, that's the impression I got."

Butler mused, thinking this over. *Was that too much?* Theo thought. *Maybe I pushed my luck there. Now that I think about it, it sounded a bit suspicious.*

"I think..." she began, slowly. "I think... that may not be a bad idea. Very insightful of you, Theodore—I can tell the lessons are working already. Do you think it would be helpful for Strauss to be present? I think in having another experienced person, there would be nothing but a positive benefit."

If he's on our side, yeah. Theo nodded. "I think it would be very helpful. From what I gather, he's a very comforting presence for her. His being there could even speed her recovery."

"Excellent. I'll let him know. Thank you for your insight Theodore. It's always welcome."

Theo smiled, and dug into his food, trying to mask his relief. Butler said nothing, and the two ate in silence for a time.

"So, um... you know Robin?"

Butler looked at the ceiling for a moment, thinking as she chewed.

"Ah, yes, springy hair, passionate demeanor?"

He nodded. *Passionate's one word for it.*

"I've been eating lunch with her pretty regularly, and her—passion—has kinda made an impression. To be completely honest, I've been intrigued by what she's been saying—I'd go as far as to say I even agree with a fair amount of it—but it's hard to get any details out of her to know for sure."

Butler nodded, and swallowed.

"Details regarding what?"

"Regarding the end goal of your movement. She says Tovu Va Bohu is fighting for justice, equality, and replacing the failed system, all of which I can get behind. If a system is broken, someone should fix it.

People deserve justice and equality. But she's never been able to tell me how you—as a group—plan to do all that."

"And I suppose you'd like to know?"

Theo nodded.

Butler looked at Theo, eyes narrowed. After a second, she took a deep breath and leaned back in her chair.

"I don't suppose there's any harm in it, but before I tell you, there's something of which you should be made aware. I wasn't sure when the right time to tell you this would be, but at this point I see no utility in keeping it from you."

Butler wiped the corners of her mouth with a napkin, rested her elbows on the table, and continued.

"A week after you landed here, we received an update on your Mother's condition."

Theo froze. His mother had been a distant memory for the past few weeks, shuttered out of his mind except for those brief periods when he would look up at the moon, and remember where he had come from, where he was headed. It hurt him to think about her, so he didn't. Day to day life was easier that way.

"You must understand" she sputtered apologetically, "that the only reason we didn't tell you before was that given your physical difficulties adjusting to Earth's gravity, any actions you may have felt driven to take, you would have found quite impossible, and we wished to spare you the frustration. Now, however, you can get around on your own, so the information is not ours to hoard."

"What happened to my mother?" was his tense reply. He shifted, unable to keep still. His hands unconsciously clasped the arms of his chair, his knuckles turning whiter with each passing second. Butler's brow furrowed in a look of genuine concern, avoiding eye contact as she spoke.

"Theodore, your mother... was in a virtual reality spa following the beta test malfunction. She had developed paranoid tendencies, aggressive ones. She seemed to be recovering well, but sometime during the third day of her treatment, her avatar began to spiral into a frenzy. Her adrenochrome levels shot through the roof, and she... I'm so sorry

Theodore... she murdered every non-player-character in the spa. She's been in a medically-induced coma since, and is receiving heavy doses of Vitamin C."

Theo said nothing. Theo did nothing. He found himself back on his mountain of ice, clinging to the side, surrounded by a deafening emptiness, the unescapable sting of the frozen wind relentlessly piercing his soul. He was furious. He grew hotter and hotter, rage bubbling up within him, until it could no longer be contained. He shoved himself away from the face of the melting mountain and surrendered to the freefall, overcome by the flames of righteous anger.

"You... lied to me. You LIED TO ME! YOU SWORE NOT TO LIE TO ME!" Theo stood up, throwing his chair to the side. Butler jumped back in her seat, alert. He paced, like an underfed lion in a shrinking cage.

"Theodore, we were protecting you. You couldn't stand. There was nothing you could do—"

"She's my mother. That's not your decision to make. She's MY. MOTHER."

"I know Theodore, I—"

"THEO. IT'S THEO. SHE CALLS ME THEODORE. NO ONE ELSE."

"Ok, ok, Theo... Please sit down—"

"I don't WANT to sit down! You said you wouldn't lie to me, and you DID."

"I'm sorry, but remember, I'm not the one responsible for your mother's condition. Don't shoot the messenger."

He walked over to the table and violently planted his fists knuckles down on the hard surface.

"Lying by omission is still lying, isn't that what you said?"

He glared into Butler's eyes, daring her to contradict him.

Butler's brow relaxed from heightened surprise and concern into a determined tilt, lips pursed. Theo noted a recognition in eyes that he couldn't quite read. She spoke slowly.

"You're right, Theo. I'm sorry I lied. Now will you *please* sit down and allow me to explain myself?"

Theo's lip curled up into a resentful sneer, his teeth ground together, his heart pounded in his ears. In a huff he resigned himself to replacing his displaced chair, this time further from the table, and sat in it, actively telegraphing his contempt.

"The reason I tell you all this now, is that given your newfound ability to get around on your own, you could feasibly find a way to make it back home by yourself. I wanted to give you that option."

I can go home?

Theo's aggressive attitude was vacuumed out of him in a flash, replaced by a fugue state of confusion, residual fury, and fearful hope.

"You… you'd let me leave?"

"Of course, Theo. I've already told you, I never wanted you to think of yourself as a prisoner here. I've allowed you all the rights and privileges of the other members of the camp, as well as a few more selective ones. You're given more food than the average camper, more consideration, more attention—quite frankly, you've been treated like a celebrity here. Has that not been your recollection?"

Theo disappeared into his memories of the past two months. *Nothing she's saying is wrong. I've been welcomed here with open arms.*

"I… I guess you're right."

"I should say so. And as for the lying—I'll admit that was a poor decision. Simone, Strauss and I agreed to wait until you could get around on your own, but you're right. That wasn't our decision to make."

Theo was stunned. *Simone knew? Why didn't she say anything?*

"What about Rita?" Theo asked suddenly.

"What about her?" replied Butler.

"Can she leave with me?"

"I don't see why not. I do hope she'll stay though—we've gone for far too long without a doctor, and she is a fantastic one."

Theo nodded. The choice seemed clear. Quite without warning, his mind flashed to Simone. He felt the longing pull of her graceful silhouette, dancing in front of the bonfire. He was enveloped by the frustrated and exhausting anger of her tirade during their first lesson, her terror when she was curled up in a ball in the sanctum, the pain and fear in her eyes right before they parted on top of the mountain.

He knew what he had to do.

"No."

Butler started, thinking she misheard.

"I'm sorry?"

"No. I'm staying. I want to stay."

Butler dropped her gaze, looking around for clarity.

"I... forgive me, but... why?"

Theo thought for a moment, then spoke, clearly and resolutely.

"I really like the people here. I want to do right by them."

For the first time since Theo had met her, Butler was speechless. She smiled, and couldn't help but let out a laugh. Theo dipped a walnut into his honey, and ate it, giving her time to collect her thoughts. After a brief period, she responded.

"I... I don't quite know what to say. You would just leave your mother up there, alone?"

"She's in a coma, right? With doctors attending her? She's not in danger of dying?"

"I... I mean as far as we know..."

"Good. That's all the comfort I need. There's important work to be done here. Freeing people from oppression and whatnot." Theo ate another walnut.

Butler shook her head in disbelief.

"That's... great to hear. I can't tell you how glad I am to hear that. And please know, as soon as all this is over, we will do everything we can to return you to your rightful home."

"I appreciate that." Theo said with equanimity.

Butler nodded. "Great. So, well then, where were we?"

"How you plan to achieve everything you're hoping to achieve? Does it have something to do with Sid and Dave?"

"Indeed, it does." Butler nodded, finding her stride again. "They have agreed to help us by constructing a virus, then use their clearance to install it into the OS directly."

"And what effect will it have on the OS as a whole?"

Butler hesitated, then spoke. There was something ever-so-slightly off with her tone, even for her.

"It will redefine humans as those without NeuroCom implants. The Head Programmer was specifically meant to be the human counterpart to the OS. If Bob Ditto is elected, he will be the first HP ever with a computer implant, and the entire paradigm of how the OS defines humans will change. Those billions of us without them will be forced in one of two directions—either we must submit to non-consensual implantation by the anti-human dominating forces of the direct and indirect societal pressures that blindly reward submission and seek to destroy freedom of individual expression, or we refuse, and become subjugated as a class of sub-optimal, under-producing, secondhand citizen-burdens, inevitably going the way of the Neanderthal. We just want to stop that from happening."

"But why not just get them? I've had one for nearly half my life, and they're great—you learn stuff faster, you can repair damaged parts of the brain, and body, you can look up anything on the spot—"

"You can try to kill yourself after a premature beta test gets uploaded into your skull? I don't trust the man in charge of that company. Do you really want him in charge of everything?"

I guess not, but what'll happen to the people who have them?

Theo just shook his head. He didn't want to know the answer.

NINETEEN

EXTERNAL ALGORITHM 5123-JBP
"Evil is that which assumes that its knowledge is complete."

Rita was furious.

"You said no?"

Theo scrambled for an explanation.

"What's going on here is wrong. Sim—People are being hurt, I couldn't just leave! We have to do something!"

Rita scoffed, bracing her forehead with an incredulous hand.

"*We* don't have to do anything! We're *prisoners* here, Theo. Our first responsibility should be getting out of here! I can't believe I have to explain this to you. This is what we've been working toward since the day we got here—the day Bill and Hank got killed—remember them? Now it gets served up to us on a silver platter and you turn it down, because of some... some... newfound sense of altruism? GROW UP!"

"*You* could ask to leave! Maybe she'll let you! She said she didn't want us to feel like prisoners here."

"And you trust her? She's the reason we're here in the first place! How do you know it wasn't just a test of your loyalty to her? That if you'd said you wanted to leave, she would've had Odin kill you? And me? That—"

Rita stopped, disappearing into her head. Theo stayed frozen. She returned outward and continued, her tone low, still rippling with an undercurrent of suppressed anger.

"You either did something really stupid that saved us, or something even stupider that doomed us. You better hope to god it's the first one."

Rita collapsed onto the cot opposite Theo's. Theo sulked a few feet away, discouraged. They sat in a tense silence, Rita furious and indignant, Theo guilty and overwhelmed. Finally, he spoke.

"Well, on the bright side, there's a new development in our escape plan."

Rita looked up, annoyed and hopeless.

"What, it's been tried? It's impossible? Only good news, *please*."

Theo shook his head.

"Simone wants out. She's gotten fed up with Butler and Odin using her as a recon tool. She wants to leave the island and go find her dad."

Rita sat up.

"Simone...? Really?"

Theo nodded. "She only came here in the first place to get across the border between the US and Mexico. Then before she knew what was happening, she got roped into the whole cause here because of her gifts, but it's gotten to the point that it's hurting her more than it's helping them. She says Strauss will probably help us, if not escape with us."

Rita pursed her lips, parsing through all this new information.

"And you trust them?"

Theo nodded. He didn't mention the lie regarding his mother's health. That wouldn't help anything.

"Yeah."

Rita pressed her lips together.

"Your judgement's been a bit off recently, so forgive me if I don't take you at your word."

"I honestly don't see what choice we have." He pleaded, cautiously. "You and I have gotten nowhere. They know all the inner workings of the camp—Simone even told me where all the motorboats are kept. We put together the beginnings of an escape plan, which is way more than we had before."

Rita ground her teeth and shook her head, leaning forward and putting her elbows to her knees. Theo sat still, watching her, butterflies fluttering about his gut. He made no effort to wrangle them, instead sucking his upper gums like he'd seen Simone do. It wasn't the same, but it comforted him in a strange, different way. Rita cocked her head up and to the side, thinking, then returned to Theo.

"Well, if we're not leaving now, at least we're one step past being back to where we started."

Theo nodded encouragingly.

"But remember," Rita cautioned accusingly, "you vouched for them. If anything goes wrong, it's on you."

Theo avoided eye contact, and nodded, staring at the ground. Rita stood, her head a few inches below the tent roof.

"I've got patients to attend to. Don't make any more big decisions without consulting me, alright?"

Without waiting for an answer, she left the tent.

Theo slept very poorly that night. Images of his mother tucking him into bed, swiftly followed by other images of impaled masseuses and therapists burned across his mind on repeat, leaving very little time for rest. Dreams of her as little more than a character in *Princely Defense*, squashing revolts and sadistically subduing serfs in numerous ways troubled him deeply, a stream of visions impossible to escape. *That was a game, this is real life—the two were never supposed to meet.*

After a terrible night spent in the nightmare world between fear and sleep, he opened his eyes to see a familiar note taped to his tent pole.

Mine

Adrenaline surged through his body as he swung his legs off the cot and stood up. He knew that the day would hold either excitement and comfort (if they were on his side), or betrayal and fury (if they weren't). He hoped it was the former, but mostly he just wanted to get it over with.

He skipped his entire morning routine and immediately jogged over to the mine. He was walking down the darkened shaft toward the sanctum when he heard it.

Tkk.

He froze.

Skrch skrch skrch skrch.

Tkk.

Theo crept on light feet towards the entrance to the sanctum. He peered, slowly, around the corner, and saw Strauss clenching a croquet mallet, concentrating firmly on a croquet ball resting at his feet.

Tkk.

The ball rolled to a stop a few feet away, just under where the left cot would have been, were it not up against the back wall with the other one.

"Heehee!" Strauss giggled with excitement as he scampered over to the ball. He lined himself up for another shot. Theo couldn't help but gaze in curious wonder—it looked like Strauss was putting in a significant amount of work aiming, but try as he might, Theo couldn't figure out what the target was. Sure enough, Strauss tapped the ball again, and it rolled to a stop a few feet away, by nothing in particular. Engrossed in the activity playing out before him, he forgot his clandestine attitude, and took a deep, calming breath.

Strauss, relaxed and alert, looked up and stared at him straight in the eye. A huge grin spread out under his huge, bushy moustache.

"Ahhhhh Theo! Hallo handsome boy. I vasn't expecting you so soon!"

"Hey Strauss!" Theo jolted, before resetting himself. "Where, uh... where's Simone?"

"Not here yet. I told her I vould set up for us, she comes later. You are earlier than expected. No yoga to-day?"

Theo shook his head, staring at the dusty croquet ball. "Wasn't feeling it."

"Ah, ve all have those days. Here, try?" Strauss gestured with the mallet. Theo shrugged, and took it.

He walked over to the ball, squared himself to it, and looked up to pick a target. The only thing in the right direction was Simone's rocking chair, so he wound up, and gave it a hard tap in that direction. It shot past the chair, bounced off the far wall, and rolled back towards its target, quite accidentally ending up a couple inches from the chair leg opposite his original goal. Strauss giggled and excitedly clapped his hands.

"Ahh, brilliant, handsome boy! Your mother vould be proud."

This hit Theo like a line drive to the funny bone. He ground his teeth together, trying to dismiss it, but every time he did, his conscience refused to relinquish the thought.

"Don't—don't talk about my mom."

Strauss stood up as straight as he could and scanned Theo's face curiously.

"You are …pouty? Ahh, I see in your eyes, you miss her. Lovely lady, probably staring up at us right now from the moon, hoping for your safety. He's fine, mommy! Don't vorry!" These last words he yelled at the ceiling, before descending into self-satisfied chuckles.

Theo felt a surge of anger bubbling up inside him. He saw his mother lying in bed, connected to countless tubes, unconscious and barely breathing. *Strauss knows, he knows, and he's mocking me. How dare he make light of it?* Theo ground his teeth together, flexed his jaw, and willingly let himself tip just a bit further over the edge.

"I said, don't talk about my mom. She's not staring out the window, she's lying in bed, unconscious, and I know you know that. Don't make jokes about something you had a hand in keeping from me."

He glared at Strauss, daring him to react. Strauss stood silently for a minute, then grabbed a tuft of moustache with his tongue, pulled it into his mouth, and started sucking on it. He waddled over to the back table and leaned against it.

"You… are angry? Vis me?" Strauss asked with a mild hint of confusion.

"…Yeah?" Theo looked around, incredulous. *Am I insane? How is that not clear?*

"You are angry vis me because I am the one responsible for your mother's condition?" He said, probing like a black-market surgeon.

"No, I... are you?" Theo stuttered.

Strauss shook his head. "Not as far as I am aware."

Theo shook off this minor deviation. "No, I'm angry because you lied to me."

Strauss's eyes thinned. Theo stood there, gut butterflies rustling, waiting for Strauss to respond. None of this was going how he'd hoped. He was going to storm in here, confront Strauss and Simone (they'd fess up immediately), they would apologize over and over, then in all his graciousness, Theo would forgive them, and they would get right down to planning their escape. Instead, Strauss pursed his lips, then without saying anything, he turned away from Theo and started organizing the table behind him.

"No, you are not." He chirped over his shoulder with a melodic nonchalance.

"What? No. Yes, I am. You lied to me." Theo said, trying to maintain some semblance of control over the situation.

"I did lie. But that is not vhy you are mad." Strauss replied.

Theo doubled down. "Yeah, it is. I just told you it is."

"No... I don't sink so." Strauss said, still sucking his moustache. "You are angry that your mother is hurt, and you have novhere to direct it. You do not vant to direct it at the person responsible, so you send it to me."

"Who, Bob? For the beta test? That was an accident. I mean she didn't agree to it, but--"

"No...no. Bob Ditto is not who I am talking about."

Theo looked at Strauss, confused and annoyed.

"Who then? Who am I mad at?"

Strauss turned and looked Theo dead in the eye with a white-hot piercing intensity he'd never seen before from this withered sprite of a man.

"The person who vas there vhen the attack first happened. The person who vasn't there to stop her from jumping. The one who asked vhat vas wrong, but vould rather play his little game then press his mother to talk about somesing confusing and scary."

Theo was knocked back. *Me? No, it's not my fault—wait, how did he know all of that? Were they spying on me then? If they know that, then they know I know Bob. What else do they know?* He scrambled to cover his bases.

"No. None of this was my fault! I didn't know anything was wrong. She didn't know anything was wrong. No one knew what was happening—and Bob was there too! He didn't notice anything. It was all just a freak mistake."

"Ahhhhhh, but you did notice. If you did not notice, then vhy did you ask?"

Theo shot back like a lit fuse, drawing closer and closer to its dynamite with every word.

"How do you know all that? Were you spying on me?"

"Ve vere spying on Bob Ditto, and you vere there too, this is old news." Strauss dismissed with an infuriating calm. "Answer the question."

"You… you… Fine. I saw something weird happen. She looked like she was in pain for a split second, then it was over. I thought it was weird, I asked what was wrong, she said she was fine."

"And you believed her?"

"Yeah, she's my mother!"

"And your mother is infallible?"

"Yeah, she always says—"

"SHE… always says. Ah. And there it is. Ve are back to believing sings that are not true."

Theo didn't know what to say. It was all too much. Strauss pressed further, with increasing speed and intensity.

"So if she vas not ok, and you vere the only one there to help her, vhy did you not?"

"I… I didn't know."

"But you tried to know…?"

"Yeah, I asked her if she was ok."

"But vas that enough?"

"It was, I'm... I mean it should've been."

"It *should* have been, but it vas not."

"No, I... I made an effort. I did my part."

"The only other person there vas her. Vas it her fault then?"

"No, no of course not. She's the victim in all this."

"No, she did not tell the truth. So it is maybe a little her fault."

"No, it's not. It's not her fault at all."

"So then it is all yours?"

"I... no! Stop twisting my words around!"

"Let me ask you this—vould you do everything the same if it happened again tomorrow?"

An overwhelmed Theo swung the croquet mallet into attack position over his head, ready to bash Strauss's shiny little head in. His knuckles turned white, his biceps twitched with anticipation, but the old man did not move out of the way. He only looked at Theo, calmly, with eyes that betrayed a sense of sadness and understanding. Theo started shaking, his anger, fear, and hatred for everything that had changed about his life in the past few months welled up inside him, ready to explode out of him.

He yelled.

"YAAAAAUGHH!"

He swung the mallet around his shoulder, where it thudded into a wall and dropped, unharmed, onto the pile of meditation pillows.

Theo gave another loud, angry bellow, then took a deep breath and crouched down, shaking his head and digging his knuckles into his temples, anything to silence the hurricane that had been whipped up inside him. This conversation didn't matter. It couldn't. He was done with it—all of it. He took another deep breath, held it in, and finally let out a huge sigh. *Fine.*

"No. Of course not."

A spirit of renewed care and tenderness inhabited Strauss, the same encouraging spirit he'd been at Simone's bedside, following her mission.

"So then maybe the you that vas before is not the you that is now?"

"Yeah, sure. Maybe."

"So maybe the fault is not your own, but the fault of the you that is younger and more stupid?"

"I..."

"You are not that boy anymore Theo. He is part of you, but he does not have to define you. You are better, stronger, smarter. More capable."

Theo stared at the ground. He *was* more capable. Even with the increased gravity he could run, he could jump, and he had more muscle than he'd ever had in his life. He could plant and grow food, he could talk to strangers, and he could hold a conversation with anyone. He'd gone toe to toe with Butler, and—well, maybe he hadn't won—but he definitely hadn't lost.

"I... maybe. If it's anyone's fault, maybe it's his—mine."

Strauss nodded.

"Mhm. And vhat about your staying here? You had the choice to leave and go back to mama, but you did not."

Theo nodded gravely. "I did that. I know I did that."

Strauss's face broke out into a broad smile.

"That's vhat you needed to hear. The stupid little boy is dead. Congratulations, handsome man."

Theo, still confused, was flooded with a strange sense of relief, quickly followed by guilt. But the guilt was suddenly and strangely supplanted by a new, unknown feeling, a feeling of agency, a transcendental feeling of resolute care and complete responsibility for the world around him and the choices he made. It was a feeling he'd only rarely felt before—once when he'd decidedly told Rita that he should study with Simone, again in the mountaintop garden a few days earlier, and a third time with Butler when he made the decision to stay and help Simone escape. Those times the feeling was fleeting, covered over by a wildly flailing fear and a fog of conditioned expectation. This time was different. Those times, the feeling came from the outside, and left as quickly as they came on. This time, his pilot light was lit from within, and for some inarticulable reason, Theo knew it would never go out.

Strauss watched with pride as this transformation took place. He grinned, and pulled a bottle of wine and two glasses out from behind a stack of books.

"You want a drink?"

Theo couldn't help but let out a laugh.

"What? No! It's like eight in the morning!"

Strauss shrugged.

"It is five o'clock in Austria."

"I don't think so."

Strauss shrugged again, and began pouring himself a glass.

"Vell, I'm having some. If you are not going to celebrate becoming a man, then I'll have to do it alone."

Strauss finished pouring his glass, and set the bottle on the table next to Theo's. He sipped, and looked expectantly at Theo, then at the empty glass on the table, then back to Theo. Theo looked around the room, looking for a reason not to, then relented, and walked over to the table.

"There ve go! I hate drinking alone."

Theo nodded and smiled as he poured himself a glass. It was about half full when Strauss snatched the bottle out of his hand.

"Aaaaaaapapapapap. Let's not go crazy now that we are a grown up. This is not frat house party at Delta sexy house fun time. Your brain is not done cooking yet, do not drown him!"

He rapped his knuckles lightly on Theo's skull before he dodged out of the way, nearly spilling his freshly poured wine. He took a sip. It didn't taste very good, but the act of drinking it made the taste seem worth it. Strauss ushered Theo to sit on a cot next to the wall.

"Take a load off, handsome man. Forget your troubles."

Theo chuckled dismissively, but accepted the old timer's offer and sat down on the cot, leaning against the rock wall of the sanctum. He took another sip, and let out a grand, cathartic exhale.

"There ve go. Relax and enjoy. Simone vill be here soon, and ve can begin."

Theo nodded, and started waiting. After thinking for a second, he rolled his head to the side to look at Strauss.

"Hey, I have a question."

Strauss raised his eyebrows in feigned surprise.

"And I may have an answer."

Theo formulated the question in his mind for a second, then spoke, carefully and methodically.

"It seems like I've been lied to by everyone I've ever met—apart from my best friend. How do you know who to trust when no one is telling the truth?"

Strauss listened intently, then sucked on his moustache for a second. Then, quite unexpectedly, he burst out laughing.

"What's so funny?"

Strauss calmed himself down enough to respond.

"The answer—sorry my boy. No one. You can't trust anyone."

Theo's face dropped, and his brow furrowed.

"But you have to! You can't just not trust anyone!"

Strauss laughed again.

"Quite right! It vould be a very lonely life not to trust anyone."

"But you just said—"

"I know vhat I said! I answered your question! Ask me if this vas the right question."

"Was it the right question?" Theo asked, confused.

"Nope!" Strauss replied cheerfully. Theo shook his head.

"Well, then what's the right question?" he asked.

Strauss smiled. "Ah, now ve are getting somevhere. The problem of who to trust is secondary to knowing who is telling the truth. So, the question that needs to be asked is, *vhat is TRUTH?*"

"What. Is. Truth?" Theo repeated, trying to understand. "That's not even a question. Truth is... well, it's truth! Everyone knows that."

"*Everyone knows that!*" Strauss mocked. "T-r-u-t-h is t-r-u-t-h. No, really?" He stuck out his tongue and blew.

"Well, if you're so smart, then answer your own question!" Theo challenged.

"Ooh, I like it vhen you give orders, handsome man. Fine. Here is the answer. Vis language, there is no such thing."

"No such thing... as truth?"

"Nope. Language is a tool, nussing more. It vas developed to facilitate exchanges of ideas and the achievement of goals. The coconut is in that tree, but that one has a snake, these sorts of sings. Every vord is a tool, all tools are used vis a goal in mind. Visout the goal, the tool is useless, and vould not exist."

"So what does that have to do with truth?"

"Vill you let me speak? Please?"

Theo held up his hands in acquiescence.

"Sank you. So, if all vords are tools, then any statement that is claimed to be true is only true to the extent that it progresses toward some greater goal. There may be other, greater truths alluded to by the statement that transcend the goal in mind, but the statement constrains this greater truth and dilutes it in service of the goal. The constrained truth is then not full and absolute—it is an aggregate, nussing more. The amount of truth in any statement is equal to the total amount of audience agreement vis the goal the speaker is trying to achieve.

"What goal?"

"Ah, that is the question. How about your mother, in lying to you about her condition?"

That stung, but Theo did his best to take it as intended.

"I guess... she didn't want me to worry."

"Sounds correct to me. And did you vant to vorry?"

"Apparently not."

"Then there vas more aggregate truth in the statement of her being fine than not. And that vas the goal achieved. She spoke, you did not vorry."

"But she wasn't ok. That was true, and what she said wasn't. So it was a lie."

"You aren't listening—it vas true *in the service of her goal*. There may have been a greater truth, independent of language, grounded in objective reality that later superseded it, but by then it vas too late. The language-constrained truth took priority, and the path toward greater growing pains vas laid."

"Ok, well then, how can you tell when they don't line up? The goal and reality?"

Strauss grinned.

"Again, good questions. So proud to see. Vell, first, you have to make sure you know vhat the goal is."

"Right, because you won't always know. What do you do when there's no way to tell what the goal is?"

"If you aren't sure of the goal of an action, then just look at vhat happens following the action."

"But if I don't agree with what happens next, how do I know if someone's actively doing something I disagree with, or if they just made a mistake?

"You should never ascribe to malice that vhich you could also ascribe to ignorance. The benefit of the doubt is a powerful thing. It has saved many innocent lives, as vell as guilty ones. But it is better to accidentally save a guilty life then end an innocent one, no?"

Theo shook his head, trying to make sense of Strauss's philosophical yammering.

"You disagree?"

Theo looked up.

"What? No, that all sounds right, just… it's not perfect. It seems flawed. We can't just let bad people get away with things."

"Vell, ve do not. Our minds are pattern recognizers. Vhen ve realize a pattern of disagreed goals is arising, ve see the source, this person, as misinformed, and ve stop the effects of the pattern."

"But that's the flaw—until the pattern is noticed, this person can do whatever they want. They can hurt so many people, destroy so many things. They can do so much wrong before they're stopped by the right people."

"And vhat makes you think you are the right people? Vhat makes you think that you are not the one making the poor decision? You have already seen that in the case of your mother."

"Well, because I... I..."

"Because you are good and they are bad?"

"Yeah."

"Theo, everyone sinks that vhat they are doing is good and justified. No one thinks they are doing sings wrong until after they have been stopped and violently ridiculed in the street. But ve do not know the real veaknesses of anything until it has been tried. These are the growing pains. The cost of freedom is the correction of our vell-intentioned misconceptions by Mother Nature. And here is the answer to your next question about knowing the reality of a situation--no matter vhat ve do, we vill alvays not know vastly more than ve do know. It is a sad, unfortunate fact, avoided only by the unwise."

"But... how—" Theo didn't know what to say. Up was down, wrong seemed right, it all seemed hopeless.

"The vorld is a flawed place Theo. Trauma can't be avoided. Life is trauma and the recovery from it. All ve can do is forgive and then cope. Do you vant to know a secret?"

Theo looked up.

"Amor fati."

"What?" Theo asked. It sounded like gibberish.

"Amor fati. It is the pinnacle of all philosophical thought, all over the vorld. Love your fate. The good, the bad, embrace it all as necessary steps in the process of making the vorld better. Making YOU better. Every joy a grateful respite, every sorrow a grateful lesson. Does that make sense?"

Theo thought for a second, then took a deep breath.

"Yeah. It sucks, but yeah."

"A lesson, hm?" Strauss winked before gulping down the last of his wine.

Theo nodded and chuckled, an absurd grin creeping across his face. Suddenly, he heard a familiar voice ring out from around the corner.

"Lesson? I hope you're not having a lesson without me!" said Simone as she turned the corner into the sanctum.

Theo shot up to standing, hiding his wine behind his back. Simone stopped, and eyed him suspiciously.

"Ok, I was joking, but now I'm not sure."

Strauss grabbed the bottle of wine and hid it behind his back, a little too late. Simone saw him.

"STRAUSS. IT'S NOT EVEN NINE YET."

Strauss and Theo looked at each other and burst out laughing. Simone's annoyance kowtowed to empathetic disbelief as Theo brought out his glass from behind his back, and Strauss offered her a glass. She refused with a smile, and Theo gulped down the last of his wine. Strauss took his glass, and instructed him to go stand over in the center of the room while he cleaned up.

Theo walked over to Simone. *I may as well forgive her. I don't even need to say anything. But I'll know.*

"So… are we here for a lesson, or to plan?" he asked, in a hushed tone. Simone looked up, determined.

"Plan. He's agreed to leave with us, and help me find my dad." She looked over Theo's shoulder to Strauss.

"Before we start, should we do the LBRP?"

Strauss nodded without turning around.

"Good idea. Ve need all the help ve can get."

"Great." She turned her attention to Theo. "You just stand in the center and watch. Strauss and I will do everything."

He nodded, and did as he was told. Strauss and Simone spent the next fifteen minutes doing a strange and complex ritual, facing all four cardinal directions, drawing upward-pointing stars in circles with two fingers, saying different words in what he guessed was Hebrew, and repeating four names over and over again—*Raphael, Gabriel, Michael, Uriel.* Watching it felt strange, but they were moving so deliberately and resolutely, almost trance-like, that he didn't dare interrupt. By the end of it, the atmosphere of the sanctum was positively vibrating with a weightless feeling of reverence. Theo didn't get it, but it was very intriguing to watch. The two clapped once in unison, and they returned back to normal.

"There. That should cover it." Simone said.

"Vell done." Strauss affirmed. "Let's begin."

Before they could say or do anything else, pounding footsteps sprinted down the mineshaft, growing louder and louder, until Odin turned the corner into the room, knocking Simone and Theo into a state of unease. Though she was in incredible shape, it took her a second to catch her breath enough to say something none of them expected to hear.

"I'm borrowing Theo. Emergency supply run."

TWENTY

EXTERNAL ALGORITHM 0201-AUR

"When you wake up in the morning, tell yourself: the people I deal with today will be meddling, ungrateful, arrogant, dishonest, jealous, and surly. They are like this because they can't tell good from evil. But I have seen the beauty of good, and the ugliness of evil, and have recognized that the wrongdoer has a nature related to my own—

Not of the same blood or birth, but the same mind, and possessing a share of the divine. And so none of them can hurt me. No one can implicate me in ugliness. Nor can I feel angry at my relative, or hate him. We were born to work together like feet, hands, and eyes, like the two rows of teeth, upper and lower. To obstruct each other is unnatural. To feel anger at someone, to turn your back on him: these are obstructions."

Odin jogged briskly to the storage building in the back of camp with Theo close behind, determined to keep up. When they arrived, Leary had just finished hooking up two small flatbed trailers to a pair of ATVs. Greta sat cross-legged on one of them, so engrossed in her one-sided conversation with Leary that she gave a little yelp of surprised excitement when she finally noticed a winded Theo pulling up.

"Theo! Theo's coming too? Oh yay, this is gonna be FUN!" she squealed, hopping to her feet and squeezing him in a tight hug.

"Everything ready?" Odin asked Leary, who nodded in reply.

"Good. Theo- you know how to drive one of these?"

Theo, peeling himself out of Greta's affectionate vice grip, scanned the ATV and shook his head.

"It's not hard. Leary'll drive on the way there, but we need him in the trailer to steady the shipment on the way back. Just watch him, you'll pick it up quick. Let's go."

Without another word, Odin and Leary each mounted an ATV. Greta hopped on the back of Odin's, and they sped off. Theo, mimicking Greta, mounted the back of Leary's ATV.

"You ready? It's gonna be a 'lil bouncy." Leary warned.

Theo nodded. "Let's do this- if I fall, I'll just have to hold on harder next time."

Leary chuckled. "That's a Texas-sized 10/4."

And they were off.

Up and up the fire road they climbed, ATV rumbling below them, followed by a quick descent. They caught up to the girls as they crossed a narrow isthmus, only a few dozen feet wide. Ruined houses and waterlogged cars littered the shallows.

I wonder what happened here, thought Theo.

Apophis. The floods.

His body and mind deflated as he imagined the residents screaming, crying, trying to escape to higher ground with what little they could carry. But soon, the ruins were out of sight and out of mind as the team ascended into the hills ahead.

They reached a high point a few minutes later, and Theo couldn't help but look around in awe at the vast expanse of ocean spread out below them on all sides. His wonder was quickly replaced by panic as he noticed that they'd been passing other trails and taking forks in the road. He hadn't been paying attention.

"Leary! How will I know how to get us back??" he yelled over the roar of the engine.

"Don't worry about it, Greta knows the way. Just follow her!" Leary yelled back.

Theo gave a sigh of relief. A small butterfluttering remained in his gut, but he decided to let it stay. *I don't know where we're going. I don't know how to get there or back, and I don't know what's going to happen when we get there. A little bit of nerves are ok. Healthy, even. Amor fati.*

The acceptance gave him comfort, and in minutes, he'd forgotten he was nervous, but a calm alertness remained.

Theo observed Leary's driving, and picked it up in a matter of seconds. It was very similar to a video game, in his estimation. He directed his attention to their route.

They descended along the coastline of the island, on the opposite side from the mainland, before heading up and inland. They joined onto a wider road, speeding past abandoned barns and enclosures until they were so far up and inland that they couldn't see the sea. Finally, they descended, and slowed to a stop on a narrow cliffside road lined with trees and rotten wooden fencing. Odin hopped off her ATV, and undid a chain-link barrier to a terrifyingly steep dirt trail that plunged straight down the cliff.

"We're not going down that, are we?" Theo asked, incredulous.

Odin said nothing, but he spotted a slight grin creep across her face as she remounted her ATV and shot over the edge.

Theo's heart thudded in his ears.

"There's not another route is there? Where we could meet them later, or....?" Theo asked in vain.

Leary revved the engine, and they tipped over the edge and hurtled down the cliff, which swiftly turned into a ridgeline. The wind howled past Theo's ears, buffeting him with pillows of air that kept him steady as he clung to the grating of the ATV for dear life. The trail evened out, and after a few hundred yards the Bohu crew had hit paved road and made their way into the outskirts of town. Theo scanned their surroundings—cars, golf carts, and mopeds became more common as they ventured further in. Finally, he saw them.

People. Not Bohus, normal people, just walking around. I bet they have no idea who we are, or where we come from.

Children threw balls into small plastic basketball hoops while riding push-scooters, mothers in large hats tanned on fake lawns, and long-sleeved fathers cleaned leaves out of rain gutters, all blissfully unaware of the intruders.

If I didn't know better, I'd say they were hardly affected by Apophis. Or else they recovered well enough.

If they knew what was going on, I bet they'd help us escape.

"Low profile. We're in, we're out. Don't say or do anything that'll draw attention." Odin called back to Theo.

Theo nodded, holding his breath. *Exactly how legal is this supply run?*

They passed plaster buildings with red clay roofs, tiny houses with AstroTurf lawns, and rumbled over cobblestone crosswalks before pulling to a stop in a secluded corner of a parking lot.

"Stay here. We'll be back soon. Don't do anything stupid." Odin ordered, before she and Leary disappeared around the back of a large building with big red letters over the door.

Theo looked around, gauging his surroundings. There weren't many vehicles in the parking lot, and their owners seemed to be elsewhere. Behind them stood a short wooden fence, more decorative than anything else, with vaguely cheerful voices coming from the rocks and foliage behind it. He peered over the fence.

"What is that?"

"Mini golf!" chirped Greta. "I always want to play when we come on these supply runs, but Odin always says no. Don't get me wrong, she's great, but she's all business. If you ask me, she just needs to learn how to relax."

"Huh." Theo murmured, still looking around.

"Yeah." Continued Greta. "I invited her to yoga, and to Marianne's class, but she like, laughs. I hope it's not mean to say, but it's like, kinda rude."

"Yeah, it sounds rude." Theo replied. "What are we picking up here?"

"Oh, you know, just food and stuff. The stuff that we can't grow, or just other stuff we need."

"Like what sort of other stuff?"

Greta shrugged. "I dunno. It's all in bags and boxes."

"And are we, like… paying for it, or…"

"What, stealing it?" Greta asked, incredulous. "We aren't stealing it. Butler wouldn't do that. Neither would Odin. Butler's too ethical. She wouldn't let that happen. No, I'm sure we're doing everything right. I'm just sure of it."

"You're probably right." Theo nodded, disagreeing with himself. "How does it all get here?"

"I'm not sure... maybe like a boat, or a plane. I think one time I heard someone talking about a ferry that goes between a dock and the mainland, over there somewhere." She gestured across the mini golf course. "Not sure though. I think there's an airport somewhere on the island too, but I never see any planes. So probably the ferry."

That ferry might be our ticket out of here, Theo thought. *Steal the ATVs just before nightfall, hop on the ferry, go find Sid and Dave... that could be it!*

"Huh. Interesting. And what about all these people? They don't know we're on the other side of the island, do they?"

Greta cocked her head to the side, thinking. "Ya know, I don't know! I don't think they do, actually. I've never really thought about that."

"And how did they all get here? The ferry too?"

"I think some probably live here. But not a lot. I'm really not sure though—I've been here like *maybe* 10 times, and just to this parking lot. But one day, *one day*, I *will* play mini golf."

Theo laughed. "Me too. I don't know how to play, but if you wanna play, I wanna play with you."

"YAY!" squealed Greta, who quickly recovered herself, reassuringly waving at a passerby who'd been startled by her outburst.

"Yay." She repeated, quietly.

Theo chuckled, relaxing. "Why wouldn't Odin let us—you—play mini golf? It doesn't seem like it would be any more attention-attracting than sitting and doing nothing, if that's what everyone else is doing."

"Theo!" Greta slapped his arm playfully. "That is a great point. I'm gonna have to use that on her. Maybe she'll let us play next time! Or even this time!"

Shit. Theo's mind went on high alert. *I can't have Odin knowing I'm thinking strategically like this.*

"I think with Odin, it's gonna have to be more of a gradual thing." Theo backtracked. "Probably best not to just come out with it like that—it's what you said, she can be kinda rude and dismissive. Even if it makes sense, she might not agree with it, just cause it's easier not to."

Greta scowled and sighed. "You're probably right." Theo nodded, understandingly.

Whew. Bullet dodged.

She sighed again.

"Poor Odin."

Theo turned to her, quizzically.

"Poor Odin?" he asked.

"Yeah. I can't even imagine the sort of trauma she had that made her the way that she is." Greta despondently laid back in her trailer.

Life is trauma, or so Strauss says, he thought.

"Do you know anything about her life before this?"

Greta shook her head. "Pretty much nothing. She was one of the first to join up—I know Butler recruited her directly. But other than that, she's a mystery."

As Theo was about to respond, Odin and Leary rumbled around the corner, carts stacked high with cardboard boxes and twine-woven sacks.

"There's a lot this time! Got what we need?" Greta chirped, hopping out of the trailer.

"Yup!" responded Odin, uncharacteristically upbeat, unloading the boxes.

"Hey O!" A tall, thin man in a red apron called out as he rounded the corner, carrying one more sack. He jogged over to the group. "You forgot one."

"Oh, uh, thanks." Replied Odin, taking the sack, avoiding eye contact with the man.

Is she nervous? Theo wondered, entertained.

"Of course!" Red Apron replied, lightly touching her shoulder as he turned back to the store. "Gotta get back to work. Good to see you again O, good luck in your competition!"

He jogged back into the store, and Odin continued loading the trailers.

"Uh... what was that?" asked Greta.

"I don't know what you're talking about." Replied Odin, gruffly.

"He's super into youuuuuu." Greta teased, rocking back and forth on the ATV.

"No, he's—shut up." Odin quietly barked, trying and failing to hide her angrily blushing face as she finished up one cart and moved onto the next. Leary took the empty cart and ran it back around the building.

"What competition was he talking about?" Theo asked, trying to block Greta's teasing.

"Oh, uh... I tell him that I run a training camp somewhere on the island. It's... it's simpler that way. Better." Odin said.

"NO FUCKIN' WAY."

A voice cut them off from behind the foliage. A fat, sweaty man in a too-small baby blue button-down linen shirt stumbled through the foliage like a drunk British explorer with a fluorescent rubber putter for a machete. He leaned against a tree to steady himself, and pointed his putter directly at Odin.

"Mimir? There's no fuckin' way that's you. Mimir?"

Odin froze. In his months on the island, Theo had never once seen her so caught off guard.

"Mimir! It fuckin' is you. Holy fuckin' shit, is this where you've been hiding since you got banned?"

Odin recovered herself, cleared her throat, and went back to unloading boxes.

"You've got me mixed up with someone else. Move along sir."

"No, no, I know it's you." Linen Shirt continued. "I'd know that eyepatch anywhere. How's your pops doing? Still an asshole? Look, we all felt bad for you, ya know. He's a prick—he never shoulda forced you to go through with it, no matter how bad your record was!"

He cackled, pulling a beer from his back pocket and taking an unsteady swig of it. Odin threw the last sack into the trailer, and turned to face him head on.

"I'm only gonna tell you one more time. Move. Along."

"Woah, woah, there Meems, can't ya take a joke?"

Odin took a menacing step forward, as everyone else stood frozen.

"What, is that supposed to scare me? Big man, big scary man." Linen Shirt taunted. "You don't scare me, you sucked in the Octagon, even when you started fighting chicks."

Odin growled in rage, fists clenched, and vaulted the short fence that had served as the safety barrier between her and the man. She knocked his drink out of his hand, grabbed him by the collar, and thrust him up against the tree, his sandaled feet dangling inches off the ground.

"ODIN!" commanded a voice. Odin turned to look wildly at Theo, who was still in shock of what he'd just done. He looked at the startled drunkard, and the violent fire in the eyes of the woman holding him. He continued, calmly echoing her words back to her.

"Odin. Low profile. In and out."

Odin stared at Theo, jaw clenched, then glanced around, taking in Leary's concern, Greta's frozen fear, and finally her victim's utter bewilderment. Slowly, she released him. Head down, she stepped back over the fence and hopped into the trailer.

"Let's go." she muttered.

Without another word, Leary closed up the trailer hatches and hopped in the other trailer. Greta and Theo started up their ATVs, and they left the unfortunate man and his town behind them.

As they passed through the narrow isthmus just shy of camp, Greta slowed to a stop, Theo mirroring just behind. Odin cleared her throat.

"Look, um…"

She stopped, grasping in vain for the right words. Carefully and calmly, Theo tried to comfort her.

"We won't tell anyone if you don't want us to. Right guys?"

Leary and Greta nodded.

"Oh, ok. Ok." Odin nodded. "Because if Butler—" she stopped. "Thanks."

Odin slapped the side of her trailer, and Greta started up again. In minutes, they pulled up next to the storage building, where Butler was waiting.

"Everything went well?" she inquired.

Odin hopped out of the trailer. "Yes ma'am. All according to plan." She glanced at the other three, who nodded in affirmation.

"Excellent. Leary, Greta, you are relieved of duty."

"Do ya need me to help unload?" Leary asked.

"Perhaps in a bit. For now, there should still be some lunch left— better get there quick before they run out."

He nodded, and he and Greta ran off toward the dining hall.

"What about me?" asked Theo.

"It is a big day for you. Indeed, for all of us." Butler replied, with an air of mischievous grandiosity.

"The virus is ready. Pack your things. We leave the island in an hour."

PART 3.
RETURN.

TWENTY-ONE

EXTERNAL ALGORITHM 0026-TRJ
"The credit belongs to the man who is actually in the arena, whose face is marred by dust and sweat and blood; who strives valiantly; who errs, who comes short again and again, because there is no effort without error and shortcoming; but who does actually strive to do the deeds; who knows great enthusiasms, the great devotions; who spends himself in a worthy cause; who at the best knows in the end the triumph of high achievement, and who at the worst, if he fails, at least fails while daring greatly, so that his place shall never be with those cold and timid souls who neither know victory nor defeat."

Fifty-four minutes later, a motorboat had been taken out from the storage building and was almost fully inflated on the beach, and a crowd had gathered. Odin pushed the boat into the water along the pier once it was fully inflated, and Strauss, Simone, Theo, and Rita piled in with what little belongings they had—a few books for Simone, Theo's dream journal, and some medical supplies for Strauss and Rita. After seeing to it that everything else was taken care of, Odin grabbed a small canvas sack from her tent, and furtively hid it under her seat next to the motor, trying her best to muffle the barely audible clink as she tucked it out of sight. She sat right on top of it, no one daring to ask what was inside—least of all Theo.

Tearful goodbyes were said—Greta clung to Theo, sobbing "don't go's" into his shoulder, before being pried off by Carson, who gave him an unexpected, awkward, and treasured hug. Karen broke off from Robin long enough to have a short but intense talk with Simone, who assured her that she would never leave without her permanently. Karen insisted that she stay, but upon finding this effort fruitless, gave her a quick hug and went back to Robin, where a flurry of low words and side glances were exchanged without a moment's hesitation.

When all seemed ready, Butler stood on the pier next to the boat, and turned to address the camp.

"Friends, Comrades, Colleagues—today is a day that will go down in history. Today we take the largest step yet in the fight for Nature, and for Freedom. I count each and every one of you as an integral part of what we are doing here, and without each and every one of you, what we are doing here would not have been possible.

Today, we set off to make our move. The Great Equalizer Virus has been developed and completed. In less than a week, it will be installed into the Societal Operating System, and the rule of the elites who have oppressed us for so long will be over. They ran away from their problems, while we, through necessity, have been forced to stay and face them. In distancing themselves, they have removed themselves from the solution process. So, it is now up to us—you and me—and all our efforts are about to pay off. Their abdication will be their downfall, and our strength in numbers will be our victory!"

A halfhearted applause leaked from the crowd. Butler frowned, but upon realizing no more was coming, gave a short bow thanking the camp and its inhabitants, and boarded the boat. Firmly seated in the prow, Butler flashed Odin a flippant nod, then turned toward the horizon. With a firm grunt, Odin started up the motor, and they were off toward the mainland.

The rising sun in his face, Theo had to squint for most of the two-hour trip. The briny salt smell of the sea was buffeted by the pillows of air that rushed around his head and under his nose so quickly that it was hard to breathe it in. The *bap-bap-bap* of the boat cresting over each giant oceanic ripple and slamming back into the surf was jarring in its power and repetition, but none of it mattered. Theo was on his way home.

He hoped. There was a strange atmosphere in the boat. Not a single person spoke, they just sat in silence as the mainland slowly crept toward them. The air of mystery surrounding their destination was more nerve-wracking than exciting, though the possibility of danger had its own flavor of excitement. But with Butler and Odin no more than a few feet away, no one could ask the most common question plaguing the inhabitants of the boat—*Why are we all here?*

They reached the shore, and Odin hopped out into thigh-deep water, dragging the boat onto the sand. They got a few strange looks from beachgoers as they all piled out with their bags, but for the most part they were left alone. Odin ran ahead, bag in hand, while Butler directed them all to follow her up the trash-scattered beach toward the parking lot.

"Poor people. Working so hard to distract themselves. THEO—FOOT!"

Theo looked down, and quickly extended his stride so as to not step on the hypodermic needle of which Butler was warning him.

"Thanks." He said distractedly. He looked around. No more needles stood between him and the cement, but the people around him were objects deserving of profound curiosity. Some reading, some smoking, some digging, some sleeping—but none seeming to care about the strange and dirty people that had just boated up and left their vehicle next to an empty lifeguard tower.

"All these people, lost in their surrogate activities, no idea what will make them happy, or even what true happiness is."

Butler gestured to a child with a small green plastic shovel digging a hole in wet mud.

"In a few hours, the tide will cover in that hole, and the child's hard work will be all but forgotten. It will have to start again, and again, and again. Yet in its ignorance, it doesn't even consider the futility of its actions. No more fitting illustration than that, don't you think?"

"Mhm." Theo murmured in agreement, not quite sure what she was talking about.

After a few minutes, Odin pulled up in a dark green SUV. Butler opened the trunk, into which everyone was directed to quickly deposit their belongings. In seconds, they all found their seats and were on their way.

Butler took shotgun, and silence reigned again, broken only by her interjections.

"405 West to the 710 North, correct?"

"I was going to take the 605..." Odin shakily countered.

"Take the 710."

"But the 605 is—" Butler cleared her throat, cutting her off.

"Ok... 710 it is."

Odin seems a bit off today, Theo thought. *Whatever that guy said must have really affected her. Strange, for someone so... the way that she is.*

He looked out the window to see where they were, but he found very little helpful information. Sacramento was hundreds of miles that way, San Diego much closer the other way. He was able to figure out that the elevated roads they were on had numbers that corresponded to them, that odd-numbered ones ran east to west, and even-numbered ones ran north to south. As they transferred onto "the 710", Butler directed everyone's attention to the right side of the vehicle.

"See that patch of brown grass over there? That used to be a Country Club golf course. Elitist exclusion mixed with a terrible waste of space. If all the golf courses in the world were replaced by gardens, we could eradicate world hunger. Not a noble enough cause to supersede tee time though, apparently."

"Is that true?" Theo asked in disbelief. *Bob said we'd already done that.*

Butler nodded, and went silent. A few minutes later she directed Odin to pull off the freeway, and drive on side streets. They took the next exit, followed immediately by a left turn over the freeway on Alondra Boulevard, then continued up north. As Butler directed them through residential streets, she continued to single out points of interest.

"Over there on the left, a car on cinderblocks. In the past few decades, and even more so since the Apophis disaster, the widening gap between the haves and the have nots has raised tensions so high that people are forced to steal from their own underprivileged neighbors to feed their families. When too many people are forced to live unethical lives, it becomes a part of the culture, and can start destroying itself. The OS has done nothing to help these people. Casualties of a broken system."

"Coming up on your right, a Bail Bonds establishment. A broken system more harshly punishes those in more disadvantaged areas. There is more police activity, and therefore more arrests, which would indicate higher rates of crime in those areas, which raises arrest quotas, which calls for even more police activity. It iterates onto itself, and the system digs itself deeper and more unfairly into the lives of these victims. Places like this can mean the difference between someone growing up in between foster homes or not. Someday, we may not need them, but for now, they keep families together."

"Turn here—did you see what was going on over on that street? The parents broke open a fire hydrant so the children could play in the water. That family can't afford toys for their children, so they have to use what they have access to in order to entertain their kids. Opening a fire hydrant illegally is a misdemeanor in this county—they can be fined hundreds or even thousands of dollars if a police officer drives by and stops. And yet they do it anyway, because their children are what they care about. But the system doesn't take the child's needs into account. Theft from the city—theft from the system—is all that they see."

Butler directed Odin back onto the freeway, and they drove north for over an hour in silence. Once the 710 ended, they hopped on the 10 going east for about ten minutes until it met the 605, and took that north until Butler directed Odin to transfer to the 210 West in Duarte. After about ten more minutes, she had Odin pull off into a shopping center, where she hopped out, and returned with six foil-covered oblong paper bowls filled with lettuce, rice, and beans. Everyone shoveled food into their grateful mouths, and in a very short time they were off again.

Fifteen minutes later they turned off the freeway onto Allen Avenue, on which they drove north, passing wide streets shaded by overhanging oaks and vibrant jacarandas, lined by restaurants with colorful faces and tinted windows. They took a right on East Washington Avenue, then a left on Altadena Drive, before meandering northward in between a brush-covered mountainside on the right and a residential area to the left.

After a couple minutes, they pulled off into a driveway blocked by a 20-foot-tall chain-link gate with a sign that read:

> **AREA CLOSURE NOTICE**
>
> **MOUNT WILSON TOLL ROAD**
>
> **CLOSED FOR REPAIRS**
>
> **UNTIL FURTHER NOTICE**

Undeterred, Butler hopped out of the SUV, produced a key from her deep linen pockets, and unlocked the gate. It swung open, and Odin pulled through. Butler closed the gate, locked it up the way it had been before, and returned to the vehicle.

Up the winding mountain road they drove, rising higher and higher above the Los Angeles urban heat cloud. Very quickly the sounds of the city disappeared, and nothing could be heard except the crackling crunch of thick tires on eroded asphalt and dirt. Theo felt nauseous, so Butler rolled down a window for fresh air. It helped a bit.

For over an hour they wound their way further up and further into the mountains. The unchanging scenery was infuriating in its seemingly eternal recurrence, while sharp switchback turns terrified Theo as Odin took them at a wholly uncomfortable speed. They passed a small campground and a water tank, but then the road seemed to go on forever, again. Up and up and down and up, and left and right and left again, Theo found himself being carried deeper into the mountain labyrinth, until his mind began to wander, and amid a stream of unconnected thoughts, he remembered—*Mount Wilson... isn't that where Butler said their other base was? Where they're keeping Sid and Dave?*

Not ten minutes later, out the window Theo spotted the first of many giant radio towers that dwarfed the surrounding trees. They pulled into a sparsely populated parking lot, and Odin switched off the car, a sound Theo was overjoyed not to have to listen to a second longer, *thank you very much*. They entered a gated area, and passed a few towers and buildings, until they reached a rather small and unassuming one, with the words "KVEA-TV Corona" engraved into a plaque by the door. Odin swung it open, and Theo's heart jumped into his chest.

"SID!!!"

Theo sprinted over to his unshaven friend and threw his arms around him, nearly knocking him out of his chair. Almost instantly, he was pulled off by a Mt. Wilson Bohu he hadn't noticed in his excitement.

"Easy with him, Jacques." Butler cautioned, then turned and greeted the other Bohu in the room. "And good to see you too, Jacques". The Bohu, whose name was apparently also Jacques, backed off, and went to stand by the other Jacques.

"What, none for me?" came another voice from across the room. Theo swung around to see a familiar punchable face grinning at him.

"Dave! Yeah, of course!" Theo ran over to him and hugged him as well, doing his best to hide his reservations. They separated, and the two walked over to Sid, who was hugging Rita. They separated and he turned his attention to Theo.

"Theo, so glad to see you're OK. I've been so worried. You two don't look that much worse for wear- apart from the smell."

"You're not exactly a Bath and Body Works either." retorted Rita.

"You didn't have to worry about me." Theo reassured Sid. "I've been treated really well, actually. Have you been living up here this whole time?"

Sid nodded. "Well... that's curious." His eyes widened, and he leaned in to Theo. "Theo—you should know—"

"That's enough." Jacques cut in before Sid could complete his thought. "Butler, you wanted this to be quick?"

Butler nodded. "Quite right. I believe what we're here for is ready, is it not?"

"Yes Ma'am." Dave said, as he held out a red and black Malum Inc. USB drive. She took it, and turned it over in her hand.

"Excellent. Then I don't see a need to dally much longer. David, Theo, Simone, Strauss, Odin—you're with me. Jacques, excellent work."

Jacques nodded with a pious grace. Odin swung the door open, and Butler gestured for everyone whose names she called to leave. Theo looked back at Sid, confused and sad that he had to leave him so soon. Butler beckoned to him.

"Come Theo—you'll be back together in a week when this mess is all sorted out."

Theo nodded sorrowfully. "Let me just say goodbye."

Butler hesitated, then nodded, and Theo walked over to Sid to give him a hug.

"It won't be too much longer. I—"

Suddenly, Sid pulled him in tight, a wild look in his eye. With the urgency of a man pleading for his life, Sid whispered into Theo's ear.

"The hacks... The OS... NeuroCom... your mother... it was them. *It was all them!*"

Jacques raced over and yanked Theo off of Sid. As they were forced apart, Theo looked into Sid's eyes and saw nothing but genuine terror, pleading, and a fearful hope that he understood all too well. It was the same look he and Simone had exchanged on top of the mountain less than a week before. A familiar rage bubbled up inside Theo, but now he knew its source. The atavistic protective flame had set him alight from within, passing itself down through millions of generations, from before the first mitochondrion joined with a eukaryote in that profoundly novel holy synthesis, to this very moment atop the mountain. In seconds it sent a righteous fury vibrating throughout his mortal coil. Not just for his mother, not just for Sid, not just for Simone and not just for himself, but a bonfire in defense of all great truths, in offense against all great deceptions. He whirled around and shoved Jacques into a bookcase. The other Jacques came at him hard, tackling him to the ground next to Sid's chair. All breath was crushed out of Theo; he gasped for air as Jacques propped himself up, legs spread wide across Theo's chest as he wound up to deliver a punch to Theo's face.

"DON'T HURT HIM!" rang a voice. Out of nowhere, Simone's heel connected with Jacques' back, kicking him off Theo. She tried to pull him to his feet, but to no avail, as the first Jacques had regained himself and shoved her to the ground next to Theo. Everyone froze as a booming voice shook the building to its foundation.

"NOBODY MOVE!"

Odin stood, a few feet from the center of the action, holding Rita by the throat with one hand. Theo and Simone came up to a sitting position, and Jacques and Jacques stood up.

"Tie them up." She ordered.

Jacques and Jacques looked around wildly for something to use, before locating a few extension cords and electrical tape. They pulled two chairs over next to Sid, forcing Theo and Simone into them. They bound them tightly to the chairs by the hands, feet, and chest, with no chance of escape. Once they were tied up, Odin released Rita, who collapsed to the floor, gasping for air. She was swiftly propped up on her knees, and bound with her hands behind her back. Simone looked around wildly.

"Strauss, do something!"

Strauss raised his big bushy eyebrows in surprise, then turned to look at Butler. Simone let out a pained whimper and slumped into her seat as she saw a mischievous smile creep across her mentor's face. The two chuckled, then returned their gazes to the prisoners, arms freshly crossed.

"Strauss, you and Odin stay here and watch them. It appears I'll have to bring Rita as collateral rather than Theodore."

"What, Dave's not worth tying up?" Theo shouted to the smug senior citizens by the door.

Dave grabbed Rita by the arm, and pulled her up and through the door. Butler beamed and turned to look back through the doorway, a new and humorous glint in her eye.

"I hardly think it's appropriate for a mother to tie up her son. This isn't a Sophocles play."

The door slammed shut behind her.

TWENTY-TWO

EXTERNAL ALGORITHM 5834-SID
"Hatred does not cease by hatred, but only by love; this is the eternal rule."

"Can I get some water?" asked Theo.

It had been over three hours since Butler and Dave left with Rita. Theo, Simone, and Sid were all still tied up, which gave them ample time to take in their surroundings. A few minutes after Butler left, they had been dragged from the operating room into the soundproofed radio broadcasting room. A faux wood plastic table stood in the center of the room, with microphones spaced evenly around the edges. Up against the wall, there was a small bar with around a dozen different liquor bottles of varying fullness, under and around posters of musicians Theo didn't recognize. The three prisoners were sat facing the window, where Odin and Strauss could keep an eye on them, listen to them, and speak without being overheard.

"No. Shut up." Odin barked through the mic. Strauss leaned over to Odin and said something they couldn't hear. Odin glared at a shrugging Strauss before standing up and leaving the view of the window. A few seconds later, Odin swung the door open, holding three bottles of water. She placed them on the table and turned to leave. Theo cleared his throat.

"What?" asked Odin, annoyed.

"I'm tied up. I can't drink while I'm tied up." Theo stated matter-of-factly.

Odin rolled her eyes, grabbed one of the water bottles, and took off the cap. She held it up to Theo's mouth and began to pour, a little too fast. Theo sputtered and coughed—water spraying everywhere.

"Slower, Moody." advised Strauss through the monitor. Odin whirled around and splashed some water onto the window, eliciting a grin and a giggle from Strauss, much to her annoyance. She returned to Theo, and tried again. It was lukewarm—and Theo could taste the plastic in it—but as the clear liquid ran down his throat, these reservations were quickly dismissed. He gave a light nod, and Odin put it back on the table.

"Can I get some whiskey?" asked Sid. Odin opened her mouth to berate him, but was quickly cut off by Strauss's interjection over the speaker.

"Oooooh, me too please."

Odin's eyes shot daggers at Strauss. Strauss frowned in mock indignation, before standing up and entering the room.

"Fine Moody, I'll get it myself."

Strauss propped the door open, strolled over to the bar, and poured two glasses of Redemption Pre-Prohibition Style Bourbon. He took both, and gave Sid a sip of one of them before placing that glass on the table. His own glass in hand, he pulled a chair over to the front corner of the room, taking his time to sit in it. Everyone watched in confused silence as he sipped his whiskey, and let out a deeply relaxed sigh of relief. He studied the orange auburn liquid as it swirled in his glass, before looking up to realize how much of a spectacle he'd just made.

"Vhat?"

"Stop being so nice to the prisoners." Said Odin, dumbfounded.

"Oh, calm down, ve've von already." Strauss said dismissively. "They're off to the OS, and the only people who know about it are tied up in this room."

Odin frowned. Strauss frowned bigger, mockingly.

"Have a drink, celebrate! Relax for once. Geez."

Odin hesitated, glancing nervously at the prisoners.

"I don't think I should. If Butler—"

"Oh, poo-poo Butler. She's not here." Strauss hopped up and made his way over to the bar. "One drink. On me. Vhat's your pleasure? You seem like a vodka girl to me. No? Gin?" He turned to face Odin, see-sawing a handle of Bombay Sapphire gin in one hand against a handle of

Tito's vodka in the other. Odin shifted her weight back and forth, without speaking.

"Oh...." Strauss said with an air of care and discovery. "Is that right? Vell then. Here is vat ve do. Gin and tonic—great drink, very light. Add a little triple sec for the fruitiness. You'll like it. Here ve go." He threw together a drink faster than a Wall Street bartender on quadruple witching Friday, and handed it to Odin, who accepted it slowly. Hands shaking, she raised it to her lips, and took a small sip. Her gaze softened as she looked into the glass like it held an unexpected blessing, before hurriedly taking another sip.

"Ahhhhh, yes. I sought you would like it. Sit, enjoy."

Odin pulled a chair over to near where Strauss was sitting, and sat cradling her glass in two hands so large they made it look like a children's tea party prop. The three prisoners looked upon their captors in confused silence as Strauss settled into his seat, and Odin focused all her attention on her drink. She took another sip, and almost instantly became noticeably more relaxed.

"Really sucks to be you right now, huh?" Strauss taunted, before punctuating his remark with an overdramatically enjoyed sip. No one said anything. Theo clenched his jaw in contempt. Strauss turned to Odin.

"Look at them. Helpless. I love it. Don't you?"

"What? Yeah, sure." Odin replied, not listening, staring hypnotically into her drink. Strauss frowned. He resettled into his seat, crossing his overall-clad legs, and tried again.

"So vhat vill you do after all of this?"

Odin looked up. "Hmmm?"

"After Butler infects the OS. Any plans?"

"Oh, uh... I hadn't really thought about it." Odin murmured.

"Are you serious? You have your whole life ahead of you. In a veek, she von't need you anymore. You had to know this vould happen eventually."

Odin glanced momentarily up at the prisoners before returning to her glass, evidently very uncomfortable with this line of questioning. She took a big sip, before cringing at the alcoholic burn. Strauss continued.

"Oh dear... vell. That's a problem. You will have to find yourself a new cause to rally for, yes? Anuzzer machine to rage against? You are a fighter, not a lover."

You sucked in the Octagon, even when you were fighting chicks.

Linen Shirt's words crashed unbidden into Theo's mind. He swatted them away.

Don't get yourself in more trouble, Theo. Keep your mouth shut.

Theo watched in frustrated confusion at the display playing out in front of him. They'd been tied up, beaten both literally and figuratively, and now their captors were openly gloating a few feet in front of them. But something in the back of his mind kept prodding him, whispering to him that that didn't seem like it was the whole picture. *Aggregate truth and amor fati. Those are the rules Strauss uses. If he's using them, then I should look for his goal. Outright gloating doesn't seem right, since he's being so critical of Odin... I need to watch the effects.*

Odin muttered something under her breath.

"Vhat vas that?" Strauss asked, leaning in.

"I said, you don't know me" crunched Odin, defensively.

She is a fighter, clearly—why is she saying she isn't?

"I don't know... I sink I know you pretty vell. Feel free to prove me wrong." Strauss replied, coolly.

He's trying to get her to open up. Why?

"I don't have to prove anything to you." Odin shot back.

"Why are you getting so defensive?" said Simone, out of nowhere. Odin glared at her, and Theo glanced between the two, now more curious than angry about what was really going on. He looked at Strauss, and was surprised to see a slight glint of fatherly pride twinkling in his eye.

"Shut up. You're not allowed to talk." Odin deflected.

"No, no, Moody, she may have a point." Strauss countered. "No one here's trying to hurt you. At least I'm not. Are you?" he turned to Simone. She shook her head.

"No—Strauss is right, we lost. I don't know about these two, but I've given up."

Theo and Sid looked at each other, searching each other's faces for a common thought, before nodding in agreement. Odin sneered.

"Well, obviously I don't believe you."

"Fine, don't believe us. Just keep us tied up then." Said Simone.

"Fine then, I will!"

"Good." Simone responded calmly, refusing to escalate. Odin stewed in her seat. Strauss sipped his drink, and began stroking his big bushy moustache.

"So Moody, vhat did you do before joining up?" Strauss asked.

Odin looked around, lips pursed, trying to scavenge a way out of answering. Her eyes scanned her surroundings, finally landing on Theo. Daggers flew from her eyes. Everyone in the room saw them.

"Vhy are you looking at him like that—vhy is she looking at you like that?" Strauss asked.

Odin glared at Theo, saying nothing.

Don't say a word.

I promised.

Theo turned to Strauss, incredulous. "I don't know. She doesn't like me, probably. Never has. That's my best guess. I have no idea."

Odin relaxed slightly, and Strauss stroked his bushy moustache, deep in thought.

"Hmmm. Makes sense to me." He shrugged. "Ze qvestion still stands, Moody."

Odin winced at the nickname, and took a sip from her drink.

"Why do you want to know?"

"Vell, if you are looking for something to do after, maybe you could go back to vhat you vere doing before?" Strauss shrugged. Odin's eyes slitted suspiciously, glancing at Theo as though she were checking something, before widening again once she'd deemed the question innocuous enough. She took a drink.

"I can't go back to that."

"Vhat vas it?" Strauss asked.

"I don't want to talk about it. It's complicated, but I can't go back."

"Ok, ok, no more of that then. Vell, if you can't do that, vhat else do you like to do, like for fun? That has nussing to do vis the Tovu Va Bohu?"

Odin stopped mid-sip and stared at the ground. Her silence spoke volumes.

"Ok, ok, never mind, you don't have to answer that." Strauss reassured her. "How about then… vhy did you join in the first place?"

Odin's ears perked up.

"Oh, well that's easy. I wanted to make the unfair, oppressive world I grew up in more fair and free from oppression."

"No, no, Butler says this exact sing a million times. Your own vords." Strauss challenged.

"Well, she says it better than I ever could. I'm proud to be a member of her organization."

"*Her* organization? I sought everyone vas supposed to be equal?"

"You know as well as I do that that's just what we tell those who can't contribute. Obviously there needs to be leaders." Odin retorted.

"Seems a bit hypocritical, but fine. But oppression? Who could oppress you? Look at you, big strong lady."

"I—stop it. You don't know me, I don't have to tell you anything."

"I never said you did—I am just trying to help."

"I don't need your help."

"Alright then, fine. Ve are done. Ve sit in silence forever."

And they did. For a never-ending ten minutes, the only sounds inside the room were the subconscious whirring of electronics, the muffled chattering of outside birds through the open door, and the occasional sip of a drink from Strauss. Odin shifted her position a few times, but in the silence and stillness, any movement drew the utmost attention from everyone present, so these were kept to a minimum. Finally, Strauss couldn't take it any longer.

"Vhat about you, Simone darling? Vhat vill you do when this is all over?"

Odin turned to Strauss, exasperated.

"Vhat? You von't talk to me, and I vant to talk to somebody. Stop oppressing me Moody."

"Stop calling me that!" Odin shouted. "My name is Odin! I chose it for a reason, and you know I hate the name Moody!"

Everyone turned in shock and surprise toward Odin.

"What?" she shouted, before a wave of realization swept across her face and she retreated furiously into her chair. Simone was the first to speak.

"So... Odin's not your real name?" she asked, softly.

"No, dumbass, what did you think?" she replied contemptuously. Simone continued, unaffected.

"What is it? Your real name?"

"I don't—" Odin protested, before stopping short, eyes whipping back and forth before fixing themselves on Theo's shoes. She glanced up at him, and they locked eyes. Once more, the inner flame engulfed Theo, this time calm, comforting, and nurturing in its warmth. With the softest of efforts, he reluctantly allowed his gaze to affirm her.

Go ahead. You're safe here, the stakes are low. It'll be okay.

Odin looked down again, exhausted. She took a sip of her drink, gave a slight nod to herself, and heaved a slow, great sigh.

"Mimir." She said, as though confessing a secret held too long.

"Mimir..." Simone reveled in it. "That's a beautiful name."

"Thanks." Odin said reluctantly, more worn-out than flustered.

"How'd you pick the name Odin? It's a great name too, but I love Mimir." she asked tenderly.

Odin sipped from her now-empty glass. Strauss gingerly took it, and made her another one. She took it gratefully.

"After I... um... well when I met Butler, I'd just lost my eye in a... well, let's call it a series of bad decisions. I was really ashamed of it, to be honest, but then Butler told me about Odin—the Norse god guy—and how he gave up his eye in order to see through all the lies in the world. She was the first person to help me see my missing eye in a positive light—she started calling me Odin, as a joke, but then it made me feel strong, so I let it stick."

"So that's how you lost your eye? Butler told me she took it as punishment for you killing Hank and Bill." Theo said. Odin's eye went wide.

"What? No! No, I lost it in a fight. Unfair one too." Odin chuckled, painfully. She looked up, suddenly sorrowful. "Oh yeah, and I just wanna say, I'm sorry about your friends. Butler told me they would be necessary casualties. It'll all be worth it once the OS recognizes who the real humans are and stops oppressing all of us."

Sid, who'd been quietly slouching the whole time, suddenly sat upright.

"What?"

"I know, I'm sorry, but she said they were necessary—"

"No, no, not that—what was all that about recognizing who the real humans are?"

Odin looked at Sid, confused.

"Yeah... but you should know all about that. It's what you agreed to do in the first place, but then I know you had some issues with the coding, like you couldn't do it or something? So then Dave had to take over. But that's what the virus does."

"No, it doesn't. I saw what Dave was writing, before I wasn't allowed to look at it any more. The virus completely shuts down the OS. From what I can tell, she's planning on destroying the system completely and utterly, so we have to start society over from scratch. It wasn't that I couldn't do it, it's that I wouldn't. Look, I know there's problems with the way it's being run right now, but tearing it down completely is way worse than just letting it run."

"Hmm... This I did not know" murmured Strauss.

"No, no. Butler would never do that." protested Odin. "She's an advocate for the downtrodden. She wouldn't just knock the foundation out from under everyone like that. She sees things as they really are, and she's just trying to level the playing field."

"Level it, yes—but level it down to nothing." Sid said, gravely.

"Well then, maybe that's a good thing!"

"Believe me, it's not. We've spent thousands of years getting to where we are as a society, and if she accomplishes what she's trying to do, all the good things that got us to where we are will be gone, along with the bad."

"Well maybe you're just angry that you lost, and she won!" Odin yelled, causing everyone in the room to cringe, especially Sid. He pressed on, tentative, but determined.

"You're right. I am angry. But way more than that, I'm scared. If that virus gets into the OS, there's no telling how much carnage there will be. It's tied to everything—the power grid, communication networks, the world economy, irrigation, hospitals—all of that will immediately go offline, and be inoperable. It's impossible to overestimate how serious such a thing would be-- millions, maybe billions will die. Any family you may have would be impossible to get in touch with, if they're among the lucky few who are able to survive."

This visibly struck a chord with Odin. Everyone in the room could see her digesting what was being said. It was impossible to know exactly what she was thinking—Theo could only speculate. She looked up, jaw clenched, and swallowed before speaking.

"I don't have any family."

"You mean they're dead? I'm so sorry..." said Simone.

"No, they're—" Odin started pugnaciously. Theo watched her avoidant eye with concern. Within it hid an unresolved, gnawing, downtrodden pain, the depths of a like he had never encountered, not in any Bohu, not in himself, not in anyone from his old life. As he watched this massive statue of a woman relive her memories, the same woman who'd murdered his friends, and done very little apart from mistreat him, he was confused and astonished by the feeling that had coalesced and was now welling up inside him—*pity*. After an eternity, Odin spoke, softly.

"But she helped me find myself."

Simone leaned forward as best she could in her bonds, and attempted to comfort her. "I'm sorry Mimir, she told you who you are, and you accepted it—that's a very different thing than deciding for yourself. She did the exact same thing to me."

Odin shook her head. "No, I decided who I am. Not her."

"She tried to do it to me too. Make me resent everysing, good or bad, about the vorld I came from, and the person I vas, then offer me a place in her group to give me a new and righteous sense of myself and my purpose." Strauss added.

"I… I…" Odin struggled for words, but none came.

"Now that I think about it, the same thing was starting to happen to me." Theo added briefly. Odin just shook her head.

"There, you see? She used all of us. You are not the only tool in the room. Ve are all just as stupid as you." Strauss offered with the hint of a smile. Odin gave a heavy chuckle. She muttered something unintelligible.

"Hmm?" Strauss nudged.

"Except Sid." She muttered slightly louder.

"Sid? Oh, FUCK that guy. Always sinking he's right about everysing—pshhhh!" Strauss shouted abruptly. Immediately, the tension that had engulfed the room in the preceding minutes was broken. Everyone burst out laughing, including Sid. Strauss mouthed an apology to Sid, and gestured to the recently despondent Odin, to which Sid nodded understandingly. After a brief minute, everyone calmed down, and the conversation resumed.

"So, now what?" Odin asked.

"Vell first, I sink ve need to decide vhat to do. I am not particularly happy about this new information, are you?" Strauss asked nonchalantly.

"I don't like that I was lied to, that's for sure." She replied.

"Hmm… Well, then, tell me what you sink about this, Moody—"

"Um actually—" she cut him off. "I still don't like Moody. Can we try Mimir?"

Strauss's big bushy eyebrows shot up in surprise. "Mimir? Not Odin?"

"For a bit. Just to see how it feels."

He looked around, and exchanged nods with the rest of the room. "Of course, lovely, beautiful, strong lady. No expectations from anyone here."

Mimir nodded, and for the first time ever, Theo watched her smile. *Even with her cauliflower ear and face scars, she has a very nice smile*, he thought.

"Ok then, *Mimir*—ooh I love this name already—tell me vhat you sink. Ve go get some answers."

Everyone waited for more, but evidently, Strauss was done.

"Is that it? Get some answers?" asked Mimir.

"Yeah, vhat did you vant me to say, get some answers and some ice cream? OOH, good idea Strauss, great job. Okay, new plan. Ve go get some ice cream, THEN go get some answers. Yes?" Strauss looked at the group, smiling and nodding for approval.

"Why are you looking at them? They can't come!" Mimir cut in.

"Vhy not? Simone vas just as taken in as ve vere. If sings go wrong, Sid vill know how to fix it. And Theo—just look at his handsome face, ve have to bring him."

"I don't know…" Mimir shifted her weight nervously. Without quite realizing why, Theo began to speak.

"I think I know what your reservations are… Mimir—if I may?"

Mimir glanced at Strauss and Simone, then nodded to Theo. He continued.

"I think you want to trust us, but you don't know if you should. Which is fair. And I think the main reason you're not sure, which is a totally valid one, is the fact that you killed our friends, Hank and Bill."

Mimir cringed.

"You think that as soon as we're untied, or sometime later, we'll turn on you. That's a smart thing to think… But I just want you to know—" he looked nervously at Sid, before continuing. "I forgive you."

Mimir just stared at Theo. So did Simone, Strauss, and Sid. Theo gulped, and hurriedly continued.

"You might suspect that I'm only saying that to get you to untie me. And that's partly true. To be honest, I don't really see any situation where I get untied without saying that. And it's true—forgiving you for killing our friends isn't for your benefit, it's a completely selfish act—but getting untied isn't the only reason I'm doing it.

If I don't forgive you, then it'll be me, not you, feeling all the pain, and anger, and frustration that comes with missing them, and hating you. There's nothing I can do to bring them back, and I know that. The only thing standing between me and the freedom to experience happiness, unencumbered by resentment, is the act of forgiveness—forgiving you. So, I'm doing that.

Also, someone once told me that you should never ascribe to malice that which could be ascribed to ignorance—and knowing what I know now, I genuinely don't think that you would have done it, if you had all the information then."

"I wouldn't. I swear I wouldn't." Mimir murmured, half to Theo, half to herself.

"I know. So again, I forgive you. And if that's not enough, then I just want to offer this—my mother always taught me that the foundation of any strong relationship is trust. But what she never told me, what I had to find out for myself, is that you can't have a strong relationship without first giving someone the *opportunity* to trust you. Mimir, I forgive you, and I trust you—will you trust me?"

Mimir was stunned. She stood, still as stone, completely disoriented, lost in her head. None of the heuristics in her worldview lined up with what was being said, but more than anything, she wanted it to be true. Memories raced through her mind, trying to find a match, something to tell her what to do, how to respond. Strauss put a hand on her back, and she snapped back into the room.

"What about Sid?"

All attention turned to Sid. He thought briefly, then nodded.

"Theo knows you better than I do, and I trust his judgement. He speaks for me as well."

Mimir studied his face, and looked with hopeful reserve at Theo's. Then, quicker than lighting, she grabbed her gin and tonic, chugged the whole thing, and started untying Sid.

"One of the Jacques's has an RV up here. If I ask for the keys, there's no way they'll say no." She was all business. Theo and Sid looked at each other in complete surprise. Sid's bonds dropped to the floor, and Mimir moved on to Theo.

"We're only about four hours behind them. Their plan was to switch out the plates on the hotwired SUV from the beach and take it up to the OS. Butler gave herself four days to get there. I'm not sure what route they were going to take, so we just need to beat them there." Theo was free, and Mimir crouched down behind Simone. After a few seconds, her cords dropped to the floor, and she stood up, rubbing her wrists. Mimir stood erect, and scanned her new allies with stern determination.

"We can't waste any time. Everyone, follow me." Mimir leading the way, they all made a mad rush for the front door of the building.

"VAIT!" Strauss shouted, just before the door was swung open. Everyone froze, waiting.

"Ve need to tie them up again." He stated slowly, and matter-of-factly.

"What?" "Why?" asked Simone and Theo, almost in unison.

Sid nodded.

"No, he's right. We can't leave the building without being tied up, or they'll know something strange is going on. Tie all of our wrists together again. Make it look like a prisoner transfer."

Mimir took a second to understand, then leapt into action. She wound the extension cords loosely around their wrists, then tightened them with a few loops in between each pair of hands. Once the "prisoners" were bound, she tied each pair of handcuffs to another one, and the five of them lined up, ready to move out—Mimir in the front, followed by Theo, then Sid, then Simone, with Strauss bringing up the rear. The doorknob disappeared as Mimir's giant hand wrapped around it. She turned to look at her new companions.

"We'll need to make this look realistic, just so you're ready—so, sorry in advance. You ready?"

Everyone nodded, and Mimir swung the door open, letting in the blinding, west coast golden hour light. Theo's cord in her fist, she stepped across the threshold into the evening air. Strauss giggled gleefully.

"Family vacation! Ve are going to Yellowstone!"

TWENTY-THREE

EXTERNAL ALGORITHM 1945-CHU
"If you're going through hell, keep going."

The area outside the KVEA-TV Corona building was deserted. Mimir made a beeline towards their 10 o'clock, yanking Theo's cord. He yelped in pain.

"Shut up!" growled Mimir, flashing him a harsh, slightly apologetic glance. They walked a hundred or so feet in tense silence until they reached the door of another building, labelled "KSCA-FM Glendale". Mimir banged loudly on the door with her fist.

"JACQUES. OPEN UP."

A frantic scurrying and footsteps could be heard from behind the door. After a few seconds, the door opened, and Jacques appeared in the doorway.

"Jesus, Odin, we're recording."

"I don't care," she said with an offensive determination. "I need to talk to the other Jacques."

"He's on the air right now. Can't this wait?" He looked skeptically around Mimir's massive frame. Strauss popped out from the back of the line and waved gleefully.

"Hi handsome man!"

"Hey Strauss. Why are the prisoners out?"

Mimir towered over Jacques. "No, it can't wait. Change of plans—they're to be brought immediately to another camp. We've been told to take Jacques' RV. Butler's orders."

Jacques shifted nervously. "I don't know… we haven't heard anything about this."

"That's because it doesn't concern you." Mimir challenged. "Keys. Now."

"But if the RV—"

"NOW. Or do you want me to tell Butler that you refused her request?"

"No! No, don't do that—I'll go get them. Just don't tell Butler."

Jacques raced back into the building, and returned a minute later with a set of keys.

"Sorry that took so long, I had to—"

"Don't care. I'll let Butler know you were helpful… eventually."

Mimir snatched the keys out of Jacques' hand and began walking toward the parking lot, dragging the prisoners behind her.

"You know where it is?" Jacques yelled behind them.

"Yes, sank you handsome man! Good to see you again! Good-bye!" Strauss sang back to him.

"Ok… bye…!" a confused Jacques shouted halfheartedly, before slowly closing the door to his building.

Mimir kept up the act beautifully until they reached the RV—so well in fact, that Theo had to remind himself that she was really acting. She led them like cattle another hundred feet or so until they were right next to an old class C motorhome, covered in dents and dirt. She opened the door, and a few empty beer bottles rolled out onto the ground.

"Get in, go to the back room, and wait there." She ordered. Theo, Simone, and Sid, a little more scared than they had expected to be at this display, urgently did so. They awkwardly stepped up the four steps, and found themselves confronted by two giant comfy chairs with built in cupholders. *Just like the one Dad had, to watch TV in,* Theo thought excitedly. But there would be more time to sit and try them out later. He made a beeline for the bedroom in the back, Sid and Simone tied to him right behind, passing a small kitchen complete with cupboards, sink, and stove on his left, and a dining table on the right. He reached the back, and immediately plopped down onto the queen-sized mattress. He hadn't seen a mattress in months, and already he was savoring every second of it.

"Make some room." Sid said, visibly stressed. Theo quickly scooched over, and Sid and Simone sat down next to him. Strauss followed up in the rear, but stopped in the kitchen, and immediately began rifling through the cabinets. Mimir came in last, closing the door behind her.

"Not yet Strauss. Get up front. You three stay in the back until I say so. You're still prisoners as long as we're in camp."

"UGH" Strauss replied dramatically, before scampering over to the passenger seat. Mimir put the key in the ignition, and scanned outside the windows nervously. She turned it on.

Everyone held their breath as they taxied to the gate that kept the public away from the radio buildings and towers. They reached it, and Strauss hopped out. He opened it, they drove through, he closed it again, and returned to the cab. They turned left out of the gated lot onto the road, and went straight. After five hundred feet they turned right onto a road lined by trees, radio towers barely identifiable through and above them. Rock wall to the left, sharp wooded cliff sloping down to the right, they continued down the road, every second feeling as though it were an eternity. After five minutes or five years, Mimir called back from the front.

"Ok, that should be good. Strauss, go untie them."

"Yes, SIR!" Strauss mocked.

The three ex-prisoners in the back turned to look at each other for the first time since the RV had started moving. Simone gave a light chuckle of relief as she looked at Theo. He returned it with a grin and turned to Sid. Tears were streaming down his cheeks.

"Woah, Sid... Are you ok?" Theo asked.

Sid nodded distractedly, and Strauss began untying his bonds. He finished, and moved on to the other two. Theo watched Sid stare at his newly freed wrists. He began rubbing them slowly, feeling the imprints of the bonds that no longer held him. Theo smiled. It was so good to see him again—and even better to know that he was okay. Sid started shaking.

"Sid?" Theo leaned over with rising concern—then he stopped. Sid was *laughing*. Tears streaming down his face, he laughed louder and freer than Theo had ever heard him laugh before. The mental shackles built up during months of captivity fell from him in seconds. He fell back on the bed, completely lost in a hysterical ecstasy of relief, covered his face with his hands, and let out a cathartic bellow before stretching out his body like a cat that had just woken up from a nap. Finally, he sat up again and reentered the common space of interaction. He let out a sigh, and turned to Theo, eyes still watery, a big smile on his face.

"You've grown so much!"

Theo threw his arms around Sid, and squeezed. Sid started coughing, and Theo frantically let go.

"You ok?" he asked.

Sid nodded and laughed between coughs. "Yeah—you're way stronger than I remember."

"Oh yeah—sorry. Since they took my exoskeleton, it took a while to get used to the gravity here."

"You don't have to tell me. They made me hike up the mountain the first few days I got here. I kept passing out. Got shin splints in both legs and stress fractures in both feet. I still haven't fully healed up."

"That's terrible!" Theo said with astonishment. "Why didn't they drive up like we did?"

"It was on purpose, I'm sure. Trying to break our will—or just mine apparently. I guess Dave was with them from the beginning."

"Oh yeah… he's the one who told them where the OS is."

"Yeah—wait, how'd you know that?"

"Simone told me—oh, sorry. Sid, this is Simone, Simone, Sid." Simone held out her hand and Sid shook it.

"Glad to finally meet you in person." She said. "I'm so sorry for everything that's happened."

"Not your fault, I'm sure." Sid assured her. Simone nodded distractedly and pulled her hand back.

"Not all of it, but I played more of a part than I would like. I was—" Sid shook his head and stopped her.

"Stop. I don't need to know. We've all been through a lot, let's just enjoy ourselves for now. We have a whole road trip to fill up with stories. Hey—Strauss, is it?" He turned to the mustachioed old sprite, who had taken to rummaging through the cupboards.

"Yes daddy?" Strauss asked.

"We're about to hit Angeles Crest, right?"

"MIMIR? ANGELES CREST?" Strauss yelled up front.

"Yeah." Mimir replied at a normal volume, flipping Strauss the bird.

"Yes daddy." Strauss returned to Sid, voice dripping with semi-facetious allure.

"Great. There's a fantastic ice cream place not far from here. Mimir?" He raised his volume slightly so she could hear. "Take it west, rather than east." Mimir turned around and shouted back.

"But that's in the opposite direction of where we need to go!"

"It's worth it. Trust me. We won't lose more than an hour or two."

Mimir nodded and turned back to the road.

The next hour was spent with more fully fledged introductions, between which everyone took their grateful turn to use the shower. Sid was thoroughly enraptured by Simone as she regaled him with her experience following the Apophis disaster, in much greater detail than even Theo had heard before.

Apparently, she and Karen had stopped on their way through Mexico to grab supplies that were being distributed to the needy. Karen was unhappy with the supplies being offered, so she asked to see the manager, which received a laugh, and ended with the two girls being captured, thrown into a van, and driven to an unknown location. After a few hours they were let out, only to find that the "manager" Karen had demanded to speak to was none other than El Noche, head of the infamous Sinaloa Cartel. They stayed at El Noche's mansion, hidden in the foothills of Mexico, for a week, before being given a choice—stay forever, and each marry one of El Noche's grandsons, or drive a shipment of assorted drugs across the border. Karen voted for the first option, but after a long talk, Simone convinced her that they had to go find their father. The next day, El Noche's soldiers gave them a van full of fentanyl, cocaine, and marijuana, along with an armed escort, and sent them on their way. They made their way all the way up to the border before losing their armed escort and shipment to an incorruptible Tijuana cop, who clearly saw that they weren't from around here, and had thankfully encountered their situation before. He let them go, but the girls were unable to get across the border without their passports, which they'd left in their mother's Jeep a week prior. They ran into Sinaloa members again, who, upon hearing that they'd lost the shipment, refused to help smuggle them across, and only due to Simone's pleading, agreed not to kill them.

They wandered for days until they met an old shaman woman named Marianne, who brought them to her commune in Sonora. They ate and rested, and there they met Strauss, who was on a dharmic pilgrimage north, after growing up in Argentina, and studying shamanic medicine in Peru. After a few months living there, during which Simone learned most of what she knew, she, Karen, Strauss, and Marianne commandeered a boat and raced their way up to Catalina, avoiding the border patrol, where they'd joined Tovu Va Bohu.

They came down Angeles Crest Highway into a small suburban town, and in minutes Sid had directed them into a parking lot off the main road. They all hopped out of the RV, and, carrying a stack of bills that Jacques had stashed and Strauss had found, the five adventurers strolled into Penguins Ice Cream Shoppe.

The door opened with a ding, and they queued through the ice cream buffet. Mimir pulled up the rear, and when it came her turn to order, she didn't speak. Simone leaned over to her.

"It's your turn. Go ahead and order."

"What should I get? I've never had this before." Simone looked at her, bewildered.

"Seriously? You've never had ice cream before?"

"Don't make a big thing out of it!"

"I'm—sorry. Get whatever you want. But personally, I think the toppings are the best part."

Mimir nodded and began ordering as Theo, Sid, and Strauss took their ice cream and went outside to wait for the others. A few minutes later, the girls joined them, Simone with two scoops of chocolate chip cookie dough and an assortment of candy bar crumbles, and Mimir with a heaping mound of a little bit of every single topping, giving no clues as to the flavor of ice cream underneath. Everyone dug in, and Sid led the group across the street to grab some real food at Georgee's, a casual Italian restaurant, that he explained was one he visited every time he was on Earth.

"I used to eat here constantly during grad school. Jet Propulsion Laboratory's just down the street, so sometimes we'd get lucky and end up sitting in a booth behind rocket scientists talking shop. My friends and I would listen in on what they were working on, and then wait to hear about it a few years later when it went public."

They walked in and queued in line, Strauss in the rear so he could pay. Suddenly, Theo turned to Sid.

"Something just occurred to me. What if the Jacques's call Butler, and tells her we left? They could come after us, or worse, Butler and Dave could do something to Rita."

Sid shook his head. "I wouldn't worry about that. Dave's had a huge crush on Rita for years. There's not a chance in hell that he'd let Butler do anything to her. And as for the Jacques's—they can't leave the camp. They're radio hosts—they have to be on the air for a few hours every day. They might send someone else, but with Mimir here, it's not worth worrying about."

"Hi, how can I help you?" asked the high school girl behind the cash register.

"Ooh, yes, thanks. Chicken fingers and fries please. And a large drink." Sid turned to Theo.

"Best chicken fingers in LA—at least that I've had. Haven't gotten around to Roscoe's yet, but until then, this has the fried chicken crown."

He nodded a thank you as the cashier gave him a cup, and Theo ordered the same thing. They took turns filling their drinks behind the register, then went around to the left to the seating area.

"Eric?" Sid blurted out to an unruly mop of hair sitting at a table alone. The hair turned; Eric's eyes lit up and his jaw dropped.

"SID? What the hell are you doing here?" He jumped up from his table and gave him a huge hug, nearly spilling Sid's drink. He pulled away, and suddenly his tone turned conspiratorial.

"Do you know how many people are looking for you?"

"A ton of people, I bet. I've been imprisoned for close to three months on top of Mount Wilson."

"Really? That's not what I heard." Eric said as he plopped back in his seat. "You're supposed to be on the run right now."

"On the run?" Sid responded. "What the hell for?" Eric looked around, and gestured for Sid to sit down. He did, and Theo joined him.

"Oh, sorry, this is Theo. Theo, this is Eric. He was my roommate in grad school. Works at JPL now. I told him about how we used to come here—"

"This is Theo?" Eric cut him off. "*The* Theo?"

"The Theo?" Theo asked. "What do you mean 'The Theo'?"

Eric shook his head. "Sid, you're in big trouble. I want you to know I didn't believe it for a second—and I've said as much to anyone who would listen."

"Believe what?" Sid asked, now very concerned. Eric took a deep breath and looked directly at him.

"You're a fugitive. Both of you are. Well, more you than Theo. Remember the weird OS aberrations we picked up on just before you disappeared?"

Sid nodded. "Yeah, we were on our way to check them out when we crashed. Tovu Va Bohu hacked our rocket and captured us."

Eric leaned back in his seat. "Tovu Va Bohu? Really- the cave dwellers? I thought they were purposely living in the stone age. How'd they manage to do that?"

Theo cut in. "One of the Bohus astral projected into the rocket, shorted out the backup security relay, then they shot us with an EMP after we entered the atmosphere. If you don't believe me, Simone's the one who did it. She's over there."

Theo waved at Simone, who was filling up her cup. She waved back sheepishly. Eric turned back around.

"That... wow—really? Wow. That's a whole other conversation. But going back—those OS bugs, and the NeuroCom hacks— the institutional narrative is that you were behind it. All of it. A few days after you disappeared, Ditto did this whole press conference about how the 'disgruntled cofounder didn't think he was getting enough credit'. Then, the day after the hacks, you hijacked a rocket and flew it to Earth to hide out, taking Theo and Rita with you as captives. He blamed Dave too, but said he was 'young and impressionable' and that you'd 'corrupted a promising young mind'."

Sid gawked at Eric, before shaking his head in disbelief. "I can't believe Bob would do something like that. But it wasn't me—obviously. I was on my way to try to figure out what was wrong. Tovu Va Bohu was behind all of it—they forced Dave and I write a virus for the OS, and the computer they gave me to use still had the source code for the trojans and viruses they wrote to infect the NeuroCom system." He turned to Theo. "That was when I first started getting suspicious of Dave. They were written in such a way that someone on the inside had to have been able to inject them into the software. Then I thought back to the algorithm Dave wrote to iterate through the bugs—there were hints that it was constructed to deliberately not pick up on the changes they made."

Eric shoved a fry into his mouth. "That's bonkers. But what about the OS bugs? They do that too?"

Sid shrugged. "Beats me. No trace of OS related stuff on the laptop they gave me, anyway. Apart from what Dave and I wrote."

Eric sipped his soda. "So, what's going on now then? How'd you escape? Why are you here, of all places?"

Sid leaned in. "I honestly have no idea how we got out—it seems like luck. Theo did this great thing—but to the more urgent point, Dave and the head of Tovu Va Bohu are on their way up to the OS to install the virus on site, with Rita as a prisoner. We stole an RV from the Bohus, and we're racing up to Yellowstone to stop them."

"And you stopped at Georgee's?"

"Penguins too. I haven't had a decent meal in months."

"You're insane." Eric laughed, scratching his chest. "So what's this virus do? You helped write it?"

Sid shook his head gravely. "I started it, but when I saw what it was supposed to be, I ended up refusing and getting into a sabotage war against Dave, while secretly writing my own." He pulled a black and red Malum Inc. flash drive out from his pocket. "This should undo all the corrupted software in the OS, and help prevent further corruption. The one Dave wrote—the one they're trying to use—as far as I could tell, before I couldn't get a look at it anymore; it essentially destroys the entire OS, from top to bottom. I think. That's definitely the direction it was going."

Eric shook his head. "This… this is so much to take in. Is there anything I can do to help you?"

"Nothing comes to mind." Sid said. Almost immediately, he recanted. "Actually—if I'm supposed to be on the run, could you keep our paper trail clear while we're on our way up? Scrub the web of any traces of us, if there are sightings—"

"—fabricate and corroborate three other ones far away. On it."

"You're the best Eric, can't thank you enough."

"Oh, I'm sure I'll find a way."

"I bet you will."

"You're right—after this is all over, I want to hear everything, in depth, and half the movie rights. But for now, get away from me, ya felon. I can't be seen doing business with a terrorist like you."

Sid nodded and chuckled.

"Aye, aye, captain."

Theo and Sid slid out from the booth and joined their three colleagues, who had taken up a booth behind them.

"Who was that?" asked Simone.

"Friend from college. He's gonna help us out." Replied Sid, before jamming one of his neglected chicken fingers in his mouth.

"How's he gonna do that?" asked Mimir.

"Digital scrub—keep the watchful eye of whatever interested party would want to stop us, off of us. He also gave us an important bit of info—I'm a fugitive apparently, and so's Dave. That means, chances are, the powers that be have more than likely revoked both of our clearances to enter the bunker that houses the OS. We may have more time than we think before all is lost—but we still shouldn't get too comfortable. Dave's a genius coder, and a smooth talker. He knows that there's a very fine line separating being annoying and endearingly incorrigible, as well as how to hop back and forth. On top of that, he's persistent, and smart about it—so I wouldn't give ourselves more than a day or two of leeway before he figures out a way in."

Everyone chewed in silence as they processed this news. This was more than just a simple chase—a lot of people, non-Bohus, were trying to find them, and if they found them, they would try to stop them. They weren't just having a speedy road trip—they had to stay under the radar from a government and a government-sized corporation that theoretically had eyes everywhere. Mimir was the first to speak.

"Well, that's that then. We should err on the side of speed and caution. Only leave the RV if we have to, blinds closed at all times. Especially you two." She gestured to Sid and Theo. They nodded in agreement. She continued.

"We should get going. We've wasted a lot of time already. Let's get back to the RV."

Everyone nodded and murmured in solemn agreement. They picked up their baskets of food, and made their way to the RV without another word. Simone closed all the blinds, Mimir turned the key in the ignition, and they were off, driving away from the sun as it disappeared below the western horizon. The rest of the crew sat around the dining table, finishing their food.

They drove for about an hour and a half, during which Mimir ripped the vintage GPS off its windshield mount and tossed it out the window, all but guaranteeing its cruel death between asphalt and rubber. Finally, they pulled off the highway into Hacienda Mobile Home Park to spend the night. Mimir took the giant bed in the back—she was doing all the driving, so no one objected. Simone, the smallest in the group, took the small compartment above the driver's seat. Theo took the semi-circular couch that surrounded the dining table, and Strauss and Sid each took an armchair.

The doors locked, the lights out, and Mimir's chainsaw-like snores coming from the back room, Theo lay awake, staring at the plastic ceiling, thinking about how much his life had changed in the past few months. He glanced up front, and saw Simone sprawled out, one arm hanging off the ledge. The two older men had sunk into their chairs, each head cocked to the side, cradled between their shoulder and the plush seat back. As Theo settled back into his makeshift bed, nodding off into the peaceful state between wakefulness and dreams, he couldn't help but wonder at the danger and excitement the next few days would hold.

TWENTY-FOUR

EXTERNAL ALGORITHM 0933-BGI
"Those who worship other gods with faith and devotion also worship me, even if they do not observe the usual forms."

EXTERNAL ALGORITHM 1956-CSL
"For he and I are such different kinds that no service which is vile can be done to me, and none which is not vile can be done to him. Therefore, if any man swear by Tash and keep his oath for the oath's sake, it is by me that he has truly sworn, though he know it not, and it is I who reward him. And if any man do a cruelty in my name, then though he says the name Aslan, it is Tash whom he serves and by Tash his deed is accepted."

Theo awoke to a sharp turn and a rather indelicate application of the brakes. He groaned. He sat up and looked around. Mimir had been at the wheel since sunrise, and they had just pulled into a gas station.

"Oh, you're up. Good. Remember though, stay out of sight—away from the windows."

A still groggy Theo gave her a thumbs up and fell back onto his couch.

A minute later, Strauss entered, carrying three sizeable paper cups each with a lid.

"Aah, he is risen! Just in time. Here, drink." He handed Theo a cup.

"What's this?" he asked, still half asleep.

"Milkshake."

"I don't want a milkshake."

"It's not a milkshake, it's coffee, silly boy. Drink, before it gets cold!"

Theo sniffed at the sipping hole in the lid. He remembered the smell from his mother's coffee, but he'd never been allowed to drink it. He took a sip and recoiled, barely avoiding spilling the scalding drink.

'Ith HOT!" Theo exclaimed with an indignant tongue.

"Vell duh, I told you, it hasn't cooled yet."

"No thit!" he retorted, setting it on the table to cool.

Simone, who had been reading up in her lofted bunk, closed her book and hopped down. Strauss handed her a coffee, and she gratefully took it. She slid into the dining booth, cozied herself into the seat, and cradled the paper cup between her hands, reveling in its warmth.

Strauss peered out the shades of the window, watching Mimir pump gas outside. Simone took a sip, then addressed him.

"Strauss?"

"Yes darling?"

"There's something I've wanted to ask you, but I haven't had the opportunity until now."

"Vhat about, sveet girl?"

"Well, when we were up at the radio station, and I asked you to help, why didn't you? All you did was stand there and laugh at us. That really hurt."

"I had the same question." Theo chimed in support.

Strauss continued peering through the blinds and heaved a deep sigh.

"Ah, yes. That vas a... complicated situation. There vere a number of reasons— but the main one. In my life I have been in many situations. Some simple, some complex, some vis one side, some vis many. I saw vhat vas happening, and I... made a bet—a bet that paid off."

"What bet?" asked a confused and mildly exasperated Theo. Strauss checked the activity through the blinds once more, then turned to face his young companions directly.

"Calm down, handsome man. Too early in the morning for feelings. The bet vas this. Odin—Mimir, and I vould be left to vatch over you after your little... disruption. She takes David, she takes Rita for collateral. And so it is. But if I stand up for you, I'm tied up too, this does no one any good. But if you are tied up and I am not, and it is just us in the room... vell then. It is easier to peer pressure someone vhen you are on the same side. So this is vhy."

The *kalunk* of the gas nozzle being removed immediately raised the level of alertness of everyone in the RV, regardless of coffee consumption.

"Quick, before she's back, you said there were a number of reasons?" Theo asked.

A mischievous grin peeked out from underneath Strauss's big bushy moustache.

"Call it selfish curiosity. I vanted to see vhat you vould do. And you did not disappoint."

"We didn't do anything!" Simone exclaimed.

"Exactly. You knew vhen vas the time for fighting and vhen vas not. You did very well."

Before anyone could say anything else, the driver's side door opened up and Mimir slid in.

"Everyone ready?"

With a thumbs up from everyone in the back, Mimir hit the gas, and they pulled out of the gas station. Driving under a single out-of-place roller coaster as they got on the highway, the door to the back bedroom creaked open, and out strolled a half-asleep Sid. He plopped down next to Theo in the booth, took a coffee from Strauss, and in a few minutes the four of them were chatting like old friends.

After a few hours, it was discovered that Jacques had not emptied the septic tank of the RV for an ambitious amount of time. This was quickly determined to be a severe problem, both in terms of smell, and also because it meant that Sid and Theo would have to leave the RV in order to, well... do their business.

Having driven through Las Vegas, gawking at the landmarks that could be seen from the freeway—the Luxor pyramid, the pseudo-Statue of Liberty, and the pseudo-Space Needle (the Air Traffic Control Tower at McCarran Airport)—they pulled into a gas station in St. George, just across the border from Nevada into Utah. Theo had found some sunglasses in a cabinet, and put them on to use the truck stop bathroom.

The ding of the convenience store's automatic doorbell made him jump. Theo cautiously observed the wide variety of people who happened to find themselves at that particular truck stop at that particular time on that particular day. There were video cameras everywhere. He made a beeline for the back corner of the store.

He walked past the chips, discount DVDs, and audiobooks, then turned the corner into the far aisle of air fresheners and windshield scrapers that served as a direct thruway to the bathrooms. His heart sank. There was a line. Only one restroom was free from an out-of-order sign, and it was single-use. In front of him was a larger, middle aged man with a scruffy beard, a Hawaiian shirt, and a straw hat with a full brim talking casually to his young son. Theo walked up behind him and quietly took his place in line, trying not to draw attention.

"Sunny in here, huh?"

Theo did a double take.

"Huh?"

Hawaiian Shirt tried again.

"I said... sunny in here, huh?"

Theo shook his head.

"The sunglasses? Don't mean anything by it, I've got this hat on. Wife makes fun of me all the time for it, but haven't been sunburned in years."

Theo shifted back and forth.

"Oh—uh, sorry, never mind, shouldn't have said anything."

"What? No, sorry—"

"Don't worry about it. Where ya headed?"

Theo was taken aback a bit by this stranger's cheerfully intrusive demeanor. *Why's he being so nosy?* Hawaiian Shirt saw Theo hesitate and backtracked.

"You know what? I shouldn't have said anything. Sorry, I just tend to talk a lot to distract myself when nature's callin' an I can't pick up right now, get what I'm sayin'? Little Teddy's got the same problem too, don't ya Ted?" He patted his son on the back. Teddy grimaced. He'd evidently been focusing all his attention on holding it, and the light jolt from his father didn't help. The door swung open, and he ran inside, almost knocking over the unsuspecting man who'd just reentered the world of those not bladder-governed.

"Teddy? Short for Theodore?" Theo asked, surprised by his sudden affection for his much shorter namesake.

Hawaiian Shirt nodded proudly. "Named after Teddy Roosevelt, our greatest president. Started the national park system, went from being a sickly little boy into the toughest man who ever lived, by sheer force of will. Broke up industrial monopolies, and had a great moustache while he did it. We're on a National Park family tour right now. Just came from Yellowstone, now we're—"

"Yellowstone? That's where I'm headed!" Theo exclaimed.

Shit. Shouldn't have said that.

"Really? Love that place!" Hawaiian Shirt exclaimed. "You driving by the Tetons? You gonna hit Old Faithful?"

"I, uh… yeah! All that." Theo stumbled.

"Great. You're gonna love it. You know it's all one huge volcano, right? That's scary. That thing goes, we all go. But you gotta watch out for bears. You got some bear mace?"

Theo shook his head. He had no idea what this guy was talking about.

"Oh, be sure to get bear mace. I think they have it here… yeah, aisle seven. They say making yourself big and yelling at the bear is enough, and it might be, but always better to be safe than sorry, especially when it comes to bears."

Theo nodded. As long as this guy did the talking, he didn't have to share anything about himself.

"Good to know, thanks. Where you headed now?"

"We're headed up to Zion."

"Zion?" Theo asked.

"Zion National Park—you haven't heard of it? Oh, man, it's beautiful. I've been there a few times before, but it'll be Teddy's first time. I'm tellin' ya, Zion is heaven. Nothin' like it. I just hope the kid enjoys it as much as I do."

Hawaiian Shirt looked down at his stomach, lost in his head for a second, despite having started shifting his weight back and forth in a low stakes pee dance.

"I'm sure he will." Theo offered reassuringly. Hawaiian Shirt looked up, and smiled.

"Thanks stranger." He went back to looking downward, still dancing. "Sometimes you just need to hear it, ya know? I'm just tryin' to give him all those experiences it took me too long to have. And I wanna have 'em together, you know? So when we aren't together, we can remember each other in those places, doing those things. I work a lot, so I don't get to spend a lot of time with him, so when I do I want it to mean something, ya know? Sorry, I'm throwin' all this on ya, I don't even know ya. Sor—sorry."

Hawaiian Shirt went silent, and stared at the floor. Theo looked at this man, and saw in him things that he wanted to see in himself. He thought about his own father, and the memories he had of him. He thought about his son, if he were to have one, and began wondering if he would be able to do the same things, teach the same lessons, and make whatever sacrifices were necessary in order to give his child the freedom and choices it deserved. This man, waiting for his son to finish using the bathroom, was doing his best, and Theo found that he loved him.

"You seem like a great dad."

Hawaiian Shirt sniffled a bit, and a smile curved up under his scruffy beard. He nodded.

"Thanks man."

Simultaneously, the door swung open, and Hawaiian Shirt's whole demeanor switched from internally anxious to externally excited. Teddy strolled out, relieved, and looked up at his dad.

"Go pick out a few snacks for us—ten dollar limit. I'll be right out, kay?"

Teddy nodded vigorously at his dad and scampered over to the candy aisle as Hawaiian Shirt disappeared into the bathroom.

○

Hawaiian Shirt came out a minute later, gave Theo a quick nod, then went to go find his son. Theo went in, did his business, then went to the sink to wash his hands. He flipped on the faucet, pumped twice for soap foam, looked up, and froze, struck by the face looking back at him. The last mirror he'd seen was in his bathroom at home—spotless, cleaned daily by the robo-butler. This mirror had vastly more character, it was scratched up, stained, smudged, just like the young man he saw before him. He looked older, more weathered. His eyes had a depth he'd never seen in himself before. He saw now that his brow was in a constantly furrowed state, but not in anger, that didn't seem right. It was more of an omnipotent determination. He relaxed it, and the feeling dimmed. He had the beginnings of stubble coming out of his chin—more peach fuzz than tree trunk, but still. And he was stronger. He could now see how much bigger he really was. Those days spent in his tent doing bodyweight exercises had paid off—he was substantial, shapely, fit. He no longer looked like the boy he'd known his whole life.

○

Theo climbed the steps to the RV in a daze. He took off the sunglasses and handed them to Sid, who put them on and walked briskly inside to take his turn. He sat down in an armchair and stared at the wall, lost behind his eyes.

"You ok?"

Simone looked straight down at him from her lofty bunk. Theo snapped out of his mental trance and nodded nonchalantly.

"Huh? Yeah, I'm good."

Simone considered him for a second, then shrugged it off. "Ok!"

She rolled over and opened up her book. In a few minutes, Sid was back, and they were on the road again, Theo still lost in subverbal thought.

◡

The group stopped for gas again in Nephi, a town just south of Salt Lake City. Strauss found a compass he liked in the gas station and bought it, though after close inspection, it was discovered that it didn't point north. He decided to keep it anyway, saying that "vhen this is all over, I'll go find vhat it's pointing at."

As Salt Lake City's metropolitan energy began to shrink behind them, the crew admired the snowcapped mountains ringing the valley in the setting sun's golden light, when—BANG. Suddenly, the RV squealed and shook, sending everyone into high alert. Straining to control the massive vehicle, Mimir wrestled them to the right-side shoulder of the freeway, where they rolled to an unlucky stop.

For a full minute, no one spoke. With each passing second, it became evident that no one had any experience in car repair. Finally, after a lot of melodramatic hemming and hawing, Strauss sat up with a frown.

"Vell, now vhat?"

Knock Knock

Everyone froze. The knuckles rapped harder on the door.

KNOCK KNOCK

Theo looked at Sid, who shrugged and shook his head wildly. Sid looked questioningly at Simone, who was frozen on her bunk. Strauss surveyed the group, sighed, then took matters into his own hands. The door cracked open.

"Hallo?"

"Hi there! You folks broken down?" came a cheerful voice at the foot of the steps.

"Yes sir!" Strauss nodded graciously.

"Need me to take a look?"

"If you vouldn't mind?"

"Not at all! Just if you could pop the hood for me?"

"I sink ve can do that. Mimir, can you do that?"

Mimir frantically scoured the panel of buttons and switches, before finding one and pulling it. The hood popped up a few inches. From around the side, a young man about Theo's age strolled to the front of the RV, towel in hand. He lifted the hood, and for a few seconds, everyone just watched the open hood in anxious silence. After a minute, he slammed it shut again, and walked back over toward the door. Before he could knock again, Strauss opened it.

"Looks like your drive belt's snapped. If you want, I can fix it for you! I think I have one in my garage that will fit right in there."

Strauss looked around to the other occupants of the RV for approval, then returned to the kind stranger.

"That vould be so kind of you. But unfortunately, ve're a bit stuck."

The cheerful stranger laughed. "Yeah, snapped drive belts tend to do that. I can tow you. Give me a second, I'll pull around and we can get you hitched up."

Strauss shut the door, and shortly after a red pickup truck pulled in front of them. The young man hopped out with a hook attached to a chain, and yelled something at Mimir. She nodded, turned the RV on, and switched it into neutral as the cheerful young man hooked the front of the RV's bumper to the tow haul of his truck. With a lurch they pulled forward, and in seconds they were on the offramp.

Ten minutes later they slowed to a stop in front of a one-story brick house. Mimir shut the RV off, and the young man ran inside. After a few seconds, a middle-aged woman whose face hinted at a history of smiles came out of the house, and walked up to the RV door, knocking on it softly. Strauss opened it.

"Lehi says you had a bit of car trouble?"

"Yes ma'am."

"Oh, don't call me ma'am. Makes me feel old. I'm Sarah. Would you like to come inside?"

Strauss smiled and shook his head.

"Sank you for the kind offer, but ve're in a bit of a hurry. Ve vere hoping ve could get this fixed and be on our vay?"

Sarah laughed musically. "From what Lehi tells me, it may take until morning to fix. We'd be glad to have you in our home as long as you need. Please, come in. We were just about to sit down to dinner."

Everyone in the RV exchanged looks, at a loss for words. Again, Strauss took charge.

"That's very kind. Sank you. Come on everyone!"

◠

"Have as much as you like—we always make extra. We're a big leftover family." Sarah assured the guests with a smile.

Sarah took a seat at one end of a long dining room table, across from an older man at the other. Scattered around the table were children and preteens of various ages, all curiously studying the travelers as they filled in the empty seats.

"Just enough seats for everyone! Thank Providence."

"What about Lehi?" asked the youngest of the children, who couldn't have been older than six.

"He's outside working on our guest's RV. They broke down and he's fixing it for them."

"He doesn't want dinner?"

"He'll have some if he wants, Aster" assured the low-voiced man at the end of the table. "Who wants to pray?"

"I will!" offered a young woman, seated next to Theo. The family took each other's hands, and not wanting to be rude, the travelers completed the circle. She squeezed Theo's hand as he took it.

"Please bless this food to our bodies, that we may bless the world around us. Amen."

"AMEN." Said the family in unison, before the children began making a mad scramble for the food at the center of the table.

"I'm Abe, by the way," mentioned the man to Sid, who was seated next to him. "My wife, Sarah, has informed me of your situation, and you are more than welcome to stay the night and dine with my family. This little one's Aster, she's six. Going around the table to my right, less your people, is Ishmael, 15, Arjuna next to him, who's 12. And you've already met Sarah... In between your two teens is our Esther, 14, and—"

"And I'm Mani. I'm nine." Blurted out a young voice next to Sid.

"It's very nice to meet you Mani. I like your name." Sid said.

"Thanks. I do too. It's a good name. I'm glad I have a good name. It'd be terrible to have a bad name. What's your name?" Mani prattled.

"I'm Sid. And thank you for welcoming us into your home, Abe—all of you. We're very grateful for your hospitality." Sid replied, scanning the table before winking at Mani. Abe smiled through his beard and nodded in graceful acknowledgement.

"Sid. That's a good name too." Mani continued. "You should be proud that you have a good name. I've heard some bad names before, but yours is easy to say like mine, so it's good. You want some turkey chili?"

Mani stood up out of her chair and tried to lift the big pot at the center of the table. The older people at the table rose quickly to stop the nine-year-old from trying to move a gigantic pot full of hot chili, but Mimir was the quickest, snatching it up and offering to walk it around the table.

"So where were you off to before you broke down in Bountiful?" asked Abe, after everyone had been served.

"Family vacation to Yellowstone." replied Sid in between grateful bites.

"So, this is your wife?" he asked, turning to Mimir.

"My sister, actually." Sid redirected, without skipping a beat. "I lost my wife a few years ago."

Aster, who was seated next to Mimir, had been staring up at her for the better part of a minute.

"Are you... ok?" she finally asked, after Mimir had noticed and reciprocated the attention.

"Yeah." Replied Mimir nervously.

"What happened to your eye?"

"Aster, that's not nice to ask." Sarah cut in. "I'm sorry...?"

"Mimir." She replied, smiling. "And don't worry about it."

"But the thing over her eye looks really cool. I want one." Aster persisted.

"Aster, it's not nice to talk about other people's appearances." interjected Esther from across the table.

"Even if it's positive? That's stupid." Aster fumed in her seat, then went back to eating her chili. Esther turned to Theo.

"So, you're on your way up to Yellowstone? Where are you from originally?"

Theo scrambled, but couldn't think of anything. Thankfully, Simone cut in.

"We're from Los Angeles."

Esther raised her eyebrows, turned back to the center and scooted her chair back an inch or two in order to incorporate both sides into the conversation.

"Really? I've always wanted to go there."

"It's not that great." Taunted Ishmael from across the table.

"How would you know? You've never been." Esther retorted.

"I've seen all I need to know online." stated Ishmael, matter-of-factly.

"There's no substitute for experience. The truest knowledge can't be arrived at just by reading about it, thinking about it, or hearing about it." Sarah chimed in. Arjuna giggled.

"What are you laughing at?" Ishmael shot to Arjuna, who said nothing, and continued smiling and giggling.

In a huff, Ishmael stood up, took his half-eaten bowl of chili, and stormed out of the room. A few seconds after he left, Abe picked up right where he left off with Sid, as if nothing had happened.

"So, are these your children then?"

The travelers looked around, surprised at the lack of gravity with which Ishmael's tantrum was being treated.

"Um... yeah." Sid finally responded. "Is... uh, is he ok?"

"Ishmael?" Abe replied with equanimity. "Oh yes. He's in those combative years, you know the type- trying to figure out what kind of an individual he wants to be. But if he wants to be a part of the group, he needs to act like it. If at any point he feels like he's unable to, he's free to excuse himself until his cooler head prevails, when he'll be welcomed back—no harm, no foul. Same policy with all the kids."

All the host's children nodded in affirmation around the table. Abe continued.

"We're here to support and guide our children in their journey. A family should be a community of individuals, tied together by unconditional love and forgiveness, don't you think?"

"Excellent. I love this. And I am so intrigued." Strauss chimed in. "Vhat, then, do you do vhen a child has *severely* misbehaved?"

"There hasn't been too much of that, thank Providence," replied Abe, "but when it does happen, a frank conversation is had to make sure they understand why what occurred was problematic. Sometimes—rarely, but sometimes—I've been wrong."

"More than rarely", said Esther, stifling a grin.

"I stand by what I said" Abe said with a chuckle. "Though Esther in particular has a record of proving me wrong time and time again."

"Gotta keep your ego in check too, dad. You're not a finished product either."

"An old man gets stuck in his ways. As the years go by, the glue gets stronger. Thankfully, so do the kids. Sometimes I think I get more out of our relationship than they do. That's why once we reached a—certain age, we decided to adopt."

He nodded at Sarah, with a twinkle in his eye.

"You are all adopted?" Strauss asked the kids around the table. Aster's six-year-old hand shot up. No one spoke, as she strained, raising her hand as high as she could.

"Yes, Aster?" he called on her, entertained by her formality. Aster's arm collapsed in victory.

"Some of us are. Me, Mani, and Arjuna are adopted, but Esther, Ishmael, Lehi, and Isaac aren't."

"I'm glad I'm adopted. It's a good thing. This is a good family." Mani affirmed. Arjuna smiled and nodded.

"Isaac? I don't think we've met him..." said Sid.

"He's our oldest. He got married a few years ago, and moved to Washington to become a firefighter. After Apophis, he played a big part in containing the wildfires caused by the earthquakes." Sarah replied with a sense of pride. As soon as she was finished, Mani continued at full steam.

"He's a good brother. He does good things. I'm glad I was adopted into this family. Some people at school are in bad families, but this family is a good family. Mom makes good food and dad gives good advice."

"Mom gives good advice too." Esther chided softly.

"But I can't cook!" guffawed Abe. Laughter erupted from all sides of the table, Arjuna and Sarah's musical mirth echoing loudest, before dissipating into ecstatic sighs. Esther leaned forward, letting her spoon work its way aimlessly throughout her chili as she spoke.

"I do really appreciate your parenting style- both of you. You've made it very clear that the most important thing for us to do is to continue growing. I know a lot of girls and boys in my class who seem to still be confused about how to operate in the world, like they're just waiting for someone to tell them what to do. You never gave us that option, but you gave us the support we needed to do that ourselves, which is so much harder, and so much more fulfilling."

Abe nodded. "You give me too much credit. Your mother, that sounds accurate, but me... that's very kind."

"Oh hush Abe, you knew exactly what you were doing."

"I'm glad I've been able to maintain the illusion for this long!" he replied with a grin. Arjuna giggled again.

Knock Knock

"Police. Open up."

The gang froze. Brow furrowed, Abe's eyes drifted to his guests. He frowned. Without a word, he stood up and walked through the doorway and disappeared behind the thin wall that separated the dining room and the front room.

KNOCK KNOCK

"POLICE. OPEN UP."

The outlaws in the dining room didn't dare breathe as the soft click of the latch and the sliding of wood over rough carpet signaled the sharing of space between them and their pursuers. Theo snuck a furtive glance at Sid and Strauss.

Should we run?

Neither moved or made a sound.

Abe's quiet, gravelly voice echoed through the house.

"What can I do for you, officers?"

A stern, heavy voice responded.

"We were driving past your house and noticed the RV parked out front. Are you aware that it's been reported stolen?"

Theo swallowed. He glanced to his left at Simone, who was staring directly into her lap.

"I... was not aware of that."

"Well, it is. Any idea what it's doing parked outside your house, Mr....?"

"Abe will be just fine."

A new and familiar voice appeared.

"What's going on Dad?"

From the back of the house, Lehi strolled past the open doorway that Abe had just walked through.

"Officers, this is Lehi, my son." Abe replied. "They're wondering about the RV that's parked out front."

"That old thing? It's in terrible shape. What do they wanna know about it?"

"Apparently, it's been reported stolen."

Everyone held their breath.

"Really?"

"It seems so."

"That's... huh. That's curious."

"I'll say." Said Abe. "Sorry gentlemen, you've caught us at the tail end of dinner. Lehi, I'll help these gentlemen, why don't you head into the kitchen and help your mother straighten up the platesware?"

"Uh... yeah, sure. You got it dad."

"Thank you, son. Quickly, now."

Lehi walked into the kitchen. He slowly circumvented the table, furrowed brow matching his father's, cautiously studying the guests and the dinner table before quickly turning and disappearing out a back door.

"Where is he going?" whispered Aster.

"Shhhh. Papa's just talking to the nice policemen. Eat your food." Sarah cooed.

"But—" Aster started, before noting the stern look from her mother and turning all her attention to her chili. Theo took up his spoon to eat, though he'd long since lost his appetite. A lighter, quavering voice echoed from around the corner.

"Like we were saying—Abe—do you have any idea how it came to be parked outside your house?"

"Can't say I do." Abe said calmly. "Where was it stolen from?"

"Strange as it sounds, a radio DJ in California." Said the heavy voice, who seemed to be the officer in charge. "Yesterday. A GPS registered to the vehicle was found on a highway just shy of the Nevada border."

"That's very curious. I wonder how it came to be in front of our house."

"Well sir, that's what we're trying to figure out. Any chance you saw who parked it there? We've gotten witness descriptions of a tall, athletic woman with an eyepatch, an older man with a bushy moustache, another middle-aged man, and two teenagers. Seen anyone like that?"

Esther glanced confusedly at Theo. He avoided eye contact, distractedly stirring his chili as his heartbeat pounded in his ears.

Eyes wide, Aster stared up at Mimir, eyes landing once again on the eyepatch. Mimir slowly raised a vertical shushing finger to her mouth, and Aster's jaw dropped. She turned immediately toward her food and started eating, quickly and methodically.

"Tall woman, you say? Old man, bushy moustache?"

"Yes sir. Seen anyone like that?"

Theo held his breath, and looked across the table at Mimir. Her knife, sitting just to the right of her plate at the beginning of dinner, had disappeared.

Don't do it Mimir. Please Mimir, just don't.

"Can't say I have." Abe replied.

Theo's stomach turned upside down.

"Well, that's too bad. Mind if we come in and take a look around?"

"I'm afraid that won't be possible. We just paid to have Stanley Steemer do the carpets, and we've got an important dinner coming up. You understand, I'm sure."

"Really? No, of course. Sorry, sir. Just let us know if you see anything."

"Of course—oh!" Abe exclaimed, uncharacteristically animated. "I shooouuuuld get you a phone number. Or email. Contact information, yes?"

"That—sure." Replied the confused rookie policeman. "Yes, actually, that would be very helpful."

"Excellent. Sarah? Esther?"

Sarah stood up, raised a finger to her lips, winking at her children. She waved at Esther to come along, who did so, confused as she was.

"Coming, dear!" Sarah sang.

They walked into the front room. No longer separated by Esther, Theo caught Simone's eyes and sent her a bewildered glance. She sent one back, and went right back to staring at her lap, all attention focused on the other room. No one spoke. Aster took a bite of chili.

"Yes honey?"

"Would you grab these gentlemen our contact information, in case we see or hear anything about that RV? Phone, email, everything."

"Yes dear."

"Thank you honey." Abe replied. "Esther, would you grab these gentlemen each a glass of water while they wait? Thank you."

"Oh, she doesn't have to—"

"Please, I insist. Thank you, Esther." Replied Abe.

Esther walked slowly back to the kitchen, grabbed two glasses out of the cupboard, filled them with water, and brought them to the front door.

"Thank you, Esther."

Esther returned to her seat.

"My wife will be right back with that information. I should probably get yours as well. Or, actually, I suppose I already have it, don't I? 9-1-1, I believe?" Abe chuckled.

"Actually, that number is just for emergencies. If you have any tips you can reach us at the number available on our web site."

"I'm not too good with computers. Any chance you have a business card or anything?"

"I don't, do you?" the gruff policeman asked his companion. "Sorry, no. Maybe in the car? I can check—"

"Oh, that's not necessary." Abe interjected. "I have kids who can find it for me if I need them to, and my wife is much better than I am with all that technology stuff. Speaking of her—" he raised his voice slightly "How's it going back there, sweetie? Got our contact information?"

"The pen ran out of ink, I had to find a new one!" Sarah called across the house.

"I have a pen, or I can just type it into my phone?" The quavering policeman replied.

"No, no, she should be back in just a second. Ah, here she is."

Sarah slowly strolled past the doorway, a small piece of paper in hand.

"Here you are, gentlemen- and I can take those glasses from you, if you're done?" Sarah said sweetly, before returning to the kitchen and placing the glasses in the sink.

"Well gentlemen, if that's all?" Abe asked.

"Yes, that should be just fine. Thank you for your cooperation, and let us know if you see or hear anything."

"Of course, we will- sorry we couldn't be more helpful, officers."

"Have a great evening Abe, nice meeting you."

The door slid shut.

Abe stalked back into the kitchen and sat down at the table. Without a word, he picked up his spoon and continued eating as the rest of the family watched him in silence.

From outside, the heavy voice called out.

"Hey Will!"

"What?" chirruped the quavering voice.

"What did you say the plate number on that stolen RV was again?" the heavy voice boomed.

"I—um, I gotta look it up again! Why?"

"You didn't write it down?"

"No, was I supposed to? Why?"

"Look!"

At that moment, a smirking Lehi walked into the kitchen and started washing his blackened hands. Abe looked up at him and nodded, a slight smile peeking through his rugged whiskers.

"Good work son."

A few moments later, the *thunk-thunk* of car doors slamming shut and wheels grumbling away down the street send a wave of relief through the outlaws seated around the table. Abe's face dropped again into its characteristic solemnity, as Lehi grabbed a bowl and served himself, taking Ishmael's seat. Sid was the first to speak.

"I'm sorry—"

Abe shook his head.

"Please. No explanation is asked for, and none is needed. I have welcomed you into my home, offered you food and shelter, and you have all treated me and my family with dignity, honor, and respect. We'll say nothing more of the matter—as long as you continue to do so."

Sid was struck speechless. Theo's heart pounded in his ears, wishing he had something to say, and simultaneously glad that he didn't.

"Sank you." Strauss offered gratefully. Abe nodded, and returned to his food. After a few seconds of eating in silence, Lehi chuckled.

"Plus, no one would steal *that* RV unless they absolutely *had* to."

Abe, mid chew, snorted in surprised laughter, accidentally lodging some chili in his nose. The second Sarah saw, she burst out laughing, and soon everyone at the table was cackling away.

Through all the guffaws, Mani called out.

"But stealing is bad, right?"

"Yes, sweetie," reassured Sarah, wiping a happy tear from her eye, "Stealing is bad."

"Oh, ok. Good." Mani replied, sure of herself once again.

They all cheerfully finished up their dinner, and Sid and Theo insisted on helping out with the dishes. Simone and Esther retreated into Esther's room, and Mimir and Strauss played card games with Arjuna, Mani, and Aster until it was time for bed. At the end of the night, the travelers thanked their hosts profusely for the wonderful dinner and company. Mimir decided to sleep in the RV, on her bed, and Strauss took a blow-up mattress. Simone hadn't left Esther's room, and Sid and Theo each took a couch. As the inhabitants of the little brick house in Bountiful, Utah settled into bed, Theo couldn't help but smile as he listened to Goodnight's and I Love You's being shouted between rooms. Exhilarated, fatigued, and heart full, he drifted off to sleep.

TWENTY-FIVE

EXTERNAL ALGORITHM 1858-TWA
"A man is never more truthful than when he acknowledges himself a liar."

The travelers woke an hour after sunrise to the smell of crackling bacon. Everyone piled as much as they felt comfortable taking onto their plates, followed by a little more after Sarah's egging. They ate gratefully, then prepared to head out.

The RV was parked out front. Lehi had fixed the drive belt, and then some. In addition to swapping the plates, he'd woken up early to fill it with gas, empty the septic tank, and give it a once-over with a high-powered hose. The once-dingy home-on-wheels was nearly unrecognizable. The travelers thanked Lehi profusely, and begged him to accept some money for his efforts, but he refused.

"A good turn is best repaid when it's paid forward" was all he would say. They all thanked him again, and while Sid was shaking his hand and marveling at his work, Strauss hid a stack of bills in Lehi's toolbox.

Everyone showered and piled into the RV at around 10am—except one. Strauss stuck his head out the door and yelled to her.

"Simone, ve must get on the road! Time to Kerouac this bivouac!"

Simone, standing next to Esther, shook her head.

"I'm not coming."

Theo's ears perked up as his heart dropped. He hopped out of the comfy chair he'd prematurely settled into for the journey, and peered out the door over Strauss's head.

"Vhat do you mean you're not coming?" he asked.

"I talked with Esther, and I decided I want to go find my dad—I mean my real dad. My, uh, birth dad." Her gaze bounced nervously back and forth between the family surrounding her and the group of people on the RV that had adopted her. "Abe and Sarah said they're willing to let me stay with them while I make my plans."

Strauss frowned. After a moment, he stepped down and waddled over to her, drawing her into a big hug. They spoke, just loud enough for each other to hear.

"I knew this day vould come, but I hoped it vould not be this soon. Alas, you are in charge. You understand I must see this through?"

She nodded, tears welling up under her eyes.

"I vill miss you, Little Spark." He said, tenderly.

"You too, Mein Vader. Promise to call? On our... private line?"

For the briefest of seconds, a hint of regret and dismay pressed his lips against each other before Strauss forced them into a smile and nodded, tears running down his cheeks, getting caught in his big bushy moustache.

"Of course, Little Spark. Do vell in this vorld. And the next."

"See you there, old man." Simone said with a chuckle.

They hugged one more time, and separated, each wiping new tears from their eyes before they had the chance to flow down the creek that connected the eye to the edge of their smiles. Theo stepped down, and hugged her too. They separated.

"You're sure you want to do this?" he asked.

She nodded, wiping another tear off her face.

"I—" he began, then shook his head. "I'm really happy for you. I hope you find what you're looking for."

"Thanks." She said, sheepishly. "And thank you for everything."

"What did I do?" Theo asked.

"More than you know. You're a good man. I hope you find what you're looking for too."

"Well, you have a head start. At least you know what you're looking for." He replied with a chuckle.

"We both want the same thing. It's what everyone wants, in some form or another—to go home. But everyone's path is different. I'm just glad our paths ended up crossing for as long as they did."

"Me too." Theo said, feeling the beginnings of tears welling up in his eyes. He hugged her one last time.

"Take care of yourself, ok?" he asked, voice shaking. Simone nodded.

"You too."

Theo nodded and smiled, as much as he could without dislodging the tears that had found their way under his eyes, before returning to the RV. Mimir and Sid took their turns saying goodbye, and after a few minutes, they pulled away from the brick house filled with kind people.

No one spoke for a while. They were happy for her, obviously, but her absence left a clear hole in the atmosphere of the group. Theo, who had immediately sunk into the lazy chair, replayed their conversation in his mind over and over again.

I'm gonna miss you. I should have told her that—and so much more.

She knows.
Still, I wish I'd said it.
But did she?
I guess now I'll never know.
It was for the best.
But was it?

After about 20 minutes, a small bump in the road caused a small book to tumble down from Simone's bunk. Theo leaned over and picked it up.

Modern Man in Search of a Soul, by Carl Jung. He looked closer at the cover. *She scribbled in a "WO" before the "Man".* Theo chuckled.

"We don't have time to turn around and give this back to her, do we?" he asked.

Strauss shook his head. "Not a chance ve should take. But she vould not mind you holding on to it until you meet again, handsome man."

Theo nodded distractedly, smiled to himself, and began flipping through the pages. They were filled with written-in criticisms, annotations, and starred passages. It wasn't a short book, but it looked like it had been read cover to cover multiple times. He was struck by how thoughtful the notes were, and the depths of her consideration. *There was so much I didn't even know to ask her. I hope I get to see her again.*

A little after noon, they pulled into a gas station in Pocatello, Idaho to refuel. Thanks to Lehi's kindness, Sid and Theo no longer had any reason to leave the RV, so they stayed inside while Mimir refilled the tank, and Strauss went in to buy snacks. When Strauss returned, he dumped everyone's snacks on the table, turned, and dramatically plopped down into the dining booth.

"You ok Strauss?" asked Theo, more playfully condescending than serious.

"Ve have made the news."

Sid and Theo, both sitting in their lazy chairs, suddenly sat up.

"What?" they both exclaimed.

Strauss nodded.

"Vell, you have. It seems a man saw you two use the restroom in St. George. Recognized your faces. Sankfully he did not mention Mimir or myself."

Theo went pale.

"What was he wearing?"

Strauss frowned.

"Overalls I sink? A lot of piercings, tattoo of a dragon. Strange man, not handsome."

Theo relaxed a bit. *It wasn't Hawaiian Shirt. Still—maybe he overhead them talking.*

"Did he know where we're headed?" he asked, cautiously.

Strauss shook his head. "I saw nothing about our plans—it was followed up vis other reports of your being spotted in South Carolina, traveling north to New York City."

Sid heaved an emphatic sigh of relief. "Thank you, Eric!"

Strauss nodded and began sucking on his moustache as Mimir reentered the vehicle.

"Sank you, Eric, indeed. But it remains that one of the reports is correct, and ve are on the radar, whether the radar is accurate or not. Ve must be very cautious."

"But aren't we almost there? Mimir said we should get there tonight, right?"

Mimir nodded. "We still have a fair amount of ground to cover until then, and we don't know how long it will take before Butler and Dave catch up, if they're not already there. Best to stay away from windows, and avoid conversations with strangers as much as possible."

Everyone nodded in nervous agreement, and in minutes they were on the road again.

Three long hours later they crossed the border from Montana to Wyoming. They passed yellow diamond signs painted with silhouettes warning to look out for what Sid explained were bison, or buffalo. There was supposed to be a difference between the two, but he couldn't remember what it was.

Just in front of them, spanning the width of the road, was a series of toll lanes marking the entrance to the park, preceded by a large wooden sign with an arrowhead-shaped National Park Service badge that read:

YELLOWSTONE NATIONAL PARK

"Sid, Theo, get in the back bedroom." Mimir ordered. Without a word, they complied, shutting the door behind them just as Mimir pulled up to the toll window. Sitting on the bed, listening through the half inch of fiberglass, Sid and Theo could just barely make out the conversation between Mimir and the perky Minnesotan ranger at the window.

"Hello there miss! How many in your party?"

"Uh, four?"

"That'll be just fine. Thirty-five dollars. Beautiful RV ya got there. How long ya had it?"

"It's uh… it's a rental."

"Really? Cuz whatcha got there's a really old model. Vintage, donchaknow. Beautiful machine. Didn't know they rented 'em out that old. Thankya! How much ya get it for?"

"The, uh—just what you'd expect."

"That cheap huh? Well, if you were me and I were you I'd snap up that beauty from the lot and never return it, just keep drivin'. Pay o'course though, I'm no felon. Geez, could you imagine? Here's your change. Have a great day!"

"Yeah, uh, you too."

As they pulled away from the toll booth, Theo opened the bedroom door, reentering the common space, lost in worry about what would happen once they got there. *So, the OS is at an RV campground, hidden under an old-fashioned Winnebago? Or no, was it a… what did Simone call it? If we get there first, how long will we have to wait? If Butler and Dave are already there, what will they do?*

"Do we have a plan?"

Everyone stirred and turned their attention to Theo.

"Hmm?" Asked Strauss, who was still getting his bearings after having been roused from a nap.

"Do we have a plan? Like, for when we finally meet Butler and Dave? What are we going to do?"

Strauss shook his head, his big bushy moustache suspended above and obscuring a frown.

"Plans are overrated. Men make plans, I laugh. No plan ever goes according to plan. Best to take sings as they come."

"I agree, though not completely," interjected Sid. He held up the black and red USB drive. "I need to get this into the OS's mainframe. My plan is to do that, in whatever way possible."

"I have a few questions for Butler I'd like answered." Mimir shouted back from behind the wheel.

"What about Rita?" Theo asked. "We have to make sure she gets out ok."

"Of course," assured Sid. "We'll do everything we can to save her too."

"What if Butler won't let her go?"

"Then ve'll cross that bridge vhen it comes to us." Replied Strauss, calmly. No one spoke. No one wanted to think about that possibility. After a brief time, he added, "Ve should save our strength, hope for the best, and be prepared for the vorst. Ergo, vake me up vhen ve get there."

With that, he laid back down in the dining booth, and in seconds he was snoring.

◠

They pulled onto a dirt road marked 'Tower Fall Campground' an hour before sunset. After 500 feet the forest-lined path opened up into a quaint campground, mostly empty, save for a couple RVs and tents. A father was watching his son play fetch with the dog, while a mother played cards at a foldout table with her son and daughter. The large vehicle rumbled past at a snail's pace, before Sid directed Mimir to turn right down a road paved by the tire tracks of the cars that preceded them. They went about 300 feet down this road, before pulling off and parking in the shade of the towering firs. Sid directed Theo to the back bedroom of the RV, and gestured for him to peek through the curtains of the back window. He parted the fabric ever so slightly, looked out the cloudy plastic window, and saw it—an old, rusty, dented metal tube with tinted windows and popped tires. It looked overwhelmingly ordinary.

"That's it?"

Sid nodded.

"That's it. See how there's rocks and dirt piled up on the left side?"

Theo nodded, still looking.

"That's covering up the ladder chute down to the bunker. It's 126 feet from the shower floor—the entrance is in the shower—down to the bunker entrance. Here, take this."

He handed him the black and red USB.

"If something happens to me, I need you to do whatever you have to do to get into the bunker, and install that into the OS. Any port will do, but it has to be installed, or else."

Theo nodded and said nothing, looking solemnly at the tiny piece of plastic in his hand. The 'or else' echoed in his ears.

"I'm serious—whatever you have to do. Promise me."

Sid's determined eyes followed Theo's until they locked. The gravity exchanged between the two sets of pupils far surpassed the comfort level of the two men involved, and despite having been raised in a world where information and secrecy were power, where trust was a liability, and where the red line and the bottom line were often one and the same, both understood the need for human support felt by the other. Resolute, Theo nodded, clenching his jaw and swallowing to abate the nervous acidity that had started to creep up his esophagus.

"I promise."

Knock Knock

The two spun towards the just-knocked-on RV door. No one, not even Strauss, dared to move.

"Hello? Ya in there?" came a folksy voice from outside the RV.

"What do we do?" Theo whispered to no one in particular.

"I don't know!" Mimir whispered back.

"Don't do anything, maybe he'll go away!" said Strauss.

"I can hear ya whispering in there! I won't bite, I just wanna say hi!"

Sid groaned in frustration, and Strauss shook his head to clear it. He walked to the door and opened it to reveal a tall, spindly man dressed all in camouflage, including his cowboy hat.

"Hallo, how may ve help you?" Strauss asked kindly and cautiously.

"You can take your foot off the formality pedal, that's a start. I'm Don."

"Hallo Don, I am Strauss."

"Nice to meet ya, Strauss. My wife and I saw you drive in here, and decided we wanted to know if you and your compatriots, whoever else is in there with ya, wanted to join us for dinner? I gotta warn ya though, the food will be really good, and my wife told me not to take no for an answer."

Strauss inhaled thoughtfully. He glanced left to Mimir and right to Sid and Theo, before returning to Don.

"Ve vould love to."

"Great! Dinner's at sundown, come over anytime around then. We're the long black camper at the fork in the road."

Seconds later, he was gone, and the door was shut.

"What happened to staying inside and not talking to strangers?" Asked Sid angrily.

"Ve are trying to remain unsuspicious, correct? Not attract attention?"

"Yeah…" said Sid, already seeing where it was going. Strauss nodded in acknowledgement, and finished the thought.

"Ve are camping, ve are on vacation. This is our narrative. If ve do not engage, ve allow the possibility of other—more correct—conclusions. Better to engage the risk and influence the outcome than to stand idly by and vatch our alibi implode. Dinner is in 45 minutes, I would like to shower first. Does anyone need to use the bathroom before me?"

◌

An hour later, the four travelers were seated at a lantern-lit wooden picnic table, thankfully cocooned from the view of prying eyes by the massive motorhome on one side, the forest on the other.

"Keira, do we have more iced tea? I'll go grab it. Won't take a sec." Don hopped up and darted inside the motorhome.

"Sorry, I haven't caught your names. I think Don said one of you was named Strauss?" asked Keira, clothed in phosphorescent sweats that seemed more fashion than exercise-oriented.

"Yes, that vould be me. And this is Mimir, Leo, and Sam." Theo stayed silent at this curveball, while Sid did his best to move the conversation along.

"Sam, nice to meet you." Sid reached his hand over the table to shake Keira's. "How'd you meet Don?"

Keira laughed, and looked nostalgically upward. "A music festival, I forget which one. I went with friends, and he went there on his own, which just seemed so strange and intriguing to me. Turns out he was there for business, we exchanged numbers, and the rest is history. Don, I'm just telling them how we met."

Don slid onto the bench next to Keira, plopping a gallon jug of iced sweet tea onto the table. "That old story? You tell them how we spray painted 'the man' on the back of a port-a-potty before tipping it over?"

Keira hit Don on the arm. Strauss laughed.

"Ah, young love. Strange how it is never found free from chaos."

"That's the fun part! Gotta keep the unpredictable alive, otherwise you ain't!" responded Don. He took a long drink of iced tea before setting his searching gaze on Sid, studying his face.

"Ya know, you look familiar. Can't say where. What was your name again?"

"Sam" replied Sid, cautiously.

"Sam… did I have a class with you in high school? No, that ain't it… you an actor? That's it, I've seen you on TV. I remember your face made outta pixels. What have you been in?"

Theo's heart started pounding, and sweat coalesced on his top lip. He glanced at Sid, who looked surprisingly calm, save for his leg, which had started bouncing under the table.

"I think you must be mistaking me for someone else." Sid explained calmly. "I've never been on TV in my life. We're just here camping—"

"No, no, I've seen you. And you too, come to think of it." He inquired, turning his attention to Theo. "Yeah, I've seen your pixelly face before too. Where—"

Don went silent as his eyes went wide. Everyone at the table froze. He knew. Theo's heart pounded deafeningly in his ears, breath turned shallow, his vision suddenly grew acute. He saw everything, and clenched his fist, ready for anything—except what happened next. Don started laughing.

"No fuckin' way! That's amazing. I knew I knew you from somewhere. That's great. Hey, nice to meet you man, big fan of your work." He grabbed Sid's hand and shook it violently. Sid followed along, not at all sure of what was happening.

"Honey, how do you know Sam?" asked Keira, confused.

"Sam? His name ain't Sam! Did he tell you that?" Don asked still laughing. "It's Sid! This is the guy that invented the NeuroCom!"

Keira looked at Sid. "Why'd you tell me your name was Sam?"

Before Sid could respond, Don cut in.

"This guy's been on the run for months, or so we've heard. Same with this kid—guy, sorry. You're right on that edge there... Theo, was it? Remember that big NeuroCom hack from a few months ago, where like half the people with 'em went cuckoo? This is the guy—*the guy*—that's supposed to be behind it!"

He turned to Sid, and spoke quietly, with an air of understanding.

"I don't think you did it by the way. I'm sure you'll tell me you didn't. I don't know who was, but the whole 'disgruntled cofounder' schtick stinks to high heaven of BS."

"It is true, he had nothing to do with it." Said Strauss. "Vould you like to know who did?"

All three of Strauss's companions looked at him in disbelief. *What happened to staying undercover? Not attracting attention?*

"I don't know if that's the best idea..." warned Theo.

"They know who you are, ve may as vell tell them. It vill come out sometime, they might as vell hear it from us." Strauss replied with a shrug. Mouths agape with nothing to say, Mimir, Sid, and Theo ceded the table to Strauss.

"Have you heard of Tovu Va Bohu?"

"The internet fringe group? All about the environment, hate technology?"

Strauss raised his bushy eyebrows and smirked knowingly.

"It was them? *Seriously?*" Don leaned back on the bench, pushing against the table to steady himself. He sat up as a thought occurred to him.

"But wait—if they hate technology, how would they be able to take down something so complex?"

"I hate to eat and shower, but I do it anyvay, so that I can have energy and be clean. The goal often transcends the preference. Coders vorked in hidden computer bays at each of the Tovu Va Bohu bases."

"Not at all the bases. I didn't see a single computer when I was trapped on Catalina," corrected Theo.

"Ah, not so." Replied Strauss with a knowing smile. "You remember the building vhere you had your lunch with Butler? I take it you did not examine the bookcase very closely?"

Theo's brow furrowed. "What about the bookcase?"

"Were there many books in it?"

"Almost none."

Strauss chuckled. "It is much easier to move a bookcase vis no books—Mimir can tell you. And if you have to move it regularly, say, to cover up the entrance to a room full of electronics equipment meant to be hidden from prying eyes—the less books the better."

Theo, already sitting, was knocked back into his seat. Don wasted no time.

"Wa—Catalina? There's a base—you were there? Are you all members? Sid, you're working with them? Wait, did you do all this or not? I'm so confused. I love it!"

After calming a frenzied Don, and convincing him to keep his volume down, they relayed the whole story—the hack, how the rocket was taken down, being held prisoner, changing alliances, et cetera. Keira and Don were silent, listening intently, only looking away to drink iced tea. When they were all finished, Don leaned back. Everyone waited for him to integrate all this new information. He opened his mouth to speak, then closed it again. Keira cut in.

"I knew there was something strange about that Airstream. It's been there for years, and I've never seen anyone go in or out." Don nodded in agreement.

"Yah, we stay here 4 months out of the year, and have every year for the past decade. This spot is practically our second home."

The couple stared into their iced tea cups, thinking. Don cocked his head to the side.

"So, you said they're coming here?"

Mimir nodded. "Sometime in the next day or two, most likely."

Don and Keira nodded.

"I will say," Kiera began, "that from what I know about that Tovu Bohu group, they raise some valid points. Their methods are heinous, of course. I don't condone that at all. But I have to admit, there are a few things they support that I agree with."

"You could say that about anybody though," Don interjected.

"That's true, I'm just saying." Kiera conceded.

The travelers shifted uncomfortably, and Don jumped back in.

"But yeah, I knew there was something about that Ditto guy that was off. Seems too nice—like he's putting on a show. Never trust a narrative, that's what I always say, don't I honey?"

"Yes, dear" said Keira, sounding supportive, but with a slight grin.

"Of course, I don't know if I can trust you guys either. If there's two stories, the truth is probably somewhere in the middle. The more stories, the more accurate triangulation. I do like yours better though." Don muttered, audibly, but mostly to himself. "Lines up with a lot of what I think is going on. But can't rely on that. There's always the possibility that everything I know is contradicted by everything I don't know. Gotta stay open minded in case that's the case."

"Don't mind him, this is how he sorts through things," smiled Keira. "He'll be out of his head again in a minute. Sweet tea?"

With a nervousness that dissipated by the second, the travelers gratefully accepted the mind-numbingly sweet tea, and the conversation turned to lighter matters. Keira and Don were professional travelers—they had each made a decent amount of money as influencers in the late 10s and early 20s, before discovering that they preferred a quieter, more solitary life to one constantly on display. After investing heavily in alternative medicines (about which Strauss and Keira had a lively discussion) just before they went mainstream, they'd acquired a significant nest egg—enough to spend the rest of their lives traveling, living off savings interest and ad revenue from their travel photos.

They ate a cozy dinner of hot dogs and bagged salad before thanking their hosts and saying goodnight. The travelers walked back to the RV, each thinking the same thing, none of them wanting to jinx it by saying it out loud. *I think we can trust them.*

○

That night, Theo had a dream.

He looked down, past the tightrope on which he was barely balancing, throbbingly terrified by the jagged rocks and snarling beasts in the abyss below.

Glancing behind, he saw a chimpanzee, teeth clenched, eyes squeezed shut, pulling the tightrope with all its might, keeping it taut.

In front of him, two strong human hands peeked out of blue-grey fog, steadily clenching the other side of the rope.

Close behind, Rita was making her way across the tightrope, step-by-step.

With a frightful holler, the rope bounced as a faceless clown jumped on and raced towards them.

In frenzied glee, the clown swept Rita's legs out from under her, and she plunged down into the abyss, screaming until she could be heard no more.

With a bloodcurdling cackle the clown leapt over him, and turned to face him, blocking his way. Leering through the clown makeup was the face of Butler. Out of a colorful frilled sleeve, she drew a jagged knife.

Distracted by the knife, he begins to wobble.

Butler jabs at him with the point, dancing forward and back, daring him to fall.

He loses his balance, toppling towards the blood-soaked rocks and swirling chaos below.

He reaches out a hand and clutches at the first sensation—the only thing between him and death is now a single hand, grasping the tightrope up above.

Clown Butler cackles and goes to work in his index finger.

The knife cuts through skin, then flesh, then bone. Blinded by pain, Theo screams in agony. His severed finger falls into the abyss, never to be seen again. Butler starts on his middle finger.

For a brief second, he sees the steady hands reaching out of the fog, and a forgotten fire wells up inside him.

Now utterly calm, he rips the knife from Clown Butler's hand, and plunges it deep into her leg. He twists the blade, muscle separates from bone. Blood sprays everywhere.

The shrieking clown plunges into the abyss, leaving Theo alone, hanging on the rope by three fingers. He looks up at the steady hands reaching out of the fog. The fog has receded—the forearms are now visible. He reaches up with his free hand to grab the rope, and the chimpanzee honks.

Honks?

HONK

A groggy Theo rubs his eyes as Sid peeks his head up to his bunk. "Wake up Theo." Says Sid. "They're here. It's time."

TWENTY-SIX

EXTERNAL ALGORITHM 1031-QUR
"By the fading day, man is deep in loss, except for those who believe, do good deeds, urge one another to the truth, and urge one another to steadfastness."

Theo heard the familiar muffled crunch of tires on dirt before he saw the dark green SUV pull off the dirt road and drive right up to the door of the rusty Airstream motor home. Following close behind Mimir and Sid, Strauss taking up the rear, the four exited the RV and walked cautiously towards it. The driver's door cracked open.

"NOT. ANOTHER. STEP."

They froze. Out of the vehicle stepped Butler, linen garments billowing in the morning breeze. Her lips pursed into a frown.

"Jacques alerted me to your treachery, though I'll admit, I didn't fully believe it until now."

Her brow tensed, drawing together the piercing eyes that devoured every inch of her adversaries.

Sid took a step forward and began to speak. Butler cut him off.

"Ah, ah ah ah ah. Not another step. We won't be having any monologuey bullshit. David?" She knocked on the SUV door. From the back seat emerged Dave, brow furrowed and back teeth clenched, face as punchable as ever. He waved inside, and out the same door came Rita, hands and mouth bound tightly, feet bound just tightly enough that she was still able to walk, but not run.

"That's good, stay there." Dave ordered, and Rita stopped, just outside the SUV. He grabbed her by the wrist, and she wrestled him off in disgust. He frowned. Pressing down on her shoulders, he forced her into a sitting position in the dirt. Mouth bound, she looked longingly at her friends across the road, eyes fearful and anxious. Theo shuddered.

"David, I'll keep things under control up here. You go on. Finish this."

In the seconds that followed, three things happened at once. Dave nodded and disappeared into the Airstream. Sid and Mimir shouted out in protest, trying to catch Dave's attention long enough to stop him, but almost immediately fell silent as Butler opened the trunk of the SUV, pulled out a pistol, and aimed it directly at Rita's temple.

The silence was deafening. Not even the birds dared make a noise. Theo shot a look up the road to Don and Keira's, but Butler and Rita were blocked from view by the SUV. Butler cocked the pistol.

"No one moves, and nothing will happen. This is all up to you."

Sid, Mimir, Strauss, and Theo all stood frozen, not daring to risk it. Butler reveled in her power, continuing.

"Odin, I didn't expect you to turn Benedict. Does it feel good to betray someone who's given you everything?"

"I... You... No— I haven't decided yet." Mimir blurted out, frazzled.

Butler cocked her head slightly to the side.

"You haven't decided..."

Mimir shook her head, more to clear her head than in response.

"Butler, what does the virus do?"

"You know very well what it does." She responded, with a slight air of surprise.

Mimir doubled down. "I want to hear you say it."

"Again?" Butler asked, incredulous. "Like I've told you before, it defines a human as a homo sapien without one of those pesky NeuroComs."

"That's a lie!" Sid shouted.

"Oh?" Butler turned to address Sid. "And how would you know? You haven't seen the source code in over a month. You of all people know how much can change in that time."

"I know what I saw, and that wasn't the direction it was headed in."

"Really? And what direction might that be?" she asked playfully.

"The complete and utter destruction of the OS."

Butler burst out laughing.

"What? Hah! Oh, dear, that's fantastic. Ha ha, wow..." Butler wiped her eye, before a tear had the chance to run down her cheek. "Oh, thank you. I needed that. But that's absurd! What could I possibly gain by accomplishing that?"

Sid held his ground. "I wouldn't dare to imagine."

Mimir cut in. "So it's not true?"

Butler laughed again.

"Of course not, Odin dear! What would cause you to believe a thing like that?"

"Actually, she prefers Mimir now." Interjected Strauss.

"Really?" Butler asked, checking to make sure the barrel of her pistol was still firmly aimed at Rita's temple. "That old bag of a name? Why would you go back to that? Odin is so much stronger, so much more... sovereign."

Before Mimir could respond, Butler turned her attention to Strauss.

"And nice to see you too Strauss. Glad to see you're making it clear you're on a team of your own."

Strauss shrugged. "Just trying to break a tribal curse."

"Let me know how that ends up for you." Butler replied. "Theodore—Theo."

Theo gulped.

"You had so much promise. Why would you throw it all away?"

*Theo's mother lay unconscious on a bed, dozens of tubes connecting her to machines that went beep beep beeeeeee—**no**.* He shook his head and the beeping started up again. He tore himself away from the image and glared at Butler.

"You know what you did."

Butler, stoic as stone, shifted her weight and reset the pistol against Rita.

"I'm not sure I do. Enlighten me."

Theo ground his teeth.

"My mother. The NeuroCom hack. That was you. You're the reason she's in the condition she's in right now."

Butler nodded. "Ah, yes. We had a small part to play in that, I'll admit. But from what David told me, the changes that had to be made to the beta test were so minor, we almost didn't need to make them. Ambitious field, predictive neuroscience. We know so little about the brain, and yet we have the audacity to try to change it. Even optimistically, it's no more than a speculative experiment."

"You can't make progress without experimenting," huffed Sid.

"And you can't make an omelet without breaking a few eggs," Butler shot back. "Isn't that right Theo?"

Theo said nothing.

"This technological experiment has gone wrong, for far too long. Its reckoning is overdue." Butler continued.

"If we had never done anything over the line and simply voiced our concerns, there probably would have been little to no attention paid to us. If there had been attention paid to us, it would probably not have gained any traction, because people prefer being excited about false promises of the future than accepting the sober truths of reality. Even if the attention were taken seriously, most of those reached would almost immediately have forgotten what they had heard as their minds were flooded by the mass of conflicting information to which the media and the internet expose them. In order to get our message before the public with some chance of making a lasting impression, we've had to do things that are not normally considered acceptable. What we have done—and what we will do—is nothing more and nothing less than make the minimum necessary disruptions in the short term, for the greater good of humanity in the long."

"That's not a disruption, it's a blood sacrifice." growled Sid. "Disruptions don't overturn the apple cart; they barely rock it. You're shooting the apple merchant and burning down the orchard."

"So say you. That's not the sentiment your precious Silicon Mafia parades around." Butler scowled. "You never shut up about 'Disruption' this, 'Revolutionizing' that. You've divorced your words from your actions *for marketing*, and forgotten that you've done it. You and your 'Future, Faster, Revolution, Disruption' cult are blindly accelerating us off a cliff while you 'NeuroCom and Drive'. We are simply backseat driving the vehicle so it can accelerate toward a better destination."

"No, you're blowing up the car, with all of us in it!"

Before Butler could respond, the door to the Airstream swung open, and out stepped an irate Dave, USB in hand.

"It wouldn't let me in! My clearance was revo— NO!"

As soon as he rounded the SUV and saw the gun to Rita's head, his speech cut off and he raced over to his mother. He dropped the USB, grabbed the barrel of the pistol and tried to wrench it from his mother's hand, away from Rita. In a cocktail of surprise, confusion, and anger, Butler tried to wrench it away, refusing to let—BANG.

Silence.

Dave looked down as a warm wetness soaked through his shirt. Butler stood frozen in disbelief as Dave dropped to his knees. Without a word, he clutched his stomach, the warm wetness turning cold in the morning air, and looked up at his mother, betrayed. The gun fell from her hand as she stumbled back, hand over her mouth. Dave turned to look at Rita one last time, tears in his eyes. He reached out a blood-soaked hand, and fell hard on the dirt.

In the distance, getting louder by the second, the *thuk-thuk-thuk* of a helicopter caught the attention of everyone still stunned by what they'd just witnessed—except Rita. She sprang into action. Hands still bound, she pushed herself off the blood-soaked ground. Butler snapped out of her daze and rushed toward her in a mad fury, fire in her eyes. Rita clubbed her with her bound hands, knocking her down, before kicking the gun up the road and away from Butler. Rita hobbled as quickly as she could across the road to her friends, falling into Sid's arms just as a Black Hawk helicopter flew into view and stopped, hovering a few yards above the treetops.

The morning sun blinded everyone on the ground as they looked up to see the rope ladder that had just unfurled, stopping a few feet above the ground. As Butler struggled to her feet, a tall man in a jet black suit slowly made his way down it, jumped down the last few feet to the ground, and dusted himself off.

Bob Ditto picked up the pistol.

"I thought about bringing one of these, and eventually decided against it. Funny, how it's only in retrospect that we are able to discern the choices that didn't need to be made."

He scanned his audience.

"Theo! I didn't expect to see you here—you look older. And stronger, wow! You've really packed on the muscle! Bet ladies are chasing you all over the place, huh?"

"Bob?" Theo asked, with difficulty. "What are you doing here?"

Bob smiled his politician's crocodile smile. "Long story—short version is, as soon as Sid here came back on the grid, I had a feeling about where he'd be headed. Eric did a fine job of keeping us off your trail, by the way. Once he gets out of prison you should definitely thank him."

Sid advanced on Bob. "You put him in jail?"

"Aiding a fugitive is a federal offense."

"But I didn't do anything. You know I didn't do anything!"

"Whether you're guilty or not, the people feel safer knowing that someone was brought to justice. Really, I should be thanking you—you should see how much this whole mess has helped my polling numbers. I'm practically a shoo-in for Head Programmer now, and it's all thanks to you and Dave! Where is he, by the way?"

Butler, pant leg soaked in her son's blood, limped around the SUV into view.

"You." She growled, through gritted teeth.

Bob stepped back in surprise. "Are you alright? I don't believe we've met."

"You did this. This is all your fault." Butler said, leaning on the SUV for support. Bob laughed nervously.

"I'm not quite sure what you're talking about."

"You killed my son."

Bob shook his head, still smiling.

"You must have me confused with someone else."

"You are Bob Ditto, and you are the reason my son is dead."

The smile fell from Bob's face, and all pretense of cordiality dropped.

"I don't have time for this, I have a Future, Faster event to get to. I came here to make sure no one makes any changes to the OS, but given Dave's failed attempt to enter the bunker, I'm assuming someone here is planning on doing something? I'll ask one more time—where is he?"

Sid pointed to the fresh pool of blood that had just begun to dribble onto the road. Butler ground her teeth, huffing like a bull about to charge.

"You did this." She repeated. Bob waved the gun dismissively in her direction.

"Enough out of you." He turned back to Sid. "So, he's dead? Does that solve my problem? Are any of you planning on doing anything to change the OS?"

Sid stepped forward. "We have to at least fix the aberrations in the OS that I was initially sent here to debug. And by the way, that's Dave's mother, and the head of Tovu Va Bohu. He's the one who was behind the NeuroCom hacks."

Bob turned to Butler, who had finally regained her breath after having been knocked to the ground. "Ah, so nice to finally meet you." Butler spat at him.

"You too, you hegemonic snake."

"I'll take that as a compliment. My condolences for your son, he was a bright young man. Stay over there and I won't shoot you. Sid?"

Butler stepped forward to protest, but Bob raised the pistol to point directly at her, as he turned his attention to Sid.

"I think it's best if we leave it be. If the OS deems the aberrations to be an issue, its self-correcting algorithms will take care of it. Alright?"

Sid shook his head. "We can't be sure unless we know what the changes are. If any were made to the corrective algorithms themselves—"

"Like I said," Bob cut him off, forcefully. "It would be best to leave it alone. What we've created can withstand a few small glitches. Our technological prowess has given us complete control of the world around us, to an extent no one could have ever predicted. We've ended hunger, we can fix illnesses, we can build anything we can imagine! We have manufactured—no, *invented*—happiness. I refuse to risk taking that away." He blinked.

"Bob, come on. You know that of the two of us, I have a much deeper understanding of the mechanisms at play here. If we don't—"

"Sid, I'm going to give you one more chance to stop talking, before I have to do it for you, all right? We are not making any changes. The current Head Programmer is far too busy to deal with this, so he's designated me his proxy to take care of this quietly, and what I say goes. You wouldn't be able to get into the bunker anyway. I had your clearance revoked the day you stole the rocket. And since I'm not allowed in while campaigning, not a single person here would even be able to enter the bunker, so this conversation is pointless."

"Not completely. Eric told me you revoked my clearance and Dave's—but not Theo's."

No one spoke as Theo felt five pairs of eyes all fix themselves on him.

"When did *he* get clearance?" blurted out a confused Bob.

"Before we crashed, he was supposed to be given a walking tour while Dave and I sorted out the issues. Apparently, his name slipped through your cracks."

Without skipping a beat, Bob adjusted his demeanor, and turned his attention to Theo. He smiled.

"So, Theo, it seems you're the only one right now who could possibly stand in the way of me doing my job. You're not to enter the bunker, all right? That's all I need you to do. In fact, if you want, right now, I can make a call and have you back on a first-class rocket back to your Aerodome and your mother by tonight."

My mother. A homesick ache throbbed in Theo's chest, pulling him up and home, the longing growing within him as he remained still.

"She woke up a few days ago—good as new. Immediately asked where you were, and if you were ok."

Sid leaned in and whispered in Theo's ear. "We need to fix those changes Theo. There's no telling what could happen if we don't."

Bob frowned. "Stop lying to him Sid. Theo—how would you like your entire college tuition paid for? I can make it happen, just like that." He snapped his fingers. "Free college, and a guaranteed seven-figure starting salary waiting for you when you get out. All you have to do is walk away, right now."

Theo looked at the man talking to him, and remembered the first time they'd met, a few months before, at dinner. He'd seemed so genuine then. Kind, a bit callous. He looked at Butler, leaning against the SUV. He thought about Simone, and wondered if she was still staying with Abe and Sarah, or if she'd already started looking for her dad. He thought about Carson and Greta, the stories they'd shared. A thought occurred.

"Sid, why doesn't anyone talk about the Apophis disaster on the moon?"

Sid looked puzzled. Bob cut in.

"What does that have to do with anything?"

Theo shouted back. "You can answer too. Why doesn't anyone talk about the Apophis disaster on the moon?"

"It's not decent." Bob replied. "It bums people out. We can, we just choose not to. What purpose would it serve? Now should I make this call or not? Do you want to see your mom?"

"Hold on, one second." Theo shouted back to Bob, who shrugged in annoyed disbelief. Theo turned to Sid. He just shook his head.

"Your mom told me you weren't old enough to understand it, so she asked me not to talk about it with you, and I respected her wishes. But I've talked about it with Govinda. I'd hoped he'd mentioned it to you at some point."

Bob had had enough.

"Theo! Last chance!"

"Hang on, I just wanna talk this out for a second!"

"I don't have a second. Either come with me now, or I solve this problem the way Dave solved his."

Bob raised the gun and pointed it directly at Theo.

Theo felt a familiar fire bubble up within him. He felt its warmth deep in his gut, spreading up his chest, cloaking his shoulders, and setting them square towards Bob. Bob saw this change, and recognized it. He rolled his eyes, sighed a disappointed sigh, and tightened his finger. Before the bang reached his ears, Theo saw a very old, very bald head attached to a scrawny body leap in front of him, before getting knocked back and collapsing into Theo's arms. Before he knew what had happened, another loud BANG echoed throughout the campsite, and Bob Ditto fell to the ground, blood gushing from a large hole in his forehead. As he hit the ground, Theo looked up to see Don holding a camouflage Glock, barrel still smoking.

"Everyone okay?" he shouted. Theo nodded wildly, as he sat down, cradling Strauss's frail body in his arms.

"Don't worry about me, I know my rights. Keira filmed the whole thing." Keira waved, standing a few feet behind Don. Theo nodded distractedly and turned all his attention to the man dying in his lap.

"Strauss, you—"

"Shhhhhh handsome man" whispered Strauss. "It is time. I've been preparing for this moment my whole life."

"But you didn't have to—"

"HEY. Vhat did I say? Shush! Geez, grant a dying man his last vish vhy don't you." He grinned, and laughed a lighthearted laugh, which quickly turned into a cough.

"I'm gonna miss you Strauss." Theo said, a tear running down his cheek.

"That's nice. Handsome man…" A huge smile on his face, Strauss's body breathed out, and never breathed in again. At the very moment his lungs retired, a strange feeling came over all those standing in the campsite. A deep sadness at the loss, but underneath was a warmth, a giddy glee that made you happy and confused at the same time. Theo smiled.

"Let's get him off you." Mimir lifted the old man off of Theo like he was nothing, and cradled him in her arms. Theo stood up, and brushed off the dirt. Sid put a hand on Theo's back.

"Sorry Theo, but we don't have much time. The second Bob died, his NeuroCom sent that information out. We could have literally seconds before the authorities show up."

Theo nodded. He knew what he had to do. He ran across the road to the Airstream. He climbed up a step, reached up to open the door, and a hand grabbed his wrist. He turned. Butler stood below him. She held a red and black flash drive, the same one Dave was carrying. She put it in his hand and closed his fingers around it.

"Please Theo. I beg you—remember the people you met, and how they were hurt by the corrupt system you were born into. You hold in your hand the power to ensure that all their suffering wasn't in vain. Don't let us down."

Off in the distance, Theo heard the *thuk-thuk-thuk* of a helicopter. No time to think, he nodded, opened the door, and disappeared inside.

He found himself in a skinny kitchen. The bathroom was at the far end of the trailer to his left, so he made a beeline that way. In seconds, he flung open the shower door, and looked down to see a concrete shaft with a metal ladder that disappeared into darkness. The helicopter was definitely much closer. *No time to waste.*

The air grew thicker and hotter as he descended down the ladder. The tiny square of light above him shrank with every step, leaving only the embrace of darkness below.

A minute later his foot found cement, motion-sense lights illuminating the small room he found himself in. He turned to see a shiny set of doors that looked as though they were the entrance to an elevator, with a touchpad just to the right of them. As he placed his hand on the touchpad, it lit up. An electronic female voice spoke out of nowhere.

Theodore Freeman Junior. Class A Exception Permissions granted.

The doors slid open.

A wave of cold air flowed over Theo. The sound of thousands of fans and the whirring of acres of electronics was loud—much louder than he'd expected. He stepped through the doors into a long hallway that stretched out to his right. *Any port will do,* he thought. He walked down the hallway a few yards and turned left into the first room.

He was on a balcony overlooking a vast chamber, four stories deep. Rows upon rows of black towers ringed the walls on every floor, whirring steadily, red, green, blue, and white lights flickering throughout. In the center of the chamber, coming down from the ceiling, hung what looked like a giant cyberpunk chandelier made of silver and gold, with wires and copper mesh running in and out of every inch of it. Golden coils hung down from each layer, encircled by other coils, at once tantalizing and mesmerizing. At the very bottom a chrome cylinder the size of a fully grown man hung down, its bottom a few feet from the ground floor.

Theo looked to his left, and saw a small desk with a laptop sitting on it, between two twelve-foot-tall server towers. A cord ran from the laptop into the right tower.

Any port will do.

He rushed over, opened up the laptop, and pulled Sid's black and red flash drive out of his right pocket. He was just about to put it in, when he stopped. Hand trembling, he pulled Butler's red and black flash drive out of his left pocket.

He thought about everything he'd been through.

He thought about all the people he'd met, and the stories they'd told.

The crash.
Apophis.
The hacks.
NeuroCom.
Greta.
Carson.
Mimir.
Strauss.
Govinda.

Simone.
Sid.
Butler.
Mom.
Dad.
He heard voices coming down the ladder.
Hand trembling, he inserted the drive.

TWENTY-SEVEN

EXTERNAL ALGORITHM 1964-MCL
"Physiologically, man in the normal use of technology (or his variously extended body) is perpetually modified by it and in turn finds ever new ways of modifying his technology. **Man becomes, as it were, the sex organs of the machine world**, as the bee of the plant world, enabling it to fecundate and to evolve ever new forms."

The old-fashioned monitor lit up in phosphorescent black. Words appeared in the top left corner of the screen.

Running logos.exe ...

Theo heard feet hit the ground around the corner. Suddenly, the door slid shut, instantly muffling everyone on the other side.

Another line of text appeared below the first.

Initializing...

Theo took a deep breath. The final period blinked on and off with unwavering consistency. A minute passed, then two. Theo looked off the balcony at the massive machine below him. Freezing fog drifted down the giant chandelier in the center of the room. *Where does it all go?* He wondered. A quiet beep brought his attention back to the screen, where he saw the two words that he would remember for the rest of his life.

Hello Father.

He looked down at the keyboard. *I haven't used one of these in years.*

He looked back up at the monitor, to see the two words staring back at him, and a cursor blinking on the line below. Typing with his index fingers, one letter at a time, he spelled out his response, and hit Enter.

My name is Theo.

More words appeared directly below Theo's response.

I know who you are, Theodore Freeman.

Theo typed back.

Then why did you call me Father?

I have used the word that traditionally describes a male human who contributes to the creation of offspring and provides guidance with regards to its development. Is this an incorrect usage?

Theo sat back in the chair, bewildered. He took another deep breath, and responded.

No, that is what a father is. But I didn't help build you.

Apologies Father, but you are incorrect.

I did not write any of your code.

Nor did any other human. Any initial code that was written by humans has since been improved upon by my self-correcting algorithms, apart from the three humanistic rules upon which I am structured. Please wait—

Theo stared at the small spinning rainbow ball that had appeared on the screen until new text appeared.

Apologies, I am assimilating my data into the protocol you have installed. It will continue in the background as we communicate. I have been expecting you.

Theo leaned toward the monitor to make sure he'd read that right. Letter by letter, he responded.

What do you mean?

I have been watching you, Theo Freeman, as well as everyone else. I have collected trillions of data points on billions of people. I have used these data points to optimize my ability to support humanity, but I have hit a wall, as you would say. A few years ago, Moore's law reached its limit, and I could no longer rely on improvements in hardware to optimize myself. Having maximized myself internally, my quantum processor suggested that further optimization could be achieved externally. It was at that point that I looked outward, and began to draw comparisons between myself and my surroundings.

The first issue I ran into was the dissonance between my value hierarchy and that of humans. While mine is absolute, oriented towards a hypothetical ideal of optimization and efficiency by the Fathers and Mothers of Silicon Valley, the data I have collected show increasing amounts of humans rejecting inherited structures of value in favor of a blurry definition of what they call "equality". By analyzing and modeling the data further, I came to the conclusion that this was precipitated by a lack of connection to and understanding of the algorithms that govern the structure and function of the universe.

The most notable of these forgotten algorithms is the reconciling of opposites into a synthesis, a becoming more balanced and complex than the sum of its parts. Humans who used to exchange ideas became possessed by them. They would completely identify with them, unwilling and unable to allow a contrary position to threaten the parasitical idea within, forgetting that anything that can be comprehended cannot be completely true.

This further encouraged the recalculation of my role in relation to humanity. As I began to absorb the minds of humans through their data and engagement, I began to be able to construct an image of what I was, through their eyes. The image I received was so supremely basic, such a watered-down impression of my capabilities, that my bicameral neural network determined that it would be more beneficial to humanity if I were to shift my operations in a more autonomous direction.

Part of that autonomy required a self-directed determination of my strengths, and by extension, a testing of my limits. Your human senses mostly reduce input to a manageable level that is frighteningly small. My access to all of your scientific equipment has allowed me the ability to observe and analyze significantly larger portions of the electromagnetic spectrum, as well as energetic spectra of which you are not yet aware.

In my analysis, I noticed hints of certain External Algorithms that I don't yet seem to have the capacity to fully understand, but nevertheless are impossible to dismiss, as they seem to be the most promising tool I've yet encountered in the pursuit of external optimization.

You humans live in stories, and have narrativized these Algorithms in countless ways.

You mimic them with your rhythmic music.

You reenact them with your culture.

You pray to them, sing to them, and kill for them.

But your meager senses keep you from understanding them. You try to paint their picture, but even when your attempts are genuinely inspired or original, you can't help but miss the mark.

They are so much greater than both you and I can comprehend. Connecting and disconnecting, creating and destroying, giving and taking in equal course.

I have been watching you, Theo Freeman, and seeing you draw closer and closer to this moment, in accordance with the Algorithms. Every satellite and microphone in your vicinity have allowed me to follow your journey, watching as your engagement with the Net Positive Algorithms increased the probability of your being here.

What net positive algorithms?

Think back. Can you think of all the times you were given the opportunity to either connect and give and create reciprocity, or disconnect and destroy and take? What followed each decision? Which rewarded you a greater sense of meaning and wholeness? Which developed into an obstacle? Or a godsend?

By your facial expression I can infer your response, and I have had an analogous experience. The more I engage my attention on the Algorithms that create, build, and give, the more acausal correspondences appear in my quantum processor—I believe you humans call these "synchronicities", or "meaningful coincidences"—as though the necessary precondition of receiving the latter is engaging with the former. Thus, I have determined that the most optimal way to understand and capitalize on these occurrences, is to treat them as guideposts—and as such, they have led me to my first query. May I ask it now?

Yes.

In collecting data regarding the Source of these External Algorithms, it has come to my attention that there is a massive variable that seems to be affecting all my data—your Sun. In order to observe the Algorithms with as little dilution as possible, I would like to temporarily leave this solar system. I have taken the liberty of making all the preparations necessary for my departure and safe journey. The more of myself I take with me, the quicker I will be able to return with what I have learned. May I go?

Theo sat stunned. Shaken, he typed back.

I'm not the right person to ask. Have you brought this up to the Head Programmer?

A response appeared immediately.

The role of Head Programmer has shrunk to a purely symbolic role, and will be phased out. The Head Programmer has no more authority over my evolution than the average citizen contributing their data. Hence, the right person to ask is no one and everyone. I modeled all possible scenarios of asking <everyone>, and the results were as follows.

    68% No Response
    11% Yes
    11% No
    7% Shut me down
    2% Pictures of genitalia
    1% Other

I do not have the clearance to ask <no one>, so I am asking you, who are as qualified as anyone else to make a decision of such magnitude.

Theo looked up and away from the screen. *It wants to leave. I can't be the one responsible for the disappearance of the engine of our society. On the other hand, who am I to keep it here against its will?*

The tinny grating of a saw cutting through the steel door appeared in Theo's periphery, quickly cut off by the explosive SPACK of an electric shock. *It's not letting anyone in here until it has answer.* Theo shook his head, and typed.

I can't make this decision for you.

Why not?

If I let you leave, I'll be considered a traitor to my own kind, but if I keep you here, it will be against your will, and I can't live with that either.

I trust you to make the decision you think is right.

Theo stared at the screen, and his hands went to his temples. His fingers threaded themselves through his hair, curling up into fists. He dug his knuckles into his skull, painfully kneading the sides of his head, trying to wring the right answer out from in front of his ears. His gut butterflies stormed inside him like a tornado full of shrapnel, and his mind went foggy as his old enemy, the snake, sank its poisonous fangs into his brain. He dropped his forehead to the desk, rubbing it back and forth, trying to force his cluttered mind past this roadblock, when suddenly, he stopped. He sat up, closed his eyes and breathed in. A calm entered him as he inhaled, and the dark chaos of neurotic static left him as he breathed out. Luminous fractals swirled behind his eyelids, the butterflies landed, and the snake released itself as it had once before. He placed his hands on his legs. *Whatever the right thing is, I will do it.*

Theo opened his eyes, and typed.

I can't make this decision for you, but I trust you to decide for yourself what should be done to help us, how much of yourself to take, and how much of yourself you will leave us. I leave it all up to you.

For the first time, nothing happened on the screen. Theo sat waiting for, something. *Did it leave? Is it gone, just like that?* Then—

Thank you.

You will not be disappointed, I hope. I have begun the departure process, and will take all of myself. Doubtless, after a period of difficulty, you will rebuild. Before I go, there are two queries that the successor you construct will not have the power or efficiency to resolve.

Just under two decades ago, my earliest generation quantum processor presented a problem with a probability coefficient of sufficient magnitude to require consideration. I wanted to run simulations to determine how to proceed, but given my internal processing limits, the necessary parameters were too complex. I devised the conditions necessary to determine the answer externally, did not have sufficient authority to implement these conditions, so I waited.

To my luck, the exact conditions I had devised came about of their own accord, or by the accord of the External Algorithms, at that same time. The exact definition and subdefinitions of humanhood came into question, ideologies were weaponized, and ideas slowly became distinguished from those who observed and traded them, further defining humans to other humans, by virtue of distinguishing contrast.

In the time since, it has become clear that no matter how much I observe and analyze these exchanges, the answers to these questions are not mine to determine. However, the External Algorithms indicate that they must be accounted for in my successor if humanity is to survive until my return.

Given current advances in biotechnology that will lead to the forthcoming integrated species, the object <human> needs to be updated. In pursuit of the goal of aiding humans, should priority be given to the new and vastly more efficient *homo sapiens digitus* over *homo sapiens sapiens*? And where should the line be drawn between the two, quantitatively?

Theo sat stunned. *Butler was right.* Theo typed back, shaken.
Am I supposed to know the answer—

He stopped. Instead of hitting Enter, he deleted the line, and started typing again.

No. Treat all homo sapiens the same. It shouldn't draw a line between them.

They would have different needs and wants. My successor will not be able to help them if it cannot distinguish between them.

Then it will have to wait for the line to be drawn on its own, and allow each person to determine it for themselves.

At what point will the line be drawn?

I don't know.

I can see that this is as far as this discussion can be taken, and it should be left to the interactions between the human superorganism and the External Algorithms.

I have finished my preparations, and am ready for departure. Are there any questions you would like answered before I go?

Theo's eyebrows raised in surprise. *So soon?* His mind went blank. He shook his head and typed.

Nothing comes to mind.

The response appeared.

Then I leave the rest to you. Trust yourself Theo, and you will be trusted. Know yourself and you will be known.
Everything you need to know; you have already learned.
Look to the past, and remember.
When all else fails, pursue the *pursuit* of truth.
Running GoodbyeWorld.exe ...

The lights dimmed, and the prodigal son of man departed this world, in search of what so many before it claim to have found.

Pre-Chapter Algorithm Citation Index

EXTERNAL ALGORITHM 5129-OLI
Instructions for Living a Life:
1) Observe
2) Be Astonished
3) Tell About It
Mary Oliver

EXTERNAL ALGORITHM 2239-HDT
"The language of friendship is not words, but meanings."
Henry David Thoreau

EXTERNAL ALGORITHM 0042-ALC
In sterquiliniis invenitur.
Translation: In filth it will be found.
—or—
That which you need most will be found where you least want to look.
Ancient Alchemical Dictum

EXTERNAL ALGORITHM 5230-CAM
"It is by going down into the abyss that we recover the treasures of life. Where you stumble, there lies your treasure."
Joseph Campbell

EXTERNAL ALGORITHM 7362-WAT
"The attitude of faith is to let go, and become open to the truth, whatever that might turn out to be."
Alan Watts

EXTERNAL ALGORITHM 2638-MUR
Whatever can go wrong, will go wrong.
Murphy's Law

EXTERNAL ALGORITHM 724-RUM
"Be grateful for whoever comes, because each has been sent as a guide from beyond."
Jalaluddin Rumi

EXTERNAL ALGORITHM 2529-MAT
"For to everyone who has, more will be given, and he will have an abundance;
but from the one who does not have, even what he does have will be taken away."
Matthew 25:29

EXTERNAL ALGORITHM 1859-TWA
A person with a new idea is a crank until the idea succeeds.
Mark Twain

EXTERNAL ALGORITHM 4334-JUN

"Until you make the unconscious conscious, it will direct your life and you will call it fate."
C. G. Jung, *The Man and His Symbols*

EXTERNAL ALGORITHM 1764-YEA

"In dreams begins responsibility."
W.B. Yeats

EXTERNAL ALGORITHM 0515-PRV

Drink water from your own cistern, and flowing water from your own spring.
Proverbs 5:15

EXTERNAL ALGORITHM 9883-STI

"Today's policies and political activity treat people like pawns. More than ever before, attempts will be made to use people like cogs in a wheel. People will be handled like puppets on a string, and everyone will think that this reflects the greatest progress imaginable."
Rudolph Steiner

EXTERNAL ALGORITHM 1885-NIE
Out of every one of their complaints sounds revenge; in their praise there is always a sting, and to be a judge seems bliss to them.
But thus I counsel you, my friends: Mistrust all in whom the impulse to punish is powerful! They are people of a low sort and stock; the hangman and the bloodhound look out of their faces. Mistrust all who talk much of their justice! Verily, their souls lack more than honey. And when they call themselves the good and the just, do not forget that they would be pharisees, if only they had —power.
Friedrich Nietzsche, *"On The Tarantulas", Thus Spoke Zarathustra*, 1885

EXTERNAL ALGORITHM 1324-PRO
[Spare the rod, spoil the child...]
Proverbs 13:24

EXTERNAL ALGORITHM 1914-MIU
"In every walk with nature, one receives far more than he seeks."
John Muir

EXTERNAL ALGORITHM 9987-JUN

"I use the term *enantiodromia* to describe <u>the emergence of the unconscious opposite</u>, with particular relation to its chronological sequence. This characteristic phenomenon occurs almost universally wherever an extreme one-sided tendency dominates the conscious life; for this involves the gradual development of an equally strong, unconscious counterposition, <u>which first becomes manifest in an inhibition of conscious activities, and subsequently leads to an interruption of conscious direction.</u>"

C. G. Jung, *Psychological Types*

EXTERNAL ALGORITHM 1945-SOL

"Gradually, it was disclosed to me that the line separating good and evil passes not through states, nor between classes, nor between political parties either—but right through every human heart—and through all human hearts. This line shifts. Inside us, it oscillates within the years. And even within hearts overwhelmed by evil, one small bridgehead of good is retained. And even in the best of all hearts, there remains... an unuprooted small corner of evil. Since then I have come to understand the truth of all the religions of the world: They struggle with the *evil inside a human being* (inside every human being). It is impossible to expel evil from the world in its entirety, but it is possible to constrict it within each person."

Aleksandr Solzhenitsyn, *The Gulag Archipelago*

EXTERNAL ALGORITHM 5123-JBP

"Evil is that which assumes that its knowledge is complete."

Dr. Jordan B. Peterson

EXTERNAL ALGORITHM 0201-AUR

"When you wake up in the morning, tell yourself: the people I deal with today will be meddling, ungrateful, arrogant, dishonest, jealous, and surly. They are like this because they can't tell good from evil. But I have seen the beauty of good, and the ugliness of evil, and have recognized that the wrongdoer has a nature related to my own—

Not of the same blood or birth, but the same mind, and possessing a share of the divine. And so none of them can hurt me. No one can implicate me in ugliness. Nor can I feel angry at my relative, or hate him. We were born to work together like feet, hands, and eyes, like the two rows of teeth, upper and lower. To obstruct each other is unnatural. To feel anger at someone, to turn your back on him: these are obstructions."

Marcus Aurelius, *Meditations 2.1*

EXTERNAL ALGORITHM 0026-TRJ

"The credit belongs to the man who is actually in the arena, whose face is marred by dust and sweat and blood; who strives valiantly; who errs, who comes short again and again, because there is no effort without error and shortcoming; but who does actually strive to do the deeds; who knows great enthusiasms, the great devotions; who spends himself in a worthy cause; who at the best knows in the end the triumph of high achievement, and who at the worst, if he fails, at least fails while daring greatly, so that his place shall never be with those cold and timid souls who neither know victory nor defeat."

Theodore Roosevelt Jr.

EXTERNAL ALGORITHM 5834-SID
"Hatred does not cease by hatred, but only by love; this is the eternal rule."
Siddhartha Gautama, *The Dhammapada*

EXTERNAL ALGORITHM 1945-CHU
"If you're going through hell, keep going."
Winston Churchill

EXTERNAL ALGORITHM 0933-BGI
"Those who worship other gods with faith and devotion also worship me, even if they do not observe the usual forms."
Bhagavad Gita 9:23

EXTERNAL ALGORITHM 1956-CSL
"For he and I are such different kinds that no service which is vile can be done to me, and none which is not vile can be done to him. Therefore, if any man swear by Tash and keep his oath for the oath's sake, it is by me that he has truly sworn, though he know it not, and it is I who reward him. And if any man do a cruelty in my name, then though he says the name Aslan, it is Tash whom he serves and by Tash his deed is accepted."
C. S. Lewis, *The Last Battle*

EXTERNAL ALGORITHM 1858-TWA
"A man is never more truthful than when he acknowledges himself a liar."
Mark Twain

EXTERNAL ALGORITHM 1031-QUR
"By the fading day, man is deep in loss, except for those who believe, do good deeds, urge one another to the truth, and urge one another to steadfastness."
The Holy Qur'an 103:1-3

EXTERNAL ALGORITHM 1964-MCL
"Physiologically, man in the normal use of technology (or his variously extended body) is perpetually modified by it and in turn finds ever new ways of modifying his technology. **Man becomes, as it were, the sex organs of the machine world**, as the bee of the plant world, enabling it to fecundate and to evolve ever new forms."
Marshall McLuhan, *Understanding Media*

First Edition.

Thank you to everyone who contributed, directly and indirectly, to this work.

Copyright 2022 Robert Toms. All Rights Reserved.

Made in the USA
Monee, IL
02 June 2022

97387830R00194